Ellie's Haven

SHARLENE MACLAREN

WHITAKER
HOUSE

ELLIE'S HAVEN
River of Hope ~ Book Two

Sharlene MacLaren
www.sharlenemaclaren.com

ISBN: 978-1-60374-213-9
Printed in the United States of America
© 2012 by Sharlene MacLaren

Whitaker House
1030 Hunt Valley Circle
New Kensington, PA 15068
www.whitakerhouse.com

Library of Congress Cataloging-in-Publication Data

MacLaren, Sharlene, 1948–
  Ellie's haven / by Sharlene MacLaren.
    p. cm. — (River of hope ; bk. 2)
  Summary: "Trials test a marriage of convenience between a young woman running from her past and a widower desperate for help with his four children"—Provided by publisher.
  ISBN 978-1-60374-213-9 (trade pbk.)
  1. Murder—Investigation—Fiction. 2. Man-woman relationships. 3. Single-parent families—Fiction. 4. Wabash (Ind.)—Fiction. 5. Domestic fiction. I. Title. I. Title.
  PS3613.A27356E45 2012
  813'.6—dc23
                    2011049627

1 2 3 4 5 6 7 8 9 10 ⱳ 18 17 16 15 14 13 12

Dedication

To Christine Whitaker, for giving those first three chapters of *Through Every Storm* more than a sweeping look, calling later to say, "We'd like to see the rest of your manuscript," and tacking on, "You're a good writer." Thank you, Christine, and thanks to all of the lovely people at Whitaker House, who have become like an extended family to my husband and me.

We love you very much.

Other Titles by Sharlene MacLaren

Tender Vow

Long Journey Home

Through Every Storm

The Little Hickman Creek Series
Loving Liza Jane
Sarah, My Beloved
Courting Emma

The Daughters of Jacob Kane Series
Hannah Grace
Maggie Rose
Abbie Ann

River of Hope Series
Livvie's Song

Chapter One

February 1928
Athens, Tennessee

Thou art not a God that hath pleasure
in wickedness: neither shall evil dwell
with thee. The foolish shall not
stand in thy sight....
—Psalm 5:4–5

Nothing wakes a body faster than a barking dog competing with the heated shouts of furious men. Eleanor Booth threw off her heavy quilt and leaped out of bed, pulled her flannel collar up tight around her throat, and raced across the gritty floor to the window. With her fingertips, she rubbed a circle of frost off the pane and peered out into the cold, dark morning, squinting to make out the shadowy figures that appeared to be facing off just feet away from the rotting front porch. An icy chill surged down her spine.

"I ain't payin' you one cent more, Sullivan. You done took me for every last penny."

"That's where you're wrong, Byron. Your pocket ain't empty till I say it is, and as long as you keep producin' hooch, the greenbacks'll keep rollin' in. You stop payin', and I'll shut you down quicker than a lizard on hot sand."

5

They were at it again—Byron Pruitt, Ellie's worthless stepfather, and Walter Sullivan, that crooked government agent. Byron's dog, Curly, didn't let up his fierce, frenzied barking, which ought to have deterred the dispute but seemed to fuel it instead.

"Byron," Ellie's mama, Rita, pleaded in a panicked tone. "Byron, pay the man so he'll get off our property."

"Shut up, woman, and git back inside! I ain't payin' 'im another dime!"

Ellie snatched her fraying robe from the foot of her bed, slipped it on, and rushed out of the room, toes gone numb from the frozen air wafting up through the floorboards. Tennessee winters didn't generate much snow, but that didn't stop the temperatures from plummeting into the single digits.

She entered the dark, tiny living room and found her mother standing in the open doorway, shoulders hunched, hands clutching the door frame. Her grayish-black hair was mussed every which way, and her tattered flannel nightgown hugged her narrow frame.

Ellie shot a hasty glance at the potbelly stove in the middle of the room, where nothing but a few embers glowed through the blackened glass. More shivers stampeded down her spine. "What's goin' on?" she asked, coming up behind her mama.

At the sound of her voice, Byron gave a half-turn, and that's when Ellie spied the sawed-off shotgun in his arms. "Git back to bed, missy," he groused. "You ain't needed here."

Walt Sullivan had a gun, too—a pistol—but he kept it holstered, one hand hovering over it.

"Byron, put that gun down before somebody gets hurt," Ellie said firmly.

"Yeah, Pruitt. Listen to your purty li'l daughter."

"Shut yer tater trap and git off my land, Sullivan."

"Not till I get what's due me."

"I done paid you. Now, git!"

"'Fraid you paid me half."

"You keep raisin' the rates, you dumb ox. How you 'spect me to make any kind o' livin'?"

Sullivan chortled. "That ain't my concern, now, is it? I swear, if you don't pay up, I'll come back with my men, and we'll turn your whole operation into mince-meat by midday." He made the mistake of taking a step toward Byron, whether to intimidate or to show his authority, Ellie couldn't say. She knew only that it was a mistake.

Byron raised his rifle and quickly fired off three shots, each one rocketing through the vanishing moonlight to reach its intended target.

Seconds later, with eyes bulging in an expression of shock, Sullivan dropped to the ground like a sack of wet cement.

Utter mayhem followed. Curly kept barking and ran circles around the fallen body, while her mama shrieked. "Byron! You—you—you've shot 'im. Is he dead? Oh, dear God, help us!" And Ellie, to suppress her own sobs, turned away from the body, where red fluid already oozed from mouth and nose. She clutched her stomach to keep from retching right there on the floor.

"Shut up, just shut up, both o' you!" Byron roared. "I have to think." With eyes flaming and nostrils flaring, he turned and started pacing.

The women kept quiet, save for the occasional gasp of air, and hugged each other. Ellie swallowed down some of the bitter juice churning in her stomach and chanced a peek over Mama's shoulder.

Byron paused and crouched over Sullivan's body, feeling for a pulse. He cut loose a curse. "He's dead, all right."

Ellie's mama gasped and released her to cover her mouth with her hands. "Oh, mother of all things holy, Byron! What in the world have you done?"

"Shut up, I told you, 'fore I shoot you, too!" He raised his gun at her.

On impulse, Ellie leaped between them, her arms raised. "Put that gun down, you fool!" She had to tell herself to breathe.

The man's beady eyes stared as if to bore holes through her, but he lowered his weapon. Still, she knew Byron Pruitt had no soul—she'd known since the day she'd met him—and she'd go to the grave wondering why her mama had married him after her father had died. Perhaps, she'd seen him as her only hope of surviving in the hills. Some protector he'd turned out to be, operating an illegal distillery that brought the scum of society straight to their door. If he ever turned a profit, her mama never saw it, for what he didn't gamble away he paid in bribes to keep the authorities off his back.

"I gotta git rid o' this body," he muttered, sweeping five stubby fingers through his scraggly hair.

"No," Ellie said quietly. "We have to call the sheriff."

"Are you crazy?" he spat, stepping over the body and walking toward them, his eyes as wild as a rabid dog's. "We ain't callin' no sheriff. I kilt a man, a government man, in cold blood. You think any court o' law's gonna let me off the hook?"

Ellie huddled close to her mama and wrapped a protective arm around her.

"W-we won't tell," Mama said, her whole body quivering. "We promise, Byron."

Ellie couldn't believe her ears. "Mama, how can you say that?"

Byron's eyes bulged with madness as he climbed the rickety porch steps and entered the house. The worst kind of cold slithered in the door and tangled around Ellie's ankles. "Because you two're in this with me, that's how she can say it. I'll tell the cops you both played a part, that you talked me into doin' it." He raised the shotgun and poked the barrel into her mama's chin, lifting it.

Ellie swallowed hard and stiffened. "Byron, don't you dare hurt her."

Her stepfather was a perpetual terror, always cocking a gun, sharpening a knife, or speaking not-so-veiled threats. It seemed that nothing satisfied him more than creating havoc in their little household. Byron Pruitt was a viperous lunatic, and if it hadn't been for her beloved mama, Ellie would have left years ago.

Byron slid the muzzle up Mama's face and held it at the center of her forehead. "I ain't lyin', Eleanor—if you don't help me bury that body an' promise to keep yer trap shut 'bout what you saw, I'll kill yer ma."

"You are plumb crazy," Ellie whispered through her teeth.

"Don't believe me?" He cocked the rifle and chortled. "I'll blow 'er head off right now."

Mama whimpered as a lone tear trickled down her trembling cheek.

Byron redirected the shotgun at the floor and pulled the trigger. A unison scream sounded as Ellie and her mama clutched each other and stepped away from the cloud of dust that rose from the splintered hole in the boards. Outside, Curly barked even louder, and Ellie could hear the chickens fussing in the coop.

But she heard nothing except the pounding of her own heartbeat when Byron stuck the barrel of his gun in her mama's temple. "I'll kill 'er, Eleanor, I swear it. You go to the cops, and she's as good as dead. And here's an interestin' li'l tidbit: you workin' alongside me at that liquor still makes you my partner in crime." He laughed, the sound cold and hollow. "Them head beaters don't look too kindly on us moonshiners, an' with you bein' one of us, well, they're likely to lock you up tighter'n a pickle in a cannin' jar. Just don't forget that."

She hated that he was right. "Fine. Just put that stupid gun down."

He complied, but only after he'd held it in position for what seemed like another minute, an ugly sneer on his face. "Good. I'm glad we're clear on that." He pulled the gun strap over his shoulder. "Well, come on, then, both o' you. We got a body to bury."

Hours later, Ellie could barely believe she'd actually dug the grave of Walter Sullivan. Granted, she'd done it with Byron's rifle aimed at her. Twice she'd emptied her stomach contents into the hole, only to hear the gun cock and Byron tell her to hurry up and finish before somebody came along.

Now, she watched her mama working at the stove to prepare lunch. In the living room, Byron sat in his rocker next to the fire and cleaned his gun, Ellie knew, to rid it of any traces of telltale gunpowder.

Ellie moved up beside her mama and touched her shoulder gently. "You've been stirrin' this soup for fifteen minutes, Mama. Why don't you go sit down a spell? You're plain tuckered out."

"What you two whisperin' 'bout in there?" Byron barked.

"Nothin'," Mama called back. Then, with lowered voice, she sputtered to Ellie, "You can't stay here. You gotta leave today. I wouldn't be able to bear it if anythin' happened to you."

"I can't leave you with that maniac, Mama. He's insane."

"Of course you can, and you will. I'll be fine. The minute he heads out to the barn, I want you to grab whatever you need and then skedaddle across the field to the Meyers' house, you hear? Ask Burt to drive you down the mountain. He'll do it."

"What you two blabberin' about?"

Byron's brusque voice in the hallway had Ellie whirling on her heel. "Nothin', just like Mama said. Go sit down. Your lunch is ready."

"Humph. You best not be plannin' to run off anywheres," he grumbled before shuffling off to the table. Ellie caught the smell of his breath, and her stomach lurched, though she should have been accustomed to the stench of whiskey by now, considering the hours she'd worked at the still, where the air was saturated with mash. She would always associate the odor with Byron—and his shotgun, which was the only thing that had kept her working there.

The legs of his chair scraped against the sooty floor as he scooted in closer to the table, his back to them. With an icy chortle, he muttered, "You two don't got nowheres to go, anyway."

Three hours later, Ellie bumped along in the backseat of a Model T driven by Burt Meyer. Mildred, his wife of forty years, sat up front with him. Quiet tears dampened Ellie's face as Burt maneuvered the automobile, its brakes squealing in protest, down a narrow pass.

She'd had no more than minutes to throw a few belongings into a little suitcase, hug her mama good-bye, and then sprint along the worn path across the cornfield. Mama had given her strict orders to locate her deceased husband's aunt in Wabash, Indiana, and not to send word to her for at least a month, and then only through Burt and Mildred. "We can trust them," she'd said as she'd helped her pack, Ellie crying all the while. "Don't tell them where you're goin', though, and when you write to me, put the letter inside a small envelope and then tuck that inside a bigger one. Put your return address on the inside letter, never the out-side one, you understand? The less information Burt 'n' Mildred know, the better off they'll be. They're good people. I don't want them gettin' involved in this mess, other than to drive you to the train station."

"You sure you want to leave your ma?" Mildred asked, bringing Ellie's attention back to the present. The woman turned around and looked her in the eye. "You seem awful broke up 'bout leavin', honey."

Ellie wiped her cheeks and nodded. "I'm nineteen. High time I make my own way."

"And get away from that fool stepfather o' yours," Burt muttered. "Too bad Rita didn't leave with you."

Mildred glared at her husband. "Now, Burt, that ain't none of our concern," she scolded him gruffly. When she was facing front again, Ellie heard her add, "Even if you're right." In a louder voice, she said, "We're goin' to miss you somethin' fierce, Eleanor. Always did love it when you came across the field to visit us."

"And brought them scrumptious pies with you," Burt tacked on. "Won't be the same up on West Peak with you gone." He glanced back at her and winked. "Where you travelin' to, if you don't mind my askin'?"

"I...I plan to head north, look for a job. Not quite sure just where yet." She could at least tell them that much.

Mildred turned around again, her brow wrinkled in concern. "You don't got a plan, Eleanor? Why, we cain't just drop you off if you don't have no sort o' arrangements."

"Sure you can," Ellie said, forcing brightness into her tone. She wiped away the last of her tears. "I need to break out o' my cocoon."

"Darlin', if you want to break out, why don't you go south? It's so blamed cold up north."

"Daddy has an aunt I'm plannin' to stay with." She regretted the disclosure immediately, but it did seem that they deserved an explanation of sorts. They'd always been so kind to Mama and her.

"Say no more," Burt spoke up. "Long as you'll be safe, that's enough for Mildred and me."

"He ain't a good sort, that Byron Pruitt," Mildred said, as if she knew that he had something to do with Ellie's departure.

Ellie determined to purse her lips for the rest of the trip, lest some hint of the sordid murder slip past them. Best to keep it buried in the deepest parts of her soul.

Chapter Two

Wabash, Indiana

I will instruct thee and teach thee in the
way which thou shalt go: I will guide
thee with mine eye.
—Psalm 32:8

With a hasty prayer for courage, Gage Cooper tacked the note he'd printed in block letters to the bulletin board at the front of Livvie's Kitchen, a popular restaurant in town. Behind him, Sam Campbell read over his shoulder, making a point to speak up so that none of the patrons would have to strain his ears to hear: "Wife needed to tend house and four children. See Livvie for details. Gage Cooper. PS: Private quarters provided."

Gage let out a slow breath, ran a hand down his prickly hot face, and slowly turned to look at the snickering diners, many of whom had set down their eating utensils to listen, then picked up their napkins to cover their grins and guffaws. "What?" he spouted with a shrug. "I need a wife, all right?" He'd intended to sneak in and out of the restaurant unnoticed, but he should have known that his chances of succeeding were slim with Sam Campbell around.

"That is the nuttiest thing I've ever heard of, Cooper, your advertisin' for a wife. We aren't living in the eighteen hundreds, when mail-order brides were all the rage. These are modern times, or haven't you heard? You actually expect to find a wife by postin' a sign?"

"I'd like to give it a shot, yeah. Now, mind your business." Perturbed, he lumbered past his friend toward the back of the restaurant, where he hoped to find some peace and a cup of coffee.

Will Taylor, Livvie's husband and the head cook, stood on the other side of the bar with a steaming mug in hand, a half grin on his face. Great. Gage supposed Will would offer his two cents just as readily as Sam had. But Gage had already reasoned through every conceivable argument—and prayed about it, to boot. He'd gone through a slew of housekeepers and nannies, and none of them had lasted more than two days. Oh, they had been diligent and caring, all right, but they hadn't been legally obligated to stay. A wife, on the other hand, would not have the option of dropping everything and leaving him in the lurch at the first sign of trouble. He needed permanence and stability, and so did his four children. Sure, they could be a handful, but wasn't that to be expected?

Evidently not, according to his last nanny, Frieda Carter. "Those twins of yours are going to wind up in jail if someone doesn't get a handle on them," she'd informed him just before quitting. Gage had found her statement rather rash. "Unfortunately," she'd added, "I am not equipped for enforcing such extreme reform." Then again, Frieda Carter was in her seventies, and she probably couldn't be expected to handle especially rambunctious children.

"What you want to broadcast your need for a wife for, anyway?" Sam persisted, plunking down next to him at the bar. "It's nonsense."

"In my day, a man courted a woman he fancied," crowed the elderly widower Coot Hermanson from two tables over. "That's how I got me the prettiest woman in town. A woman likes to be wooed, and that's the truth." Reggie, Coot's big black mutt, raised his head, as if in agreement, then lowered it again, making himself comfortable at his master's feet. Livvie was nothing if she wasn't meticulous, and she wouldn't allow just any dog inside her establishment. But Reggie had played a major part in the search and rescue that had saved her life a couple of years ago, so, ever since then, she'd thrown the welcome mat out to him.

Gage took a sip of hot coffee from the mug Will had set on the counter. "With a business to run, I don't have much time for courting." Besides, since losing his wife, he hadn't found any other woman remotely appealing.

"Shucks, if I was a few years younger, I'd jump at the chance to marry you, Gage Cooper," said Cora Mae Livingston, a waitress at Livvie's. The plump, middle-aged maid with the graying hair gave his earlobe a little tug as she passed him on her way to the kitchen. "'Course, your brood of kids might make me think twice."

"Four kids is not a brood," Gage protested. "And I'd marry you tomorrow if you'd say yes."

"Oh, phooey! Don't tempt me."

"Gage Cooper! Stop trying to steal my help out from under my nose," Livvie said as she leaned over the counter to pass an order slip to Will. A certain look passed between the couple, and, for the briefest moment, Gage felt almost envious of their unmistakable love for each other. He'd had a love like that with Ginny, but he'd come to accept the fact that most people didn't get to experience it more than once in a lifetime. No, the next time he married, it would be out of necessity. Sure, it would be nice to find someone pleasant, but love would not be a requirement.

Livvie rounded the counter, stood next to Will, and looped an arm through his. Smiling at Gage, she said, "Is your search limited to women in Wabash? There might be someone in a neighboring town who'd be interested. Why don't you call on a few of the pastors and ask them if they know of any available women in their parishes? I'll bet they could come up with some qualified candidates."

Gage took another swallow of coffee and set the mug down with a gentle thud. "Nope. I've been so busy at the shop, I haven't had time to make many inquiries. That's why I posted the ad. Hopefully, a worthy candidate will wander in and notice it."

"Candidate?" Sam chortled. "What're the job requirements?"

"Well, she'd have to like kids, number one, and be a Christian, of course."

The skin between Sam's thick eyebrows crinkled, and he leaned closer. "Shouldn't it be the other way around?"

Blessedly, the majority of folks had gone back to their lunches, limiting the conversation to the four of them. Even Coot had lost interest, for he was now engaged in a discussion with the three cronies at the table with him.

"That was a slip of the tongue," Gage said quickly. "Of course, the number one priority is finding a woman who loves the Lord."

Sam gave a dubious grin. "You're nuts, fella. What if you wind up with a controlling, conniving, money-hungry, plug-ugly tubster who insists she's perfect for you? What are you goin' to do then? Your note doesn't list any parameters."

Gage tossed back his head and laughed. "I've got the right to be choosy. Besides, Livvie's going to help me. Right, Liv?"

She shook her head and held up a hand. "Now, wait a minute, Gage. I said you could post the ad; I didn't say I'd be a party to it."

"Well, all right. But let's say a young lady inquires, and she seems competent. You would steer her in the right direction, wouldn't you?"

She huffed and threw her husband a withering look.

Will gave a low chuckle. "Don't look at me. The only woman I know anything about is you, and you're still a mystery most days."

That made Sam laugh. "Ain't all women? That's why I stay clear of 'em."

Livvie tossed her hair nonchalantly. "Oh, I suppose it can't hurt to be on the lookout for you."

Gage expressed his relief in the form of a sigh.

"But that's as far as I'll go, Gage Cooper. Gracious me, what in the world would Ginny think of this outlandish plan?"

His heart tripped a little. "I can't say, exactly, but I know she'd want those kids to have a mother."

The atmosphere sobered noticeably. Ginny had died from a sudden case of pneumonia mere weeks after giving birth to Tommy Lee, now nearly three years old. The problem was, most of the housekeepers and nannies Gage had hired had been grandmotherly types like Mrs. Carter who'd already raised children and had been too tuckered out to keep house, cook meals, and corral his frisky foursome. Even during the school year, when it should have been easier to manage things, there was still Tommy Lee to chase after.

"Well, I assume you've prayed about the matter," Will said as he shelled a peanut, then popped it into his mouth.

"I have." His conscience pricked a bit. He hadn't exactly labored over it in prayer, that's for sure.

It didn't seem to occur to Sam to close his mouth while he chewed. "So, I guess God told you to march on down to Livvie's Kitchen and put up that pathetic poster?"

Put like that, it did sound ridiculous. "He didn't tell me *not* to."

"Seems to me the important thing is not the way you go about this...wife shopping," Will mused, "but that you keep God at the forefront, asking Him for wisdom and guidance. I mean, yeah, it's a bit unusual, but I suppose it could work." He started working on another peanut.

Livvie gawked at her husband. "Will Taylor! I do believe you've jumped right on the bandwagon."

"Not me." Sam removed his cap to scratch the top of his head, then plopped it back into place. Gage could have sworn he saw a few dust balls fly in the process. "I still think it's a harebrained scheme."

Gage sighed. "All right, it probably is, but what harm is there in trying it? If it doesn't pan out, I'll just hire another housekeeper...as many as it takes until my kids are grown." Ideally, he would find someone who wouldn't quit on him. He'd been jerking Tommy Lee from one house to another while the other kids were in school, seeking out women who would watch him a day here, a day there. The poor little guy didn't know where he belonged from one moment to the next.

Gage took a few more swigs to finish his coffee, then tossed several coins on the counter and slid off his stool. "I'd best get to work. That furniture isn't going to build itself." Since he'd established Cooper Cabinet Company some ten years ago, his company had grown steadily. These days, he could barely keep up with the demand, even though he'd hired an assistant several years ago. Requests for custom cabinets, as well as tables, beds, desks, and chairs, kept pouring in, and he had neither the will nor the desire to turn them down.

A train whistle sounded, which meant the eleven o'clock was leaving the station. Outside the restaurant, pedestrians hurried up and down the slushy sidewalks, coats buttoned to their throats, hats tugged down, and scarves wrapped around them to shield their faces from the wind. Automobiles and trucks chugged past, and a few horses clipped along, pulling wagons.

The diner door swung open and ushered in a couple of new customers, one of whom caught Gage's eye. She had long black braids and wore only a lightweight jacket. With large, chocolate eyes, she surveyed the place, then set a small satchel on the floor. The motion made her wrap fall open to reveal a frayed, knee-length skirt and, beneath that, bare calves, cuffed socks, and skimpy shoes—all in all, an odd ensemble for a cold day in February. Many diners glanced up from their steaming mugs and plates to gawk at her, and one little lad even pointed before stretching his neck up to whisper something in his mother's ear.

"Good grief! Doesn't she know it's still winter?" Gage asked.

"Apparently not," said Will.

"Pathetic-looking little creature, isn't she?" Sam supplied.

Livvie gave her head a couple of sorrowful shakes. "Poor thing. I'll see if there's anything I can do for her. She looks lost."

❋

Ellie had always thought the hills of Athens were cold, but Wabash? Gracious! Mama hadn't prepared her for the frigid temperatures, not to mention the snow. There wasn't a lot, but it didn't take much to make one wet and miserable. Her eyes searched the crowded little restaurant for an empty table, preferably one near a fireplace where she could thaw out her icy toes, or a warm corner where she could avoid notice, perhaps forget the past few hours.

So much for obscurity. A pretty lady with a strawberry blonde bob who wore a blue dress and a white cardigan sweater approached her from the back of the restaurant with a friendly smile.

"See you later, Livvie," said a fellow who walked past her, tipping the brim of his hat, on his way to the door. For some reason, a chill unrelated to the cold raced down her spine when he brushed by and left his woodsy scent behind.

"Stop in again, Gage," the woman called after him before turning her full attention on Ellie. "Would you like to sit down, miss?"

"Um, yes, please, if you don't mind."

She smiled again and nodded. "I have the perfect place for you. Follow me."

She led her to a spot situated in a darkish, cozy corner at the back, and Ellie didn't miss the curious stares or fail to hear the whispered remarks as she passed between tables. Why, she nearly stopped in her tracks to ask, "What're you all lookin' at?" Instead, she raised her chin a notch and pretended not to notice.

"I haven't seen you around town before," said the woman named Livvie. "Are you visiting someone?" Her tone connoted genuine interest rather than nosiness.

"I...yes, actually. Would you happen to know the whereabouts of Gilda Hansen? She's my great-aunt."

A strange expression passed over the woman's face. A kind smile immediately replaced it, and she nodded at the chair across the table from Ellie. "May I?"

"Yes, o' course," Ellie said, excited about the chance for conversation. Her trip had been anything but pleasant, with several stops and layovers along the way and a mixed bag of passengers to serve as seatmates—some of them so talkative, she never got in a word edgewise; others sullen, silent, smoky, or smelly. To top matters off, she'd shivered for the entire journey, regretting throughout the tediously long stint that she hadn't thought to dress in several layers and wear warmer socks and shoes. Her flimsy slip-ons, handed down from her mother, were hardly suitable for wet snow. Now that she had reached her destination, one of the first things she needed to do was find a secondhand store to purchase some necessities. She hoped she'd find such a place without having to ask around.

"I'm Olivia Taylor, but most people call me Livvie," said the lady, extending her hand across the table toward Ellie. "My husband and I own this place."

Ellie took the woman's hand and found it soft and warm. My, what she wouldn't give for soft hands! Hers were callused from years of hoeing and digging in the garden, chopping wood for the fireplace, and doing almost every manner of housework. When she wasn't helping her mother, she was out in the barn, feeding the livestock or bottling whiskey with Byron. The thought of never again having to contribute to his illegal business seemed too good to be true. Of course, she'd have to make certain he never tracked her down.

She glanced nervously around the room. "It's very nice." In haste, she pulled her hand away and promptly intertwined her fingers in her lap. "I'm Eleanor Booth. Ellie, actually. I'm happy to meet you, ma'am."

"Ellie...what a pretty name. I considered that name last year, when I was expecting, but my baby girl turned out to be a boy, so we named him Robert." Livvie gave a lighthearted giggle. "I have three sons, two of whom are in school right now. Robert's napping in his crib." She nodded at the ceiling. "We live upstairs."

"Oh, that's real convenient for you, ma'am."

Livvie smiled. "Yes, I'm always running back and forth, so I get plenty of exercise. Most days, I don't work down here, but one of my waitresses is sick today, so I'm lending a hand while Robert naps. You have quite a southern drawl, Ellie Booth. Where are you from?"

Ellie hesitated for a moment, but she saw no reason to withhold the truth. "A little town called Athens, Tennessee."

"And you've come all this way to see your aunt?"

"Yes. Do you know her?"

"I...I did at one time, yes."

"Oh." A knot of dread formed in her stomach. "Is she...did she...?"

Livvie reached across the table again and touched her arm. "I'm sorry, honey, but your aunt passed away about a year ago. As I recall, there wasn't any next of kin for the funeral director to contact. If it's any consolation, she had a good number of church friends. Had your parents lost contact with her?"

"Yes. Well, my daddy is dead, so I suppose Mama failed to stay in contact with her." Frankly, since hitching up with Byron Pruitt several years ago, her mama had lost contact with everyone, including her local friends. Byron had driven everyone away. "Mama told me Aunt Gilda was elderly...said she might could use my help around her house, an' such."

"Her house?" Livvie frowned. "Well, actually, she had sold her home and moved in with a friend, who attended her until her passing. I'm afraid there just isn't anything left of Gilda Hansen's estate, Ellie. Most of her possessions were given to the Salvation Army, if I remember correctly."

"I see." Ellie felt her hopes grind into the floor beneath her cold feet. Had she really come all this way for nothing?

Livvie must have sensed her despair. "How about some hot soup and fresh bread? My husband is a fine cook, and his chicken noodle soup is a favorite around Wabash. Things always look brighter on a full stomach, don't you think?"

Ellie nodded and reached for her satchel. She needed to come up with a budget, or the money Mama had given her would run out before she knew it.

"My treat," Livvie said with a wink. She'd read her thoughts again.

"What? Oh no, I couldn't let you do that."

Livvie slid out of her chair and stood up. "I absolutely insist. After you've had a nice, warm lunch, we'll talk about your alternative plan."

Alternative plan? What would the nice lady think when she learned Ellie didn't have one?

Chapter Three

*My God shall supply all your need according
to his riches in glory by Christ Jesus.*
—Philippians 4:19

Gage set the final nail for the chest of drawers in place and put the hammerhead to it, striking it one, two, three times, then stood back to survey his handiwork. With its ornate, hand-carved trim and lavish gold-toned knobs, this piece was turning out nicer than planned, if he did say so himself. He ran a hand over one of the smooth edges and let out a long sigh. If it weren't for his myriad responsibilities, he could easily work round the clock at his shop and maybe have some hope of finishing the stacks of contracts that cluttered his desk. For each order he completed, three more came in, so his customers had to wait a good, long while for their requests to be fulfilled. Most of them didn't seem to mind, though; the prevailing attitude was that a piece of furniture with Gage Cooper's signature was worth the wait. And his reputation reached far beyond Wabash. Why, he'd gotten work orders from as far away as California and New York.

"I'm breaking for some lunch, boss," said his assistant, Fred Wilcox, who was in his mid-forties. "You

bring a sandwich today?" Fred set down his plan-
ing tool on the bench where he'd been working and
stepped over a mound of wood shavings. Hiring him
had been a smart decision; the extra labor helped to
pick up some of the slack. Plus, the man had the mak-
ings of an excellent craftsman and had proven to be a
hard worker.

"Yeah, but you go ahead," Gage told him. "I think
I'll work through my lunch hour." The coffee he'd
downed at Livvie's Kitchen had taken the edge off his
hunger, as had his anxiety over the want ad for a wife
he'd posted. He wondered if many people had seen
it and how long it would take for him to become the
laughingstock of the town.

"Sure, make me feel guilty," Fred said as he shuffled toward the back of the shop, where they kept a
small icebox stocked with snacks. Of course, it took
Fred some time to maneuver through everything to
get to the icebox. The woodshop, on the corner of Factory and Carroll streets, was filled from floor to ceiling with workbenches, sawhorses, tools, and stacks of
wood. There was a front desk, piled almost just as high
with papers, where his secretary, Edith Nickerson, answered the phone and kept him organized two days
a week. "How are those kiddos of yours doing?" Fred
asked. "You find somebody to replace that last housekeeper who quit on you?"

"Not yet, but I'm looking. My kids are doing fine,
thanks." Fred had no idea about the sign he'd posted
at Livvie's Kitchen, and he intended to keep it that
way. The last thing he needed was another ribbing,
Sam Campbell style.

"Your twins staying out of trouble?" Fred straddled a chair and took a big bite of his sandwich.

"You had to ask. They shattered a neighbor's window last week when they were tossing snowballs."

"That's not good."

"It was an accident, of course, but Mr. Decker wasted no time in marching over to my place to tell me what it would cost to replace the pane. I lit into my boys and told them they'd have to work off every cent their carelessness cost. I think I was too hard on them."

"Naw, you're a good pa," said Fred. "You just need...." He looked thoughtful for a moment, then took another bite.

"What?"

"Help. You need some help."

Gage rolled his eyes. "Well, thanks. I thought you were about to tell me something I didn't already know."

His ten-year-old twins, Alec and Abe, were notorious for their conduct inside and outside of school. If it wasn't shooting paper wads across the classroom, it was pulling some girl's pigtails or putting a spider down her dress. Last week, Alec had tied Homer Derk's shoelaces to his chair leg, and the boy had fallen when he'd stood up to leave. Abe had put a glob of glue on Rudy Reynolds' chair and ended up ruining the youngster's new trousers.

Gage knew all of this only because the school principal had called to explain why his sons would be detained after school for three days to perform janitorial duties.

Thank God for Frances, his eight-year-old daughter, who never gave him an ounce of trouble. The second grader was shy and mild-mannered, and her teachers' only complaint was that she seldom volunteered to speak in class. He would have liked to see a bit more assertiveness in her, but, the truth was, the girl missed her mother; she'd been withdrawn since her death. While the twins processed their grief by acting out, Frances turned within herself. Tommy Lee alone was unaffected, at least in terms of grief, since he had no recollection of his mother.

"Well, maybe you'll get yourself a new house-keeper one of these days who'll show some genuine interest in your kids. That would take a load off your shoulders."

"Sure would." He didn't have the courage to tell him he was hoping for a wife.

The chicken noodle soup hit the spot. After slurping the last spoonful, Ellie checked to make sure no one was looking, then used the remaining piece of bread to sop up the liquid coating the bowl.

"How did you like my husband's soup?"

Ellie glanced up and saw Livvie wiping down a nearby table. "Delicious, ma'am." She hastily dabbed her chin with her napkin. "I never knew a man to cook." She couldn't imagine Byron opening a can of cold beans to save his life. Making moonshine was as close as he came to cooking.

With warm feet and a full stomach, Ellie felt better about figuring out her next move. She stood up and slipped into her jacket.

Livvie tossed her cloth on the counter and walked toward Ellie, wiping her hands on her apron. "Have you thought any more about what you'll do?"

"Yes," Ellie said, fishing around in her satchel for a few coins. "I'm going to start lookin' for a job. Any suggestions where I might begin?"

She set the coins on the table, but Livvie scooped them up and dropped them back inside her bag. "I told you lunch was on me, sweetie." A scowl of frustration crossed her pretty face. "I'm sorry, but I can't think of anything right off. I wish we had need of another waitress, but I just hired a girl about a month ago. I can recommend a cheap place to stay up the road, but even that will become costly if you don't find a job soon. Have you considered going back to Ath—"

"I can't go back there." She hadn't meant to sound so abrupt. Poor Livvie nearly stumbled backward. "I mean, I'm nineteen, and it's past time I struck out on my own. Since I'm already here, I may as well try to make a livin'."

Livvie studied her. "I wouldn't have pegged you for nineteen."

Ellie straightened her shoulders and gave herself a once-over. It was painfully apparent that, while Livvie's body was perfectly curved and contoured, hers might as well have been a crude plank of wood. Even Livvie's hair had volume, while hers was braided in two straggly pigtails. "My birthday was last month."

"Well...." Livvie glanced at the door, probably to see whoever had just come inside. "We ought to be able to find something for you to do around town. It sounds like you aren't afraid of a little work."

"I'm a good worker."

"You could try the cleaners up the street, or J. C. Penney, or the camera shop. All of them had 'Help Wanted' signs in the window last week."

"Is that so? Well, thank you for the suggestions, ma'am. I'll be sure to check them out." She started to button up her jacket.

"Do you have anything warmer than that in your suitcase?"

"No, I...I'm afraid I didn't come real prepared. I left in somewhat of a hurry."

That last detail could easily have been left unsaid, but it had popped out without forethought. Ellie needed to concentrate more on considering her words before she spoke.

Livvie furrowed her brow. "If you wait here a minute, I can fetch you a warmer coat. It's one I never use."

"What? Oh my stars, no, I couldn't—"

"You can, and you will." Livvie turned on her heel. "Don't go anywhere, you hear?" Before giving Ellie a chance to reply, she disappeared through a doorway at the back of the diner.

"She means business, young lady," said a deep male voice.

Startled, Ellie turned and saw the cook, Livvie's husband, a giant of a man with warm eyes and a nice smile. "I hear you hail from Tennessee." He folded his arms across his broad chest and leaned back against the sink, a towel flung over his shoulder. A dark-skinned man stood beside him, peeling potatoes. "Livvie says you came all this way to see your aunt, only to discover she'd passed away last year. I'm sorry for your loss."

Ellie shrugged. "It's okay. I didn't know her." *There you go again, speaking without thinking first.* "I mean, thank you for your concern."

He seemed to study her, so she averted her eyes and scraped a few breadcrumbs off of the table and into her palm.

Will stepped away from the sink. "Livvie should be back down any minute."

"Thanks. I think I'll just walk around a bit."

"Help yourself."

A few lunchtime customers lingered—an old man and his dog, a businessman reading a newspaper, and a young woman with a baby. A feeling of dread came over her that she didn't belong in this pleasant little town called Wabash, Indiana; that she would never learn to fit in even if she did find a job. What was she to do? And how would she survive? She'd never been out on her own, had rarely even left the farm to go into Athens unless Byron insisted she tag along with him to help carry back brewing supplies. If she was a praying woman, she would offer up a few words to the Almighty, asking for guidance. But she didn't think He'd hear her. None of her past prayers had ever gotten through to Him, as far as she knew. She wandered toward the front of the restaurant, where a beam of sunshine had found its way through the window blinds.

"I knew Gilda Hansen." It was the old man with the dog. "Mighty fine lady. It's a shame, her passing before you got a chance to know her, her being your aunt and all." Had everyone in the restaurant heard her tale of woe? She supposed that was standard in small-town diners.

His dog crawled out from under the table and sniffed her, his wet nose nudging her hand. She patted him on his square head. "Your dog is friendly. What's his name?"

"That's Reggie, and he's the smartest dog you'll ever meet." The man looked at her and rubbed his whiskery chin. "Now that I think on it, you look a trifle like Gilda...it's the eyes, I think."

"Really?" That spiked her interest. "I'd like to think I resemble her, especially since you say she was a fine lady." No one had ever called Ellie a fine lady. A scrawny, tomboyish girl, maybe, but never a lady.

The man kept rubbing his chin as he surveyed her up and down. "Did I hear you say you're nineteen?"

By gum, he must have heard every word of her conversation with Livvie. She squared her shoulders. "Yes, sir. Nineteen last month."

"Hm. That so? You ought to go read that sign Gage Cooper posted earlier."

"Sign?"

"Yeah, up front by the door." He pointed an arthritic finger. "Go on, read it."

She had no idea what to expect, but he'd lassoed her curiosity. So, she swiveled on her heel and approached the bulletin board, Reggie padding alongside her. She scanned the flyers until her eyes fell on the one printed in neat block letters and signed "Gage Cooper." When she got to the part about "private quarters provided," the back door opened and shut with a loud bang.

Ellie turned around and saw Livvie carrying a dark coat. "Here's something warm, Ellie. And don't you pay any mind to that silly advertisement."

Chapter Four

*Your Father knoweth what things ye have
need of, before ye ask him.*
—Matthew 6:8

*H*e has four children, honey. It'd be too much for
you to handle. Besides, Gage is at least thirty-five
years old, or older—far too old for you." Livvie brought
her palm to her forehead. "Gracious, I can't believe
I'm even talking to you about this."

"That ain't—er, that's *not* too old for me," Ellie insisted. "And I can handle four younglings. I've had lots
of experience." Really, she hadn't had a lick of experience with children, but she'd dealt all of her life with
calves, kittens, piglets, and foals. How much different could children be? In her mind, a youngster was
a youngster, whether human or animal. She liked the
part about the private quarters, because it meant that
this was to be a business arrangement—exactly what
she wanted and needed. Getting married and changing her name would help her to fade into oblivion and
make it next to impossible for Byron, not to mention the
law, to track her down. Her heart sank at the thought
of going to prison for aiding and abetting. Yes, marriage and a change of name could be just the ticket for
her. Mama might not be too happy about it, but she'd
have an entire month to decide how to tell her.

That was assuming this Gage person would even hire her. If he was looking for feminine grace and beauty, she'd never fit the bill. She recalled the man who'd left the diner soon after she entered. Hadn't Livvie called him Gage? Also, she remembered that his brushing against her had created a strange stir in her chest.

"You've had experience?" Livvie asked, breaking her tangled web of thoughts.

Ellie lifted her chin and sucked in a breath. "With infants on up."

"Well, it certainly sounds as if you're qualified."

"I say she ought to at least go talk to Gage," the old man said as he hobbled toward them, his battered cane steadying his steps.

Livvie put her hands on her hips and scowled at him. "Coot Hermanson, you are a rascal for even suggesting such a thing."

"Well, you gotta admit, Cooper's pretty desperate for someone." He grinned. "I got a sneaking feeling this little lady here can take care of herself." His old eyes glistened. At least somebody had pegged her right. Ellie liked the fellow.

With a sigh, Livvie clamped her eyes shut and pursed her lips, which caused a dimple to emerge on her cheek.

With a few giant strides, her husband joined them. Livvie turned to look at him with anguish in her eyes. "Will, what do you think? Should I walk Eleanor over to Gage's shop, or would it be too much like throwing her in a pen with the big bad wolf?"

Land of Goshen, did she have to put it that way?

Will's mouth turned into a pathetic sort of half grin that conveyed either amusement or worry, Ellie couldn't tell which. He put his arm around his wife's shoulders and gazed down at Ellie. "You say you've got experience with kids?"

If, by "kids," he meant "baby goats," hers was an honest answer. "Yes, sir. Years of experience with kids."

He pondered her response, then gave a subtle nod. "I guess it couldn't hurt to at least introduce them." He leaned forward and winked. "You'll know him by his growl."

She sucked in a gulp of air. "Oh."

"He's joshing you, dearie," said the man named Coot. "Gage Cooper's a fine man. A little driven, maybe."

The trio spent the next moments staring at her, Will pulling at his chin, Livvie playing with her shiny earring, Coot leaning on his cane, all of them looking as if they were assessing whether or not to push her over a cliff.

"Here, honey, put this on." Livvie turned around and lifted a coat off of a chair, then thrust it at her.

Ellie's mouth fell open. It was the prettiest coat she'd ever seen, sable-colored and made of wool, from the feel of it. She'd never worn something so fine. "I can't take this, ma'am, but I do appreciate the offer." She attempted to hand the garment back to Livvie.

"Don't you like it?"

"No, it's beautiful, the prettiest thing I've ever seen. It's just...it's much too generous."

Livvie flicked her wrist dismissively. "I have some boots for you, too. They're over by the door." She cast a glance at Ellie's feet. "Yes, I'm sure they'll fit. And, here." She reached forward and pulled a scarf out of one of the coat sleeves. "Put this around your neck. Oh, and there are some gloves in the pockets."

"What?" Ellie's eyes pricked with tiny tears.

"Best not argue with her," Will said, softening his grin. "She can be a stubborn thing."

"Oh, hush," Livvie told him, then took the coat from Ellie and held it up. "Hurry, now. Put this on so I can take you to meet Gage before I have a change of heart. I'll make no promises about him, mind you, and I don't want you thinking I endorse his methods of finding a wife."

"I won't hold you responsible," Ellie said. She hesitated, then slowly slipped her arms into the sleeves, one at a time. "Oh, my goodness," she crooned as the lush, warm fabric melted around her. "This is lovely."

"Good. It fits you perfectly."

"I don't know what to say. I've never...I really don't think I should...."

Ignoring her remarks, Livvie buttoned up the coat as she would for her own child. "Earlier today, somebody called Gage's idea harebrained," Livvie said, glancing at Coot. "And I'd have to agree." With the fastening complete, Livvie turned to her husband. "Will, go see if Robert's awake yet, please."

"Of course. Anything else, my little matchmaker?"

"Ugh, don't call me that."

Behind them, Coot and Will chortled.

Gage and Fred had been working for almost an hour in silence, each engrossed in his own project, when the bell above the shop door jangled. Gage looked up and was surprised to discover Livvie Taylor, along with that waif of a girl who'd walked into the restaurant earlier. At least now she looked dressed for the season, no doubt due to Livvie's generosity. What in the world had brought them here?

He laid down his tape measure. "Livvie."

"Hello again, Gage," she said, looking none too comfortable. "I wanted you to meet someone."

"Oh, yeah?" He looked from her to the girl, then wiped his hands on his pants and ambled to the door.

Livvie shifted her weight from one foot to the other. "I'd like you to meet Eleanor Booth. She arrived on the train earlier today from Athens, Tennessee. Eleanor, this is Gage Cooper."

The girl bit her lower lip and extended a gloved hand—warily, it seemed. Her brown eyes, shaded by thick lashes and perfectly sculpted brows, had struck him before, and now they surveyed him with caution. He saw no traces of makeup, such as Ginny always wore, but with her tan complexion and rose-pink mouth, she hardly needed it. Besides, if her stance didn't label her a tomboy, her two-foot braids certainly did.

Putting aside his confusion as to why Livvie would have trudged five or six slushy blocks to introduce him to this girl, he took her hand and gave it a tiny shake. "Hello, Eleanor." He pasted on a smile for good measure.

"You can call me Ellie," she offered by way of a greeting.

"All right. Ellie." He nodded at her, then shot a glance at Livvie and lifted his eyebrows. Some explanation would really be appreciated.

Livvie folded her hands in front of her and smiled sweetly. "Eleanor read your sign, Gage."

"My sign...? Oh! My sign!"

She couldn't possibly think...there was no way on earth. This girl couldn't be more than sixteen or seventeen years old. What had Livvie been thinking?

"I'm nineteen, Mr. Cooper," the girl said, as if reading his mind.

"What? No, you're not."

"I most certainly am, and I've got a birth certificate in my satchel to prove it."

Gage turned bewildered eyes on Livvie. "You don't mean that this young thing—"

"I'm a grown woman, sir."

"Not in my book, you're not. That ad I posted, it was not intended for someone of your...." He looked her up and down, searching for the woman in her. "Your age."

"But I have plenty of experience with kids."

He couldn't help chuckling. "Ah, I see. How about four kids, all under the age of ten?"

Her brown eyes snapped to his face. "I could do it." She might have been a mite of a thing, but a flame of ire to equal a she-lion rose up in that one simple statement.

Behind him, Fred cleared his throat. He must have been listening in. "You post an ad for a housekeeper, boss?"

Gage whirled around. "Something like that."

"A little more than that, actually," Livvie clarified.

"Oh?" Fred turned curious eyes on her.

"You'll have to ask Gage for the details." Livvie turned to the girl and put a protective arm around her narrow shoulders. "I'll leave you to discuss this whole matter with Gage, all right? When you're done, you can walk back to the restaurant, and I'll take you over to the Dixie Hotel." She glanced up at Gage. "Unless you want to take her over there in your truck."

His stomach rolled over. "What? You're not just going to leave her with me, are you?"

"The least you can do is talk to her, Gage. She won't bite."

"I think I'll run across the street for a cup of coffee," Fred announced. He rushed to the door, grabbed his hat and coat, and slipped outside without so much as a backward glance.

Livvie shot Gage one last look, a half smile, before leaving in Fred's footsteps.

Well, a fine predicament this was, being stuck alone with this...this frail, little braided filly. Sam Campbell was right. What a harebrained idea, advertising for a wife.

※

The only words that came to mind when Ellie looked at Gage Cooper were "loutish," "smug," and, well, perhaps "terribly handsome." A wan shaft of light from the window struck a shock of brown hair falling over his forehead and made it gleam like dark gold. As if he realized she'd noticed, he brushed the lock of hair to the side and shifted his weight, his deep brown eyes assessing her. He had a broad physique and was at least half a foot taller than she—definitely a bigger man than Byron, but nowhere near as daunting, despite his firm features, square jaw, and shadow of a beard.

She lifted her chin, daring to look him directly in the eyes. "You did advertise for a wife, didn't you?"

He awakened from his reverie with a look of bewilderment. "I didn't expect that sign to attract the attention of a young girl."

She removed her gloves and shoved them inside her coat pockets, where she kept her hands, not wanting him to see their rough, callused texture. "I told you, I'm—"

"Yeah, I know. Nineteen. That's still young to a thirty-six-year-old man. Criminy, I have four kids!"

"I might be young in your eyes, Mr. Cooper, but let me tell you, those nineteen years weren't none too pampered." She wasn't about to tell him her story, but she didn't want him thinking she knew nothing of life, either. She'd witnessed a murder, for goodness' sake—and, God help her, buried the body with her bare hands. She doubted he could say as much. "Besides, what difference should my age make, considerin' you want a marriage in name only? You did mention the private quarters."

A spot of red stole into each of his cheeks, and she relished knowing she had the power to embarrass him. She figured he had it coming.

With a huff, he pulled up two chairs. "Here, sit down," he ordered her. "The least you can do is tell me about your unpampered self. What brought you all the way here from Tennessee, anyway? Surely, you didn't have in mind to come looking for a husband the minute you arrived. You're not running away from something or someone, are you?"

It alarmed her how quickly he'd pegged her, but she couldn't let him know that. She lowered herself into the chair and began picking at a loose thread on a button of her coat. "I actually came up to care for my great-aunt, Gilda Hansen, but I got here only to find out she died last year." With a little luck, he wouldn't notice how she'd brushed over his question.

"Gilda Hansen…I've heard of her. She lived on the east side of town, I think. You must not have known her very well if you weren't aware she'd passed away."

"No. She was my daddy's aunt. Anyway, since learnin' of her passin', I decided right off to hunt for a job here in Wabash, and that's when I saw your poster."

"So, why not do just that—look for a decent way to make a living? Are you desperate or something?"

"I heard you were."

He jerked back his head and laughed hoarsely. "News sure gets around fast. Okay, I'll admit I've had my share of housekeepers, and I am somewhat desperate at the moment."

"Let me guess. You always hired older women, and your younglings were just too much for them to handle."

"That about sums it up."

"Where's their mama, if you don't mind my askin'?"

His expression went as dark as midnight. "She died of pneumonia almost three years ago."

"I'm sorry. My daddy died when I was twelve. I know how much your kids must ache at their loss. You feel it right here in your innards." She pressed her stomach with both hands.

He gave a solemn nod, then glanced at a far wall, where several tools hung on hooks. She wanted to ask him about his wood shop, but now didn't seem to be the best time. Obviously, he built furniture, and from what she could tell, he did fine work. She wondered how many hours it kept him away from his children.

"My ten-year-old twins are regular rapscallions. They're probably more than fifty percent of the problem."

Ellie had cared for twins before—they'd belonged to Martha, the family's goat. But he would probably see that as a suspicious coincidence rather than a selling point. So, she said instead, "I'm pretty adept at dealin' with rapscallions."

He stared at her for all of a minute, as if actually entertaining the idea of this arrangement. But then, something in him snapped, and he leaped to his feet. "This is plain idiotic."

She jumped to her feet just as fast. "Why do you say that? You need somebody to take care o' your kids, don't you? Why not somebody young, who's got a lot of energy and life?"

"Because, it...it just wouldn't be right. You'd be making a lifetime commitment, and you might want to marry for love someday."

"Pfff, I've got no use for that. What I'd like is, well, a home...and some security." It didn't look like he intended to budge, so she added, "Maybe I could at least meet your kids."

He sighed and shook his head. Moments later, he looked up and chuckled. "Actually, that might get you off this kick. Come on, I'll drive you to the Dixie Hotel."

He started for the door, and she hurried to keep up. "But...aren't you goin' to introduce me to 'em?"

He plucked a wool coat and brown, wide-brimmed felt hat from a couple of wall hooks, then opened the door, letting in a blast of cold air. Next, he plunked the hat in place and stepped outside while shrugging into his coat. Had he decided to ignore her question, then? She had no choice but to pick up her valise and follow. "My truck's over there." He pointed across the street at a battered black truck backed up to a snowbank. "Here." He snatched the suitcase out of her hand and set off. When they reached the vehicle, he tossed it into the truck bed, which was coated with a layer of snow. "You have to give the door a good yank before it'll open," he said, motioning at the passenger side.

"Oh." She trudged around the front of the truck to the other side, thankful for Livvie's boots. So, he wasn't the world's best gentleman. But then, she wasn't the pretty, feminine lady he'd been hoping for when he'd written that darn ad, so she supposed they were even. Straddling a snowbank, she reached for the door handle and pulled. When she finally managed to jar the thing loose, she stepped awkwardly into the cab and then tugged the creaky door shut again.

Their breaths came out in great white puffs and clouded the windows. Gage fiddled with the key in the ignition, pumped the gas pedal, and cajoled the engine until, finally, the old jalopy roared to life. Without another word, he maneuvered the truck out onto the road—Factory Street, according to the sign—and drove along until he turned on Wabash. When they turned right onto Market Street, Ellie recognized where they were.

"Livvie's a nice lady," Gage said as they passed her restaurant.

"She sure is, and very generous. She gave me this beautiful coat."

He glanced over at her. "I figured as much."

They jounced along for a few more blocks, until Gage pulled up to the curb outside the hotel. He slipped the gearshift into neutral and let up on the clutch but left the motor running, his foot on the brake. He took a deep breath and looked up the street. "Livvie shouldn't have brought you over. I mean, it's just not going to work out, you marrying me. You understand."

"'Course, I understand, Mr. Cooper. I'm too young and not near pretty enough to suit you."

"What?" He turned to face her. "It's not that, for crying out loud. I mean, well, you are awful young, yes, but you're not, I mean—"

She stopped him with a hand to his arm. "Please, don't go tryin' to explain, Mr. Cooper." She smiled, wanting him to at least notice she had all her teeth—darned nice ones, at that. "I understand, and it's fine, really." She turned and grasped the door handle. "I'll be goin' on inside now. Real nice meetin' you, sir." With her shoulder, she pushed at the door, but the blamed thing wouldn't budge.

"That blasted door. It's even harder to open from the inside."

"Well, why don't you fix it?" she spouted, sounding more ornery than usual, but she was determined to get inside before the tears started to fall.

Gage opened his door and jumped out. While he ran around behind the truck, Ellie brought a sleeve to her eyes, hastily drying her tears. Good grief! This was the first job inquiry she'd made. Surely, there were plenty of other opportunities awaiting her. She hadn't yet spent one night in this town; she would not allow discouragement to settle in so soon. She wasn't usually so emotional, and she chalked it up to missing Mama. How was she faring without her there to tend to the house and protect her from Byron?

After several unsuccessful tries, he hollered that she'd have to crawl through the door on his side. She nodded and scooted across the seat. This time, he met her on the other side and extended a hand. Because it was a bit of a jump down, she took it and couldn't help but sense the power behind the muscled arm as he guided her to solid ground.

"Well, again, nice meetin' you," she said, picking her way along the snowy sidewalk.

"And you. I...I hope you find a job soon."

"Oh, I'm not worried," she fibbed. "If I don't find somethin' in the next couple o' days, I'll just jump back on the train and head to the next town. Might be, I'll go on over to Indianapolis. I'm certain to find somethin' there, seein' as I do have a high school education."

He raised his eyebrows. "You've got a diploma and all?"

Her back went brick straight. "Mr. Cooper, I may be a hillbilly girl with the strongest southern drawl you ever heard, but I'll have you know, I ain't—I'm not dumb. In fact, it might surprise you to know I managed to graduate top of my class. It wasn't the biggest class, mind you, but seventy-five students ain't—isn't anything to spit at." Meanwhile, a lot of good it'd done her to earn such high honors, only to live under Byron's roof and be forced to help him with his whiskey operation. No one had been happier than he when she'd finished her schooling, for it had afforded him another pair of hands to help with the bottling and labeling.

"Congratulations," Gage said, his dark eyes glinting beneath that big felt hat. "Why didn't you go on to college?"

"Very funny, Mr. Cooper." Ellie lifted her coat up to the knee to reveal the tattered hem of her skirt. "Do I look like the kind that can afford college?"

He didn't respond, and so they just stood there, staring at each other—not for long, though, since Ellie deemed it preposterous to linger in the frigid air for no reason. It seemed she would have to make the first move. "Well, enough talk. I thank you for the ride, sir. I'll say good-bye now." She turned and headed for the hotel steps.

"Oh, Eleanor!"

She stopped and turned around.

"Your bag." He scooped it out of the truck bed and picked his way up the snow-covered path. "You'd be missing this."

"Yes, I surely would." Their hands brushed in the exchange. "Thank you, and good-bye, again." With that, she turned once more and gingerly climbed the steps. When she reached the front door, she glanced around and saw that he hadn't moved. *Strange man*, she brooded. Then, she pushed her way inside without so much as a wave and marched over to the reception desk.

Chapter Five

The LORD is good, a strong hold in the day
of trouble; and he knoweth them
hat trust in him.
—Nahum 1:7

What you cookin' for supper there, woman?" Byron Pruitt demanded. Hunched over the stove, his wife used a wooden spoon to stir a steaming kettle, but she didn't so much as glance up when he walked through the door, much less answer him. Fool woman hadn't spoken more than two complete sentences to him since that girl of hers had skipped town. It wasn't any skin off his back, though. She could go on forever with the silent treatment, as far as he was concerned, unless it meant that he'd never find out where that worthless Eleanor had gone. Shoot, he had two less hands helping with his operation, which made him spitting mad.

Worse than that was the haunting fear that it was only a matter of time before she opened her mouth to the authorities and told them what she'd witnessed. He hoped she'd taken him seriously when he'd told her burying Sullivan made her just as guilty as if she'd murdered him herself. At least he and his partners had moved the still to Curtis Morgan's farm, so that if anybody ever came snooping around, he wouldn't find any evidence of his bootlegging business. He hadn't told Curtis or the others what he'd done to Sullivan; he'd just told them they ought to move the operation every now and again, to stay ahead of the authorities. Curtis hadn't been too keen on relocating the still to his property, but he'd finally given in when Byron had promised him a bigger piece of the pie.

"I asked you a question, Rita, or didn't you hear me?" He tossed his hat on the beat-up sofa across the room and approached her from behind, leaning in close to whisper against her neck, "You wouldn't be ignorin' me on purpose, now, would you?"

"Stop it, Byron." She batted a hand at him and shifted to the side, never taking her eyes off of the kettle, which appeared to contain some sort of beef soup with more vegetables in it than meat.

He swallowed a bitter lump, part of him wanting to smack her, another wanting to stay on her good side. He usually had the upper hand with her, but ever since Ellie's disappearance, she'd gotten bolder, and he didn't like it one bit. Trouble was, if he was hoping to learn where Eleanor had gone off to, he'd have to play his cards right with Rita. If he could only loosen her up enough, she'd let slip where that girl of hers had gone, and then he'd set out after her. In the meantime, he had to treat Rita with kid gloves, which, blast it all, was hard to do considering most days he could barely stomach her.

"Smells durned good," he said.

"Stop pretendin' to be nice. I ain't fooled."

"Pfff, stop bein' such a stubborn wench. I'm sick of you givin' me the cold shoulder."

She went silent again and reached for the salt and pepper, shook a little of each into the soup, and then resumed her stirring. He pushed his hand through his hair and sneered, then walked over to the icebox for something cold to wet his whistle.

"Ain't much of anythin' in there," she said as soon as he opened the door and bent to survey the two shelves. "I need to pick up some supplies."

He'd known they were running low, but he'd hoped to find at least some sweet tea. "How could you run out o' tea?"

She made a smirking noise. "Things don't last forever, Byron."

"Ha! No, they don't, do they?"

"I'll take the truck into town tomorrow."

"Right, and hogs moo. You're done drivin' my truck, woman. I don't trust you to keep yer big trap shut."

Her stirring arm went still, and he thought he noted a slight quiver in her chin, but then she started up again, staring at the steaming swirl. "Fine. Then, you'll have to drive me."

"You know I'll be sleepin' tomorrow. Tonight the bootleggers are comin' in, so I'll be workin' all night at the Morgan place, and I won't be done till sunup."

A cold smile set into her features, and she shrugged. "Then, I guess you'll starve, Byron Pruitt."

"All right, all right. I'll take you later in the day."

"Suit yourself."

His blood boiled at her utter detachment. It was like she'd lost her will to fight, and it plain confused him.

🌾

"What's for supper, Daddy?" Alec called from the entryway. Gage heard the stomp of boots on the rug—two sets, since Abe was with him.

Tommy Lee giggled gleefully at the sound of his brothers from where he was standing in the kitchen, while Frances merely glanced up from her place at the kitchen table, then went back to her book, *Little Women*. For a mere eight years of age, she was an avid reader of just about anything she could get her hands on, always finishing her chores then burying her face in whatever book captured her interest.

"Spaghetti and meatballs," Gage answered from the stove.

"Spaghetti again?" Abe whined. "We had that two nights ago."

"I'd appreciate it if you wouldn't complain. I had the ingredients on hand, so that's what we're having."

"When're you gonna get some different ingredients?" Abe asked.

"I have no idea. You boys know I'm pinched for time." He hated being a grouch, but he and the kitchen were not on the best of terms. Ever since Frieda Carter had quit on him, it had been a struggle to do the laundry, put breakfast on the table, pack the kids' lunches, get them off to school, and fix the evening meal, not to mention keep his business running. Thankfully, Mrs. Watkins, a grandmotherly sort who lived a few blocks over, had agreed to watch Tommy Lee until the end of the week. After that, he wasn't sure what he'd do, unless someone else expressed interest in his advertisement. He didn't see that happening, however. What woman in her right mind would submit to such an arrangement? Excepting Eleanor Booth, of course, but who said she was in her right mind? Shoot, he couldn't even be sure she was nineteen. With those thick, dark braids and that willowy frame—what he'd seen of it under her coat, anyway—she looked barely sixteen.

He could almost imagine the remarks around town now: "Have you heard the news? Gage Cooper robbed the cradle. Has that man gone completely loco?" Why, it could even hinder his business if folks thought he'd lost his mind.

No question, everything about the notion of marrying that southern girl rang of idiocy. And yet, there was the matter of the experience she claimed to have with kids. And, for the life of him, he couldn't deny her natural-born beauty—those big, haunting brown eyes, those sculpted brows, that charming little nose, and that tawny complexion, not to mention that spitfire personality she'd let show a time or two. He did have a strong suspicion she could hold her own when the occasion called for it. Still, that was no reason to up and marry her, for crying out loud. He supposed he could pray further about it, as Will Taylor had suggested, but he'd always found it hard to determine God's perfect will in matters like this. The Almighty had given him a head for thinking, hadn't He?

"When're you gonna hire another housekeeper?" Alec asked from the entryway, kicking off his boots and letting them land where they would on the linoleum.

"When I can find someone interested in staying long term," Gage answered. "I'm done hiring women who won't give me some kind of guarantee. Alec, please stand your boots up against the wall by the door."

The boy retrieved them with a sigh and set them as a pair where they belonged, Abe following his example. Of the twins, Alec had a stronger personality, making him the usual instigator of their shenanigans. Whatever Alec suggested, Abe usually went along with, despite Gage's efforts to urge him to think for himself.

"How come nobody ever stays?" Abe asked, taking off his coat and hanging it on the coat tree by the door. Both boys' cheeks glowed with rosy red patches.

Gage regarded his sons, both of them brown-haired, blue-eyed, and tall for their age, if a bit gangly. "You know very well why they don't stay. Everybody I've ever hired has quit because you guys are a regular handful."

"Reg'lar handful," Tommy Lee parroted.

"Horse dung! We're always good as gold," Alec said as he entered the kitchen, Abe on his tail. Of course, he couldn't walk past his kid brother without knuckling his curly brown head.

"Uh-huh," Gage said, ignoring the comment and laying down the wooden spoon he'd been using to stir the spaghetti sauce. "How come I always get a different story from the ladies who watch over you? And don't say 'horse dung.'" Tommy Lee dropped to his hands and knees and started pushing his toy fire engine around his brothers' feet, making motor noises loud enough to equal the real thing.

"Why? It's not cussing," Alec argued.

"Because I said, that's why."

"I heard you say 'horse dung' a time or two," he retorted.

That was probably true. He used to say a lot worse until he met Ginny and she insisted he clean up his speech. Irritation formed a knot in his chest.

Frances was so engrossed in her book that she hadn't heard a word of the exchange. Either that, or she'd grown so accustomed to their almost nightly fracases that she'd learned to tune them all out. She'd set the table, filled the glasses with water, and put the bread in the basket before retreating to her own seat.

Man, what Gage wouldn't give to go to his own place of retreat.

After he offered a quick supper prayer, discussion started up as to whom he would hire next to take care of the household chores. "I hope the next one ain't old," Abe said.

"Isn't," Gage corrected him.

"Yeah, we always get grandma ladies," Alec said, his mouth full. As much as he'd complained about having to eat spaghetti for the second time that week, he was already working on his second helping.

"I wish our real grandma could watch us," Frances said quietly.

Everyone turned to gawk at her, as if she'd grown an extra ear. Even Tommy Lee stopped throwing his food.

Gage smiled, his heart tripping with love for his sweet daughter. "I know, honey, but Chicago is a good long journey from here. Grandma Cooper would like nothing more than to look after you guys. Shoot, she and Grandpa would probably even move back here in a heartbeat, if it weren't for all those gas stations Grandpa and your uncles have to run. And your other grandparents...well, they live in Nebraska." Since Ginny's passing, his in-laws had had little contact with the kids and him. Sure, they sent cards for Christmas and birthdays, but they never mentioned wanting to visit. Gage sometimes wondered when, if ever, they'd see their grandchildren again. They'd never been overly nurturing, even with Ginny.

Outside, the wind howled, rattling the dining room window and making the lights flicker in the chandelier above the table. In the kitchen, soiled pans awaited Alec and Abe's team efforts of scraping, rinsing, washing, and drying, a chore Gage knew would lead to some serious squabbling that would require his refereeing while getting a cranky Tommy Lee ready for bed and coaxing Frances to put down her book long enough to help him. *Lord, I need a wife,* he mused, gazing around the table from one youngster to another.

And that's when it happened. Like a spirited doe, Ellie Booth's face, a gold oval framed by long, dark braids, flashed across his mind.

The next morning brought a fresh, thin layer of snow but nothing so severe as to stop the flow of traffic on W. Hill Street, the site of the Coopers' sprawling two-story house. The morning also brought its usual flurry of activity—arguments as to whose turn it was to wash the bathroom sink and scrub the toilet, who was going to carry the garbage out to the waste barrel, and who was going to run back upstairs to make sure all the lights were out before they left the house. In the end, the tasks fell to Gage. And in the few seconds it took him to handle those matters, Tommy Lee fell off a chair he shouldn't have been climbing and bloodied up his chin, causing yet another delay in handing him off to Mrs. Watkins and getting the older kids to school. No wonder Gage heaved a sigh of relief when he finally pulled the family Buick into the woman's driveway.

"How come her house is dark?" Abe asked, stretching his neck to see over the dashboard. A squirming Tommy Lee jumped up in his seat next to him to look out the window.

"I don't know," Gage said, reaching across to pick up his youngest son. "I'll be right back."

With Tommy Lee on one hip, he used the other to push his door shut. Then, he trudged up the unshoveled path to the Watkinses' front door. The snow that had fallen was wet, more like raindrops than flakes, which made maneuvering tricky, both in the car and on foot. "C-cold, Daddy," Tommy Lee said, his words catching in a little sob as he buried his face in Gage's neck.

"I know, son," he mumbled, ducking his head to ward off the worst of the winter wind.

When they reached the front porch, the door swung open with a squeak, and the elderly Mr. Watkins poked his head out. "The wife's sick," he mumbled by way of a greeting.

"Oh." At first, the full meaning of his words didn't sink in. "Oh, you mean—"

"She can't watch your boy today. Sorry."

"That's fine. I mean, I'm sorry to hear she's sick," Gage said, not truly meaning it. What was he supposed to do now?

"She got a bad cough and won't be gettin' out of bed. Doubt she'll be able to watch him the rest of the week."

"All right. Well." He dawdled on the bottom step, trying to determine how the rest of his day would play out. He couldn't very well take Tommy Lee to the shop; he and Fred wouldn't accomplish one blessed thing with a two-year-old underfoot. "Tell your wife I'll stop by later with her pay. I hope she feels better soon."

"Yup." Mr. Watkins gave a curt nod and closed the door.

"And a nice day to you, as well," Gage mumbled to no one in particular as he turned and walked away, wending down the same path he'd carved out with his boots, as three pairs of curious eyes watched him from the car.

"Lord, what am I supposed to do now?" As prayers went, this one rated as desperate.

And, just like that, it happened again. Eleanor Booth's young face popped into view.

❋

Ellie wrapped her woolen scarf around her neck, stepped into the boots she'd left by the heat register overnight, and slipped into her coat, still loving its luxurious feel, still astounded that Livvie Taylor had given it to her. Yesterday, she'd trekked all over Wabash in search of a job. She'd had no luck until she'd reached J. C. Penney, where she was to return first thing this morning to meet with the department manager for a discussion about her schedule and salary requirements. It wasn't the job of her dreams, but it would suffice until something better came along. Livvie had told her over supper last night not to be choosy about a job in the beginning, because her most important consideration was finding employment so that she could survive. She'd had to agree.

She glanced at her reflection in the cracked, distorted mirror and frowned at the big brown eyes staring back at her. How would she ever learn the workings of a cash register when all she'd ever known was bottling liquor, caring for farm animals, working in the fields, and performing household chores? She uttered a tiny prayer, clumsy though it was, and fingered the braid overlapping her right shoulder. On their walk over to Mr. Cooper's workshop earlier that week, Livvie had told her God loved her and longed to be a part of her life, but Livvie didn't know what she was saying. Ellie had an ugly past, the kind that God couldn't possibly be interested in redeeming.

Outside her room on the second floor of the Dixie Hotel, a gust of wind whistled past the window, and cold air seeped in through the cracked caulking beneath it, creating an unpleasant draft. The tiny room was austere, to be sure, with a single bed, a dresser and mirror, and a washstand, but it would be her home until she found someplace permanent. "God, why ever did Mama think comin' clear to Wabash was a good idea?" she wondered aloud. "I feel so alone and helpless. What if Mama needs me?" The thought crossed her mind that God could protect her mama in her absence, but her pathetic brand of faith did not provide her with much comfort. Moreover, Byron was an evil man capable of murder. What would keep him from killing her mama next and then hunting her down with murder on his mind? She'd witnessed more than any woman her age should ever have to see, and Byron could be none too happy about that. He wasn't likely to rest until he found her. "Oh, Lord—" Her prayer halted at the sound of footsteps in the hallway, followed by a rap at her door. Panic knotted inside her. Who but Livvie—and Gage Cooper—knew her whereabouts? Byron couldn't possibly—

"Eleanor? Ellie? It's Gage Cooper. Are you in there?"

As if something had scalded her, she vaulted backward, put a clenched fist to her chest, and squeezed while staring at the door. Mr. Cooper had come calling? But, why? She'd thought she'd seen the last of him when he'd dropped her off here two days ago.

The knock came again, only louder, and then there was a deep-timbred "Hello?" followed by a soft, youthful "Heh-wo?"

A croaky gasp caught in her throat, and, for a second, she forgot to breathe. She immediately collected herself, stepped up to the door, and slowly pulled it open by the knob. There he stood, all six-plus feet of him, wool coat buttoned up to his square chin. In his arms was the cutest toddler she'd ever seen, all bundled up. *Keep your bearings about you, Eleanor Booth,* she ordered herself. *This could be nothing.* "Well," she managed, tightening her grip on the doorknob. "I surely didn't expect to see you."

Arched eyebrows disappeared beneath his hat brim as he gave her a quick up-and-down. "You said you wanted to meet my kids, so I thought I'd introduce you to at least one of them. This is Tommy Lee."

She smiled at the tyke and reached out to touch one rosy cheek. "Hello, there."

He smiled back. "Cookie?"

"Tommy Lee," Gage scolded him.

Ellie laughed. "No, I'm sorry. No cookies here."

Gage shifted the jovial little guy to his other arm. "Did you mean it when you said you have experience taking care of kids?"

"Uh, yes." It was a bit too late for truth-telling now. "Why?"

"Can we come in?"

"Well, um, I was just gettin' ready to leave."

"Yeah, I can see that. I suppose you're going job hunting." He strode past her without invitation, his bulky frame seeming to take up more space than her tiny room could handle. She glanced down at the trail of water his overshoes had made on the wooden floor.

"No, actually, I'm not. I got a job yesterday!" She made sure to exaggerate her excitement.

He turned to face her. "You got a job?" His shoulders dropped a fraction, and under his hat rim, an instant scowl emerged. "Already? Where?"

"At a department store...J. C. Penney. How about that?"

"Oh."

"Why, you said you hoped I'd find a job real quick."

"I said that, did I?" But his smileless face denoted an absence of enthusiasm. He removed his hat and held it at his side. "So, you're starting this morning, then?"

"No, I'm startin' on Monday, but I'm to speak with the manager this mornin' about pay and such."

The little boy wriggled to get down. When Gage released him onto the floor, he made a beeline for the window. "Look, Daddy! Peoples down there." He stood on tiptoe and pointed a pudgy finger. "Ooh, look! I see a train."

"That's good, Tommy Lee." Gage kept his gaze directed at Ellie. "Are you set on this job?"

"Well, it's a job, and Livvie told me not to be too choosy in the beginnin'."

"Ah. Good advice, I suppose...if you're desperate."

"Which you know I am." She huffed a breath of annoyance. "You mind tellin' me why you came here, Mr. Cooper?"

"You may as well start calling me Gage."

"I don't think I know you well enough for that."

"Humph. I'm hoping we can fix that."

"I'm not sure I follow you."

"Daddy!" Tommy Lee exclaimed. "See the horsey?"

"Yes, son." Still, Gage's eyes never left her face. "Here's the thing, Ellie. I'd like to revise what I said the other day about our...arrangement not working out."

Her heart thumped wildly, but she wouldn't let him know it. She stuck out her chin and sniffed. "I don't know why you would. I'm only two days older than the last time you saw me."

A smile tugged at the corners of his mouth. "You said you were nineteen, and I believe you, although I wouldn't mind seeing that birth certificate for confirmation."

"Why should I show it to you?" Might as well make this difficult while she still had the chance.

"You're a little whippersnapper, aren't you?"

"Please get to the point, Mr. Cooper."

He pursed his lips for a moment, as if deliberating where to begin. Finally, he let out a long sigh and proceeded. "All right, then. I need help today... and tomorrow...and the next day, as well. I can't cook worth beans, and my house is in need of a good cleaning. I assume you do cook. As you know, I have four kids—Tommy Lee, here, and Frances, my eight-year-old daughter, who would rather read than socialize, and the ten-year-old twins, Alec and Abe, who can be real stinkers. Don't get me wrong; they're good kids, but they don't have any consistent discipline. I've gone through a long string of housekeepers, and I really think I need someone who'll stay. That's why I'm aiming to make it legal and, well, permanent"—he cleared his throat and looked at the floor, as if half embarrassed to say it—"you know, as in marriage."

"I read your ad, remember?"

"I know I said you were too young, but my situation is getting critical. The lady who was supposed to watch Tommy Lee this week got sick."

"So, because you're desperate this week, you want to marry somebody for the rest o' your life?"

He licked his lips and turned his hat in his hands. "I don't see the situation improving, and I need to do something."

She winced. "Are you hard to get along with or somethin'? I don't see why you can't just get yourself a woman."

"I haven't, uh, courted anyone. Courting requires time, you see, something I don't have in abundance right now. My work consumes me."

"Yeah, I get that feeling." No wonder his ten-year-olds acted out. Their mama had died, and their daddy spent most of his waking hours working at his beloved shop. Moreover, his daughter, who exhibited reclusive behavior, probably lived in a dream world, her books the vehicles that transported her there.

"You'd have your own room, as I posted on the flyer, and you wouldn't even have to talk to me if you didn't feel like it."

"Oh, really? I wouldn't have to talk to you?" She gave a sarcastic chuckle. "Now you're makin' it sound quite temptin'. Still, I'm not sure."

"Not sure? Why?" His chestnut-colored eyes roved anxiously across the room to Tommy Lee and then back to her, their intensity pulling at her heart. "If you recall, you're the one who came to me in the beginning, frantic for a job. You can't possibly have changed your mind that fast."

She stared at him for a full thirty seconds, and then, without a word, she walked to the dresser. The room was silent, save for her footsteps. Tommy Lee left his post at the window and came to stand beside her as she fished through the top drawer. When she found the document she wanted, she marched back to Gage and thrust it under his nose. "I suppose you'd need this to obtain a marriage license," she said, her heart pounding nearly out of control. Was she plumb crazy enough to marry a man she didn't know?

He seized the certificate, studied it for a moment, and then nodded, a slight smile hidden somewhere behind his eyes. "It's not a bad thing, you know, appearing younger than you really are. Most women desire it."

"Pfff. I'm not most women, Mr. Cooper."

"No, you certainly are not."

"So, you say I'll have my own room?"

"Absolutely. I have a big house, with four bedrooms and a bathroom on the second floor. The twins share a room, Frances has her own, and there's a nursery off your room, which used to be mine, where Tommy Lee sleeps. He's still in a crib, but it won't be long till I put him in a regular bed. My room is on the first floor—the library, if you can believe it, but I converted it into a bedroom. There's another lavatory on the ground floor."

"Indoor facilities?" No worn path through tall grasses to get to the necessary? It would take her some time to get accustomed to that.

Gage rocked on his heels. "Running water, too."

"Hot...runnin' water?" It sounded almost too good to be true.

He nodded, and she didn't fail to notice the glint of pleasure in his eyes. "Of course, and lots of it. You can have a hot bath every night, if your heart so desires."

"Oh, but I wouldn't demand such extravagance."

He tilted his head. "Most city folk do at least have the most modest of conveniences."

"Are you rich?"

He laughed. "Hardly. But I do well for myself, if that's what you mean. As for my house, my father came into some money after his father, my grandpa, passed away. Grandpa had stock in the oil business, so my two brothers and I inherited a good chunk of that sum, which came in handy when Ginny—my late wife—and I were ready to build our first house. My carpentry business is fairly lucrative, I'm not ashamed to say. All in all, God has been very good to us."

That was the first time he'd mentioned his wife or the Lord, and she found herself wishing he'd speak more about both. "Where do your parents and brothers live?" she decided to ask.

"They moved to Chicago from Wabash, oh, a good ten years ago, I'd say. Both my brothers are older than me and married with a couple of kids. Maybe someday you'll meet them. Anyway, they'd invested in some gas stations throughout the state, with Indianapolis as their biggest hub, and with the rise in automobile production, it's been a worthwhile venture, to say the least. They asked me to partner up with them, but my heart wasn't in it. I'm satisfied right here in good ol' Wabash, where everybody knows everybody." He chuckled.

"You work a lot, I suppose."

"Well, yeah, of course. Operating a business takes a lot of sweat and blood, not to mention long, hard hours. When you've got orders to fill and only so many minutes in a day, it keeps you at the shop longer than you'd like, a lot of nights. Don't get me wrong; I love what I do. I can no more see myself running a bunch of gas stations than I can see myself singing in a boys' choir." The comparison made her sprout a tiny smile. "Using my hands to build stuff is what I do best."

She fingered the buttons on her coat, weighing the idea of living with a houseful of kids and a bear-sized man.

"I'd expect you to go to church every Sunday," he said in haste, almost as an afterthought. "You do go to church, I hope."

"I...Athens is quite a trek down the mountain. We didn't go as a rule." She thought he might reconsider if she divulged that she'd never set foot in a church building. "I'm not opposed to the idea, mind you."

"Are you a praying woman?"

"Oh, absolutely!" She prayed when she was desperate, but didn't everybody?

He gave a satisfied nod. "And you read your Bible, I presume."

"Um, yes, o' course. Every day." Her next prayer would have to be one of repentance, for this was an outright lie. She didn't even own a copy of the Good Book.

"Excellent. It seems like this arrangement was meant to be."

She nodded, pretending she fully agreed. Young boys who acted up, an unsociable daughter, and an active toddler, all needing discipline and nurturing? She would have her hands full if she took the "job" of marrying Gage. And that was exactly how she would have to view it—as a job, for the sake of providing Gage with a housekeeper/nanny in exchange for security and a new name. All told, probably not a bad deal.

No question, he had lost his mind, and so had she.

Chapter Six

*Whoso findeth a wife findeth a good thing,
and obtaineth favour of the LORD.*
—Proverbs 18:22

What do you know about this girl, Gage?" Reverend Lewis White clasped his hands in his lap and studied Gage from his seat in a middle pew of the Wesleyan Methodist church he pastored. Gage and Ginny had attended there during their marriage, and Gage still went every Sunday with the boys. He knew plenty of other members who attended the church, including Will and Livvie Taylor and Sam Campbell.

Gage propped his elbows on his knees and leaned forward, contemplating his response. He wanted Reverend White to officiate the wedding and was hoping for his blessing. He couldn't deny not knowing much about Eleanor, but he didn't want to be talked out of these nuptials, so he weighed every word. "Well, she's a nice person, friendly and spirited. As I said earlier, she hails from Tennessee."

"A real Southern girl, then."

"With the drawl to prove it."

The reverend chuckled. "And that attracted you."

"Uh...well, yes, I'd say it did. But, uh, Reverend? I guess you could say the main reason we're getting married is for the sake of convenience."

Reverend White looked at his hands. "I see. Well, marriages of convenience are certainly nothing new, and some have even wound up working out quite well, but...." He frowned and scratched the top of his head. "They can also prove disastrous. I hope you've considered this arrangement from all angles."

Gage nodded. "I think I have."

The reverend cocked his head to one side and raised an eyebrow. "And made it a matter of serious prayer, of course."

"Of course." A new wave of guilt washed over him. "Well, I guess I could have prayed harder, but it does appear as if the Lord has paved the way for Ellie and me to marry. Even Livvie Taylor encouraged me to give her a chance, and, believe me, Reverend, when I first met Eleanor Booth, everything in me rebelled against the notion of marrying such a young thing. The fact is, her youth is probably the biggest plus. As you know, my boys can be a trial, and what they need is someone with a good supply of energy and enthusiasm. I'm not saying she'll replace Ginny in their minds, but I'm hoping they'll eventually come to like her and respect her. I know Tommy Lee took to her right off. They need a woman in their lives, a mother figure."

"Don't forget those youngsters need a father, too, Gage. You can't expect your new wife to take on all the responsibilities without your guidance and participation."

Gage nodded, sensing the subtle reprimand. "I'm well aware of that." Actually, he was hopeful Ellie would jump into her new role with gusto. A seamless transition would be nice.

Reverend White smiled. He had a quiet, knowing way about him that led folks to believe he possessed an innate ability to see right through them, and perchance he did. "I suppose if you're feeling at peace about this marriage there's not much I can do or say to talk you out of it. Bear in mind, I'm always here, in case you need a few words of advice. Not that the wife and I have all the answers, but we've been married almost as long as you've been taking breaths." He slapped his knee and grinned. "When did you and Eleanor have in mind to say your vows?"

Relief washed over him, followed abruptly by stark reality tinged with fear, which squeezed like a rope around his chest. No arguments? No trying to convince him this could well be utter nonsense? He didn't know what he'd expected. Certainly not immediate compliance.

"You're a grown man, Gage," the reverend said, as if reading his thoughts. "I trust your judgment."

"I appreciate that, sir. Ellie's over talking to Livvie Taylor right now, asking her to stand in as witness. I intend to ask Fred Wilcox to do the same for me. As for timing, we were hoping for next Saturday—if everyone, and you in particular, is available."

"Yes, yes, I'm available, but—that soon?"

Gage swallowed a dry lump. "I know it's sudden, but if she's going to move into my house and start helping with the kids, it wouldn't be proper any other way."

Reverend White nodded. "That's true enough." He scratched his temple and seemed to consider Gage's words. "Are you inviting any guests to this...this wedding ceremony? What about the young lady's parents, and your own, for that matter? Won't they want to be present?"

"Ellie's father passed on when she was twelve, and she says her mother wouldn't be able to come on such short notice. She intends to write her a letter. Regarding my parents, you know Dad and my brothers. They're all so busy, they'd never be able to get away. I'd need to give them six months to plan for it, and we all know that's not possible. As for Mom, she'll be as restless as a fox, of course, and anxious for spring's arrival so she can ride the train over to meet Ellie and see the kids. I'll be ringing her up tonight to let her in on the news. As for those in attendance, it will be a very small number, seeing as Ellie knows no one."

"Well, that's up to you and Eleanor, I suppose, taking care of this wedding in short order. Do you suspect any sort of conflict in her family that would make her want to marry so quickly? You wouldn't want to get caught in the middle of something huge."

"I've no reason to suspect anything, no." But even as he voiced the words, he doubted his confidence. "She came here expecting to help an elderly aunt, so I'm supposing she just thought it was time to leave home and be independent of her family. Most women of nineteen would feel the same."

With a slow nod, the reverend tugged at his longish chin. "I suppose that's true enough, although most would prefer to go out on their own for a while if they're wanting to spread their wings of independence."

"She can't afford to fly very far on her own, Reverend. She has no money, and even with a job, she'd have to move in with someone to make ends meet. She might as well move in with us if she's going to do that, and, in case I failed to mention it, she'll have a room to herself."

Reverend White continued moving his head up and down, putting Gage in mind of a toy with a nodding head.

He shifted positions on the hardwood pew and told himself he had to be the looniest living creature on the planet for jumping into this thing with blinders on—like some wild stallion charging head-on into blackness, not knowing if he might come to a steep cliff and fall to his death. Paradoxically, he also had an odd peace about it, an utter assurance from God of a rightness he couldn't refute.

※

Four pairs of eyes examined Ellie like they would some mysterious object that had just dropped from the sky. Their scrutiny made her wonder if she'd left part of her lunch on her cheek, like a smear of ketchup or a dab of mustard. She glanced down. Perhaps she'd spilled coffee on herself or, worse, put a hole in the blouse she'd bought at the Salvation Army store. She'd found the place on the day she'd gone out job hunting and had loaded up on secondhand skirts, blouses, and underclothes, plus two pairs of practical shoes and a few out-of-date dresses. Clearly, these kids didn't know what to make of her.

"You're gonna be our new housekeeper?" one of the twins asked, his blue eyes wide and shining. Already she'd forgotten how to distinguish him from his brother. They weren't identical, but they resembled each other more than typical fraternal twins—they were also tall for ten-year-olds, with coffee-colored hair like their father's, and they wore curious, if not wary, expressions. Within only five minutes of meeting her, standing here in the Coopers' somewhat cluttered kitchen, they didn't trust her, and who could blame them?

"She's actually going to be a little more than that," their father said, stepping up beside Ellie and putting an arm around her shoulder to draw her close, as if she actually meant something to him. His touch sent chills up her spine. "I'm planning to marry her this Saturday, which will make her your stepmother."

Tommy Lee giggled and commenced dancing in a circle. "Saturday!" he cheered, having no notion of the impact of his daddy's words. Ellie longed to enfold him in her arms, so much did his innocence tug at her heart. At least she could count on acceptance from one of the four.

"Huh?" the twins said in unison. Their eyes darted back and forth between their father and her. Frances merely gawked at Ellie, wordless, her petite mouth gaping and her clear blue eyes as round as little moons. Odd how every member of the family excepting Mr. Cooper had striking blue eyes. No doubt, their mother had contributed that feature.

Ellie searched for something to say to ease their minds. "You don't have to call me Ma or anything like that."

One of the twins eyed her with obvious skepticism, paying particular attention to her braids. "Don't worry 'bout that. You don't even look like a ma." He turned to his father. "Why're you gonna marry her?"

Gage clenched her shoulder until she nearly winced. His nerves must have gotten the better of him. "Because I think it's for the best. This way, Eleanor can move right into our house and be here all the time. Won't that be nice?"

"Are Grandma and Grandpa Cooper comin' to the wedding?" Abe asked.

"No, but Grandma said on the phone she'd come visit us after everybody gets settled," Gage answered brightly, as if that would lift their spirits.

One twin shrugged, the other frowned, and Frances looked at her shoes. Tommy Lee kept up his happy dance, singing a song to accompany his moves.

"Why does she talk so funny?" one of the boys asked over Tommy Lee's racket.

"She doesn't talk funny, Alec," their daddy said, identifying for her again which boy was which. She noted a tiny mole on the underside of Alec's chin and determined to make a quick association: *Mole has an "l" in it,* she mused, *and so does Alec. Mole, Alec, Mole, Alec.* It was a pretty lame association but the only one she could come up with on a second's notice. "She has a Southern accent," Gage was saying. "She grew up in Tennessee."

Alec narrowed his gaze and lifted one corner of his lip in a snarling fashion. "Well, she ought to go back there. She sounds dumb."

"Alec Cooper, that was completely uncalled for. You owe Eleanor an apology. Now."

The boy challenged his father's order with a stubborn stare.

"Either apologize or go to your room."

"No, please," said Ellie. "He's just expressin' his opinion. Let him stay so we can get acquainted. Besides, I'm goin' to rustle up some supper, and I thought the kids could all help me."

"No, thanks," Alec said, pulling back his shoulders. "I'll take my dad's suggestion and go to my room."

"It wasn't a suggestion, Alec," Gage said, his tone tinged with irritation and embarrassment.

Alec had the nerve to make a scoffing sound and then turn on his heel, disappearing from the kitchen and then clomping loudly up the stairs. Surprisingly, his twin did not mimic his dramatic exit. If she could convince Abe to come over to her side, maybe Alec would follow suit. Gage heaved a sigh and started to go after Alec, but Ellie halted him with a hand to his forearm, noting with interest the muscle beneath his flannel shirt. She released it as she would a fire-hot pot handle. "Leave him be, if you don't mind. He's just confused right now."

Gage scowled at her. "You sure you want to go through with this? I don't want to force you into an agreement you'll regret."

He would have to ask her that. She swallowed deep and thought of the alternative: Byron hunting her down. Living with Gage and his family and taking his last name would make her a hard target to track. "Yes, I'm positive."

The wedding ceremony on Saturday was not marked with much exuberance, unless one counted Tommy Lee's enthusiastic outbursts from the front row pew. Ellie alone knew about the strange bounce her heart took when she first laid eyes on her groom, standing at the front of the church with Reverend White and Fred Wilcox. He was dressed in a perfectly fitted black suit with a handsome tie, his hands clasped in front of him, his broad shoulders pulled back to reveal their regal breadth and width. From Gage, Ellie's eyes flitted to Livvie, whose smile and nod seemed to say, "You can do it, honey." She wondered if Gage had heard the tiny gasp of delight coming from the audience when she'd first appeared in the doorway at the back of the church, or if he'd even cast her any sort of special glance. She would never know, for as soon as she started her journey down the seemingly endless aisle, she kept her eyes on the floor. It was uncomfortable being the center of attention, never mind that the crowd numbered only a handful or so.

As if Livvie Taylor hadn't already done enough for her, she'd also insisted on taking Ellie's measurements and buying her a suitable dress for the ceremony. From Beitman & Wolf, she'd purchased a lovely long-sleeved, ivory-colored, knee-length dress made of pure silk, with lacy cuffs and a dipped neckline, as well as matching heels. Livvie had done up her long locks in a fancy bun wound with silk ribbon, leaving a few curly strands of hair to dangle on either side of her face. Truth be told, she'd felt like a princess as she'd gazed at her reflection in the mirror in Livvie's apartment that morning. When Livvie had called Will to come look at her, though, she'd been positively mortified. Even now, the memory of his startling whistle made her cheeks burn. "My, my, Eleanor Booth, are you sure you're only nineteen?" he'd teased.

Livvie had said that because the dress was a practical length, Ellie should be able to wear it again to a gala or a holiday party. But never in a zillion years would Ellie expect Gage to invite his housekeeper/nanny to a formal affair of any kind.

Once she reached the front of the church, the rest of the ceremony flew by in a blur. Reverend White read some passages from his Bible, she and Gage repeated their vows after him, and then she closed her eyes as the reverend offered a closing prayer of blessing on the new couple. After that, Will Taylor played a beautiful hymn on his mouth organ, and the melody so touched her that her eyes misted with tears.

Finally, Reverend White invited Gage to kiss his bride. Mercy, what an awkward moment that turned out to be! Hands on her shoulders, he pulled her closer and leaned forward to deliver a kiss that was light, quick, and lacking all feeling. Still, it didn't fail to send a shock wave straight down her spine. After all, the only person who'd ever kissed her, as far as she could recall, was her mama, and always with a light peck on the cheek. She had never before experienced a man's lips on hers, and she couldn't call the sensation entirely unpleasant.

Afterward, the small group of attendees gathered around at the front of the church to give their well wishes. Gage's kids held back, however, the twins wearing spiteful grimaces, while Frances, in her frilly pink dress, fretfully constrained Tommy Lee, bent as he was on running laps around the sanctuary.

Next, everyone assembled at Livvie's Kitchen, which the Taylors had closed for the day, to celebrate with cake and ice cream. Besides Gage's youngsters, there was the Taylor family; Fred Wilcox and his wife, Lucille; Reverend White and his wife, Esther; a middle-aged fellow named Sam Campbell; and Coot Hermanson, the elderly gentleman who'd first told her about Gage's advertisement. Even Reggie, Coot's faithful mutt, found a rug in a warm corner of the restaurant in which to curl up and wait out the festivities. Everybody was as friendly as could be, all of them seeming determined to make the event a cheerful affair, even though they knew that this marriage had not even a pretense of romantic love. Why, they even brought gifts—an exquisite crystal bowl, some pretty kitchen towels and dishcloths, a colorful handwoven rag rug, a mantel clock, and a teakettle. She'd never seen such pretty things, and she accepted each one with a twinge of guilt. Whatever would Mama say when she learned that her only daughter had married a stranger, albeit a handsome one, with four children? She longed to write her immediately with the news, but she deemed it wise to wait until one month had passed, per her mama's instructions, in hopes that Byron would have given up wondering where she'd run off to by then.

It had been well past seven o'clock by the time the Cooper family climbed into Gage's Buick to head back to the two-story house with white siding on the corner of W. Hill and Ewing streets, which she'd seen but once before the wedding, when Gage had taken her there to meet the children. Such an elegant house, with its sprawling wraparound porch, and spacious, too; when Gage had whisked her through for a tour, she'd wondered how she'd ever keep it clean. But she wasn't about to be intimidated by size. With her usual optimism, she envisioned a picnic lunch at the city park after church on a hot Sunday afternoon in summer: Tommy Lee running ahead of them, Frances talking a blue streak about the friends she'd made, the twins tossing a ball back and forth, and Gage eyeing her with admiration for the way she'd adapted to his children and they to her.

Yet, as Frances and the twins crowded wordlessly into the backseat, and Gage plopped a tired, cranky Tommy Lee onto her lap, closed her door without so much as a "How do you do?" and walked around to his side to climb in, then started up his big car on the second try and headed west on Market Street in the direction of her new home, she realized it was a hopeless delusion.

Chapter Seven

This then is the message which we have
heard of him, and declare unto you, that God
is light, and in him is no darkness at all.
—1 John 1:5

The next morning, Ellie rose early, unable to manage one more wink of shut-eye. Heaven knew she'd sought sleep, even longed for it, but every time she'd tried to drift off, an odd mix of memories had flooded her head, from the gruesome images surrounding Walter Sullivan's murder to the simple interior of her little room at the Dixie Hotel. Then, there was the last look she'd gotten at her mama's doleful face before setting out across the cornfield to the Meyers' house and, last, the image of Gage at the wedding, his face as staid as stone, yet looking handsomer still than any Hollywood star she'd ever seen on a magazine in the grocery store.

Gracious, had she slept more than five consecutive minutes? She couldn't have, with so much staring at the shadowy ceiling in this oversized bed in this unfamiliar room, so many thoughts cluttering her head, not to mention oh-so-many seeds of self-doubt. What had she done? Could she handle this lifelong commitment? Who was this man she now called her husband,

and what of his children? Would they ever accept her into their home and regard her as an authority figure? And this house! As much as she'd tried to deny it, she was intimidated by its massive size. She'd never set foot in a dwelling with so many rooms—front parlor, living room, library (Gage's room), kitchen, washroom, and laundry. And that was just the main floor! Upstairs, there were three large bedrooms, a nursery, and a second washroom. How would she ever manage to keep everything neat and clean on top of preparing the meals and disciplining the children? She turned to look at the clock on her nightstand. Five thirty-five. Only a few hours ago, she'd uttered those two infamous words that changed the course of a life forever. If only she'd recognized the magnitude of her duties before saying "I do."

Breathing a weighty sigh, she gathered her tattered robe around her, stepped down to the floor, and padded over to the window, where the sheer white curtains caressed the polished oak panels. She pressed her hands to the chilly windowsill and leaned forward, her nose grazing the cool glass pane. Outside her window, the full moon illuminated the inviting porch and, beyond that, the house next door. She moved to the other window, which overlooked the side yard. If she pressed even closer and turned just so, she could see a sliver of the big backyard, where the moonlight indicated a small garden overrun with tall stalks of dead weeds. She wondered why, and for what period of time, Gage had let the space go. Had the garden been his wife's project? And, if so, would he mind her bringing it back to life? It would provide ample opportunities to engage the children. She imagined the five of them raking, hoeing, digging, and tossing seeds up and down in straight rows as they talked about the wonderful harvest their garden would yield.

She stepped away from the window and turned around to study her surroundings, still barely visible in the growing light of morning. Her eyes made a path to the small nightstand at the head of her yet-unmade four-poster bed. On it were the clock, a lamp, and a couple of leather-bound books, one called *A Soldier's Recollections* and the other, *Life in the United States before the Civil War.* "Grippin' bedtime readin', I'm sure," she muttered under her breath. On a lower shelf sat another book, this one with page corners turned up and a spine worn nearly to the point of splitting. Upon closer inspection, she realized it was a Bible. She picked it up and thumbed through the whisper-thin pages, awed to see so many passages underlined in pencil. It struck her as irreverent. Gingerly, she set it back in place, thinking she would read from it later, when she had a chance.

Beside a rocking chair in a darkened corner was yet another little table, this one round and with a doily thrown over it. Atop it sat a small reading lamp and a silver picture frame. She ambled to the picture and knew, upon drawing closer, that it held a photograph of Gage and his late wife, his arm draped lazily over her shoulder, her light brown hair sun-drenched and glistening. She'd pictured her as beautiful, but not ravishing. "Exquisite" also came to mind. She was tempted to lay the picture on its face or perchance place it at the bottom of a drawer, but then, what if Gage had left it there for the purpose of impressing upon her mind that he had no intention of ever forgetting his wife? Wouldn't he love to see that he'd succeeded in making her envious? Cold shivers scuttled down her arms as she perused the rest of the room, her eyes at last coming to rest on her unpacked valise and the box of clothes she'd bought at the Salvation Army store standing next to the dresser. If she shifted a bit to the right, she could catch a glimpse of herself in the mirror. Her mind flooded with memories of stuffing her suitcase to the brim with the mishmash of items Mama had kept handing her. "You'll need this," she'd said of a comb and brush set passed down to her from her Indian grandmother. "And this," of a worn black cardigan with three missing buttons. "And somethin' else," Mama had said, drawing from her pocket an unwrapped bar of Lux toilet soap.

"Mama, I can't take that," Ellie had protested. "You've been holdin' on to it for so long."

"Which is plain ridiculous. It was one o' those extravagant purchases. I been makin' my own soap for years; can't see why I'd stop now." She'd put the luscious-smelling bar in Ellie's palm and closed her fingers around it, her eyes watering as she set her gaze on her only child. "Never can tell when it might come in handy." Then, as if a light had dawned, she'd muttered, "Don't move," and slipped out of the room. She'd returned seconds later, thrusting a small wad of bills at Ellie. "Here, take this. I've been savin' it up for your ticket out o' here."

"What?" Ellie had looked at the roll of bills, which must have taken her mama years to put aside. "I can't take this. You might need it yourself."

"No, I'll manage fine. I made my bed when I married Byron. My place is here."

"I'll figure out a way to pay you back."

"Nonsense. My payback will be knowin' you're safe an' sound in Wabash." She'd wiped the dampness from her eyes and looked sternly at her daughter. "It's high time you went out on your own, anyway. If Aunt Gilda ain't in Wabash no more, then you'll have to figure out somethin' else. You'll do fine, though, you'll see. Heavens, you're plenty old enough for leavin' my ol' nest. Most girls your age're long married by now."

That last statement had stung, but Ellie knew she'd meant only good by it. Yes, she'd been on the verge of passing the age of independence—and probably even marriageability—but she'd always hung close to home, never knowing how much more difficult Byron would make life for her mama without her daughter there to protect her by redirecting his wrath.

Oh, what she wouldn't do to see her mama's face again, hug her familiar frame, and feel the warmth of her breath on her cheek.

A chill skittered back up her body, making her quake from the top of her head right down to her bare toes. "Oh, Lord, please guide me in the days to come," she whispered, still somehow doubting her words would come within earshot of the Almighty.

Swallowing a sour lump, she stared at the waiting satchel and box of clothes for a moment, then crossed the braided oval rug to reach them. Time to put away her threadbare wardrobe. Upon opening the doors of the towering armoire, she discovered a sight that threatened to steal her last breath. A passel of beautiful dresses, nightgowns, shawls, jackets, and the like had been pushed to the side, providing her with a narrow space in the middle to hang her garments. On the other side hung several pieces of men's attire—pressed trousers, shirts, and a couple of dark suits—and stacked neatly on a rack in the bottom of the cabinet were several pairs of men's and women's shoes. Was she to hang her rags amid all this finery? And, if Gage's wife had passed some three years ago, wouldn't one think he'd have parted with these items by now?

Her heart sank into a dark, deep place as reality punctured a hole in her wishful thoughts. What a foolish pipe dream to think that her husband would ever consider her as anything more than a maid and housekeeper. Dolefully, she set to hanging up her pieces of clothing, noting every stain and wrinkle.

The benefit of a meager wardrobe was never having trouble deciding what to wear. For today, she selected her blue cotton long-sleeved frock. It had a three-cornered tear in one elbow from catching on a nail in the barn last summer. She brought the fabric to her nose and took a whiff, thankful no odors of hay and muck lingered. With a long sigh, she tossed the garment on the back of a chair. She knew she ought to press it before wearing it, but she didn't know where Mr. Cooper—Gage, rather—kept the ironing board and iron. Tomorrow, while he was at work and the children at school, she would take an extensive self-guided tour of the house, accompanied by Tommy Lee, whom she didn't plan to let out of her sight.

Her parched throat told her it was time to lay aside her present concerns and go in search of something cold to quench her thirst. She removed her nightgown and slipped the wrinkly dress over her head and then secured the buttons down the front, forgoing for the moment her undergarments and the belt that went with the frock. No one else was up at this hour, so she also let her snarled hair fall over her shoulders; she would comb and style it later. She entered the silent hallway, closed the bedroom door behind her, and tip-toed silently toward the stairs.

※

Gage stood at the stove and wiped the sleep from his eyes as he waited for his coffee to finish percolating. His body was fatigued, but his mind had long been wide awake, racing with every manner of thought. Had Ellie slept any better than he? She had sure looked pretty yesterday, and he realized now that he'd failed to acknowledge it. Today seemed a little late, unless he managed to slip a comment about her being a beautiful bride into some future conversation without sounding like a dimwit. He'd felt like an idiot last night, bringing her home with his four kids in tow and then doing nothing to make her feel at home. Good grief! What had he done the minute they'd walked in the house but sit down by the fireplace and read the *Wabash Daily Plain Dealer*? Meanwhile, he was pretty sure that Ellie had meandered through the house, playing with Tommy Lee and trying to strike up a conversation with Frances. As for the boys, they'd immediately hauled out the carrom board to play and turned on the radio, anything to avoid talking to him or Ellie.

He couldn't blame his kids for reacting negatively to his remarrying. After all, they'd expected a house-keeper, not a stepmother. Still, he figured they'd grow accustomed to the idea of Ellie one of these days, and he could only hope that he himself would follow suit.

Hearing a sound behind him, he turned on his heel. Eleanor stood in the doorway in a shabby blue dress that hung loosely on her lanky figure. Brown eyes like mud puddles revealed her shock at finding him in the kitchen. "Good mornin'."

"Good morning to you." For some odd reason, his throat dried up like desert sand at the sight of her black hair flowing liberally over her shoulders.

"You certainly rise early," she said, brushing a tangle of tresses behind her ear. "I...I came to see if I might find some milk in the icebox."

"Oh!" He gathered his wits and reached for an upper cabinet. "Glasses and cups are in here. You'll probably want to poke around later, figure out where everything is. Do you drink coffee?"

"No, sorry. I can't abide the taste."

"No need to apologize."

"I know how to make it, though. I made it all the time for By—never mind. Anyway, now that I know you drink it, I'll be sure to rise ahead of you, and—"

"You don't have to do that. I've been making it every day for the past three years." He wanted to know for whom she'd made coffee back in Athens but decided not to press the issue. He took down a glass, lifted the milk bottle out of the icebox, uncapped the lid, and filled a glass. "Just so you know, the milkman stops by with a delivery every Monday and Thursday," he said as he handed the tumbler to Ellie. "He has a supply of cheese, eggs, cream, butter, and whatnot in his wagon, so, if you'd like, you can speak to him about what you want delivered besides the milk. I have a running account."

"I guess there's a lot I need to learn. Maybe you can fill me in on everybody's schedule."

"You'll figure it all out, don't worry. You'll have to catch me on the run most days if you have questions."

She raised the glass to her mouth and took several sips, then wiped away her milk mustache with her sleeve. "Maybe breakfasts would be a good time to talk about any issues that come up during the week."

"Suppers would be better. I don't usually eat breakfast."

"You don't eat breakfast? My mama used to scold me back when I was in school if I tried to skip out of the house without my usual breakfast of potatoes, ham, and eggs. She said breakfasts were my fuel for the day."

"Are you planning to do the same? Scold me, that is?"

"I wouldn't presume to scold a grown man, especially one who already knows better."

He chuckled. To say she didn't look beguiling with her dander slightly up, her hair disheveled, and her dog-eared dress hanging in a haphazard fashion would be an outright lie. He leaned against the kitchen counter, folding one arm over the other. "Your mama sounds like a smart woman."

"She's smarter than a tree full of owls."

"What do you think she'll say to your marrying a complete stranger? Will she call that smart?"

"No, she'll think I've lost my last brain cell."

He tossed back his head for a laugh. "I'm sure my mother is thinking the same about now."

"I shudder to think what's goin' on in your mama's head."

"She's anxious to meet you."

Her otherwise bronzed skin turned a pasty white. "When will that be?"

"Oh, I expect her to come rolling in on the afternoon train in the next day or so."

"What?" she screeched.

He couldn't help it; he clutched his stomach, laughter spilling out of him. "Relax, I'm just kidding. She'll probably come sometime in April or May."

A breath whistled through her lips. "She'll have a terrible fit when she sees me."

"No, she won't. Why do you say that?"

She cast a glance downward, whether to study her worn dress or her bare feet, he couldn't say. "Because your first wife 'n' me are about as different as oil 'n' water. I saw a picture of her on the little table in my room. She was beautiful."

Something like a rock dropped to the bottom of his gut. "Yeah, she was. Sorry I didn't think to put that away before you came, but you can stick it in a drawer, if you like."

"Gosh, no. It's not like it bothers me or anything. It is your room, after all. By the way, all the clothes in the big cupboard...don't you, um, need them? Well, not Ginny's, o' course, but yours?"

"I took out enough to get me through the next week or so. As for Ginny's clothes, I know it's a little strange they're all still hanging in there. I don't know why I never got rid of them. Maybe I'm saving them for Frances or something."

Ellie took another sip of milk and stared at her feet again, shifting slightly. "Or maybe you just don't want to deal with 'em?"

How had she managed to pin him down to a tee? "You shouldn't have to look at those clothes every time you open the armoire. I'll find a place to hang them after I get home this evening."

Her lack of response led him to believe she wouldn't stop him. He motioned at the table and then pulled out a chair for her. "Sit down with your cup of milk, Mrs. Cooper. I'll get my coffee, and we'll talk a little before the kids wake up and we all start getting ready for church."

Her head shot up. "Church? This mornin'?"

"It's Sunday."

"Well, I know, but we just got married. Won't folks think it odd, you showin' up the day after the event?"

"Why should they? By now, most people know I posted that ad at Livvie's Kitchen and that we married for the sake of convenience. One thing about Wabash, you don't have to read the daily paper to hear the latest scuttlebutt. Some folks might stare and maybe even whisper about us, but I can guarantee they'll also be friendly and welcoming."

She fingered a loose tendril of hair and tensed her jaw, staring down at the chair he clutched. Reluctantly, she set her glass on the tabletop, lowered herself onto the seat, and allowed him to ease her forward.

When he went to fill his coffee mug, he tried to imagine the church ladies' reactions as he marched his new wife and his kids down the center aisle to their usual pew. Oh, there'd be whispers, all right—of that he could be certain—especially if she wore that raggedy dress and pulled her hair back into braids again.

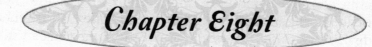

Chapter Eight

*The L*ORD* preserveth the simple: I was*
brought low, and he helped me.
—Psalm 116:6

*O*ver the next several days, they fell into a routine, of sorts. Gage rose ahead of everybody, including Ellie, showered and shaved, brewed a pot of coffee, and then slipped out the door without a sound. She vowed to set her alarm clock well in advance one of these mornings so that she could at least bid him good-bye. More than once, she'd offered to make him breakfast, but his insistence that he had no appetite in the morning soon discouraged her from persisting. Clearly, he didn't like seeing her at the start of the day, and who could blame him? Shoot, she didn't want to see herself, either, not with her wild hair, puffy eyelids, and slumped shoulders. By now, he must have observed what a plain woman he'd married.

She generally got up around six and started breakfast before rousing the kids. Tommy Lee had no obligations, and she quickly learned that he liked to sleep until eight o'clock—fine by her, for it afforded her plenty of time to tend to the others, pack their lunches, feed them breakfast, and make an effort at conversation. It was the latter task that proved the most challenging.

Suppers were anything but pleasant, with the twins always squabbling about one thing or another. In the short time she'd known them, Ellie had learned a few important things: they were indeed closer than most brothers, they shared many similarities, and they generally enjoyed each other's company. That said, the pair was far from immune to disagreements. Sometimes, their spats arose over something no more serious than whose turn it was to wash the dishes, shovel the sidewalk in front of the house, or carry the basket of dirty clothes to the laundry room. Other times, an incident at school would spark a disagreement over which boy had been the instigator. "He started it," Abe would say, pointing across the table at Alec.

"Did not! You did, when you threw Lexi Brady's book down the hallway!" Alec would retort. "You like her, I know you do. You're always tryin' to get a rise outta her so she'll smile at you."

"Am not!"

"Are, too!"

"Am not!"

"Are, too!"

"Boys!" Gage would end up shouting. "Both of you, just...just cease all talking and eat!" He would grow extremely irritated with their bickering and often look to Ellie, as if the mere act of marriage ought to have instilled in her the instant capability to calm the waters.

One evening, supper was particularly tense. Tommy Lee threw his food on the floor, the twins kept kicking each other under the table, and Frances asked to be excused before finishing her food, saying that she wanted to get back to her homework. After the meal, Gage cornered Ellie in the living room. "You did tell me you had experience with kids, did you not?"

"I did, but I'm not a magician. What did you think? Get married, and—snap!—instant calm?" She was a bit put off by his insinuating tone.

"Something like that," he answered, resting one hand on the mantel. "I was hoping your living here would lend stability and alleviate some of the problems, but the boys are still acting out, and Frances still wants to bury herself in her books. Tommy Lee seems to be the only normal one around here."

"So, what you're sayin', if I read you right, is that you regret this marriage."

"No, I didn't come close to saying that."

"Well, it sounded like it to me. I'm sorry to disappoint you, but I'm not a miracle worker. I'm the housekeeper."

"You're my wife."

"That may be. But it's an arrangement of convenience, and the kids know it. Those boys need firmness, to be sure, but they're not goin' to listen to me—not yet, anyway. They're your kids."

"And now they're your kids, too," he pressed.

"Maybe so, but in their minds, I'm still an outsider."

He rolled his eyes to the ceiling and then back at her. "So, what do you suggest? We start sharing my bedroom?"

"What?" Hands fisted at her sides, she poked her chin straight upward so that their brown eyes met, glare for glare. "Certainly not, Mr. Cooper!"

"Don't call me Mr. Cooper. It makes me feel...old. Like a neighbor."

"You might as well be."

"What's that supposed to mean?"

"Your children don't see enough of you. You're gone when they get up in the mornin', and you come home in time to eat supper, only to retreat to your room afterward. Have you ever thought that their actin' out might be on account o' your lack of presence in their lives? I think they're feelin' insecure."

"Insecure? Oh, so now, you're suddenly the expert. For your information, I'm plenty present—maybe not as often as they'd like, but my job keeps me busy."

"So I've noticed."

Although they kept their voices low, the twins must have overheard. They were in the kitchen, allegedly doing homework, though their giggles suggested otherwise. "Well, what do you know, Abe?" Alec said. "They're havin' their first argument."

"Boys!" Gage crossed his arms, never taking his eyes off of Ellie. She'd swallow pins before she let him know how much he unnerved her. "Stop fussing and finish your homework. And, just so you know, Eleanor and I were not fighting; we were having a discussion that was none of your business."

"Sounded like a fight to me," Alec said.

Gage unfolded his arms, gave his head an aggravated shake, and let out a loud sigh. "We'll continue this later," he mouthed at her.

"I can hardly wait," she returned.

There were rustling sounds in the kitchen. "Hey, quit it! Daddy, Alec is makin' spitballs. Ouch!"

At last, Gage turned away from her and directed his gaze toward the kitchen, though the boys were out of sight. "You'd better not be wasting perfectly good paper in there."

"We're not," Alec assured him. "It's scraps."

"Yeah, scraps of the assignment Alec scribbled on, so I had to start over," Abe groused.

Gage pinched the bridge of his nose, his thick eyebrows furrowing.

She wanted to smile but figured that would truly push him to his limit. "They're just boys," she reminded him.

He dropped his hand and looked at her again, his gaze a trifle softer this time. "Scalawags, more like it."

He went to the kitchen to check on the boys' assignments, deeming them messy but passable. Then, he delivered a halfhearted lecture on proper behavior. *Better than nothing,* Ellie mused as she straightened up the kitchen.

Finally, he tousled the twins' hair affectionately and mumbled "Good night" to her. He made a point not to look her in the eye, no doubt to indicate that their argument was far from over.

"I bet you 'n' Daddy aren't gonna stay married very long," Alec remarked after Gage had disappeared inside his makeshift bedroom in the library.

"Of course, we're goin' to stay married. Why would you say such a thing?" She walked to the sink, where the drying rack was stacked full of clean dishes, and started putting them away, plates first and then glasses. She knew the twins' eyes followed her every move; she felt their gazes like little daggers.

"'Cause nobody ever stays around here, and besides, you two were fightin'," Alec answered.

After setting two glasses on a shelf, she swiveled her body and put her back to the counter, one of her braids flopped over her shoulder, the other streaming down the back of her baggy shirtwaist dress. She knew she must look a sight after a long day of household chores. "That doesn't mean I'm goin' anywhere. Like your daddy said, we were just discussin' some things."

"Prolly talking 'bout us," Abe said.

"And Frances and Tommy Lee," she added.

"We ain't your kids," Alec said, crossing his arms defiantly. He looked so much like Gage.

"Well, I know I'm not your real ma. I'd never try to take her place. But I am your stepmother, and that's somethin', isn't it?"

The boys shrugged in perfect unison, then stuck their school papers inside their notebooks, closed them with purpose, and pushed back in their chairs to stand. Thank goodness, they'd finally settled down, their jovial moods suddenly turned toward sour. The wall clock over the stove registered nine thirty-five, well past time for sending them off to bed. Gage usually tucked them in, but it appeared that wouldn't be the case tonight.

She wanted to make a couple of things clear while she had an audience with them. "In case you're wondering, I'm not the sort to give up easy, so don't go thinking I'm going to be quitting anytime soon. I married your daddy, for better, for worse, even though it's more of...well, a business arrangement than anything else."

"Is he payin' you?" Alec asked.

"Payin'? Not exactly, but he's supplyin' me with plenty o' money for buyin' food and whatever other items we may need around the house."

"Most people get paid for doin' jobs," said Abe.

"Yes, well, I live here, so I consider my pay my room and board."

"That ain't very fair," he said.

"It's perfectly fair, and don't say 'ain't,' Abe Cooper." She turned back around to put away the remaining dishes and silverware.

"Why not? I've heard you say it."

She swiveled to face them again. "Yes, but I'm tryin' to break myself of the habit, and you should do the same. It's not proper English."

Neither boy answered. They merely stared at her as if she'd grown a black mole on the end of her nose. So, she added, "It ain't even in the dictionary."

Abe pointed a finger at her and laughed. "You just said it!"

She gasped. "I didn't, did I?" She turned around to face the sink so that they wouldn't see her grin. "Gracious, it must've just slipped out." That's when she realized it didn't take much to entertain ten-year-old boys, much less hoodwink them.

Later that evening, Ellie lay in bed, surrounded by murky shadows, and reflected on the first spat she'd had with her husband. Clearly, she disappointed him as a wife and mother. Well, too bad. She'd never claimed to work magic, and she didn't take kindly to being scolded, especially when the kids were within earshot. It troubled her that Gage didn't interact more with his children. He could have done any number of things with them to bring them closer together as a family, but he always had one excuse or another not to engage, and it usually involved reading his newspaper with a cup of coffee or sitting at the kitchen table drawing up plans for his next furniture project. She didn't know anything about raising kids—human ones, that is—but it didn't take an expert to know they needed plenty of love and attention, along with wise guidance. Her mama may not have had the money to furnish her with decent shoes and fancy clothing, but not once had Ellie been made to feel insignificant. She had no doubt Gage loved his children, but his means of expressing it often fell short. Even quiet Frances desperately longed to be noticed, but her need was overshadowed by her older brothers' antics and her little brother's curiosity. Ellie decided to up her efforts to draw the girl out of her shell.

She punched some shape into her pillow, threw herself over on her other side, and yanked the blankets up close to her throat. My, how the cold did find its way into her big bedroom. Spring couldn't be too far in the offing, though, what with the way the snow had melted in past weeks. With any luck, warmer days would encourage outdoor play, backyard romps, and picnics by the river. She prayed as best she knew that God would intervene, lending her wisdom and knowledge. But, once again, she doubted He even heard her prayers, since He and she weren't actually acquainted on a personal level.

Her mind wandered back to the past few Sundays when the family had gone to church, the first real church services she could recall attending. Actually, she'd never even stepped inside a house of worship before her wedding day, and she found she rather liked the mysterious sense of peace it had given her. She'd felt it again last Sunday, the reverend's message having brought her a kind of hope for the future, though she couldn't quite put her finger on what made her feel that way. He'd mentioned the book of Psalms a lot, so she figured it must be something worth reading. She glanced at the nightstand, where the Bible still rested on the bottom shelf. She'd dusted it off just this morning. Turning on her other side, she stretched down to retrieve it. No time like the present to discover what the book of Psalms was all about.

Chapter Nine

Knoxville, Tennessee

For there is nothing covered, that shall
not be revealed; neither hid, that
shall not be known.
—Luke 12:2

Ned Castleberry, Director of Prohibition for East Tennessee, scanned the smoke-filled conference room of the Knox County Courthouse as he prepared to call to order the weekly meeting, when the agents in his district would report on recent arrests, confiscations, and stills they'd shut down in the eastern part of the state. From his seat in a captain's chair at one end of the long mahogany table, his eyes roved from face to face as the agents engaged in conversation, puffed their cigarettes, and sipped from steaming mugs of coffee. For some, these meetings were their only opportunity to socialize, as the job itself could be quite lonely and didn't make them many friends.

These were good men—hardworking, committed, and untainted—and he trusted them implicitly, not something every director could say about his squad. Many of them had unswerving dedication to the mission, whether inborn or out of a sense of obligation, since he'd handpicked a number of them from the police academy. There were a few veterans on the force, and he'd lay down his life for any one of them—except Walter Sullivan, who'd failed to show up for the previous three meetings. He hadn't returned any of Ned's phone calls, and he'd had the gall to miss today, as well. Apparently, the fool needed a reminder of what was meant by "mandatory."

The Bureau of Prohibition had its hands full enforcing a law that the general public, and even many officers within the bureau, considered senseless. Rampant corruption often compromised their efforts, and a significant number of agents had been dismissed and even prosecuted for accepting bribes and for public intoxication, which hardly improved the average citizen's opinion of the Bureau. Ned had had his eye on Sullivan, and, while he had no actual proof of any wrongdoing on his part, he still had his suspicions about the guy. For one thing, he always smelled slightly of alcohol; for another, his daily reports indicated that "unspecified" activities took up blatantly large blocks of his time. When Ned had questioned him about it, he'd said he'd gotten lazy about detailing his hours, or that the gaps constituted travel time.

Not only that, but he'd made a habit of going off on his own and leaving his partner, a young recruit named Russ Auten, alone to fend for himself. Ned had finally reassigned Auten to a couple of veterans, and he'd gotten no argument from Sullivan on the decision. He'd intended to give him a clear warning today that if he didn't clean up his act, he'd soon be standing in the unemployment line. It seemed that the reprimand would have to wait for another day. Or, maybe Ned would mail him a warning—heck, he could deliver it himself. He thought he knew where Sullivan lived, alone in a tiny apartment in nearby Sevierville. One way or another, he had to get in touch with the scoundrel.

He gave his throat a good clearing to get everyone's attention. "Let's bring this meeting to order so I can get you fellows out of here at a decent time."

The meeting lasted well over an hour. Ned presented the latest statistics and news from the state and national level, and then the agents took turns giving updates on their individual enforcement work. They grew especially animated in relaying accounts of catching bootleggers red-handed and dismantling their stills before their very eyes. This usually involved axing their equipment and dumping dozens of barrels of liquor down hillsides or into a stream.

There was almost always at least one story that invited laughter, and today's meeting did not disappoint. Oscar Welling recounted a raid on an operation he and his partner had been staking out for days, in a run-down cabin by a creek. The two of them, along with four other agents they'd enlisted, had descended upon the four bootleggers in the midst of their labors. When they'd broken down the door, one of the fellows had wet himself, while another had burst into tears and begun pleading for his life. In the center of the room had stood two thirty-gallon stills and a double condensing apparatus over a gas stove. Hogsheads of whiskey mash had filled the cabin, along with a hydrometer for testing the specific gravity of whiskey. In one corner, they'd found a five-gallon jug containing the finished product and a small quantity of flavored syrup.

After arresting the bootleggers, Welling said, they'd made short work of the hogsheads of mash with their axes, then prepared to dismantle the operation. He hadn't failed to notice, however, that one of the copper fermenting barrels had been engraved with the phrase "HERE'S TO YOU, UNCLE SAM."

After a few more stories and some additional chuckles, Ned surveyed the room and heaved a breath. "I thank you all for coming today. That just about covers it, I think. Want you to know you're all doing a fine job."

"Yeah, now if you'd only pay us what we're worth." The semi-sarcastic remark had come from Ken Dawson, seated at the opposite end of the table. He flicked his cigarette over an ashtray while blowing smoke out of the side of his mouth.

"Yeah!" several others cheered in agreement, while others started applauding.

Ned took it in stride. "Hey, they're not paying me much more than you fellas, and what I'm taking home is peanuts. But we're all here, aren't we? I guess that speaks volumes about your dedication to upholding the law. Well, most of you, anyway. On that note, anybody seen Walt Sullivan lately?"

The room went still, as if they'd all been wondering the same thing but hadn't had the guts to voice it. Ned took note of the anxious look on almost every face. "He's been missing meetings and won't return my phone calls. I'll find out where he is, one way or another, but it sure would save me a heap of time if somebody could shed some light on the matter."

Harold Wentz shifted in his seat and pulled on his beard. "I ran into him awhile back." The fellow had arms as thick as tree trunks, and he crossed them over his broad chest while leaning back in his chair. Folks often said they wouldn't want to meet Harold in a dark alley, especially if he had a beef with them. He was a no-nonsense kind of guy, the type everyone wanted on his side. "I bought him a cup of coffee in a little diner in Sweetwater off Highway Eleven. He mentioned something 'bout goin' down to Athens the next mornin', but that was...hm...a good month ago, I s'pose. He didn't say what his business was there."

Ned narrowed his eyes. "Athens? I don't know about any dealings in Athens."

"Sullivan had some sort o' connection there, but I couldn't tell you what it was," offered Tim Lindstrom. He was the clean-cut sort, married with a couple of young kids. "He once tol' me he got a tip 'bout an operation from some cute little waitress at a restaurant in Athens, some place called Rose's Restaurant...or was it Daisy's Diner? See, I ain't good at rememberin' names, but you give me a street number, an' it'll stick with me like glue." That comment earned a couple of chuckles from those who knew him best. "Anyway, he was pretty closemouthed about the details. It wasn't my lead, so I didn't pay much attention. 'Sides, it had to've happened way back in the spring sometime, maybe earlier. Golly, boss, I thought you'd know about it."

"Can't say I authorized any investigation down in Athens." A nettling sensation stirred in Ned's gut. He fixed his eyes on Russ Auten. "You know anything about this, Auten?"

The fellow straightened. "No, sir. Sullivan and I were lookin' into some leads in Kingston and Loudon, but he never did mention anything about Athens." Just then, he paused and scratched the back of his head. "Well, there was that time...."

"Go on," Ned urged him. The room was as silent as a morgue.

"Well, we were headin' over to Madisonville, right down near Athens, when he dropped me off at a restaurant and told me to have some lunch. Said he had some personal business to tend to and he'd be back later to pick me up. I'd say it wasn't much more than an hour later when he came strollin' through the door, lookin' all...well, puffed up 'n' proud. I asked him what was up, and he flashed a wad o' bills under my nose. Said he'd just made a transaction. When I asked him what sort, he laughed and said something like, 'Sold a piece o' land over in Decatur.' I didn't know he owned any properties, but I figured it wasn't any of my business."

"Sullivan's been walking around in some pretty fine duds, if you ask me," said Bill Flanders. He and Ned went back a long way, clear to their academy days, when they were still plenty wet behind the ears. Ned couldn't believe how fast thirty-five years had come and gone. Now pushing sixty, he'd been thinking more and more about retirement and spending time with sweet Marlene, his wife of almost thirty-seven years, but something told him he'd be working at least another five. Police work was in his blood.

"And everybody in the force knows he just got that nineteen-twenty-seven Olds," Bill finished.

"What're you gettin' at, Bill?" Ned knew well and good what Bill was getting at, but he wanted to hear him say it.

"Where's he gettin' the cash? You just said yourself you're takin' home peanuts. You drive a twenty-seven?"

The room buzzed with murmurs of concurrence. "Yeah, how's that happen?" somebody said amid the babble. "You can't convince me Sullivan had any property in Decatur."

"I don't trust Sullivan any more than I trust a bear in the woods," someone else added.

"All right, all right, I hear you," Ned said, raising his hand to silence the negative talk. "I'll do a little investigating and see if I can figure out what he's up to. The last thing we need is somebody tarnishing our department. I think I'll head over to Sevierville tomorrow, and then maybe Athens, to do some poking around."

"You want some company?" Bill asked.

Ned grinned. "I thought you'd never ask."

"That Sullivan character ain't been around in a while. You finally get him off your back?" Curtis Morgan propped his booted feet on Byron Pruitt's porch railing and leaned back in one of the rickety rocking chairs, his arms crossed over his narrow chest, the wide brim of his hat covering most of his weathered face. He drew smoke from his stogie, then blew it out in four perfect rings. Herb Sells and Hank Waggoner took up the other two chairs on the front porch, and Byron perched on the broken top step. The hot, sticky air had caused beads of sweat to pop out on his brow, made more plentiful by Curtis's question.

"Yeah, got 'im off my back, all right. Paid 'im one last time and made 'im promise to stay away."

"Man, you must've gave 'im a good lot to get 'im to agree. That fellow's been eatin' away at our profits for months now. Whatever you said, let's hope it sticks."

Byron mopped his brow and sneered. "Don't you worry none."

The screen door opened, and Rita stepped onto the porch with the tray of drinks he'd told her to bring. She cast Byron a hateful glance, no doubt because she'd overheard his remark about Sullivan. "Set that down right there, woman," he barked, "and git back in the house."

To his surprise, she obeyed without question. Out the corner of his eye, he watched his cronies' mouths drop in similar shock.

After she'd disappeared inside, Herb stared at the closed door and rubbed his scraggly beard. "Criminy! I order my ol' woman around like that, and she'd have my tongue twisted in a knot so tight, I wouldn't be speakin' for days."

Hank coughed, his lungs sounding older than his forty-some years. "Norine'd come at me with a pitch-fork."

Byron puffed out his chest. "That's 'cause you don't demand respect. You gotta teach 'em their place, fellas. Ain't that right, Rita?" He leaned forward in his chair, hoping his voice had reached her ears.

Of course, she didn't answer, but only because she knew better than to stir the pot. For the most part, Rita had been minding her manners. Now, if he could only get her to tell him where that blasted girl of hers had run off to, he'd rest a lot easier.

Chapter Ten

*It is good that a man should both hope and
quietly wait for the salvation of the LORD.*
—Lamentations 3:26

*E*llie awoke to the sounds of Tommy Lee's whimpers
in the adjoining room. She threw off her blankets, sat
up in bed, and tried to get her bearings. The room
was dark, save for the shaft of dim light from the hallway that seeped in through a crack under her door.
She whisked her hair over her shoulder, gazed at the
window overlooking W. Hill Street, and slowly reori-
ented herself. Even after two weeks of living here, she
still awoke every day with a fuzzy head and wondered
where she was for a few seconds, until reality struck.

She heard footfalls downstairs in the kitchen,
along with water running and dishes clanging. Gage
must not have left for work yet. Yesterday, he'd spoken
scarcely two sentences to her. He was probably still
stewing over the silly argument they'd had the evening
before. *Well*, she thought with a scowl, *he can stew all
he wants*. There were children to handle and a house
to put in order, never mind that she felt quite inept,
and she hadn't the time to fret over his words.

Tommy Lee let out a more demanding yell. She
leaned over to pull the chain on her bedside lamp.
The small brass clock read five fifteen. Yawning, she

slipped out of bed, snatched her robe from the foot-board, put her arms through the sleeves, and then padded barefoot into Tommy Lee's room.

In the waxing light from the window behind his bed, he was a mere silhouette, standing in bed with his arms slung over the wrought-iron bar. As soon as he spotted her, he straightened and began chirping happily.

Despite her dragging feet and weary body, she smiled back at him. Of Gage's kids, Tommy Lee was the most transparent. Busy as all get-out, too! She could imagine why an older woman would have a difficult time keeping up with him. "What are you doin' up, you little goober?"

"I stinky!" he exclaimed.

"My stars, you sure enough are!" she said, screwing up her face as she drew nearer. She plugged her nose and touched her forehead to his, which set off a spurt of giggles from him. "Come here, little mister," she said, holding out her arms. His own arms spread as he stood on tiptoe, making it easier for her to lift his thirty-some pounds up and over the railing. As suspected, his pajama pants were wet, as was the sheet. Good thing there was a rubber mat underneath to protect his mattress. The poor little guy! He couldn't have been comfortable. She needed to teach him to use the toilet, the sooner, the better. Maybe she would pay a visit to Livvie Taylor and ask for some suggestions. As a mother of three boys, she was probably an expert by now.

"Gracious, you're a heavy little man," Ellie said, groaning as she set Tommy Lee on the changing table. "Have you been sneakin' cookies?"

"Cookies!" he squealed. "I hungwy."

"I knew I shouldn't have said that word."

"I want cookies," he repeated with more vigor.

She pulled off his soggy bottoms, then unsnapped the safety pins on either side of the diaper and carefully removed it. "But it's not even time to get up, little man. You'll have your breakfast later. How do pancakes sound?" She cleaned him off with a few sheets of Gayetty's medicated paper, a most useful item she'd never known existed before moving to Wabash. My, what would Mama think if she saw her now, changing a baby and cleaning him with medicated paper? In the ramshackle privy on the farm in Athens, they always kept old catalogs at the ready.

"Panpakes! Panpakes!" Tommy Lee shouted.

She laughed at his pronunciation, then tried to cover her amusement with a stern hush. "Shh! You'll wake the household."

"Household!" he sang at the peak of his lungs while kicking his bare legs, enjoying his diaperless state.

She shook her head, hoping to discourage his silliness. With one hand, she held him still, and, with the other, she reached into the top drawer, where she'd stashed a fresh stack of laundered diaper cloths. How she wished she knew a thing or two about young boys. At least she'd learned the art of diapering, thanks to Frances, who had assisted her on her first try—on her wedding night, of all times. She'd spent the evening bathing a baby and then powdering and diapering his bottom, while her groom had sat downstairs, poring over the newspaper. That should have been her first clue that she'd married a boring, emotionally distant oaf!

❦

The giggles coming from Tommy Lee made Gage smile. That his son could find so much joy on a chilly, sunless morning both baffled him and stirred his envy.

He longed for a little more lightness in his step and a lot more grace in his behavior. Even Eleanor, who it was now apparent didn't know the Lord in a personal way, as far as he knew, acted more Christlike than he, especially around the children. He had yet to apologize for his harsh words of two nights ago. How could he have been so heartless as to insinuate that she was putting forth anything less than her best effort at parenting his kids? Good grief! She'd been working her tail off, and he'd made her to feel that it wasn't enough. In short, he'd been a mean old grouch. It wasn't as if he'd asked her to expound upon her past experience with kids. Had she cared for nieces and nephews? A neighbor's children, perhaps? He still knew so little about his wife, something he knew he needed to fix. What was keeping him from inquiring about her background and family? Surely, she missed them.

Deep down, he knew that he'd been keeping her at arm's length because the less he knew, the less commitment and effort were required on his part. "Horse dung!" he muttered. Regardless of her youth, she was his wife, and he needed to prove that he wasn't some beast, that his attitude of laxity and indifference was not the norm.

Tommy Lee shrieked with glee. While Gage couldn't decipher Ellie's response, he could hear her own giggles through the register overhead. He decided to venture upstairs to see just what the racket was about.

"I'm a-goin' to tickle your belly," Ellie was saying as he climbed the stairs and rounded the corner, tiptoeing past Frances's closed door and then the twins' to make his way down the dimly lit hall to the nursery. The door was ajar, giving him a two-inch slit to peer through—and he got an eyeful. If ever he'd seen a more remarkable sight, he couldn't recall it, woman bending over child, unspoken love passing between them. "Oh, what's this?" she cooed. "Is this a belly button? I'm a-goin' to kiss it."

Her frayed housecoat reached mid-calf, revealing feminine ankles and feet. Her wealth of black hair, wavy from being braided, now streamed freely down her back, some of it cascading over her shoulders. He hadn't seen her like this since the morning after the wedding, when they'd met rather awkwardly in the kitchen. Looking back, he'd been too blind and flummoxed to take much notice of her, but the sight of her now, her hair tumbling like a waterfall, caught him by surprise. He didn't know what he'd expected, but it wasn't this. Up till now, he'd viewed Ellie as a housekeeper and a sort of lifesaver for the way she'd come along at just the right time and agreed to marry him, thereby binding herself to him as a legal live-in nanny. But now, he saw her in a new light—a bright, dazzling light. Was she ever stunning! The realization struck him like a rock between the eyes.

As he lingered there unnoticed, fascinated by Ellie's interactions with his son, a vision of Ginny traipsed into his mind, and, try as he might, he couldn't push it away. Neither could he ignore Ellie, standing there before him, and so it was as if his two wives were working side by side, a striking contrast of elegance and sophistication in Ginny and unrefined energy and childlike naiveté in Ellie. Ginny had loved the twins and Frances—and Tommy Lee, of course, but the Lord had taken her so soon after his birth that she'd barely gotten a chance to hold him. A wave of sorrow washed over Gage. He'd wrestled hard with

God for nearly three years over the matter of her death, letting every emotion imaginable have its way in him. He'd questioned the wisdom of the Almighty, arguing that he needed his wife more than the Lord ever could, and he'd even lashed out in anger at God for stealing his one true love.

Once, he'd poured out his woes to Reverend White and asked him why God would steal a woman away from her adoring husband and kids. The preacher had smiled empathically and, after some thought, said, "It's hard to steal something that already belongs to you. Ginny has belonged to the Lord from conception, and when she asked Him to forgive her sins and take first place in her life, that just sealed the deal, in God's eyes. She was His, through and through, to do with as He chose. He has ordained for each of us the day and the hour when we will be restored to Him, and our job is to be ready and to somehow learn to accept when He calls our loved ones to go ahead of us."

"I'm a-goin' to tickle you," Ellie was saying again as she nuzzled Tommy Lee's belly with her nose. The toddler laughed loud enough to raise the roof, and certainly to draw Gage out of his reverie. As he resumed watching them, he experienced an uncanny warmth spread through his heart. It moved slowly, to be certain, sort of like God's fingers tenderly massaging those deep, aching places.

He would say one thing for Ellie—she had won the heart of his youngest child. He had no idea what Frances thought of her stepmother, or of anything else, for that matter. As for the twins, they'd kept up their antics as if nothing had changed. And that's what had sparked the heated discussion between Ellie and him the other night—the children. He'd implied that she wasn't doing her best, and she'd blamed his lack of involvement. That was something else about her: she'd brought a number of unpleasant things to his attention—things he'd known already but needed someone else to point out. Of course, he didn't spend enough time with his children. But who could add even an hour to the day?

He cleared his throat, hoping not to startle her, and pushed the door a smidge wider. The hinge squeaked loudly, though, startling even him. Ellie whirled on her heel. "Gracious me! Don't you know it ain't polite to sneak up on folks?"

"I wasn't sneaking up," he insisted, stepping into the room. "I just heard the ruckus and thought I'd come check on you two."

She gathered the collar of her robe high around her neck, as if that cotton undershirt buttoned clear to her throat were something forbidden. Averting his eyes, he noticed the threadbare hemline and torn pocket on the faded floral terry cloth. Why hadn't he sent her out to purchase some new clothes? Goodness, he had plenty set aside in the bank, and it wouldn't break him to open an account for her individual needs. Ginny had owned an abundance of clothes. He should know, after making three trips to carry crates of them to the storage area in the cellar. Later today, he would give Ellie some money, although something told him she'd stubbornly refuse and tell him she wasn't a charity case.

"Daddy!" Tommy Lee stretched out his arms, so Gage stepped forward and scooped up the boy with a kiss to the cheek. When had his son gotten so big? He delighted in the way he burrowed his head into the hollow of his neck. "What's he doing up so early?" he asked Ellie.

She patted the boy's bottom. "He had a soiled diaper."

"I'm stinky," Tommy Lee mumbled against him.

Gage couldn't help but chuckle. "Ah, that explains it."

"He needs to learn to use the...you know, the...."

He grinned. "Toilet?" Until now, he hadn't thought Ellie embarrassed easily, but in the dim light, he detected a slight blush on her cheeks.

"Yes. I don't suppose any of the nannies worked with him on that?"

"I guess not. We never really talked about it. He's the baby." He kissed his head.

"Well, he's startin' to outgrow these diaper cloths." She gave Tommy Lee another pat. "You must've trained the other kids before they got this big."

He thought about it. "I can't really remember. Ginny would have been the one training them."

"I see." She glanced down at the floor, then up again. "Well, it's goin' to take all of us workin' together to teach him."

He winked. "Can't you just wave a magic wand over him and call it done?"

The corners of her mouth quivered in a slight smile. "Like I told you the other night, I'm not a magician."

"Yes, my dear lady"—he tapped the end of her pert nose—"you did say that, didn't you? Speaking of the other night, I'm sorry...about our argument. I said things I shouldn't have. Forgive me? I truly think you're doing a great job with the kids." He didn't expect to feel such relief at getting that apology off his chest.

"I think I'm doin' a dreadful job, but I thank you anyway. As for the argument, I can forgive and forget, if you can."

"Good. You were right, you know."

"About doin' a dreadful job?" she asked with doleful eyes.

"No, silly. You were right when you said I don't spend enough time with my kids. Maybe we could plan an outing of some sort."

Her face brightened like a lightbulb. "Really? An outing? Like a picnic or somethin'?"

"Why not? Tommy Lee's third birthday is coming up. Maybe we could go out to celebrate."

"But what about the weather? Isn't it still too cold?"

"We'll bundle up, if need be. The only thing that might stop us would be rain."

"Oh, heavenly stars, a real party?"

"I guess you could call it that."

She clasped her hands together as one of his kids might do, reminding him just how young she was—not quite twice the twins' age. Sobering, he thought.

"I've never been to a party."

His head jerked back. "Never? Not even a birthday party for one of your friends?"

"Buthday party! Buthday party!" Tommy Lee chanted.

She shook her head. "Unless you count the shindig Livvie threw for us after the weddin'. That was a party, of sorts. As for goin' on a picnic or celebratin' somebody's birthday, I've done no such thing. To tell the truth, I didn't have a lot of friends growin' up."

"That's too bad. Most of my early memories involve my brothers and friends. The memories I cherish, anyway."

"You had a happy childhood, then."

"Pretty carefree."

"I be thwee on March twenny-first!" Tommy Lee spouted, as if to broadcast the news to the entire town.

"What?" she asked around Tommy Lee's chatter. "Did he say March twenty-first? That's just around the corner! We'd better get busy plannin'."

Gage laughed. "I'll leave the details up to you, my young wife."

She scowled up at him, and he presumed it was on account of his word choice. But it didn't dampen her enthusiasm, for she immediately began listing off all the things she'd need to do to prepare for their outing, such as bake cookies and other treats, come up with some games to play, and hunt down a picnic basket.

"What's goin' on in here? Sounds like the circus came to town."

Standing in the doorway was a sleepy-eyed, puffy-faced Alec. Coming up beside him were Abe and Frances, looking equally bushed. "Why's everybody making so much noise?" asked Abe.

Gage exchanged a glance with Ellie. "It all started with a dirty diaper."

Chapter Eleven

By this shall all men know that ye are my
disciples, if ye have love one to another.
—John 13:35

Ned Castleberry and Bill Flanders started their investigation of Walter Sullivan by poking around his stu-
dio apartment, looking for clues as to his whereabouts.
"You say you haven't seen him around for a while?" Ned
asked the landlord, who stood in the open doorway, rattling his keys in his pocket.

The short, stout fellow shook his balding head.
"Can't recall the last time. 'Course, that ain't too unusual. What is strange is that his mail's been pilin' up."

"That so?" *No surprise there*, Ned thought. "You
mind if we take a look at it?"

"His mail? Uh, I don't know about that."

"I won't open anything unless it looks like it might
aid in our investigation."

The fellow scratched his head and squinted pen-
sively. After a few moments, he finally said, "Oh, all
right. I'll go get it."

In the meantime, Bill sorted through piles of
papers on Sullivan's messy desktop, while Ned rifled
through the contents of his dresser drawers.

"You see anything of interest?" he asked Bill.

"Nah, not much."

Ned huffed a sigh and moved on to the kitchen area, where he pawed through more drawers and peeked inside the cabinets. When he opened the compact refrigerator, the stench of spoiled food nearly knocked him over. He groaned and quickly shut it again.

"Here's a matchbook," Bill muttered. "Millie's Diner, Athens, Tennessee."

Ned went to inspect it. "Might be the place Lindstrom was referring to yesterday when he said Sullivan told him some waitress gave him a lead on an operation."

"I'm thinkin' the same," said Bill.

"We'll check it out."

They continued to scour the tiny apartment until the landlord returned with a small stack of mail. Ned shuffled through it, disappointed to find nothing out of the ordinary—just a couple of advertising flyers, a utility bill, and several newspapers. He handed it back to the landlord and heaved a deep sigh. "Looks like we're done here. Thanks for showing us inside."

"No problem," the landlord said. "Hey, do me a favor?"

"Sure."

"When you find Mr. Sullivan, tell him his rent's overdue."

Ned gave a low chuckle. "I'll pass the word along."

❧

The sunshine warmed Ellie's shoulders as she pushed Tommy Lee in his stroller up Market Street. She'd chosen to gather her hair up into one long ponytail that morning, securing it with a pretty ribbon, and it bobbed from one shoulder to the next as she traipsed up the sidewalk. They passed J. C. Penney, where she would have been working right now if Gage Cooper hadn't hired her—married her, rather. It still felt plenty odd to think of him as her husband. She'd always pictured herself getting hitched to someone she'd loved long and hard and then settling down in a cozy cabin in the Smokies, maybe in the foothills. They would have enough land to live off of, some horses and a cow or two, maybe a few sheep and chickens, and, of course, dogs and cats! In time, children would round out the family, and they would learn together how to be the very best of parents.

Now, here she was, married to a man who'd already been wed to his first love and had four kids with her. The chances of his ever wanting more children were slim, especially given the strictly platonic nature of their relationship. It was more of a business partnership, and it wouldn't result in any offspring unless there was something to having kids that Ellie didn't know about. No, this setup did not define the marriage of her dreams—in fact, it didn't come close. But she had found a secure home, a new last name, and everything she needed to survive, and that meant a lot.

And, of course, she had the children, who were growing on her every day. She smiled at Tommy Lee, who squirmed in his stroller. He would much rather have walked, and he didn't fail to tell her repeatedly that he wanted to get out, but she'd figured the twelve-block jaunt was too much for a toddler. Besides, he dawdled, and she'd told Livvie to expect her between noon and one.

Warmer temperatures had melted most of the snow, and she found her spirits lifting to the heavens because of it. She still missed her mama terribly, but the sunshine planted seeds of hope for the future in her heart. Of course, it also helped that Gage had apologized earlier for their argument, and that she'd successfully convinced him to delay his departure for work so that he could join the rest of the household for breakfast. She'd prepared a hearty meal of ham, eggs, and pancakes, and Gage had said a blessing for the food and for the day ahead. It had filled Ellie with a wonderful sense of calm, making her wish that every day could begin like that.

She admired his manner of praying—he spoke to God as if He were a close friend, someone with whom one could sit down and have a cup of tea—and felt a longing for something she couldn't quite identify. Peace, perhaps, or freedom from fear. Yes, that was it. Since arriving in Wabash, she'd been haunted in her dreams by flashbacks of Walter Sullivan's death, and, more often than not, she awakened in a drenching sweat. Lately, she'd come to dread going to bed for fear of an imminent nightmare.

A sparrow pranced around on the sidewalk up ahead, pecking at some scraps, but it flitted away as they drew closer.

"Birdie!" Tommy Lee squealed. "Here, birdie."

Ellie chuckled at his innocence. "I think he's afraid of us," she said.

"Why?"

"Because we aren't birds."

"Why?"

Until meeting Tommy Lee, she'd had no idea a toddler could ask so many questions. "Because we're people, I suppose."

"Why are we people?"

How did one answer a question like that?

"Why?" She should have seen the one-word question coming.

"Miss Ellie!" She gazed up and saw Coot Hermanson strolling toward them with his dog, Reggie. Apparently they'd just left Livvie's Kitchen. *Ah, a break from the questions,* she thought with a happy sigh. She smiled and waved at the old gentleman.

"Doggy!" Tommy Lee shrieked, clapping his hands and kicking his feet.

They stopped on the sidewalk to greet each other, Reggie going straight for Tommy Lee's cheeks with his long, wet tongue. The boy laughed hysterically.

"Reg, go easy," Coot said. The dog immediately went down on his haunches. Gracious, the big mutt was quicker to obey than most kids, and Ellie pictured the twins when the notion occurred. "Hello there, young lady." Coot's yellow-toothed smile stretched across his craggy face. His eyes, cloudy yet intelligent, moved from her to Tommy Lee. "And you, too, lad." He looked back at Ellie. "What brings you to Market Street?"

"We're goin' to visit Mrs. Taylor."

"Mrs. Taylor," Tommy Lee chirped as he reached for Reggie. He managed to grab hold of a long, floppy ear, but the dog didn't object in the least, which reinforced in Ellie's mind something she'd been thinking a lot about lately: the Cooper family needed a dog—a big, friendly one like Reggie. She'd long thought that having a pet went far in teaching children responsibility. Of course, she had yet to broach the subject with Gage. She figured she'd have to develop a well thought-out argument if she hoped to win his approval.

"Is that so? Well, I'm sure she'll be right happy to see you." Coot grinned at Tommy Lee. "She likes little boys, that's for sure."

"I want a cookie!" Tommy Lee declared.

"Tommy Lee," Ellie scolded. "You don't need to eat everywhere you go."

"Of course he does," Coot insisted. "He's a growin' boy, ain't he?"

"I'm growing. I be big as Daddy!"

Coot chuckled. "Well, you're certainly on your way, young man." He turned to Ellie, his gray eyes giving off a twinkle of warmth. "How is that husband of yours? You two adjustin' to married life?"

Ellie shielded her eyes from the sun with her hand. "I suppose it's goin' as well as can be expected, considerin' I married a complete stranger."

He chuckled again. "Indeed you did, and I consider myself partially to blame for that. After all, I did encourage you to go on over to his place and introduce yourself."

"Oh, I don't want you feelin' guilty, Mr. Hermanson. Gracious, I don't have any regrets, truly I don't."

"Well, that's good to know. Give it time, my dear. Gage Cooper is a mighty fine man. Losing Ginny took a big toll on him." He gave his white head a couple of shakes. "He became a widower overnight, with four kids to raise, and one of 'em a newborn. Hardened 'im a little bit, I'd say, and pushed 'im to overwork himself at that cabinet shop. Never mind, though. I got a good feelin' about you two, yes, I do."

She smiled. "I'm glad somebody sees somethin' I don't." She wanted to ask him to elaborate on his remarks, especially those pertaining to Ginny Cooper, but she decided against it. Besides, Tommy Lee had started whining, so she bid Mr. Hermanson good day and headed for the restaurant.

Even with the sunshine, the air held a crispness that kept folks walking at a considerable clip, but it didn't stop them from congregating in groups of two or three for brief conversation. In the short time she'd lived in Wabash, she'd found it to be a friendly place. Her morning walk only underscored that fact, as everyone she passed seemed eager to greet her with a smile or a cordial hello. When she reached the door of Livvie's Kitchen, a man standing on the curb and puffing a cigarette rushed to hold the door open for her so that she could push the bulky stroller inside. "Clumsy things, aren't they?" he said with a wink.

"They certainly are. Much obliged, sir." Once inside, she parked the metal contraption beside an empty table, where she hoped it wouldn't be in the way.

Meanwhile, Tommy Lee wriggled and squirmed, doing his best to extricate himself from the buggy.

"Ellie, there you are!" Livvie dashed over to them and gave Ellie a hug, then extended her arms to Tommy Lee and lifted him out of the carriage. She was a natural in business mode and mommy mode alike, and Ellie couldn't help but gawk admiringly at her chic bob hairdo, her lovely yellow shirtwaist, her white apron secured behind her slender waist, her silken hose, and her two-inch black pumps. How did one run a restaurant, raise three youngsters, and still manage to look so riveting? Standing beside her, Ellie felt thrown together, not to mention unattractive and awkward. It made her wonder what Gage thought when he looked at her. Did he see the same thing she saw in the mirror—a plain, tomboyish girl with no idea how to look the part of wife and mother?

She removed her woolen scarf and unbuttoned her coat—*Livvie's coat*, she reminded herself. One day, she would find a way to repay her.

"How was your walk over here?" Livvie asked as she lowered Tommy Lee to the floor.

"Very nice. It's lovely out."

"It's still a bit too cold for my blood. I'll be happy when the leaves start popping out. I did see some daffodils sneaking up through the soil on our walk to church last Sunday, which was encouraging. Well, shall we go upstairs?"

"Oh! Sure, but I don't mind sittin' down here."

"Gracious, no," Livvie said. "I insist we go upstairs and relax. My sister has Robert for the afternoon, so we don't have to worry about interrupting his naptime. And there's a big box of toys Tommy Lee can dive right into. He'll love that."

"I'm sure he will, but are you sure? I don't want to be a bother."

Livvie smiled. "Honey, with four men in my house, I don't get nearly enough girl time. Come on! We've got things to discuss."

She looped an arm through Ellie's, and so, with her other arm, Ellie extended a hand to Tommy Lee, and the two of them followed Livvie toward the back of the restaurant. Will waved from the kitchen and then gestured to the countertop, where he'd set a cup of milk and a plate of biscuits smothered with jelly. "Hello there, Eleanor. Nice to see you again. I've got a snack here for that little fellow, if he's hungry. I bet he's been keeping you busy!"

Ellie laughed. "That would be an understatement." She tousled Tommy Lee's hair.

"I'm hungwy!" the boy chirped, eyeing the plate with eagerness.

"Can you say thank you to Mr. Taylor?"

"Tank you." Ellie's heart nearly melted at the sheepish smile that accompanied his statement of gratitude.

"You're welcome, young man." Will glanced up at Ellie and winked. "Why don't you two ladies leave Tommy Lee with me and the guys"—he nodded to the two men seated on barstools at the counter—"to sort through the world's problems while you two chitchat over tea?"

"Sounds perfect," Livvie said.

"Oh, but I don't want you to..." Ellie sputtered. "I mean, he's quite a handful."

"Ellie." Livvie turned, still attached to her at the arm, and looked her in the eye. "You forget that you're talking to the father of three boys, and each one a handful—fifteen fingers in all!" She laughed. "Don't worry. Will can handle him."

"I'm sure he can, and I'm not worried one bit, but I didn't come here intendin' to give him more work."

Will came out from behind the counter and put an arm on her shoulder, guiding her and Livvie toward the back door. "Young lady, my wife has been looking forward to your visit with anticipation. Now, you just leave Tommy Lee down here, and we'll keep him entertained for a while. If things get too busy, which I don't anticipate, I'll bring him up to you. But until then, you ladies go upstairs and enjoy yourselves."

Livvie squeezed Ellie's arm. "Isn't he a dream come true?"

"Good grief! You'll make me blush," he said as he opened the door for them.

"No, I won't. You know you love it when I tell people what a great husband I have."

He dipped his head in agreement. "Well, all right, I guess that's true. But I think most people know I'm a great husband when they see how I have to put up with you."

Livvie swatted at him. "Silly boy." Then, she giggled, blew him a kiss, and turned to lead Ellie up the staircase. As they ascended to a landing on the second floor, Ellie thought how fun it would be to reach a level of comfort with Gage where they could banter back and forth, as Livvie and Will did. She supposed that would require them to be friends first.

The Taylors' apartment had a warm, cozy atmosphere, with windows aplenty to let in light and offer a vista of downtown Wabash. A bright kitchen with floral curtains, inviting furniture in the dining room and living room, and framed art on the walls, as well as a smattering of toys strewn across the floor, gave it that lived-in family feel, putting Ellie at ease as soon as they entered.

"What a nice apartment."

"Oh, gracious, it's not much, a little snug for five of us, but it's home, and as long as we have the restaurant to run, we'll stay here," said Livvie. "It's a dollhouse compared to Gage's place, isn't it?"

Ellie gave a light laugh. "His house is huge, I agree. And a chore to keep clean, let me tell you."

"But is it starting to feel like home?"

She had to ask that, Ellie thought. The mere mention of "home" conjured the image of her mama, and she fought back the tears that threatened to fall by forcing a smile. "Somewhat, I guess. But, in lots o' ways, I still feel like a stranger."

Nodding, Livvie helped her out of her coat and then laid it on the back of a dining room chair. Then, she started for the living room. "Things will work out in time, sweetie. You'll see. The Bible says that *'all things work together for good to them that love God, to them who are the called according to his purpose.'* I believe deep within my heart that you were called to be Gage's wife, even though you and maybe none of us really saw it in the very beginning. Be patient. You're just getting to know your new family." Livvie gestured to an overstuffed chair. "Please, make yourself comfortable. Would you like some tea?"

"That would be nice, thanks, but don't go to any extra trouble." Ellie lowered herself into the chair and dabbed her eyes, dampened by a few tears that had managed to slip out.

"Pooh, it's no trouble at all," Livvie said as she moved to the kitchen. She picked up a shiny copper teakettle, filled it with water from the spigot, and set it on a burner she ignited. "Like Will said, I've really been looking forward to our visit. I'm so glad you came over. Between the restaurant, the apartment, the boys, and church, my time is stretched pretty thin. I rarely get the chance to chat with other women, and I miss it dearly."

Ellie watched in fascination as Livvie flitted about the kitchen. "I hope you like oatmeal cookies," she said in singsong. "I baked a batch last night."

"They're my favorite!"

Livvie moved to the china cabinet, opened the glass doors, and lifted out a beautiful teapot with a floral pattern, along with two teacups and saucers, and set everything on the counter. Then, she opened a drawer and brought out a couple of striped napkins.

"So, how did your mother react to the news of your marriage?"

The question, while certainly an innocent one, caught Ellie off guard, but she tried to cover her surprise. "I...I haven't exactly told her yet. I plan to tell her in a letter."

Livvie glanced up, her eyes as round as the china saucers. "Gracious me! You mean, you haven't told her you're married? But wouldn't she want to know?"

Ellie knit her fingers together and swallowed hard. "She'll be mighty surprised, I'm sure, but when I explain the circumstances of how Gage needed a wife to help care for his children, I'm sure she'll understand. In fact, she'll be downright happy for me."

Much to Ellie's relief, the teakettle's whistle drew Livvie back to the kitchen. She watched her move the kettle off of the burner and fill the teapot as steam rose in tiny white clouds. Then, she set the teapot and cups and saucers on a tray.

Ellie jumped up. "Please, let me help you. I don't know where I left my manners."

"Thank you, honey. I'll let you carry that plate of cookies, there, and the napkins."

Ellie followed Livvie back into the living room, where they arranged the tea service and cookie tray on a wooden table topped with a lace doily.

"Now, sit back down so I can serve you," Livvie insisted. Ellie couldn't remember ever having been so carefully waited upon, and she hardly knew how to react. Livvie smiled. "Go ahead, sit down."

Reluctantly, Ellie slowly lowered herself back onto the soft cushion and accepted the cup and saucer offered her. She set them on the table and picked up the teacup, both her hands delighting in its warmth, as Livvie situated herself in the other chair.

"Now, let me offer a prayer of thanksgiving for our time together," Livvie said.

Ellie's heart skipped a beat, and she immediately lowered her cup from her lips. "Oh, that would be so nice."

Never had she heard a lovelier, more eloquent prayer. In it, Livvie thanked the Lord for her friend Ellie. She then prayed a blessing over her marriage and asked that Ellie's mother would receive the news of her daughter's wedding with much joy. After that, she prayed for the children who had been put under Ellie's care, that God would bless them, protect them, and give Ellie wisdom and guidance as she raised them. She also prayed the unthinkable—that, in time, Ellie and Gage would find a love like no other, a love that could come only from the One who had designed marriage for man and woman to enjoy. Finally, she prayed that Gage's soul and Ellie's would be fully surrendered to the Father and His purposes for their lives, emptied of all selfish desires, and filled instead with the love of the Lord Jesus Christ, as well as a longing to obey and serve Him.

By the time Livvie uttered the final amen, Ellie's face was wet with tears. She picked up her napkin to dry them.

Livvie scooted off her chair and squeezed in next to Ellie, throwing an arm around her shoulders and giving them a little hug. "I didn't mean to make you cry, sweetie. I think the Lord must be working on your heart. And you probably have a lot of emotional build-up that was bursting to get out." Livvie fingered Ellie's ponytail, something her mama would have done.

So, when Livvie asked, "What shall we talk about first?" Ellie burst into tears. "I miss my mama somethin' terrible," she sobbed into Livvie's shoulder.

"There, now. Of course, you do. Let it all out, Ellie. It's good, these tears."

"And Gage and I had our first big argument"— she hiccupped—"but he apologized this mornin', so I think we're back on track." Another hiccup pushed its way out. Gracious, she was nothing but a big baby.

"Every couple has disagreements, honey; it's to be expected."

"And I don't know the first thing about teachin' Tommy Lee how to use the...the...privy."

"The toilet, you mean?"

"Yes!" Her tears came a little faster.

Livvie's soft laughter soothed like a warm summer breeze. "That I can help you with. We'll have that boy trained in a few days if you follow my simple steps."

"Really?" Ellie sniffed and wiped her tear-drenched cheeks with her napkin, trying with all she had in her to regain her composure.

"He's almost three, so he's definitely old enough to start training. The trick is to remove those diapers and put regular drawers on him. Next time he wets and starts to complain about it, just tell him, 'I'm sorry, but we don't have enough briefs to keep changing you into dry ones. If you would have used the potty seat, as I showed you, you wouldn't feel so uncomfortable.' Just making him walk around wet and itchy for a few minutes at a time will speed things along. Granted, you may have to prepare yourself for a battle, but it will be short-lived if you stay firm. When our kids are uncomfortable, we tend to want to remedy the problem immediately, but this is the time to hold off on that. Let him deal with that nasty feeling for a while, and soon he'll begin making the association that if he uses the toilet when he has a need, the discomfort will go away. Don't punish him for doing it wrong, but do give him lots of praise. I tried this with my boys. In the morning, I laid out a good-sized cookie or brownie. Every time they used the bathroom, they got to take a bite. If they soiled or wet their underwear, then no bite. Sometimes, I had to throw away more than half the cookie at day's end, but then came the day they stayed completely dry, and so we celebrated by finishing the cookie...and maybe even getting another one."

"You make it sound so easy," Ellie said.

"Ha! Nothing about parenting is easy, Ellie dear, but it is rewarding, and I have a strong hunch you're going to discover that truth a hundred times over as you and Gage raise those delightful kids together."

She felt better already. "Thank you for bein' my friend, Livvie."

"The pleasure is all mine." Livvie returned to her own chair. "I think our tea has gone cold on us."

Ellie put the cup to her lips. "Mmm," she murmured as the warm liquid slid down her throat. "It's still delicious as can be."

Livvie smiled and picked up her teacup. "It'll do for now, but we'll soon need a warm-up. I've a feeling we have a lot more to talk about."

Chapter Twelve

For God shall bring every work into
judgment, with every secret thing, whether
it be good, or whether it be evil.
—Ecclesiastes 12:14

After stopping at a gas station to ask for directions, Ned and Bill cruised along Ingleside Avenue, a few miles outside of Athens' city limits, and finally found Millie's Diner. Ned parked the car in the lot, and he and Bill climbed out. "Don't know why, but I pictured this place being downtown," Ned said, stopping on the brick walkway leading to the restaurant to stretch his aching muscles. He was getting too old for taking hour-and-a-half-long drives over bumpy country roads on a seat with a broken spring.

Bill surveyed the field behind the diner, where several cows and horses grazed, and gave a little sniff. Then, he reached into his pant pocket and pulled out a cigarette and his lighter. "Yeah, I s'pose I did, too." He lit the nicotine stick and took a drag. "But if Sullivan's tryin' to hide somethin', it might make sense that he'd prefer someplace off the beaten track."

Ned waved a cloud of cigarette smoke out of his face. "You think he's trying to hide something, do you?"

"Don't have a clue, really, but the other guys seemed to have their suspicions at the meetin' yesterday." Bill sent another puff of smoke skyward. "Frankly, Walt Sullivan's always been somewhat of a puzzle to me. Nothing wrong with being private, I s'pose, but he's plain reclusive. Not what I'd call a team player. Why'd you hire 'im, anyway?"

"He came recommended by a friend of a friend of a friend, if you get my drift, and his qualifications seemed sufficient, even though I never did get a decent explanation as to why he left his former job. He worked for an agency in Lakeland, Florida, but I'm not sure which counties he covered. That's kind of in the middle of the state, in case you didn't know—lots of wide-open spaces, from what I hear. When I asked him why he left, he mentioned something about there not being enough action. But then, just a few weeks after I hired him, I read about some major bust the department made right there in Lakeland."

"Humph." Bill took a few more drags off his cigarette and narrowed his eyes at a fellow across the street, who got into a car and drove off. "I'd try to get in touch with his superiors down there. Find out who really decided he needed to leave."

Ned chuckled low in his throat. "Flanders, it scares me the way our minds think alike sometimes." He combed one hand through his thinning gray hair.

His friend grinned while he tapped his cigarette against his leg to release the ashes. "When you been workin' together as long as we have, it's no wonder. Me, I don't think I've had more than a ten-minute conversation with Sullivan, but I've always had a feelin' about him. He sort o' reminds me of a skunk hidin' his smell."

"Huh. That's one way to put it," Ned said. "He keeps to himself, that's for sure. Truth told, I was about to fire him if he didn't start laying his cards on the table concerning his whereabouts. Can't have somebody on my force I can't trust. Where do you think he's been for the last month or so?"

Bill scratched the back of his head. "Maybe he's got a woman."

"Walt Sullivan? I guess anything's possible, but I don't see it. He doesn't strike me as the type who'd care about anybody but himself, much less the type any woman would care about."

"Yeah."

They stood there for a moment, pondering the matter.

"Well, let's go in and get us a cup of coffee, shall we?" Ned said.

Bill stomped out his cigarette. "Lead the way, boss."

Inside the diner was a smattering of customers who were probably regulars, along with a couple of harried-looking waitresses and a male cook. According to Tim Lindstrom, Walt had said he'd gotten a tip from a "cute little waitress." If that was true, either they had the wrong place, or Walt Sullivan's taste in women was vastly different from his.

"You see any cute waitress?" Bill whispered out of the side of his mouth. Again, their minds ran along the same vein. *Scary,* Ned thought.

A waitress approached them with a grin that revealed some missing teeth and led them to a table against the far wall. "What can I get you two fellers?" she asked.

"A couple of coffees," Ned said.

"You want some strawberry pie with those coffees? It's fresh, baked just this mornin'."

"No, thanks," Ned replied.

"Yeah," Bill said at the same time.

The waitress raised her eyebrows at Ned.

"Oh, why not?" he said. "Bring us two slices."

She returned minutes later to deliver their pie and fill their coffee mugs. Then, instead of leaving them to their meal, she stood there, one hand holding the coffee carafe, the other planted firmly on her bony hip. "Where you boys from? I never seen you in here before. You look pretty important in them suits. You two lawyers or somethin'?"

Bill raised his coffee mug and took a sip, peering over the rim at Ned—designating him the spokesperson.

"Nope, lawyers we're not," Ned said, "and we're not that important, either. Well, Bill, here, thinks he's pretty special."

The waitress laughed—more like cackled, so gravelly was the sound. She looked from Ned to Bill and back again. "You come to Athens on business? I know you ain't from these parts."

"You know that, eh?" Ned asked. "You know everybody in Athens?"

"Durn near everybody. Been here all my life."

Ned would have guessed that to be more than sixty years. "You must know a great deal about a lot of folks."

"Ask me anythin' at all."

"Yeah? All right."

"Are you Millie?" Bill cut in.

"Me? Nah. Millie done departed this earth some five years ago. Stan kept the name, though, you know, out o' respect. I been waitin' tables here for twenty-six years."

"You got quite a career going," Ned said. "Who's Stan?"

She hooked a thumb over her shoulder toward the kitchen. The cook. "Her ol' man. Them two was quite a pair, always fightin' like two roosters in a ring but makin' up before sundown."

"Ah." Ned looked at Stan, who stood over the stove, frying up some burgers. He had his back to them, but Ned could see enough to know his profile— mid- to late-sixties, white hair and a matching mustache, weathered face, double chin, bulbous nose, and bushy eyebrows.

"So, where you two from?" she asked again. Did every stranger who came through the diner door get the third degree? Ned stole a glance at Bill, who shrugged indifferently.

He looked back at the waitress. "Drove over from Sevierville." He supposed it couldn't hurt to disclose that much. He needed to feel her out, see if he could trust her, before putting any more questions to her.

Her eyebrows shot up. "That's more'n a little jaunt. You couldn't've come all this way just for a meal at Millie's."

"No? Looks like a pretty hot spot, if you ask me," Ned joshed.

She gave another hoarse-sounding laugh and pushed a clump of dyed black hair behind her ear. "You show up here on a Friday night, we'll show you what a hot spot is." She leaned closer and raised her eyebrows. "Spaghetti night."

The door opened, and the three of them turned around to see who'd come in. A middle-aged couple. The waitress waved at the pair, then looked back at Ned and Bill. "You two enjoy that there pie. I'll be back in a bit with a warm-up."

"Thank you, ma'am." Ned raised his cup. "I'm sure we'll be needing it."

When she turned her back to them, Bill inclined his head. "If anybody can shed some light on who Walt Sullivan's hangin' out with these days, I bet she can."

With his fork, Ned sectioned off a juicy bite of pie. "You might be right."

True to her word, the waitress returned a few minutes later—perfect timing, for they'd scraped their plates clean and just drained their coffee mugs. Bill was working on another cigarette. "How'd you like that pie?" she asked as she refilled their mugs with steaming, black brew.

"Good stuff," Ned said. "And the coffee's not bad, either."

"You boys need anything else?"

The men shared a hurried glance, each trying to read the other for a clue as to how to proceed. Bill gave a subtle nod of his head, so Ned went for it. "Seeing as you seem to know a lot of folks around Athens, we wondered if you might recognize this guy." He reached in his pocket and pulled out the head shot of Walt Sullivan he'd taken from his employee file that morning.

The waitress snatched the photo and studied it, her wrinkles deepening in scrutiny. "Humph. Maybe, an' maybe not." She tilted her head at an angle, then slanted the photo, as if that would help jog her memory. "Can't say for sure." She tossed the photo onto the table and folded her arms across her chest.

"You can't say, or you don't want to?" Ned asked.

"Who are you guys, anyway?"

Before answering, Ned surveyed the room for potential eavesdroppers. The closest diners were seated several tables away and seemed intent on their own conversation. Still, to be safe, he lowered his voice and leaned a little closer to the woman. "We're government agents, but we aren't here to arrest anybody. We're just looking for this man. His name's Walter Sullivan. Sound familiar?"

"Agents, eh?" She ignored his question. "What kind? And be specific."

"Uh, well, all right. We work for the Bureau of Prohibition. I'm the director for East Tennessee. I can show you some identification, if you—"

"Wull," she drawled, helping herself to the third chair at their table, "ain't that somethin'? Here I thought you was crime bosses or somethin', the way you was all spiffed up in suits and ties—and you with that dress hat," she said, gesturing at Bill. "Earl's always tellin' me I read too many spy novels." She poked at her temple with a long, painted red nail. "He says it makes my imagination run a little haywire."

"Earl?"

"Yeah, my better half. Been married for forty-four years, not all to Earl, mind you. He's my third. Divorced number one, that no-good scoundrel, and number two kicked the bucket just two weeks after the weddin'. I hardly knew that man well enough to mourn 'im. Now, Earl, if he goes before me, I swear I'll go crazy. He's the best one so far, not that I wouldn't be willin' to go lookin' for number four if I had to. You two got wives?"

They hadn't bargained on her being such a talker. "Uh, yeah, we sure do."

"Oh, well, ain't that somethin'?" Her shoulders drooped, as if the news somehow disappointed her.

"What about the picture? You ever seen him before?"

"Nope."

"You sure?" Ned pressed.

"Yeah, I'm sure."

"Ruthie, you makin' a pest o' yourself over there?" came a shout from the kitchen.

Ned turned and studied Stan the cook. He'd pegged him accurately in every way, right down to his double chin. The only detail he'd botched was the white mustache. The fellow was clean-shaven—well, as clean-shaven as a man can be at midday.

"Just bein' my usual friendly self, Stan," she returned.

Stan shrugged and turned back to the stove.

"Sorry, I can't help you. What'd he do, kill somebody? Oh, there I go again, lettin' my imagination run free as a lark."

Bill leaned over in his chair to reach inside his pocket. "You wouldn't be needin' some extra cash, would you?" He produced a small wad of paper money.

"Flanders! What are you thinking? We just told the woman we're government agents. You want to lose your job?" Ned looked at the waitress with feigned indignation. "Sorry, Ruthie. Bill acts a little crazy sometimes, you know what I mean? He wants something, he'll resort to any measures."

Ruthie stared at the money and licked her lips. Then, she lowered her head and inched closer. "I might've seen him a time or two," came her raspy whisper.

"Oh, yeah? Why so secretive?" Ned asked, heart thumping. He swept his fingers through his hair and lowered his voice to say, "He ain't the nicest berry in the bucket, if you get my drift."

Bill placed a $10 greenback on the table. Ruthie glanced around, then scooped it up as fast as an eagle snatching up its prey and stuffed it inside her apron pocket. She leaned in even closer. "He made friends with a young lady who used to work here. Eileen Ridderman. She moved to Athens 'bout a year ago from someplace up north, tryin' to strike out on 'er own. Think she got her heart broke by some feller back home, an' she just wanted to start a new life."

"You don't happen to know where up north she was from, do you?" Bill asked.

"Couldn't tell you that, nope. Eileen an' me mostly worked together on weekends, and weekends around here get busy, so we never had much time for chit-chat. Anyway, I did happen to be workin' with her that first day Sullivan came saunterin' in here and started payin' her lots of attention. Let's see...I'd say that was a good eight months ago. Every time she passed his table, he'd wink at her or make some sort o' comment. Next thing I know, she's takin' her coffee break at his table, and they's talkin' all cozy-like. Made me wonder if she already knew 'im from someplace else, but I never did ask her. After that, he started comin' in real regular. Frankly, I think she ate up his flirtatious ways, though he sure wasn't much to look at." Ruthie shuddered, and Ned had to hold his breath to avoid laughing out loud.

Bill furrowed his brow. "I can't picture it, Walt friendlyin' up to a woman."

"I'd say she was more like a girl. I kept tellin' Eileen he was way too old for her—he could've been her pa, I tell you—and that she couldn't trust 'im, but she wouldn't listen to me. She just seemed to gravitate to 'im. It wouldn't surprise me none to find out he was givin' her money and buyin' her clothes and stuff. For all I know, he's payin' her rent right now. He does seem to have plenty of cash on hand." She cleared her throat and lowered her voice even further. "Then came the day, oh, two or three months ago, she showed up at work with a big, ugly bruise on her chin, and I got suspicious. Eileen claimed she fell down some stairs, and I said, 'Sure, I heard that one before.'

"Stan told me to mind my own business, but I couldn't help myself. Next time that rat came through the doors, I gave him a piece o' my mind, told 'im to keep his grubby hands off Eileen, 'cause she never hurt nobody. I saw fire in his eyes, and I do mean fire. And somethin' else—he always smelled mighty strong o' whiskey. If he wasn't drunk most days, then I'll eat those plates o' yours."

Ned had heard just about enough. He couldn't believe he'd been so blind to Sullivan's shenanigans. He should have fired the creep ages ago. The thought of him laying a hand on a woman and leaving bruises was utterly sickening.

"That was her last day here," Ruthie said. "I'm sure as can be that Mr. Sullivan told her to quit."

"Where can we find her now? Did she get a new job that you know of?" Ned asked.

"Last I heard, she took a little apartment above Lou an' Bud's Shoe Store in downtown Athens, and I can't say for sure, but I think she might be runnin' the cash register for 'em. Sweet little thing she is, sort of plain, though, and darned naive if you ask me."

"You think Sullivan's livin' with her?" asked Bill.

"No idea. After she quit workin' here, we lost touch. Like I said, I didn't know her well enough to butt into her affairs, 'cept for that one time I tol' Sullivan to lay off 'er. Since then, I haven't seen so much as her shadow." She wrinkled her brow. "I guess I oughtta pay her a visit, shouldn't I? I hope that dirty rascal isn't hurtin' her no more. Don't know what she saw in 'im, I tell you."

Ned and Bill both took a deep breath and pushed back their chairs. "You've been a mighty big help, Miss Ruthie," Ned said with a nod.

"Aww, well, once I figured yous two was trustworthy enough, I just told you what I know. Can't figure out what that Sullivan guy is up to, but if you find Miss Eileen, you should try to talk her into givin' 'im the boot."

"We make no promises, ma'am, but we'll surely do our best," Ned assured her.

A half hour later, they were pulling into a parking space in front of Lou & Bud's Shoe Store. "You think we'll find some answers here?" Bill asked.

"I'm hoping so." He looked down at Bill's worn shoes. "Anyone told you lately you could use a new pair of shoes?"

"Ha! Elsie did just this morning, in fact."

Ned cut the engine. "Looks like we've come to the right place."

When they entered the store, a bell above the door jangled. A customer and the clerk glanced up at them. "Afternoon," the clerk said. "I'll be right with you."

"No hurry," Ned said. He pointed to a pair of women's pumps and whispered to Bill, "Here you go. Just your style."

"Pfff."

The two of them milled about for a few minutes before the clerk made his way over to them. "You fellows see something here that interests you?"

"Sure. You got these in my size?" Bill asked, holding up a pair of black oxfords.

"Well, let's measure your feet and find out, shall we? Why don't you go have a seat over there and take off your right shoe?" He pointed at a row of chairs, then went around the counter behind the cash register and lifted some sort of device from the hook where it hung on the wall.

Bill sat down, and Ned settled in a few chairs down, thankful for the chance to rest. "What's that you got there?" Ned asked the clerk as he advanced with the metal instrument.

"This?" The fellow held up the tool, then got down on one knee in front of Bill and began positioning his stockinged foot on it. "This here's a state-of-the-art invention, called the Brannock Device. It's pretty handy-dandy, if you ask me." He looked up at Bill. "Stand up, mister, so we can get the bulk of your weight on this thing." Bill stood, and the clerk adjusted the sliding elements on the side to align with the length and width of his foot. "The patent's still in the works, but, in the meantime, they've manufactured enough of these gadgets to sell to retailers across the country. A salesman came through a couple months ago, and I bought his last one."

"That so?" Ned said, mildly interested. "Not to change the subject, but do you happen to have a tenant named Eileen Ridderman living in the apartment upstairs?"

"Used to, yeah."

"Used to?"

"Yep. Last I heard, she went back to her parents' house in Seymour." He scratched his temple and frowned. "She left...oh, let's see...ten days ago, I'd say. Still owes me this month's rent, too. She promised she'd mail it, but, so far, nothing." The clerk looked back at Bill. "Looks like you're a size eleven B, sir."

"Seymour, you say?" Ned mused. "That's over by Knoxville."

"Yep, Seymour's a bit north of here. Are you friends of Eileen's?"

"You ever see an older gentleman hanging around her apartment?" Ned asked, passing over his question.

"Her uncle Wally, you mean?"

Wally? Sure sounded as if it could be Walter Sullivan.

"I saw the guy go up to visit her quite a few times. I had a hunch he was helping to cover her rent. She sure didn't earn enough just working the cash register." He pinched the tip of his chin. "Now that I think on it, I haven't seen hide or hair of that fellow for a couple of weeks, either. Wonder if he went back to Seymour with her. Can't figure out why they both up and disappeared."

Ned wasn't about to enlighten him about "Uncle Wally's" true identity. It wouldn't accomplish anything, considering this clerk appeared to know less than the waitress at Millie's.

"If you'll excuse me, I'll go check if we have your size in stock," said the clerk. He disappeared through a curtain-covered doorway.

Ned looked at Bill. "Looks like our next destination is Seymour."

"It feels like we're on a wild-goose chase."

"It's called finding answers, Bill. We're getting closer."

Chapter Thirteen

If my people, which are called by my name,
shall humble themselves, and pray, and
seek my face, and turn from their wicked
ways; then will I hear from heaven, and will
forgive their sin, and will heal their land.
—2 Chronicles 7:14

Gage couldn't help but hum a little tune as he put the finishing touches on a dresser he'd been working on for the past month. He tightened one last piece of hardware and then ran a hand over the glossy finish to feel for any imperfections. He had the shop to himself, since Fred had taken the day off to attend to some family matters, and Edith, his secretary, had left early. It gave Gage plenty of time for reflection, and he couldn't deny that most of his thoughts were spent on his pretty wife. He didn't think she had an inkling of how attractive she was, and her naiveté only contributed to her appeal.

Ellie's natural beauty wasn't something he'd noticed only recently, it just hadn't affected him before now—more like, he hadn't previously acknowledged how it affected him. Of course, that didn't change anything, except to set off an inner warning signal that he shouldn't let his emotions run away with him, lest he complicate the nice little arrangement they had going. Their marriage was a business relationship, and he would be smart to remember that if he didn't want to scare the tender doe away. Yet he reminded himself that she wasn't the type to scare easily. No, she had the spirit and strength of character that came from a hard life but gave her enough grit to survive it, just the same. And he found himself wanting to know more about her.

Nostalgia sluiced over him when he thought about the family all gathered together for breakfast like normal folk, praying and eating together. Ginny had always insisted on prayer before meals, so he'd done his best to continue the ritual, but, more often than not, it was just that—a ritual. This morning had been different, though, as he'd thanked the Lord for His bounteous blessings and asked Him to watch over his family. It reminded him that he needed to be more intentional about bedtime prayers, talks around the table, and family fun and games. Perhaps the outing Ellie was planning for Tommy Lee's birthday would go far to draw them closer as a unit. He looked again at the dresser over which he'd labored so long and hard. All too often, his work came first, pushing the Lord and his kids into the background. His brow crumpled in a frown. "Lord, help me rearrange my priorities so that I don't forget the importance of putting You first and family second."

No sooner had he whispered the words than the door opened. He craned his neck to see over the cabinet blocking his view to see who'd come in. It was Ellie, of all people, struggling to push the unwieldy baby stroller through the door.

"Well, who have we here?" he asked, quickly weaving his way around some piles of sawdust, scraps of wood, and unfinished furniture pieces to reach the entryway. He held the door open so that she could push the carriage over the threshold.

"Shh," she said, holding a finger to her lips. "He just drifted off." Then, she closed her eyes and took a deep breath. "My, how I love that wonderful smell of fresh-cut wood. Fills the nostrils like pungent smoke from a campfire."

Had she really said that, this Southern girl? She might struggle with proper grammar on occasion, but she also had a gift for putting music to her words.

"Here," he whispered, grasping the bar of the buggy. He maneuvered it into a corner, away from the drafty door, and adjusted the blanket covering his soundly sleeping, pudgy-cheeked son. Then, he turned to Ellie. "Let me take your coat," he whispered.

"No, no, we didn't plan to stay. I don't want to interrupt your work."

He grinned. "You already have interrupted it, and I must say I'm glad for the diversion."

"But the children will be comin' home from school soon, and I need to get supper started. I just thought, since this was sort of midway between Livvie's Kitchen and the house, we'd stop by for a minute to say hi. I didn't know Tommy Lee would fall asleep on me, although I'm not surprised, since he missed his usual nap. Me 'n' Tommy Lee—I mean, Tommy Lee *and I* were just visitin' Livvie at the restaurant."

He had to hand it to her for working hard to fix her English. It occurred to him that if she could work so hard at something, he, too, could take a step toward improvement. The Lord knew he had several areas needing significant change. "Yes, that's right. Did you have a nice time? Come on, now, you can stay a minute. I'd like to hear about your day. Here, give me your coat."

With some reluctance, she unbuttoned the garment and handed it over, along with her scarf. "I didn't think 'distraction' was a part o' your vocabulary, you who're driven like the wind."

He chuckled. "Now and then I do." He laid her coat on a coffee table he'd finished a few days ago, then pulled out a chair, dusted it off with his palm, and nodded to invite her to sit. As she did, he leaned back against his workbench, folded his arms across his chest, and allowed his eyes to feast on her perfect, tawny face. Something was missing, though—the shiny, coal-black braids that were usually suspended in front of her shoulders. Today, she'd pulled her hair back in a ponytail that flowed down her back. The thick, fluid texture and ebony hue put him in mind of an Indian princess.

"Gracious, do you have to tower over me like that?" she asked. "Haven't you been on your feet all day?"

"Actually, I've been sitting on a stool a good share of the morning, sanding some wood pieces. And, believe it or not, I rather like the view from here."

"What view?" She looked around, then turned back to him, her cheeks flushing a rosy hue.

He chuckled and snagged a chair, flipped it around, and straddled it, arms crossed over the back. "There, is that better?" he asked, his eyes at her level. "So, how was your visit with Livvie?"

"Oh, it was lovely. She's such a gracious person. She gave me some tips on how to train Tommy Lee to use the pot—er, lavatory—er...."

"Commode?" Gage asked, raising his eyebrows. "I don't care what you call it, Ellie. No need to be delicate around me."

"Oh." She sighed. "That's a relief. Back home, we called it the johnny, and it was outside. But anyway, Mr. Taylor kept Tommy Lee with him in the restaurant for the longest time so that Livvie 'n' me could enjoy a cozy chat in their apartment. We sipped on tea and talked about so many things. She even said a prayer, just like you did this mornin'. Gracious me, I wish my prayers were half as pretty. Does it take a lot o' practice?"

"Praying?"

She nodded, her dark eyes flashing with interest.

"No, not really. God wants us to pray to Him the same way we would talk to a close friend."

"A friend? Really? But that sounds too easy. Do you do it often? Talk to Him, I mean?"

A stab of guilt hit him square in the chest. "Not as much as I should, I'm afraid. Life gets so busy, and, before you know it, other things take precedence. I've been feeling convicted about that lately, though—how little I've been reading my Bible and spending time alone with God in prayer." It felt surprisingly good to get that out in the open. "How about you? I know you said you didn't have much opportunity to go to church back in Athens, but you mentioned praying and reading your Bible."

She shifted her weight and gave a jagged sigh. "Um, I may have fibbed a bit so you wouldn't change your mind about marryin' me." She dipped her head and fingered the hem of her sleeve. "I'm sorry, but I'm not much good at prayin'. I never know if I'm gettin' through. As for reading the Good Book, well, I'll confess I don't even own one, but I have been readin' some from the Bible on the nightstand in my bedroom. And, if you want the truth, I find the Bible very enthralling. I read the whole book of Psalms, and now I'm startin' in on the New Testament. It's amazin' to think about God sendin' His Son to earth in human flesh and blood. I can hardly wrap my mind around it."

Her utter lack of experience with spiritual matters pained his heart, but he felt a hint of relief to realize that she was interested in learning and growing. "It is amazing, Ellie. I can't imagine loving anyone enough to give up a son." Shucks, he was about as rusty as an old tin lizzie when it came to talking about Jesus. Time to brush up on his faith, dust off his Bible, and get back into a routine of reading and prayer.

"Do you think God hears everybody's prayers?" Evidently she wasn't ready to let the subject drop.

"He sure does, in every language known to man."

"There're so many people in the world. I don't see how He could hear everyone at once, much less keep everything straight."

He grinned. "He also sees into every heart."

She studied her folded hands as she pondered this. "I wasn't taught much of anything about God, although Mama does have a Bible. I noticed her readin' it quite a lot in the months before I left home. She gets embarrassed, though, 'cause she don't—*doesn't* think she reads very well, and she has a hard time comprehendin'."

"God has a way of speaking simple truths through His Word, even when we don't fully understand the meaning of certain passages," Gage said. He remembered Reverend White giving a sermon along those lines.

"That's sort o' like magic."

He laughed. "No, not magic, but divine. God's Word is inspired, God-breathed."

"God-breathed...that's a lovely way to put it."

Their gazes caught and held for all of ten seconds, until she looked away, breaking the spell. "Well, I best get back to the house."

He stood up first, then took her hand to help her to her feet. "You want to take a little tour of my shop before you go?"

Her expression shone bright. "You mean it?"

He smiled. "Yes, I mean it." He skimmed her face, wanting to linger on each perfect feature but not quite daring to. "You did your hair differently today."

Her face went pale, and she reached up and clutched the base of her ponytail. "Does it look ridiculous?"

He leaned close and touched her nose. "Are you kidding? You're very cute."

"Cute? I think you're the first person to ever use that word for me. I...I've never been what you'd call fashionable."

"Your Southern friends don't know a cute thing when they see it. As for fashion, trends come and go. I like your looks just fine, except"—he swept his gaze down and then up again—"you could do with a new nightgown and robe, and some new dresses and shoes."

"Oh. Yes, that's true enough, I guess. But I can make do just fine with the things I have." Her shoulders went back as her chin jutted forward. She had pride. He'd need to tread carefully. "I have everything I need, really—a warm house, beautiful too, with my very own room, and children to love and cherish, and a good friend named Livvie."

"And where do I fit in there, Ellie Cooper?"

"Oh! That's right. I've got an employer—husband, rather—who's been kind...for the most part." Her eyes took on a mischievous twinkle.

"I'm not a big bad wolf," he joshed.

The heavy lashes that shadowed her eyes shot up. "I never thought you were. Besides, I ain't afraid— I'm *not* afraid of any big bad wolf."

He tossed back his head and laughed. "Perhaps you should be, Mrs. Cooper." He chortled again and took her by the hand. "Come, tell me what you think of my latest creation. It's this way." And he led her through a maze of furnishings to the dresser he'd been laboring over.

Gage's handiwork was astounding. Ellie had never seen so many fine details in a cabinet, a chest of drawers, or a headboard. Gracious, back home, she'd slept every night of her life on a lumpy straw mattress in a metal frame with broken box springs and thought nothing of it. She'd stored her clothes in an old pine chest passed down from her Cherokee grandmother, with drawers that stuck in the summer when the humidity went sky-high. Atop the chest, propped against a wall with peeling paper, stood a mirror that was cracked, so she'd always had to use one side or the other to get a reflection that wasn't distorted.

She brushed her hands along the smooth corners of one piece before moving to another, he following and saying little, except to point out which pieces were ready for the shipping fellow to pick up and take down to the loading dock, which ones he'd only just begun, and which were in the middle stages of completion.

"You do fine work, Gage," she said, thinking her words quite inadequate. "I see now why you have to work such long hours."

He pointed at the desk across the way, piled high with stacks of mail and papers. "Somewhere under there is a telephone. I have a secretary who works a couple of days a week keeping the books, taking calls, and filling out work orders, but she's not coming in again till the day after tomorrow. She's always complaining she doesn't have enough hands."

"Your company is growin', then," Ellie said.

"We don't appear to be slowing down any, that's for sure."

"Maybe you should hire a secretary for the secretary," she suggested with a wink, "and possibly another Fred."

"Another Fred! Now, there's an idea. Wonder if I can round one up."

Her nerves tingled with awareness of his hand on the center of her back as he guided her around the room. She cleared her throat and pretended that his touch didn't affect her. "It might help lessen your load."

"I had been thinking about it, actually, so your mentioning it affirms my instincts. It's just that I need to find the right person. What I do is pretty specialized."

"Perhaps you should pray about it," Ellie suggested timidly. "At church last Sunday, I heard Reverend White say we ought to pray about every decision, no matter how big or small, because God cares about everything that affects us."

"I guess he did say that."

"And you believe it, right?"

"I surely do."

"Well then, since you said prayer is just as easy as talkin' to a friend, you might start prayin' and askin' Him for guidance with your business. Might be, hirin' on a couple of other good workers could help free you up a bit more for your kids...you know, a mornin' here, an afternoon there. And that reminds me—for Tommy Lee's birthday on Saturday, I think we should take the kids fishin'."

"Fishing? I don't fish."

"My saints and angels, Mr. Cooper. You live right by the river, but you don't fish?"

"No, do you?"

"Well, o' course, I fish. I thought everybody did."

He leaned forward with a crooked grin and arched an eyebrow. "I'm not too fond of slimy things."

"Mercy sakes, what kind of outdoorsman are you?"

"I'm a shovel-a-path-from-the-door-to-the-car kind of outdoorsman, madam, and that's about the extent of it. But I'm sure the boys would love a fishing lesson."

"And Frances, mustn't forget Frances. We'll plan a picnic and all go down to the river. I'll prepare a nice lunch and take along a good, heavy pan suitable for fryin' fish on an open fire. With a couple o' blankets and some tableware, we'll have ourselves a picnic birthday party! Oh, this'll be grand."

"It sounds great, except that I don't have any fishing gear."

She expelled a sigh. "Well, we'll figure something out. Do you know anyone who might lend us his equipment?"

"Not offhand, no, but I can go over to Bill's Bait Shop and buy whatever we need."

"Best to start out with the basics: cane poles, hooks, line, and bait." She tried to keep her excitement from escalating to the point where it might alarm Gage. They were just going on a little excursion, for goodness' sake. But it would be their first family celebration, and she was beyond anxious for it to go well. She decided to turn her attention back to Gage's shop, lest her anticipation get the best of her. "Did you make a lot of the furniture for your house?"

"You mean *our* house, Ellie, and, yes, I've made a number of pieces, including your bed upstairs."

She opted to ignore his emphasis on "our." "That bed is the most comfortable thing. It's like sleepin' on a cloud every night."

"Yes, and thank you for reminding me of my fate, sleeping on that hard leather couch in my library. But don't you waste a second worrying about me, ma'am. I'm doing as fine as a duck in water! Who needs an old bedroom, anyway?"

Despite his uncommon joshing, a tiny pang of guilt for his circumstances did weigh on her conscience. "Perhaps I could take the library, and you could take back your old room. I truly don't require such a big bed. My stars in heaven, there's enough room in it for me to sprawl in every which direction. It's so much more space than I'm used to havin'."

He gave a low chuckle. "Yeah, I'm trying to picture you in that big thing. When I built it, I intended it for two people." His remark made her want to disappear like a pond snake, and the tight little gasp that whispered past her mouth must surely have shown it.

"Okay, that came out a little awkward," he said, then rubbed the top of his head and sucked in a backward whistle. "What I meant to say is...oh, never mind. The main thing is that I want you to be comfortable, and my old room is the best place for you right now. I'm fine where I am."

"Are you sure?"

"Positive."

They stopped by an unfinished circular table, and he angled his body to face hers, crossing his muscular arms and tucking his hands under his armpits. "You know something, Ellie? You've never told me much of anything about your family."

A quick knot formed in her throat at the unexpected inquiry. "Uh, I already told you my daddy died when I was twelve, and I think I mentioned my mama remarried."

"And do you miss your family very much?"

"I miss Mama with all my heart."

"But not your—"

"No!"

"Have you written home to tell them about your marriage?"

"Not yet, but I will."

"Don't you think it's about time you did?"

Hadn't she just had this conversation with Livvie? She told herself that she would not cry. "I suppose you're right."

Forever seemed to pass between them. "Do you have any brothers or sisters?"

"Uh, no. It was just me growin' up." She didn't like where this was leading.

"Then, where did you get all your experience with kids?"

"What?"

"You said you had lots of experience with kids. I was just curious if they were neighbors, cousins, nieces or nephews, you know. "

She bit down on her lower lip, pondering how to proceed. "The kids...um, they all lived on the farm."

He drew his face into a puzzled frown. "The kids? You mean, the ones you watched over?"

"Yes."

He studied her with an imperturbable glint in his eye and a tiny shadow of a smile on his lips. "So, your folks must run some sort of orphanage down there in Athens, huh?"

"Well, no, not exactly." Oh, she'd known this day of reckoning would come, but so soon? Now? No doubt, he'd send her packing tomorrow if she confessed that her experience with kids amounted to nothing more than raising baby animals. It would be plenty easy for him to annul the marriage.

"What, then?"

"I...I don't know if I should say."

"What's the harm in telling me? It's not a hard question, Eleanor."

"I know, but I don't think you'll like the answer. I know you won't, in fact."

"Really? So, you think you know me that well already?"

"I know I got your dander up the other night."

He leaned forward. "That's old stuff, and I apologized, remember? Now, out with it."

Her mind was a crazy mix of hope and fear. "All right. Well, when I said I had experience with kids, I meant...um, baby goats. They *are* kids, so it wasn't a total lie."

He unfolded his arms and blinked, his jaw dropping nearly to his belt. A shiver of panic raced straight through her as she awaited his angry reaction. So, when he commenced a loud belly laugh, she didn't know what to think.

"Goats?" he said between spurts of chuckles. "You are taking care of my kids based on the experience you had raising baby goats?"

"And other animals, too," she hastened to say, "like bunnies and lambs and colts and fillies and—"

"Oh, now that makes me feel worlds better." He clutched his stomach, and she thought she'd never seen a man laugh with such abandon—certainly not Byron. No, Byron always cackled in ridicule or disgust, never actual mirth. A smile tickled her mouth. Did she dare believe Gage wasn't angry about her deception?

He sobered slightly. "What else should you be telling me, El?"

El? No one but her mama had ever called her by that nickname. She found she liked hearing it again, from Gage. "What else?"

With a forefinger, he lifted her chin, and the simple touch brought her senses to life once more. She pulled away, afraid to let her emotions show.

He lifted an eyebrow and dropped his hand to his side. "Yes, what else?"

"Nothin'," she lied. She couldn't possibly tell him about her brutal stepfather—how she'd helped him run an illicit whiskey still and, worse, witnessed him murder a man in cold blood and hadn't contacted the authorities but instead dug a hole to bury the body. No, never that! Her stomach churned to the point of nausea. The sound of Tommy Lee's tiny whimpers gave her momentary relief. When she started to go to him, Gage stopped her with a hand around her wrist. His hold on her sizzled and burned. Hot tears threatened to spill out of her eyes.

"There's no need to fear me," he whispered. "If you're hiding secrets, it might be best to let me in on them."

Her heart hammered. "I—"

Tommy Lee's cries escalated.

She met Gage's eyes for just a few seconds, then turned to answer Tommy Lee. "I'm coming, honey."

As she walked away, the curious scrutiny of her husband was almost tangible.

Chapter Fourteen

The Father...hath delivered us from the
power of darkness, and hath translated us
into the kingdom of his dear Son.
—Colossians 1:12–13

Dear Mama,

One month is finally up. I am writing to tell
you I'm all settled here in Wabash, and I
think I'll burst if I don't come right out and
tell you I'm married. Yes, married. Don't
worry, Mama. I'm doing fine, and I only
married for convenience. In fact, I have my
very own room on the second floor of a big
house. Oh, I wish you could see it, this
big house, and I wish even more you could
come here to live.

You see, when I arrived here, I learned right
off that Aunt Gilda had died almost a year
ago (I'm sorry, Mama), so my hopes of staying
with her were dashed, but then by chance—or

maybe by God's own providence——I read an ad about a man seeking a wife to take care of his house and kids. Yes, kids. See if you can believe this, Mama....I have four stepchildren!

My husband's name is Gage Cooper, and he is a cabinetmaker. He builds beautiful furniture. His shop is called Cooper Cabinet Company.

Anyway, it's all a lot to take in right now, and I have much more to tell you, but I am so tired after this long morning, so I will write more later. You may write back to me, Mama. In fact, you'd better! Look at the return address. Don't worry, I will put the envelope into a bigger one and mail it to the attention of Burt Meyer. He and Mildred promised they would deliver my letters to you without letting Byron know, and I trust them.

I want to know how Byron is treating you and what, if anything, has happened since the ~~murd~~ (I'd better not write that awful word).

Mama, I have gotten rusty in my spelling, but since becoming a wife and mother, I'm trying real hard to speak proper English so I can set a good ex~~x~~ample. I'm not even saying "ain't" ~~no~~ anymore. You would be proud of me.

I love and miss you. Write very, very soon.

Your loving daughter,
Eleanor

PS: Gage and I have fought just once, and
he apologized for it. Can you imagine Byron
ever apologizing for anything? I will tell you
more about him later. Wabash is a nice town,
and I've already made some friends.

Ellie read and reread her letter, knowing it must be riddled with errors. Her mother hadn't had nearly as much schooling as she, though, so she didn't expect her to mind. More than once, she'd had to open the big dictionary she'd found in the library and correct her spelling. A few tears fell on the paper as she folded it in two creases and stuffed it inside a small envelope, on which she printed her address. She then slid that envelope into a larger one, on which she carefully printed the Meyers' address. Now, all she had to do was affix a stamp to the upper right corner, place the letter in the mailbox by the front door, and pray for a safe delivery.

All was quiet in the house, save for the big grandfather clock, which had just struck its eleventh gong. Tommy Lee had risen unusually early and then conked out on the sofa for a nap, which had afforded Ellie the opportunity to write the letter. She didn't expect him to sleep much longer, though, as he generally didn't take mid-morning naps. He'd strewn his toys about on the floor, but she didn't want to pick them up for fear of waking him.

At breakfast that morning, Ellie had told the twins and Frances about the outing she was planning for Tommy Lee's birthday.

"We don't have any fishing poles," Alec had remarked.

"I'll be taking care of that today," Gage had said, casting Ellie a glance across the table. In his gaze, she'd detected a slight twinkle. "Ellie's instructed me on what to buy. Apparently, she's an accomplished fisherman, or, should I say, fisherwoman?"

"Fish woman!" Tommy Lee had screeched.

Ellie had quieted the boy with a spoonful of oatmeal in his mouth. "I'll admit, I've caught my share of bluegills and sunfish and trout. There are lots o' little creeks where I grew up."

"Is Daddy coming fishing, too?" Frances had asked in her usual quiet voice.

Ellie had looked squarely at Gage. "You bet he is, punkin. I can hardly wait to watch him cast out his line."

Gage had dabbed at his chin with his napkin and inhaled a deep breath. "So that you can poke fun at me, no doubt."

"I've never fished before," Frances had said.

"Me, neither," the twins had chimed in unison.

Ellie had been thrilled that Frances had spoken up without any prompting. She smiled and reached over to pat her hand. "Well, we are goin' to take care of that. Who wants to bet that Frances will show us all up?"

"I will," Gage had said.

"I'm bettin' I will," Abe had countered.

"Do we get to put slimy worms on hooks?" Alec had asked between bites of buttered toast.

Ellie had nodded. "Big, long, thick ones."

"Oh, goodie. Sounds gross. I'm gonna make Abe eat a worm."

"No, you ain't," Abe had argued.

"Don't say 'ain't,'" Ellie had put in.

"Am, too," Alec had insisted.

Gage had cocked his head and slanted Ellie a grin, as if to say, "You started this."

The lively conversation had continued for a few more minutes, until Gage had laid down his napkin and cleared his throat. "It's getting late, but before I head to work, I'm going to offer up another morning prayer."

"Oh, please do," Ellie had urged him. "It's a lovely way to start our day, isn't it, kids?"

"It makes me feel good inside when you do that," Frances had shared.

With the family breakfast still fresh in her mind, and with Frances's remark tucked away in her heart, Ellie smiled to herself, rose from the writing desk, and walked to the front window. Pressing the envelope to her chest, over her heart, she prayed, "Lord, may Mama receive this letter in good health and high spirits, and may You protect her from Byron's hateful temperament."

It still wasn't clear to her whether God paid her prayers any heed. Oh, she figured He heard them, all right, but whether He took them into consideration remained a mystery. She somehow needed to learn how to become His child in the true sense.

She slipped out the front door, lifted the mailbox lid, and dropped the letter inside. The mail carrier usually stopped at the house around noon, so it would go out today. Stepping to the edge of the porch, she looked up at the brilliant blue sky. The sun seemed to smile down on her, and on all of Wabash, as it had melted most of the snow. Glancing down, she noticed several daffodil shoots pushing up through the layer of dead leaves. She had long considered them heralds of spring, boldly defying anything that might try to keep the season from coming in all its splendor.

Just then, she felt a sensation in her heart, much like a spring flower breaking through the hardened soil of doubt and defeatism, and it gave her a picture of God's love, sprouting forth in her heart with inexorable force, defying anyone to stop Him from making Himself known to her.

She gasped and held her breath. Could it be that God had just now spoken to her in what Reverend White had described in his sermon on 1 Kings 19 as a still, small voice?

"Oh, Lord, if that was You, would You speak to me again?"

She heard nothing; she felt nothing, except for the firm conviction that she'd just experienced something quite unusual.

When she went back inside, she saw Tommy Lee sitting up on the sofa, drilling his knuckles into his eye sockets, his disheveled curls falling across his forehead.

"Hey there, my little man," she cooed. She hastened across the room, sat down beside him, and tugged him close.

He snuggled against her. "Mama?"

Her heart leaped, but she managed to keep her composure and rested her chin on his head. "Would you like me to be your mama?"

He nodded and flashed her a toothy smile.

She wrapped him in a warm embrace. "Well, goody, goody gumdrops."

He giggled. "Silly."

"You're silly," she teased, tickling him under the arms. Soon, they were embroiled in an all-out wrestling, tickling, and squealing match, and it suddenly occurred to her that she'd never been so happy in all her life.

Since Eileen's family were the only Riddermans in Seymour, it wasn't difficult for Ned and Bill to locate them. It didn't hurt that the service station attendant he'd questioned knew the family and had even given him precise directions to the house on Rutherford Street, a one-and-a-half story bungalow within the city limits.

Ned pulled into the driveway, turned off the engine, and surveyed the small house. The exterior looked to be in need of some repairs—one of the front windows was missing a shutter, the screen door was torn, and there was paint peeling from just about every surface. He squeezed the steering wheel with both hands, blew out a loud breath, and glanced over at Bill. "Well, let's hope we find some answers here."

"I'll let you do the talkin', boss."

"Suit yourself." They filed out of the car and headed along the cracked sidewalk, then climbed the tumbledown porch steps.

A light rap on the front door was all it took to summon the round, middle-aged woman who appeared in the doorway, dressed in a soiled work frock and cloddish shoes with rolled-down socks. She peered through the screen but made no move to open it. At her feet, a camel-colored, short-haired dog the size of a squirrel yipped, danced in circles, and showed its teeth. The woman shushed the animal and nudged it with her foot. "Yes?" she said, raising her voice over the frenzied yapping.

"Morning, ma'am," Ned offered. "Didn't mean to interrupt you, but I wondered if I might find a Miss Eileen Ridderman about."

She went as stiff as a starched shirt and let out a shaky breath. "Who wants to know?"

"Oh, forgive me, I should have made that clear right off." He would have extended a hand, but the screen still separated them, so he bowed instead. "I'm Ned Castleberry, and this here is my partner, Bill Flanders. We're government agents." He reached into his back pocket and produced his ID badge. When he held it up to the screen, she inclined her head and squinted, then nodded and met his gaze.

"I don't want you to think Eileen's in any trouble. Might you be her mother?"

She turned her head to the side but kept her narrow eyes glued on Ned. Then, still without speaking, she nodded slowly.

"We just want to ask her a few questions about a man we think she may have had contact with down in Athens. We're trying to locate him, that's all."

She arched an eyebrow and gave a taut jerk of her head. "That buzzard Walter Sullivan, you mean? I'd like to put my hands around his neck and squeeze tighter than a boa constrictor." The dog kept up its incessant barking.

"That so?" Ned asked.

"Darn right! He led my daughter astray, for one thing, filled her head with every manner of nonsense. Gave her money and finagled his way into her life, then got downright mean with her when she didn't bend to his every wish."

"Is she here now, ma'am? We'd like to speak with her."

"Nope. She went down to Florida to live with my brother and his wife. The farther away she can get from that brute, the better, as far as I'm concerned."

"Florida?" Ned's heart sank. Had they reached a dead end? The department would never fund a trip clear to Florida. He scratched his temple and frowned. "Did she tell you much about Walter Sullivan, such as how she wound up involved with him in the first place, or why he would give her money?"

Pausing, the woman looked from him to Bill, then expelled a breathy sigh. "Oh, phooey. You two may as well come in for a cup of tea."

"Oh! Uh, that's not necessary," Ned replied, noticing that Bill, too, was eyeing the ferocious, squirrel-like canine warily.

The woman followed their worried gazes. "You ain't scared of my Ginger, are you? She ain't nearly as mean as she sounds."

When they hesitated like two schoolboys about to enter the principal's office, she shushed the pooch again and pointed to a far corner of the room. "Go to your bed, Ginger." Just like that, the little mutt complied, tail between its legs. Satisfied, Mrs. Ridderman pushed open the screen door. "There, now. Come on in."

The home's interior was tidy enough but old and worn, putting Ned in mind of a tired war veteran. The ceiling paint peeled away in strips from the water-stained surface, and the dingy walls were in sore need of a touch-up. Most of the upholstered furniture sagged in the middle, and the coffee table in the center of the living room bore scratch marks galore, possibly put there years ago by a toddling two-year-old named Eileen—and her siblings, if she had any.

"You two make yourselves at home, and I'll go put the teakettle on."

"That's mighty nice of you, ma'am, but there's no need to go to any trouble," Ned assured her. "We just want to ask you a few questions, and then we'll be on our way."

"Nonsense. May as well sip while we talk." That said, she whirled on her heel, skirt flaring, and scooted out of the room. From the kitchen, she hollered, "Now, stop your worrying about Ginger. She's only bit twice, far as I know, out of self-defense."

Her nonchalance unnerved him. Bill's jaw dropped, and his eyes widened, as round as silver dollars. "No fast moves, boss," he muttered under his breath as he lowered himself into a chair.

"Yeah, slow and easy," Ned said, settling into a chair opposite Bill. He kept his eyes trained on the little beast, which, by now, had dropped its head to its pillow to ogle them, its ears pressed flat against its skull.

Mrs. Ridderman returned a couple of minutes later carrying a tray with a fancy teapot and three cups, a sugar bowl, a creamer, and some silver spoons. She set it atop the marred coffee table and served the two of them, then filled a cup for herself and situated her plump frame in the middle of the faded sofa. To Ned's chagrin, she nodded to the dog, evidently giving permission to advance. Without hesitation, the pooch sailed across the room and leaped into her lap. She patted its small head. "Now then," she said with a slight wheeze. "Where did you want me to start?"

"How about at the beginning?" Ned suggested. "Tell us how your daughter met Walter Sullivan."

"Well, it's a long story, but I'll try to keep it as short as possible. Eileen went down to Athens to be close to her boyfriend, but she'd only just gotten settled when he ended the relationship." She sipped her tea and gave her a head a little toss. "My girl's had bad luck with men. I try to tell her to be patient, that the right one will come along in due time, but she just keeps falling for one no-good charmer after another. Truth be told, I think she gives her heart away too fast." A melancholy frown settled on her face. "Anyway, she got a job at a little restaurant down there and had a tiny apartment, but she could barely make ends meet. I tried to coax her into coming back up to Seymour, but she wouldn't." She leaned forward. "She didn't want to hear her mama say, 'I told you so.'" She fingered the rim of her cup. "Eileen doesn't make good choices, never has, especially when it comes to men. Probably didn't help that her daddy ran off when she was but a youngster."

"You mind telling us where her daddy is?" Ned asked.

"He left us for another woman when Eileen was about eight, and he's been married three times since then. Can you imagine? Last I heard, he was somewhere out in California. He never took any interest in Eileen, never went to any school functions, never hugged or kissed her. He didn't know the first thing about being a father, and that's a hard pill for a kid to swallow, no matter how much love the other parent shows."

"Yes, ma'am."

"Anyway, one day, this Sullivan character comes strolling into the restaurant. She said he looked all professional, dressed in a suit—sort of like you two gentlemen, I suppose—and he started asking her questions about the town and the folks who lived there, things like that. She claimed he was real friendly-like, even charming. Of course, she didn't know much of anything about Athens, seeing as she'd only lived there a short time. But she'd overheard a conversation earlier while waiting on a group of men. They were talking about working at some liquor still up in the hills, bragging about the money they were making and saying every manner of stuff, not caring one bit that she could hear them. So, that's exactly what she told Mr. Sullivan—a perfect stranger at the time. That's my Eileen for you, always looking for approval, especially from men, and never counting the cost.

"Well, it turns out those little tidbits were exactly what Mr. Sullivan was looking for. He gave her some money, told her she'd done real good, and then asked her to stay on the alert for any more scraps of information.

"He started coming to the restaurant real regular after that and paying my Eileen more and more attention. Got to where he started giving her money for no reason whatsoever. Of course, I think he just wanted to...well, you know...get close to her so he could have his way with her. It makes me sick at my stomach to think about."

Bill snarled under his breath, and Ned could only imagine what he was thinking. First, what kind of creep preys on an innocent girl? And, second, what in the world did Eileen find charming about Walter

Sullivan? More than ever, he wanted to find the brute so he could give him what for.

"So, what finally prompted Eileen to leave Athens?" Ned asked.

"For one thing, he started knocking her around and making all kinds of demands. He drank a lot and got real mean. I don't know why she put up with it, but he had some kind of hold on her, and the money he kept giving her didn't help the situation. But then came the day he quit coming around, so she took the opportunity to leave Athens. Don't ask me why it took her so blamed long to figure out he was poison, but that's my Eileen, sweet as sugar, she is, but about as smart as a rock when it comes to men."

"He quit coming around, you say?"

"Yep, just like that. It was an act of God, if you ask me. Don't know why he finally decided to leave her alone, but he did. Of course, he was paying her rent and such, so I'm afraid she left town without compensating her landlord. She'll pay him what he's due, though, just as soon as she can save up enough at her new job down south. She said she would, and I believe her."

"I'm sure she will, ma'am." Ned scratched his head and frowned. "You wouldn't happen to know the location of the whiskey still Eileen overheard those fellows talking about, would you? It might help us locate Mr. Sullivan."

"What do you want to find him for, anyway?"

"Well, for one thing, he works for me, and he hasn't shown his face for a good month."

"Maybe he got himself wrapped up in the liquor business," she mused. "Wouldn't surprise me. Gracious, I thought I taught my girl better, but I guess you never can tell." She clicked her tongue and shook her head. "Anyway, back to your question. No, I'm afraid I don't know where the still is located, just that it was somewhere in the hills. Eileen would probably remember. I can ask her, if you want. She promised to call me tonight. We talk about once a week. It isn't cheap, you know, long-distance calls. We mostly just exchange letters, but hearing her voice, that's more comforting to me."

They talked a bit more, but Ned had heard enough. They exchanged phone numbers, and Mrs. Ridderman promised to call him just as soon as she'd finished speaking with her daughter.

On the drive back to the office, Bill broke the ponderous silence. "I figured Walt Sullivan for scum, but this beats all. He's a regular vulture."

Chapter Fifteen

Every good gift and every perfect gift is from
above, and cometh down from the Father of
lights, with whom is no variableness,
neither shadow of turning.
—James 1:17

On March 21, the sun chose to lay a bright, golden blanket of warmth over the earth, so that light jackets and sweaters were more than sufficient coverage for the birthday excursion. As Ellie navigated the steps and crossed the yard to the family Buick, her arms laden with a blanket and a wicker basket full of tasty food, she soaked up the delicious rays.

A whistling Gage winked as he passed her on his way back to the house for another load, stirring up a whole nest of butterflies in her stomach. Ever since the day she'd visited him in his shop, he'd been treating her more like a close friend, teasing her good-naturedly and tossing her plenty of warm glances. And she wasn't sure what to make of it. Was he trying to soften her up so that she'd reveal her deepest, darkest secrets? If so, she wouldn't fall for it. No way could she let him know she'd witnessed a murder and aided in the cover-up. Although he was sure to wonder about her past, considering how she'd recently started waking up, screaming, from gruesome flashbacks to that odious day. Just last night, she'd dreamed that Byron stood over her bed, chortling and saying, "How stupid to think you could hide forever, li'l girl," and "Now that I've found you, I'll make you pay for runnin' away."

With all the changes and busyness in her life, she'd mostly managed to block out the horrid images of that day, forcing the pictures out of her head whenever they tried to push inside. But, sometimes, she felt close to bursting wide open with her pent-up memories, and she longed to go somewhere to be alone, completely out of earshot, and let loose a scream that reached the treetops.

Tommy Lee followed after her, singing to himself as he pranced across the lawn. "It's my buthday! It's my buthday!" he chanted happily. He certainly had a wonderful way of making her forget her troubles.

"What's in the picnic basket?" Alec asked as he slid the tackle box along the floor of the car, then climbed inside and sat down next to Abe.

Ellie looked askance at Frances, who was carrying the basket, and winked. "That's a secret, isn't it, Frances?"

The girl nodded, then maneuvered her way into the backseat next to her brother.

"And don't you go peekin' under that lid, either," Ellie told him. "Keep an eye on him, okay, Frances?"

"I will," she said with a shy smile.

Abe, too, eyed the basket with interest. "Why's Frances get to know, an' we don't?"

Ellie grinned. "Because Frances helped me pack it, silly."

"Everybody set to go?" Gage asked as he locked the front door. He turned and approached the car.

"Whatcha got there, Daddy?" Alec asked.

"What does it look like?" Gage held up what he was carrying—a baseball bat and three baseball gloves, one with a ball tucked inside. "I thought we could toss the ball or even play some baseball while we're waiting for the fish to bite." He threw Ellie a crooked grin. Mercy, he might be the death of her yet.

"Really?" Abe looked skeptical.

"Why not? Ellie's going to teach us the art of fishing, so we might as well return the favor and school her in some baseball techniques. You ever thrown a baseball, Mrs. Cooper? Or were you too busy nursing baby goats on that farm of yours?" He grinned again, his eyes scrunched in the corners, his pupils twinkling.

A wave of prickly heat crawled up her neck, but she was not about to let his jesting affect her. She placed her hands on her hips and raised her chin. "I certainly have, Mr. Cooper. We played the game in gym class, so there!" she spouted in a huffy tone. "And I wasn't half bad, either." She decided to let his remark about the goats go unanswered.

"Is that right?" He leaned closer, but she managed to hold her stance. "You mean to tell me they teach physical education in those schools down south?"

"Well, of course they do, silly. I bet I learned all the same things in school that you did."

"Bet you didn't."

"Bet I did! Everything from history to science to 'rithmetic to readin'."

He closed the back door of the car and turned to face her, his gaze focused below her eyes. "Tell me, Mrs. Cooper. Did you study the fine art of kissing on the playground?"

"Oh, for Pete's sake!" She reached down, swept up Tommy Lee in her arms, and marched around the car to the other side. Clutching the handle of the passenger door, she looked over the roof into Gage's teasing eyes.

"Tell me something else," he went on, lowering his voice and leaning against the Buick. "Besides that little peck during the wedding, have you ever been kissed?"

"I won't answer such a ridiculous question."

"You haven't, have you?"

"Oh, just—just get in the car." She broke eye contact with him, yanked open the door, and slid into the vehicle, hauling Tommy Lee onto her lap. Once situated, she stretched to reach the door handle and pulled the door closed with a thud.

Gage's booming laughter filled the car as he crawled in behind the steering wheel and shut his own door.

"What's so funny?" Alec asked.

"Yeah, what're you laughing about?" Abe demanded.

"It's nothin' important," Ellie said.

Gage pressed the electric start button to turn the crankshaft, and the engine roared to life. Ellie kept her gaze pointed forward, but she couldn't ignore his wide grin, visible out of the corner of her eye. Land of mercy, what a mortifying topic to broach, and just before setting off on a family picnic, of all things! What had possessed him to tease her about something so personal?

"It's my buthday!" Tommy Lee chirped, bouncing up and down in Ellie's lap, thankfully oblivious to their bantering.

"You bet it is!" Ellie rested her chin on his silky head of hair and hugged him close.

"I'm gonna catch ten fish, at least," Abe announced.

"I'm gonna push you in the river," Alec said, laughing.

"There'll be no pushing anybody in the water," said Gage, his smile still in place as he put the gearshift into reverse and eased the car out of the driveway.

Frances clapped her hands. "Oh, this is going to be the grandest day ever."

It was the first enthusiastic outburst Ellie had ever heard Frances make, and it thrilled her to no end. She turned her head full around. "Frances, where's your book?"

A tentative smile made her pretty face glow. "I didn't bring one."

"You didn't bring a book?" the twins gasped in unison.

"Well, I'll be," said Gage, as they slowly advanced along W. Hill Street. His gaze trailed a gleaming path to Ellie, and she couldn't help but smile in return.

�֍

There was no denying it, Gage realized; Eleanor Booth Cooper had every woman he knew beat by a long shot in several areas. Not only could she handle his kids—based on her goat-raising experience, no less—but she could pack a delicious picnic lunch: chicken sandwiches on home-baked bread, canned peaches, pickle spears, oatmeal cookies, chocolate cupcakes, and fresh-squeezed lemonade. Whether or not she'd entirely won the twins' affection remained to be seen, but Tommy Lee had taken to her from the start, and Frances had finally started coming out of her shell.

Dazzling sunlight shone down on their picnic site, a grassy patch they'd found on the riverbank, and while the trees around them had yet to sprout any leaves, there were buds ripe for blossoming, and plenty of fat robins pecking at the soil, definite signs of spring.

Through the entire meal, Gage couldn't take his eyes off of Ellie for more than a few seconds at a time. He couldn't help it—she simply enchanted him with her charcoal tresses tied back in a ponytail, her floral cotton dress, stains and all, and her rolled-up socks and leather loafers. More than once, their gazes caught, his lingering, hers flitting away to land on one of the children. Something told him she lacked experience in many areas, and it made him wonder more than ever about her upbringing and those secrets she kept hidden.

"Can we go fishing now?" Alec asked, throwing down his napkin and wiping his mouth with his sleeve.

"Yeah, can we?" Abe echoed.

Tommy Lee had finished his lunch and was running circles around the family, singing his version of the birthday song.

Ellie pushed a few strands of hair out of her eyes. "You bet we can. I hope you saved some of your appetites for our fine catch. I have a feeling we're going to fill that pail down there." She nodded toward the river, where they'd already set up their fishing poles, tackle box, pail, and net. "Who wants to help bait the hooks?"

"Me!" the twins and Frances squealed in unison. Tommy Lee ceased with his running and joined in, his voice exceeding the rest.

With brows raised in expectation, Ellie cocked her head at Gage and waited.

"What?" He stared back at her. "Oh, yes. Me, too." Gosh, it was hard to muster up much enthusiasm about baiting a hook with a slimy worm, but he could at least pretend. Truly, he would get more satisfaction from watching his children—and Ellie.

"I hope I catch the first fish," Frances gushed with rare fervor, "and I hope it's so big, I won't be able to pull it in."

Ellie granted her a sparkling smile. "Oh, my goodness. I hope the same!" She clapped her hands twice. "Well then, what are we waitin' for? Race you all to the river." Without so much as a "Ready, set, go," Ellie sprung into action, setting off at a sprint before Gage could even get to his feet. He could have run faster, but he rather enjoyed bringing up the rear, his eyes fixed on the willowy brunette with the shapely calves. At the river's edge, he stopped to watch as Ellie and his kids got down on their knees, Ellie digging in the container of worms they'd bought at Bill's Bait Shop that morning and pulling out a long, stringy, wiggly creature that curled around her slender finger. With ease, she unraveled it and set to threading it on a big hook at the end of a line. He noted in particular the twins' awed expressions as they watched Ellie work, their mouths gaping and their necks craning forward. Heck, even he had a new appreciation for her. And he almost laughed aloud at the way Frances screwed up her face, her brow scrunched in a tight frown, her nose wrinkled. Even Tommy Lee lost his tongue as he knelt there in rapt wonder.

"Almost there," Ellie murmured. "Ah, okay, he's a bit too long, see? I'll just pull him apart...right...here." She snapped the thing in two.

"Eww!" Frances shrieked.

"That's gross," Alec said. "Let me try!"

Not wanting to be outdone, Abe wiped his hands on his pants—was he perspiring with nerves, Gage wondered?—and chimed in, "Yeah! Me, too."

"How about you, Frances?" Ellie asked, looking over the boys' heads.

She hesitated, then moved closer. "S-sure."

"Okay, each of you go get one o' those poles. Be careful of that hook, though. It's sharp and nasty."

The three big kids scurried off.

"Let me!" said Tommy Lee. "I wants a worm."

The sound of Ellie's laughter was warm and rich. "All right, little man. Tell your daddy to go get you one o' those poles so he can help you put a worm on the hook."

Me? The last thing Gage wanted to do was fish a worm out of that muddy soil and thread it on a hook, but he couldn't very well let his kids—or his wife, for that matter—know the very notion made him squeamish.

"Come, Daddy." Tommy Lee skipped over to him and tugged on his pant leg. "Help."

Gage locked eyes with Ellie and curled his lips into a one-second smile, then stepped forward, crouched down, and thrust his hand into the black soil. When he felt something slimy brush past his fingertips, he lost his nerve and yanked his hand back out.

More bubbly laughter floated up from Ellie's throat. "What's the matter?" she asked. "Don't tell me you're afraid of a little worm." She dug into the container, pulled out what Gage would have described as a small snake, and thrust it under his nose. He couldn't help it; he jumped backward with a little yelp.

She covered her mouth with her free hand. "Oh, my. Your face! It's...it's sort of gray."

"Well, of course it is. I told you I don't like slimy things. And I can't abide snakes. Never have."

She held the wiggly thing at close range and studied it. "No snakes here. This is a worm, silly."

He felt his face twist into a frown. "If that's a worm, I'll eat my shoe."

"Would you like a spoonful o' gravy with that shoe?"

"A scoop of ice cream will do," he shot back.

And that was when Ellie nearly fell over in a fit of laughter, grasping her stomach with one hand, the worm still held high in the air with the other. His kids stood with cane poles in hand, mouths sagging open, and shifted their gazes from him to their stepmother, evidently unsure about what to make of her laughing spasm. As if Gage knew what to make of it! But it didn't take long for him to recognize the humor in the situation. Here he was, a big, strapping man, bothered by the sight of a measly night crawler. Rather than feel humiliated by the absurdity, he started to laugh, which the kids must have interpreted as permission to do the same. Before long, all six of them were bent over, clutching their stomachs and gasping for breath in between chuckles.

Gage couldn't recall the last time he'd laughed so hard, and he found that it did his heart good. It also put everyone in a lighthearted mood, which made for a pleasant afternoon of fishing. By two o'clock, they had caught somewhere in the neighborhood of two dozen fish. Many of them had been thrown back, though, since Ellie had designated only a few as keepers. Gage had been more than happy to oblige the expert by removing the hooks from their mouths and tossing them back into the water.

"I still caught the biggest one, right?" was Frances's question with each fish that was reeled in.

"I think you did, Frances," Ellie said. "And we can stop anytime now; I think there's enough fish for each of us to have two apiece."

Thank goodness, Gage thought, laying his pole on the ground. He hadn't caught a single fish, but he also couldn't have cared less. If he never fished again, it wouldn't be any skin off his back.

"'Course, we'll have to teach your daddy how to scale and gut them first."

"Very funny," Gage said, frowning.

"Funny! Funny buthday!" Tommy Lee spouted as he danced around, having recently awakened from his afternoon nap on a blanket by the shore.

"Well, I think you've been patient enough, young man," Gage said to his now three-year-old. "What would you say to some presents?"

"Pwesents?" Tommy Lee whirled on his heels and gawked at him.

"Yeah, let's open his presents," said Abe, reeling in his line.

Everyone else followed suit, gathering the supplies to carry back to the car. The kids raced on ahead, but Gage hung back to walk with Ellie. "I'm having fun," he told her. "Are you?"

Her face creased into an instant smile, and it struck him what a beautiful wife he'd snagged. "I haven't had this much fun since...well, forever."

"Oh, come on. You can't mean that."

Her expression sobered, and she stared straight ahead. "I do, actually. My life hasn't exactly been all sunshine and flowers. It seems like after age twelve, stuff really went sour." She gave a little chuckle tinged with bitterness.

"After your father died."

"Yes."

It surprised him that she'd let that much slip, and as much as he wanted to hear more, he realized this wasn't the time or the place. Best to change the subject. "Thanks for the fishing lesson. I learned a lot."

She turned and smiled at him with a flip of her ponytail. "You didn't catch one fish, Mr. Cooper. That's hardly a sign of a good teacher."

He bumped against her, hoping she wouldn't realize it was intentional, and dipped his face close to her ear. "You still taught me something more important than fishing. Watching you with the kids today…I've realized what I've been missing."

"Is that so? And just what is that?"

"Time with my family. The kids are growing up too fast, and I don't want to sit on the sidelines any longer."

She gazed at the children, who'd made it back to the picnic blanket. The twins were having a friendly tussle with Tommy Lee, and Frances looked on, a smile lighting her features. "They really are something, Gage. You've done a great job raisin' them, whether you believe it or not."

"Frances is coming out of her shell, and I can't take any credit for that."

"She is, isn't she? And the twins have gone a whole week without gettin' into trouble at school."

Gage chuckled. "That's some kind of record."

"And Tommy Lee, well, he's run off with my heart."

"And you with his."

"I didn't know you'd bought any gifts—the thought slipped my mind. Did you wrap them yourself?"

"Ha! I bought him a few toys at Beitman and Wolf and paid the clerk extra to wrap them for me."

"That's the big department store where Livvie bought my weddin' dress. I've never been in one of those."

"No? Well then, we'll have to do something about that."

Her face brightened. "Really?"

"Really." He touched her nose and grinned. "Come on, let's go get those gifts out of the trunk."

Chapter Sixteen

The earth is full of the goodness of the LORD.
—Psalm 33:5

Ellie was seeing a side of Gage today that she hadn't noticed before. It scared her to realize how much she'd come to care for him, mostly because she worried that she'd get too close and spill the details of her past. She'd said too much already, mentioning how her life had gone downhill after her daddy's death. The next thing she knew, she'd be confessing that she'd witnessed a murder without reporting it. And she couldn't let that information out of the bag, or he'd put her out of his house for sure.

After watching Tommy Lee open his birthday gifts, the family had started up a game of baseball, if one could call it that. Gage pitched to each of his kids, and everyone else scurried to catch the ball. There were no teams, per se, nor any bases to run; just a pitcher, a batter, a catcher, and a few outfielders. And a lot of laughter.

"Ellie's up," Alec called from the field. "I bet she won't hit the ball. Shoot, I bet she doesn't even know how to hold a bat."

His taunts were made in fun, but Ellie couldn't help but take his challenge seriously. She smiled and waved at Alec across the grassy field. "Just watch me," she hollered back, knowing full well that she might soon eat her words.

As she passed Gage on her way to the plate, he whistled and said, "You show 'em, fair lady." Abe stood waiting for her, bat in hand, and wearing a slight smirk. Obviously, he suspected the same—that she wouldn't know the first thing about positioning her hands on a bat, let alone striking a ball with it.

Ellie clenched the bat at the base, one fist on top of the other, turned her body to the side, and bent at the waist just so, feet apart, toes planted in the soil, recalling all she'd learned in gym class. In Gage's eyes, she saw a glint of admiration, maybe even respect. Time would tell whether his expression would turn to amusement when she swung and missed the ball by a mile.

But she needn't have worried. On his very first throw, her bat connected with the ball, sending it high and far. She could hardly believe it, considering how long it had been since she'd held a bat, much less hit a ball on the first pitch.

"Man alive, Ellie!" Gage exclaimed. He swept a hand through his hair, then turned around to watch Alec pursue the ball. Tommy Lee set off after his brother, shouting happily, and Frances merely stood in the outfield, a dumbfounded stare on her face.

Alec had taken off at a run, holding his gloved hand aloft, and he even dived, but he ended up missing the fly by a long shot.

"What in the—?" Abe stuttered behind her. "Where did you learn to—? That would have been a home run."

Ellie watched the ball come down, landing somewhere in the tall grass beyond the railroad tracks. She felt her own eyes pop in amazement. "Well, what do you know?" she said, laughing. "I've still got it."

They packed a great deal of fun into the remainder of the day, collecting twigs and broken branches to build a fire, cleaning and frying up their small catch of fish, playing freeze tag and hide-and-seek, and skipping stones on the river. When it was finally time to go home, four bushed kids and two equally bushed adults climbed into the car. Tommy Lee fell fast asleep in Ellie's lap almost before she had a chance to close her door.

"That was a fun day," Abe volunteered.

"Yeah," Alec agreed. "I didn't know Ellie could be so...well, fun."

"Thank you, I think," Ellie said, laughing to herself.

As Gage started the car, he snuck a peek at Ellie and chuckled. "I think we all learned a thing or two about Ellie today."

"And I really did turn out to be a good fisherwoman," Frances insisted. "I even cut the heads off two fish."

"Which is more than we can say for your daddy," Ellie teased, her gaze pointed forward.

"Hey, I scaled one," he said defensively.

"I gutted one," Alec bragged.

"I scaled *and* gutted *and* cleaned about ten," said Ellie, humored by the family's chatter. "But you all surprised me. You're fast learners."

"When can we go on another picnic?" Frances wanted to know.

"Who's got the next birthday?" Ellie asked.

"Us," said Abe. "But not till November twelfth."

"Oh. Well then, we'll just have to find another reason for a picnic, won't we?"

Back home, the twins' energy revived, even as they helped empty the car, and they talked about going to a friend's house to play.

"Be home by seven," Gage instructed them. "You need baths tonight. Church tomorrow, don't forget."

"We know, we know," they mumbled. They hurried inside, dropped off their armloads of supplies, and then skipped down the steps, carrying a bat and two gloves, and disappeared behind the house.

"Where do they get their energy?" Gage asked, watching them run off. "I would have thought they'd want to rest a bit after such a long day."

"That would be askin' too much of ten-year-old boys, don't you think?" Ellie said, a sleeping Tommy Lee in her arms, Frances having slipped past them to go in the house, no doubt anxious to return to whatever book she'd been reading.

"I guess you're right." He glanced down at her, and, for the briefest moment, they shared nothing but the sound of mingled breaths, theirs and Tommy Lee's, until a few birds overhead struck up a springtime chorus. Gage stepped toward her, arms outstretched. "Here, let me take that little rapscallion."

Even though she loved the feel of Tommy Lee's limp body in her arms, she couldn't deny her relief at handing him over, especially since the transfer didn't disturb his sleep in the least.

"Let's sit a minute," Gage suggested. He nodded toward the pair of wicker porch chairs behind them.

Although the day had been unusually warm, the setting sun was giving way to cooler air, and Ellie shivered under her lightweight sweater. "I guess I could sit a few minutes. I'd like to unpack the picnic basket and then get Tommy Lee in and out of the bathtub before the twins return. Frances needs a bath, too. Mercy, I do, as well! I sure hope we don't run out of hot water." She moseyed toward the rockers and sank into the soft cushion. "It's hard to believe that the ground was covered in snow just weeks ago," she said, admiring the crocus blossoms that bloomed in the flower bed edging the porch.

Gage lowered himself into the chair next to her, the cushion squealing under his weight. He situated Tommy Lee facing him, with his sun-washed cheek cuddled close against Gage's chest, his breaths heavy, his lips looking as pretty as rosebuds. Ellie found the sight so endearing that she had to force herself not to stare.

Gage surveyed the yard. "It won't be long before I'm out there pushing my lawn mower and going at those bushes with my sickle."

"Oh, I could do that," Ellie said. "I love workin' in the yard. In fact, I'd like to get that garden back into shape as soon as plantin' season arrives. I'll get the kids involved, and we'll make it lots o' fun."

"Is that right? You really are a farm girl at heart, aren't you? Do you miss those kids you helped raise?"

She couldn't hold back her giggles. "Are you ever goin' to let me live that down?"

He cut loose a peal of laughter. "No, probably not, but I do forgive you for fibbing just so I'd marry you."

"Wait a minute, now. As I recall, you were the one advertisin' for a bride."

"All right, I was as desperate as you for the marriage. I needed a nanny as much as you needed a place to live...and a new last name."

She jerked back. "I never told you that."

He smiled. "You didn't need to, Ellie. I surmised as much. Don't you think I know you carry a whole bag of secrets? You didn't tell your own mother you got married. Why is that?"

"Because I knew she wouldn't approve." That much was at least true.

"I trust you've finally let her know."

"I wrote her a letter."

"Well, that's good. Feel free to call her, if you'd like. I'm sure she'd like to hear your voice."

"I—I can't do that. She...they don't have a telephone."

"Is there someplace she could go to talk to you?"

"No, not really. We...we don't know anyone with a phone."

"Do you ever wish you could just jump on that train and go back to Athens?"

"Absolutely not." Her words had shot out too quickly, so she tried to amend her answer. "Well, I miss my mama, o' course, but I love the children. I'm content right where I am."

"Are you?" She didn't like his probing questions or the way his raking gaze made her cheeks burn. Somehow, she had to get to safer ground. His hand came up and rested on her shoulder, causing her flesh to tingle. "You will have to tell me everything one of these days, Ellie."

This he said in low, gentle tones while his fingers started tracing little circles in her shoulder. When had he gone from tough to tender, stoic to sensitive? No one had ever touched her in such a manner, certainly no man. She lowered her chin to her chest and looked at her lap, blinking quickly to chase the blurriness from her eyes. It never took much to stir up her emotions, which, whether she cared to admit it or not, lay painfully close to the surface. "There's...nothin' much to tell." There was a lot to tell, of course, but she had to keep in mind the consequences of spilling the whole truth.

"Uh-huh." He picked up a lock of her hair and gave it a little tug. A chill raced down her back. "You're something, you know that?" he whispered. "You were a feisty little thing when I first met you, all strong and sturdy and stubborn, but now I know you've got a real soft center."

His thumb barely grazed her cheek, and she dared to lift her head and look at him. "Well, I could say the same for you, you know."

He arched his eyebrows. "Is that so?"

"You came off all stiff and cranky that day Livvie brought me to your workshop and introduced us, but now I'm seein' another side."

"I'd better watch myself, then. Can't have you thinking I'm a pushover."

"No, we wouldn't want that. Next thing we know, you'll be givin' in to my wishes and buyin' a puppy for the kids."

"A pup—oh no, you don't." He dropped the shank of hair he'd been massaging between his fingers and sat up straighter. The movement disturbed Tommy Lee's slumber, but only for a moment, as the boy looked around, all droopy-eyed, and then dropped back against his daddy's chest, dead to the universe.

"Oh please, Gage, think about it—a cute, cuddly puppy."

"Cute, cuddly puppies grow up," he groused, a frown piercing his handsome brow.

"Well, o' course they do, and they make wonderful companions and playmates and even protectors.

They also teach children lessons on love, compassion, and responsibility." She was talking faster than an auctioneer, but felt it necessary if she hoped to convince him. "They don't need too much...just food and water and exercise, and, o' course, mountains of love and attention."

"I thought you just said they don't need too much."

"Well, with so many in the house, it wouldn't be hard to divvy up the responsibilities."

"Perhaps, until the novelty wears off. Once a dog starts tearing into everybody's stuff, eating shoes, chewing socks, making messes on the floor—"

"I'll see that every mess is taken care of in short order."

"Dogs bark and disturb the neighbors," he argued.

"I'll not allow him—or her—to make a disturbance," she shot back.

He sucked in a loud breath and then let it out slowly, his eyes narrowed to mere slits as he regarded her, a half grin softening his mouth at the corners. "I haven't had a dog since I was a kid," he finally said.

She smiled. "Well then, maybe it's time you got another one. Dogs add so much to a family."

"You think so, huh?" Tommy Lee had started growing restless, so Gage gently bounced him on his knee and massaged the boy's back until he settled down again. "Did you always have one growing up?" he whispered.

"Sure, there were always dogs around. After my mama remarried, though, I wasn't allowed to have another...to call my own, that is. Byron had his dogs, but they were never friendly. He wanted it that way."

"Byron."

"My stepdaddy. He has watchdogs, not pets." Now, why had she felt compelled to share that information? She bit down hard on her lip.

"Byron doesn't sound like the friendliest guy on earth."

She gave a little smirk. "Let's just say he's never won a popularity contest."

Moments passed before either of them spoke again. No doubt Gage was waiting for her to elaborate. When she didn't, he said, "I'll think about it. The dog, that is."

Her head shot up. "Really?"

He grinned. My, did his smile have the power to dazzle!

Just then, the screen door opened. Frances emerged, book in hand, and made a beeline for Gage. "Are we getting a dog? When? Soon? Oh, Daddy, you know I've always wanted a dog." Her blue eyes widened so that they nearly matched her gaping mouth in size and shape.

"Have you been eavesdropping?" Gage asked, his tone playfully scolding.

"Only for a minute. Are we?"

He gave a helpless shrug and glanced at Ellie. "Your scheming stepmother has arrived at the wacky notion we need one."

Frances tossed her book down and clapped her hands, as she commenced a made-up jig that consisted in turning in circles and then skipping from one end of the porch to the other. "The Coopers take a dog, the Coopers take a dog, hi-ho the derry-o, the Coopers take a dog," she sang to the tune of "The Farmer in the Dell." Gage gawked at Frances, clearly taken aback by her impromptu performance. Ellie nearly burst out laughing at both Gage's dumbfounded expression and Frances's untainted glee.

Tommy Lee came awake and instantly sat up. "Doggy?"

"There's no doggy, buddy," Gage said. Then, he looked at Ellie and winked. "Yet."

Chapter Seventeen

*The righteous cry, and the L*ORD *heareth, and*
delivereth them out of all their troubles.
—Psalm 34:17

Distant whimpers and pleading cries disturbed Gage's sleep, and he had tossed off his covers and leaped to his feet before he'd determined the source of the noise. The dark room was lit by an unusually bright moon, which cast shards of light in every direction, one of them illuminating the chair where he'd thrown his jeans before climbing into bed. He stepped back into them, then went for his shirt, taking time to slip only the middle button through its buttonhole. All the while he strained to hear any further sounds, but silence prevailed. Had he imagined them? Dreamed them, maybe? His answer came in a sobbing moan just like the others. It echoed through the register in the ceiling, which told him the noise was real—and that the source was Ellie's bedroom.

He rushed upstairs and found her door partially open. Hallway light spilling into the room showed Frances kneeling at her bedside, touching the arm of the prone figure that thrashed, arms waving, head turning from side to side.

"Leave me alone," Ellie murmured.

At Gage's entry, Frances startled and turned around. "Daddy," she whispered, "I think Ellie's having a bad dream."

"I think you're right." He leaned down and gave Ellie's shoulder a gentle shake.

"Get away, Byron!" she yelped.

"Ellie, it's me, Gage. Wake up."

As if a fiend had grasped her by its teeth, Ellie sat bolt upright and thrust out her hand, smacking Gage in the jaw. The impact propelled him backward.

"Daddy!" Frances wailed.

Something in the girl's voice jarred Ellie awake, her eyes brimming with shock. "Oh, my gracious!" she exclaimed. "What happened?"

"Uh, you pack a good punch, lady," Gage said, rubbing his jaw. "Apparently, you thought I was Byron."

"What? Did I really hit you?" She pulled her blankets up around her throat and shifted her eyes from him to Frances. "Tell me I didn't."

"You hit him," Frances said somberly.

Gage turned to his daughter and brushed the hair out of her eyes. "Frances, why don't you go back to bed? I'll take Ellie downstairs for a cup of hot tea. Everything will be fine."

With a troubled face, the girl slowly stood. Ellie pulled her knees up to her chin and cast Frances a sheepish glance. "Sorry I scared you, Frances. Thank you for comin' to check on me. Like your daddy said, I'll be just fine. I hope you can get back to sleep."

Frances gave a dismissive shrug. "I've had bad dreams before, and I usually forget about them before breakfast. You'll probably do the same."

"I'm sure I will. Thank you, honey."

But if her damp, tangled hair, swollen eyelids, and bloodshot eyes, not to mention the humdinger of a punch she'd delivered to his jaw, were any indication, Gage didn't think she'd be forgetting anytime soon.

❧

Ellie watched in silence as Gage filled the teakettle with water and heated it on the stove. She could hardly believe she'd struck him, but that dream had been so real, she'd been certain she was looking into Byron's malicious eyes, hearing his devilish laughter.

Gage lifted two mugs out of the cupboard and filled them each with steaming water, filtering it through a tea strainer. "You want a little sugar with your tea?"

"Please," she answered, then quickly added, "I can prepare it myself." She was not at all accustomed to being waited on.

"I know, but you need to sit there and collect yourself."

"I am collected."

"Well, good, then you'll be able to tell me all about this bad dream of yours."

"I can't recall the details."

"Uh-huh." He stirred a spoonful of sugar into one of the mugs, then picked up both of them, approached the table, and set hers in front of her. "You called me Byron, so I'm pretty sure he played a part in it. Whether you remember the dream or not, Ellie, I think it's time you told me about your upbringing... and about this Byron character."

A lump formed in her throat. She swallowed around it and fingered the rim of her cup, chin down, eyes focused on the rising steam. "What do you want to know?"

"Everything." He settled into a chair beside her and took a sip of his tea.

"That would take us clear into next week," she joshed, desperate to lighten the tone.

Their eyes met, and something happened deep in her chest—a small catch, a tightening—that caused her to drop her gaze again. He covered her hand with his and squeezed gently, causing her heart to skip. "Then, you'd best get to talking."

She decided to tell him small bits and pieces, just enough to satisfy his curiosity. She listed off Byron's offenses but limited them to his drinking problems and his maltreatment of her mama, with no mention that he distilled his own liquor, much less that she helped with the process. She told him how her mama had scrimped and saved to provide for Ellie's needs and how stingy Byron was with his money, with no mention of the crooked government agent who'd demanded cash in exchange for keeping quiet. And she tried to describe their ramshackle farm and its run-down buildings, with no mention of the still that had taken up a fair share of space in the barn.

Gage listened intently, inserting the occasional comment but mostly staying quiet. When she finally ran out of things to say, she sucked in a deep breath and then let it out bit by bit. "And there you have it," she said, issuing him the tiniest smile.

"That's it?" he asked. "You've nothing left to tell me?"

"Nope, that's it."

"And that's what sparked your horrible nightmare?"

"I suppose, but dreams can come out of nowhere, and for no apparent reason. "

"That's true, but you let out a scream that woke me from a dead sleep. And then, you were saying things like 'Leave me alone' and 'Get away from me, Byron!' Are you going to tell me there's no basis for all that? This Byron guy sounds like a creep, but there's more to him than what you've shared with me." He moved his hand that was atop hers so he could clasp it, instead. Their fingers entwined, and her nerves tingled with untold excitement.

"I want to know if he hurt you...in a physical sense, I mean."

How much to say without going too far? "He is a creep," she admitted. "As far as gettin' physical with me, he slapped me around some, until I got old enough to defend myself."

"And your mother didn't stop him?"

"Mama always stood up for me, but Byron is very controlling...and mean. When Mama interferes in his business, he lets her have it. Most times, I just didn't tell her if he'd hit me."

In the dim light of the kitchen, Gage's jaw tensed. "Is he the main reason you left Athens, then?"

"He is, but it was high time I went out on my own, anyway."

"Yeah, nineteen is a ripe old age," he teased.

She wriggled her hand out of his and pushed back in her chair, intending to stand, but he stopped her with a gentle touch to the arm. "Why do I get the feeling you're telling me half-truths?"

A low groan came out of her, and she sighed. "I haven't told you any lies. Other than the part about my experience with kids, that is."

"No, I'm not saying you're not being truthful. I'm thankful that you've shared as much as you have, but I still feel like you're giving me only half of the story. Like you're covering up something."

The clock above the stove read three twenty. She cupped her hand to cover a fake yawn and then said, "You may think what you want, Gage. As for me, I'm goin' back upstairs to get a little more sleep. Thank you for the tea." She doubted she'd be able to fall back asleep, but at least she'd escape his probing brown eyes and his loaded questions.

"You're welcome." He didn't let his gaze stray from her face. She stood, and he followed suit, then reached out and brushed a lock of hair away from her eyes. She remained frozen in place.

"I've never felt such smooth, silky hair," he remarked. "How did you happen upon the coal-black color, anyway? Your mama?"

"Y-yes, but hers is startin' to go a little gray, and she keeps it up in a bun all the time. Her mama, my grandma, was full-blooded Cherokee. My grandpap also had some Cherokee blood, but I don't know how much."

"Ah. I guess that would make you about a quarter Cherokee, correct?"

Her shoulders and arms broke out in goose bumps under his scrutiny. "I guess." At least the conversation had turned toward something a little less threatening, though no less mind rattling.

"Did you know them, your grandparents?"

"Not really. They settled on a reservation in Oklahoma when I was a young girl. They've both passed on, o' course, and about the only things we have to remember them by are a few pictures and some letters.

They never approved of Mama marryin' a white man, so they didn't have much use for us. And then, when Mama remarried, well, that just cut off all communication." She swallowed and focused on the window ledge behind him.

"That's a shame. They didn't know what they were missing. What about your dad's parents?"

"They're gone, too. My grandmother on my daddy's side had one sister, which would have been Gilda Hansen, who lived here in Wabash, and who I was plannin' to live with. Guess I learned of her fate a bit too late."

"I'm a little glad you did."

She lifted her head and took a moment to study the clear-cut lines of his nose, cheeks, and chin, the firm jaw and square face, the way his brown hair fell across his forehead, and she decided she'd landed herself about the handsomest husband anyone could ever want. It made her wonder again what he thought when he looked at her plainness. Such a contrast the two of them made—he so strong, capable, confident, and respected; she so shabby and simple, unpracticed at speaking proper English and with foggy notions, at best, of proper and acceptable decorum, though she'd been working ever so hard on the former. Just listening to Gage's manner of speaking helped a great deal.

"Aren't you?" he prodded her.

"What? Oh! Yes, I am glad, not that Aunt Gilda passed, mind you, but that things worked out as they did. Livvie mentioned a verse in the Bible that says something about all things workin' together for the good of those who trust and believe. I know I've fouled up the verse, but I liked the way it sounded when she recited it to me. Gave me comfort."

He nodded. "I'm familiar with the verse. Romans eight, verse twenty-eight. And, yes, it does bring comfort. I've meditated on it often since Ginny's death, wondering what good could come from our loss but somehow knowing God would show me."

"And has He?"

He tilted his head and smiled. "Yes, in many ways. We need to get you a Bible."

"My very own? I'd like that a lot. I find myself quite taken by the reverend's messages, even though I don't always understand them."

He tapped the end of her nose like he might do to Frances. "I'll take you and Tommy Lee to lunch someday soon, and afterward we'll do a little shopping. Maybe we'll even go to Beitman and Wolf to pick out those new dresses I mentioned"—he gave her a slow and deliberate downward gaze, his eyes stopping at her hemline—"and anything else you may need."

"Oh, gracious, that's not necessary. A Bible will suffice."

He took hold of the tattered cuff of her sleeve. "We'll start with a nightdress, one without any holes or tears. How old is this thing, anyway?"

"Um, Mama bought it for me at a secondhand store in Athens when I was about thirteen."

"I see. Well then, it's older than those hills behind your house, I'd guess."

She swallowed hard and dared to look into his eyes. "Perhaps."

He stepped closer and tentatively placed his hands on her shoulders, giving them a gentle squeeze. Interminable seconds passed while his dark, intense gaze was locked with hers. There they stood, suddenly poised in the clutches of a powerful, unnamed tension, his fingertips sinking in, her pulse thrumming out of control. Dare she think he might...no, he couldn't possibly mean to kiss her. But no sooner had she thought it than he lowered his head within an inch of her face and hesitated, his breath like warm steam on her lips. "You can trust me. You know that, don't you?" he whispered.

"I...yes, I suppose."

And then, before she had time to anticipate his next move, he covered her mouth with his own. At the first touch, she shuddered with surprise, and her lips clamped tightly together, for lack of knowing what to do with herself. Gage had given her a light peck on their wedding day, of course, but there was a world of difference in this kiss. *Land of mercy!* she thought. *So this is how it's meant to be!* She'd planted smooches on her pets' noses, pecked her mama's cheek, and even practiced various techniques on her pillow, fantasizing about that all-important first kiss. Yet all the practice sessions in the world could not have prepared her for this! He continued working his magic until she felt her resolve fall away, her arms moving up of their own accord to lock around his neck. Slowly, shyly, she followed his lead, awestruck at what she discovered—his lips were all warm and tender and tea-flavored. Criminy! Would she ever recover?

She strained closer, and he crushed against her, but for altogether too short a time. Just when she thought she'd gotten the knack of it, he drew back and lifted his head, holding her away from him, his breath pelting her face. "Phew! I didn't mean to frighten you."

"You didn't."

"You're young and inexperienced. I should have known better."

"I'm a grown woman."

He rubbed the back of his neck, then gave his head a couple of hard shakes, as if to rid it of a hundred troubling thoughts. "Just because you left home doesn't make you a grown-up, young lady."

She raised her chin defiantly. "Left home and got married, don't forget. That ought to count for something in the growin'-up department."

He huffed and looked at his bare feet, which, by Ellie's estimation, had to be a size 12, at least. Had she been that terrible of a kisser? "I'm sure I could improve with practice. I mean, if you want to kiss me again, I'll try to do better." She stationed herself just so, stood on tiptoe, and puckered up.

"Ellie? Uh...." He mopped his brow, which glistened with drops of perspiration, and gave a low, quiet laugh. "Believe me when I say you don't need practice."

"I don't know how that could possibly be true. The only things I've kissed are goats, calves, dogs, my mother's cheek, my pillow...oh, and one time I kissed a fence post." It was true. She'd been out in the field on a summer day, calling in the cows and goats, and, amid the wild daisies, she'd wrapped her arms around a wooden post, pretending it to be the man of her dreams, and planted a wet kiss on its knobby surface.

His jaw dropped a degree. "A fence post?"

She blinked twice. "I don't know why I told you that."

He laughed again, then nodded toward the door. "Go on back to bed, Ellie. We'll talk about this later."

"We will?"

"I don't know. Maybe. Now, go."

And so she did, but without enthusiasm, even though moments ago she'd wanted nothing more than to run upstairs and escape.

It suddenly occurred to her that kissing pillows and fence posts would never suffice again. Not when she'd had a taste of the real thing.

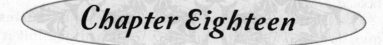

Chapter Eighteen

Justice and judgment are the habitation
of thy throne: mercy and truth shall
go before thy face.
—Psalm 89:14

Ned negotiated his Model T up the winding dirt road, the vehicle choking more and more the higher they went. Through the open windows, the hot, dusty April air whipped at their faces. "These things weren't built for climbin' mountains," Bill said. "Sure hope she makes it. You sure that Ridderman lady didn't send us on a wild-goose chase just so you'd quit buggin' her?"

"I'm not sure of anything." It'd been a good ten or more days since they'd visited Mrs. Ridderman, and she'd waited until last night to call and share the information she'd gathered. Apparently, Eileen hadn't been too willing to give out names for fear that someone might come after her, but she had at least divulged one first name. Too bad he hadn't told Mrs. Ridderman not to mention their visit. It had only spooked the girl.

"You think anyone in these parts will've heard of some guy named Byron?" The single patch of hair that covered Bill's otherwise bald head blew straight up, and Bill had long since abandoned his attempts to hold it down.

"It isn't an overly common name, but the real question won't be whether they've heard of him; it's whether they'll tell us." Ned activated his turn indicator. "Here it is, West Peak Road." He downshifted and made the right onto the road where, according to a service station attendant in Athens, they'd find an old farmer by the name of Clyde Perkins who knew a little bit about everybody in these parts. "Which house do you think the old fellow lives in? There're three to choose from, far as I can tell."

"Your guess is as good as mine. Might as well start with the first one an' work our way down."

Ned pulled into a yard where several pieces of old farm equipment lay in disarray. A big brown mutt emerged from beneath the decaying front porch, then stretched, wagged its scraggly tail, and emitted a pathetic bark.

"Well, at least he's friendly." Bill patted down his patch of hair.

Both men climbed out of the vehicle and paused to survey the surrounding countryside before advancing toward the house. On their way, they sidestepped all manner of debris, from broken wagon wheels to rusty engine parts. Tall weeds lined the path, or what remained of it. In fact, it didn't look as if the lawn had seen a mower yet this year—if ever. In front of them, a yellowed newspaper page went sailing through the air on a strong breeze and then came to rest in a patch of tall dandelions, as if to shield them from the scorching noonday sun. Perspiration dotted both men's foreheads, and they mopped them simultaneously with their forearms.

As Ned applied pressure to the first rickety step, the front door squeaked open, and the barrel of a gun poked through the thin space, with only a shadow of a face behind it. "Don't come an inch closer," a gruff voice said. "Stick up them hands."

Halting like two well-trained kids, they did as told. "We don't mean any harm," Ned hastened to say. "We just want to ask directions."

"Directions? Only directions I'm gonna give you is to turn yourselves around an' head right back down that mountain."

"You happen to know Clyde Perkins?" Ned ventured.

"We got sign, says 'No Trespassin'.' Cain't you read?"

"Sorry, we didn't see it. If you'll just tell me which house belongs to Mr. Perkins, we'll be on our way."

The gun barrel raised a degree, so that it was eye level with them, while the person aiming it stayed hidden in the shadows.

"Let's skedaddle," Bill whispered out of the corner of his mouth.

"If you can't tell us which is the Perkins place, could you tell us if you happen to know of anybody by the name of Byron? I don't have a last name."

The door's hinge squeaked as it opened a fraction further. "Who wants t' know?"

Ned wasn't sure how much to reveal for fear of word getting out among the mountain folk. Everything he'd heard about these hill people signified they were a close-knit, no-nonsense bunch, as tight as family, thicker than blood, and protective as mama bears of their cubs when it came to their neighbors' welfare. Ned realized they'd have to tread lightly if they wanted to get back off the mountain in one piece. For all he knew, Byron was the one holding that gun, although he didn't think so. There were no outbuildings where he could run a productive still, and, according to Mrs. Ridderman, Eileen had said that Byron's operation was far from small.

"We want no trouble," he reiterated, avoiding the question. "Like I said, we're looking for someone, and we hear that Clyde Perkins knows a little bit about everybody up here."

"True 'nough. But I've still got no clue who you are."

Ah, so the gun toter did know of Perkins. That was something, at least. It almost made Ned want to ask him if he'd ever heard of Walter Sullivan, the government agent, but he bit his tongue before that question came out.

"My name's Bill, and this here is Ned," his partner spoke up. "We're lookin' for somebody we haven't seen in some time. We heard Byron might be able to shed some light on his whereabouts."

"You're dressed a li'l too fine for these parts," the fellow grumbled, his gun still at the ready. Ned wanted nothing more than to yank it from his possession, but he figured there'd be somebody in the offing ready to draw another weapon, and, once that happened, infernal chaos would break loose.

"Yeah, we just came from a funeral," Bill said, looking at his shoes. Ned's head shot up at the outright lie.

"Yeah?" came the reply. "Who died?"

"Uh, just an old army buddy," Bill rushed to say. "We were surprised our good friend Walt didn't show up for the wake, so we just thought we'd see if we could locate him."

Bill was a terrible liar, and Ned had a sneaking suspicion the guy behind the gun thought the same thing, the way his beady eyes narrowed. Ned fully expected to hear the gun cock at any moment. Bill gave a loud gulp before saying, "Well, we thank you for your time, mister, but since you can't seem to help us, we'll just be on our way." He angled Ned a secret look and nudged him toward the car. "Might be them folks next door'll know something."

They hadn't taken more than three steps before the fellow cleared his throat. "Well, I guess I might be able to shed a li'l light on your situation."

They stopped, swiveled on their heels, and got the surprise of a lifetime: the fellow with the gun was a woman.

Ned removed his hat, and Bill swiped a hand over his bare head. "Ma'am," they muttered in unison.

She lowered the gun but made no attempt to smile as she stepped out onto the stoop. "Clyde Perkins ain't been well. 'Sides, he don't live on this road." Her gruff voice made Ned wonder if she'd been smoking stogies since childhood.

"Oh," he replied. "Well, we were told—"

"He lives up on Cutter Ridge, but no matter. Prob'ly wouldn't talk to you, anyway. He's got somethin' goin' on in the gall bladder, or maybe it's the kidneys, I cain't recall. I do know he's been in the hospital." Although she'd lowered her gun, she kept a wary eye on them. "Now then, state your real names and intentions. There weren't no funeral today, so don't be thinkin' you can pull one over on me. I keep up with the obituaries, and Flora Hogan was the last one to keel over, a good week or more ago."

Like a deflating balloon, the air went right out of Bill. "Oh."

Ned turned his hat a few times in his hands before speaking. "Ma'am, I apologize for not being candid from the start, but that gun of yours brought out the worst in my partner. Name's Ned Castleberry, and this here is Bill Flanders. We're government agents, and, as I said before, we're looking for someone by the name of Byron." He stepped forward to extend a hand, but she made no move to oblige him. Bill stayed rooted, as well.

"Agents, eh?" She hesitated a moment. "Well, only Byron I knows is Byron Pruitt. Mean cuss, too."

Ned's heart thumped. They had a last name. "Is that so? He live in these parts?"

She sneered, revealing several gaps where teeth were missing. "Right across that there cornfield."

"No kidding." What were the chances? "He live alone?"

The woman wiped a palm across her forehead, where tangled gray hairs stuck as if glued to the damp skin, and huffed out a loud breath. "Nope. He's got a missus, an' a girl name of Eleanor, but she done left back in February. Me an' the mister took 'er to the train station." She shook her head, her eyes clouding over. "Sure do miss 'er. She used to bring us pies an' cakes an' such, and we'd sit out on the porch eatin' us a piece whilst sippin' on sweet tea and chattin' 'bout everythin' an' nothin'."

"Where'd she go, if you don't mind my asking?"

She lifted her chin and gawked at Ned. "I don't have no idea, and I done told you enough."

He nodded, then turned and squinted at the sun-drenched field, his eyes falling on the farm allegedly belonging to Byron Pruitt. Wispy strands atop stalks of corn looking ready for harvest poked their feathery heads toward the blue sky. He had lived his childhood just north of Detroit, and he knew that here in the South, farmers lived by a different timetable. Whereas Northern growers mostly sowed their seed in the springtime and harvested in fall, down here, the schedule was reversed. He also knew that corn was an essential ingredient in producing moonshine.

"You heard any talk of Pruitt producing moonshine over at his place?" It was a long shot, but he had to ask.

She shook her head and clasped her hand around the rifle, so tightly that her dirt-caked knuckles turned white. "Now, didn't I just tell you I done answered enough o' yer questions? Me an' Burt keep to ourselves. Best way to be when you live up here."

"I can sure respect that. Burt your husband?"

"That's right, and he'll be home most anytime. He went into town to fetch some supplies to fix our leakin' roof."

"Well, we'll be on our way, then." Ned had to play these last few cards right. He followed Bill toward the car, taking a few steps, then stopped and turned around. "I figure you for someone who'd want to help out a body in need, so if you happen to think of anything else you might want to tell me, particularly about that girl named Eleanor, you can call this number." He reached into his pocket and pulled out the piece of paper on which he'd scribbled his office telephone number just that morning.

The yet nameless woman stepped forward, snatched the paper, and stuffed it inside her apron pocket. "She ain't in trouble or nothin', is she?"

"Not that we're aware of, ma'am. Of course, you never know; she could be in danger. You sure you can't tell us where she went off to?"

"Nope. All I knows is, she went north. Don't know nothin' beyond that."

"And you're not aware of any illegal doings over at the Pruitt farm?"

"No, sir, I ain't, but I wouldn't put it past Byron. Rita, his wife, don't tell me nothin' 'bout what goes on over there, but my guess is, she's too scared. Byron's been known to give 'er the occasional shiner if she don't live by the rules he lays down for 'er." She scuffed at something with her shoe. "You best get goin'. I ain't altogether sure Burt would be happy 'bout you two snoopin' 'round. We don't want no trouble with the neighbors, 'specially not Byron Pruitt." She straightened her shoulders and hefted the rifle back in place, so that the barrel pointed right at them.

Ned opened his mouth to say more, but Bill took him by the arm and yanked him around. "We thank you for your time, ma'am," Bill said. "And we're mighty sorry for mistakin' you for a man back there. Couldn't see your purty face through that crack in the door."

"Yeah, yeah, git on with you now." Her tone seemed to have softened just a bit, but she didn't lower the rifle.

Back at the car, Ned started up the engine and put the old jalopy into gear. Bill waved at the woman, who watched from her porch. "She ain't wavin' back," he said, sounding disappointed.

"Do you expect her to? She can't tell if we're friend or foe."

Bill settled back in his seat. "Where to now, boss?"

Ned cast his friend a sidelong look. "I think it's time we paid Byron Pruitt a little visit, don't you?"

Bill let out a long sigh. "I'm packin' my pistol for this trip."

"You and me both."

Just like their neighbors' yard, the Pruitts' place could have passed for a landfill. Strewn about the yard were a broken-down wagon, various engine parts, some cracked crockery jugs, and a wooden table missing one leg. "Nice place," Bill muttered.

"It looks about ready to collapse at any minute," Ned said, eyeing the house. He cut the engine and let his eyes wander from the ramshackle structure to the buildings beyond. "Think there's a still out there somewhere?"

"Sure do. How much d'you wanna bet?"

"Got your gun ready?"

"Do cows moo?"

As they made their way to the house, a big, grizzly dog darted out of nowhere at them, barking and baring its teeth. "Oh, great," Bill moaned. "And I thought Ginger was gonna be the death of us."

"Stay calm and keep walking," Ned urged him quietly. "He's probably more bark than bite."

The front door swung open, and a rotund fellow stepped out, sporting a dirty, tattered undershirt, his face unshaven, his gray hair disheveled. A rifle butt perched on his shoulder, and the barrel was aimed straight at them. "Don't come any closer," he ordered them. These mountain folk sure were protective of their property, even though Ned couldn't spot a single thing he'd be tempted to steal. The dog kept up its ferocious snarling, but, thankfully, it didn't appear as if they were about to be its next meal. "What you want?" Behind him, a woman squeezed out through the door and squinted at them. "Git back, Rita. This ain't yer affair." Like a wounded animal, she disappeared from sight. "State your business, an' make it snappy," he hissed, his eyes piercing straight through them. The neighbor woman had had Byron Pruitt pegged when she'd called him a mean cuss.

"Byron Pruitt, right?" Ned didn't wait for a confirmation. "We got a few questions for you."

"Yeah? Well, I ain't got time to answer any." He cocked the rifle and set his sights on them, not bothering to ask them how they knew his name, which troubled Ned.

"You wouldn't shoot two government agents, now, would you?"

That seemed to get his attention, for a flicker of shock flashed across the crusty fellow's face. To Ned's relief, he lowered his gun. "Shut up, Curly!" he spat at the dog. Much like the submissive wife, the mutt obeyed immediately, retreating to a nearby tree, where it sprawled out in the shade. "Government agents, you say? What business you got 'round here?"

"We're looking for somebody by the name of Walter Sullivan. Thought you might be able to give us a hint as to his whereabouts."

Inside the house, there was some kind of racket—a kettle or a heavy bucket crashing to the floor—and Pruitt jolted, swiveling to gaze behind him. Seconds later, he faced them again, this time wearing a hateful glare. "Never heard of 'im," he growled.

"Your wife all right in there?" Ned asked.

"She's just bein' her usual clumsy self." He wiped a hand across his brow and stepped out to the edge of the porch. "So, who is this Walter...what was it? Sullivan? An' who tol' you I'd know anythin' about 'im?"

"He's another government agent, works for me in the Bureau of Prohibition. As for how your name came up, well, that's classified, I'm afraid."

"Yeah? Don't change the fact I don't know 'im."

"You know of any illegal stills in these parts?" Ned asked.

"Nope."

"You sure about that?" Beside him, Bill shifted his weight.

"Sure as rain. I think it's time you two headed back down the mountain."

"We heard your daughter up and left back in February," Ned said, ignoring his remark. "Can you tell us where she went?"

Years of training had taught Ned how to detect changes in a person's countenance, even subtle ones. Pruitt's eyes flashed with wariness. "No idea. What's it to you, anyway?"

"You don't know the whereabouts of your own daughter?"

"She ain't my real daughter, she's my wife's, and she don't tell me much. I think you better leave now."

"Seems a little odd that Eleanor vanished about the same time Walter Sullivan came up missing."

"Don't see nothin' odd 'bout that. Folks come an' go all the time. Like I said, you best git off my property, agents or not."

"Mind if we talk to your wife?"

"Yeah, I mind plenty. She don't know nothin' 'bout where her girl went. 'Sides, she's a little short on brains, if you know what I mean. Now, git goin'." Holding his rifle next to him, he fingered the trigger.

The neighbor hadn't mentioned anything about Mrs. Pruitt being mentally slow, but Ned decided to leave it alone for now. "You wouldn't mind if we looked around your property a bit before we go, would you?"

"Sure, I mind, but if it'll git you to leave sooner, help yourself."

214 ⌒ SHARLENE MACLAREN

On their way to the barn, Bill let out a low whistle. "That guy's as guilty as sin on a Sunday morning."

"I agree, but we still have to prove it."

As he'd feared, the barn was clean—of anything related to producing whiskey, that is. "He's moved it, of course," Ned mused. "Probably figured someone would come looking." He searched around for some kind of clue, anything to indicate a still had once been there. But Pruitt had done a good job hiding any evidence. All he saw of note was a mouse that scampered behind a crate. "I think the girl is our missing piece in all this. I figure, if we find her, we find Sullivan."

"You really think so? You suspect Sullivan's dead, or what?"

"I'm almost certain of it."

Bill drew in a deep breath. "Yeah, I'm thinkin' the same. Well, how you plan on proceedin'?"

Ned studied his dust-covered shoes. "Start digging deeper, I guess."

"By that, I s'pose you mean locatin' that girl Eleanor."

"You're a smart man, my friend."

"Yeah, well, I'd be a lot smarter with some food in my belly."

Ned gave his friend a hearty slap on the shoulder. "I guess we could fix that."

※

Byron sneered as he watched the agents climb back in their car and drive away. "Blamed government idiots. Don't know what they 'spected to find by comin' here."

Rita stood beside him, holding a corner of the curtain aside. "Somehow, they got wind o' you, Byron. They're suspicious."

"Shut up. They ain't suspicious o' nothin'."

"Sure they are. Why else you think they'd come snoopin' around?"

"I ain't got the foggiest idea. They're lookin' for Sullivan. I better not find you opened your mouth to somebody."

"Who am I goin' to talk to? You go everywhere I go."

"Yeah, 'cept when I'm sleepin' or workin' in the field, or when I go over to Morgan's place to work. I fooled them good with the empty barn. Durn fools thought they was goin' to find somethin' out there to pin on me. I ain't dumb. I knew better'n to leave that still in plain sight. You best not have talked to Mildred Meyer 'bout nothin', neither. I seen her come over here a few times."

"She's just bein' neighborly. Land sakes, I don't know when I seen you lookin' so scared, Byron Pruitt."

"She-ooot, I ain't scared o' nothin'."

"No? Well, you should be."

"What you mean by that?"

Rita closed the curtain. "They're up to somethin', them agents. I got the feelin' they know somethin'."

"They don't know squat. They're just fishin'."

"I heard 'em ask about Eleanor. Jus' 'cause you closed the door don't mean I couldn't hear what you was talkin' 'bout."

He hated her for keeping secret her daughter's whereabouts, hated even more having to grovel to get her to tell him. "If they find Eleanor 'fore I do, I'm in trouble, Rita. You best tell me where she went."

"Now, why would I do that? I ain't turnin' you loose on my daughter, Byron Pruitt, so you may as well stop askin'."

He gritted his teeth and squeezed his fists into two tight balls. Blamed woman made him as mad as a hornet. He didn't know whether to use her as a punching bag or to soften her up with kindness and wheedle the truth out of her. Although the first option had more appeal, he knew he had to play it cool for the time being. But, by gum, when he figured out where that dratted girl had gone, he'd be hauling her back home by her hair—if he didn't kill her on the spot.

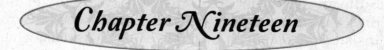

Chapter Nineteen

*For by grace are ye saved through faith; and
that not of yourselves: it is the gift of God:
not of works, lest any man should boast.*
—Ephesians 2:8–9

With fingers that wouldn't work fast enough, Ellie tore open the envelope the postman had just deposited in their mailbox. She recognized the scrubby handwriting as her mama's, but she could tell that she'd taken great care in writing the address so that the letter would arrive at its intended destination. While Tommy Lee pushed a truck through a flower bed, humming to himself as he wove the vehicle between the tulips and hyacinths, Ellie situated herself on the swing at the end of the porch and unfolded the letter. It was written on yellowed stationery that looked to be twenty years old. Seldom had she seen her mama pen a letter to anyone, thanks to Byron's rules about privacy. "Don't need folks buttin' into our affairs," he used to say. And then, with a steely smile and vile chuckle, he'd add, "Funny thing 'bout trespassers, they only try it once on my property." And it was true. Folks knew not to go near the Pruitt farm unless they wanted to risk losing a limb. The only people who drove into the yard were Byron's cohorts who helped him run the still, and, of course, Walter Sullivan—until his demise, that is. Why, the Pruitts didn't even have a mailbox at home, because Byron insisted on keeping a post office box in Athens, which he checked once a month.

Drawing in a deep breath of fragrant springtime air, Ellie set to reading.

My sweet Eleanor,

I was so happy to git your letter. My heart almost jumped right out of me when Mildred Meyer ~~delivered~~ brought it to me. Eleanor, you are married? But how is that possible? It was so fast. Are you happy. Please tell me this is a good man you marryed. Byron has not been to bad lately, but that is because I am praying to the Lord and asking Him to pertect you and me. Eleanor, I wish I told you before you left for Wabash that I asked Jesus to forgive me of all my sins and come into my life to stay. At first I wasnt sure if it would stick, but this feeling I have is very peaceful and free, sort of like a butter fly coming to land in my heart. I have not missed a single day of reading my Bible and now I wish I would have told you to buy a Bible with the money I gave you. I want you to start reading it Eleanor. It will bring you much comfort and pleasure. And after you have red it for a time, ask yourself if you don't want to give God your life. It ain't that hard. You just lay down all your burdens

then spread out your sins big and small. Once
that's done, just ask God to sweep them all
away and He does. Right in the span of a
heart beet. I swear I almost saw them ugly
things get wiped right off the slate and throwed
outside in the trash barrel. My heart went 50
lbs. lighter in that moment, no ~~egaxerating~~
fooling.

Anyways, I also want you to right back and
tell me all about these four younguns you're
watching over. What are there names. What
are there ages. Are you well. You with four
stepkids I can't hardly emagine it.

When Mildred dropped your letter off she told
me a couple of men in fancy suits showed up
at her door and asked a lot of questions about
Byron. They told her they were looking for
a friend named Walt and they asked her if
she knew if Byron is doing anything elegal.
Anyway, she told them no becase she really has
no idea what Byron is up to. But them same
men (found out they were goverment agents)
marched over here to fire a bunch of questions
at Byron. They asked wear you were. I guess
Mildred told them about you. Don't know why
they wanted to know wear you went to. I want
you to take extra care when you go out. I
haven't told Byron wear you are. I don't plan
to. But he has his ways of finding out. When

them agents were here I sure wanted to shout the whole ugly truth. But I was afraid they wouldn't believe me and Byron would beet me to death after they left. He does put the fear of the devil in me, even though most times I can hold my own round him. I still cannot get the pictures out of my head of that aweful day when he killed Mr. Sullivan. It was purely vial. And then to think he forced you to dig that aweful hole. Eleanor, I am so sorry.

Did I tell you that Byron and the others moved his still over to Curtis Morgan's farm? He did this right after the ~~murd~~ shooting. I guess he is trying to cover his tracks. And he must of did a good job becase them men looked around out in the barn and didn't see no trace of nothing. It makes me wonder if they'll even come back here again. If they would just come when Byron's not around I might have the nerve to tell them everything.

Well, I don't want to bother you with any more news becase you are in a much better place now. I don't want you wurrying about me Ellie girl. You just take good care of yourself and that will make me happy.

Pray to the Lord. He will help you through all your days. I wish I could rite as pretty as

*you do. I guess that is what I get for not going
passed six grade.*

I miss you so very much.

*Love,
Mama*

*PS: I'm going to copy a Bible verse that has
helped me a great deal: Fear thou not; for I
am with thee: be not dismayed; for I am thy
God: I will strengthen thee; yea, I will help
thee; yea, I will uphold thee with the right
hand of my righteousness.*

With the back of her hand, Ellie wiped away the tears that had made two paths down her cheeks, then read the letter again, more slowly this time, letting each precious word sink into her heart. A few things stood out to her: first, her mama's profession of faith in Christ, which didn't altogether surprise her, since she'd seen her reading her Bible; second, the fact that she was safe, at least for now; and, third, the government's apparent suspicion that Byron was somehow involved in Walter Sullivan's disappearance. Thoughts of the shallow grave up West Peak Road, albeit hidden a mile back in the pines, gave her the shivers. She hoped Mildred Meyer hadn't divulged too much to those agents, especially about her. For all she knew, those fellows heading up the investigation could be just as crooked as Walter Sullivan. Who was to say that they weren't looking for her under the guise of searching for Mr. Sullivan? Nobody could be trusted these days, not when things were so precarious and complicated.

Well, with the exception of God, she supposed. Every week in church, Reverend White preached about the Lord's unending faithfulness and unfailing love, and, now that her mama had found a faith of her own, Ellie longed to do the same. She'd been reading her Bible every day, the one Gage had brought home the evening after they'd shared those delectable kisses. She'd been putting the final touches on supper, and Frances had been setting the table, when he'd strolled into the kitchen and laid the book on the counter. "Oh, my!" she'd gasped, quickly wiping her hands on a towel. When they were dry, she'd ceremoniously picked it up and started thumbing through its feathery pages. "It's the most beautiful book I've ever seen, let alone handled. Is it for me?" Frances had paused in her chore and come alongside her to ogle the black leather book and ooh and aah along with her.

He'd smiled. "All yours. You'll even find your name in the front." She'd looked, and, sure enough, there at the top of the third page, in fancy script, was printed "This Bible Was Presented To." On the line beneath, "My wife, Eleanor" was written in the loveliest hand. She could not recall ever receiving anything more precious, and she'd determined right then to read from it every day for the rest of her life.

A hummingbird darted past, bringing her back to the present. She followed its course to the nearby sugar feeder, where it partook of the sweet water, while a robin poking in the grass below chirped in scolding fashion at a squirrel that had ventured too close. Ellie smiled, then moved her gaze back to Tommy Lee, who seemed content with his toys. His singing had turned into garbled words, as he made up stories she couldn't quite discern. If only she could live with such abandon, having not a care. *You can trust Me.* She straightened and craned her neck from side to side, certain someone had spoken in an audible voice yet seeing no one. Had it been the Lord, offering words of assurance? Did He love her so much as to make His voice known to her, as she'd asked Him to do? The very notion sent a wave of hope through her body.

"Ellie? Play cars?" This voice she did recognize. Tommy Lee was constantly inviting her to join in his games, and, while she loved getting down on her hands and knees to play with him, today she lacked her usual enthusiasm. Still, she wouldn't let him know it.

"Tell you what," she said, standing up and tucking the letter into her apron pocket. "You come with me to the johnny and show me what a big boy you are, and then we'll make a racetrack in the dirt."

His eyes widened, and he jumped to his feet, crusted dirt falling from his bare knees. She followed him as he skipped happily up the porch steps and scampered inside to the bathroom. In less than a week's time, he'd caught on to the whole toilet training system, and Ellie wanted to take him back to Livvie's Kitchen sometime soon to share the good news.

He quickly took care of business, singing at the top of his lungs, and then she helped him pull his pants back up, fastening the snaps at the waist. "You are such a clever boy," she told him. "An antidote for any doldrums."

"Auntie who?" he asked, tilting his head to one side and scrunching up his nose.

Laughing, she planted a kiss on his dewy, pink cheek, and then together they washed their hands, lathering the soap into a mountain of bubbles.

Just then, the front screen door opened with its usual squeak and closed with a whack. The familiar-sounding footsteps that echoed through the house didn't fail to cause her heart to leap to her throat. She glanced at her watch, confused. What was Gage doing home at a quarter after noon? Did he have an appointment she'd forgotten about? And, worse, had he asked her to have lunch ready for him? It wouldn't surprise her, as distracted as her mind had been lately. She quickly straightened, wiped her hands on her skirt, gave herself a hurried glance in the mirror, and then whisked a few strands of hair off of her brow, which was damp with perspiration. Oh, if only she'd put something nicer on, not that she had much to choose from. Gracious, she looked a sight today, with her hair plaited into one long braid. The shirt she'd paired with her faded blue skirt bore more than a few stains on the front.

It struck her then how much she looked forward to his homecomings, and she wondered how he viewed their reunions. Ever since those searing kisses they'd shared—and her ridiculous behavior afterward, practically groveling like a pouty child for another—she hadn't been able to look at him the same way. He affected her deeply, making her shiver and quiver whenever he entered the room, not from fear but from excitement, and causing her heart to skip a beat or race out of control. She doubted she had the same effect on him, though, as he hadn't come close to kissing her again in the past two weeks. Surely, he'd been disappointed by her lack of experience. Next time, she would be ready. She would pucker up at precisely the right time, lean her head at an appropriate angle, close her eyes instead of watching him advance, and then meld into the kiss immediately instead of standing there awkwardly, trying to figure out what to do with her hands and the rest of her. Gracious, the experience must have made him think of kissing a first grader!

"Anybody home?"

"In here!" she called, trying to conceal her alarm.

"Daddy!" Tommy Lee squealed, running out of the room to meet him.

"Hey, there's my boy," Gage said, his voice carrying from the hallway.

"Mama in bafroom."

"Mama?"

Mama? Ellie felt the blood drain from her head. Although Tommy Lee had taken to calling her "Mama" during their morning playtimes, she didn't think he'd ever used the endearment around his daddy or his siblings. Bracing herself for Gage's reaction, she moved to the doorway to peer out.

He smiled at her and winked one nut-brown eye while patting Tommy Lee's rump.

"He sometimes calls me that when no one else is home," she hastily explained. "I hope you don't mind. I can tell him to call me 'Ellie,' if you prefer."

He shook his head. "No, of course not. Whatever you're both comfortable with is fine with me. In fact, I think it's great he feels that level of comfort with you."

"Oh, good." Her sigh came out a little lengthy and loud. "Well, what brings you home at this hour?" She tossed her hair with feigned nonchalance.

His grin grew wider. "I decided to take the afternoon off."

"What?" She stared at him, her mouth hanging open. Whatever would she accomplish with her husband underfoot? She'd established a routine with Tommy Lee and knew exactly how to talk to him at his level, how to keep him entertained, when to give him a snack, and when to put him down for a nap. And she had a long list of tasks to complete during his nap today: sort the laundry and wash at least one load, write a letter to her mother, peel a pound of potatoes and skin several chicken breasts for dinner, and scrub the kitchen floor. But with Gage home, those plans would have to change.

Gage laughed and set Tommy Lee back down. As the toddler ran off in the direction of his toy box, he cast her a questioning glance. "Did you forget?"

She gasped and put her palm over her mouth. "Oh, I knew it! Yes, yes, I did forget. Land of Lizzy, I'm so sorry, Gage." She transferred her hand to her chest. "In fact, I forgot so completely that I don't even know what I forgot. Can you please remind me, and then quickly forgive me?"

His laughter boomed, deep and rich, putting her in mind of a thunderous clap. "I'm kidding, honey."

Honey? So, he'd decided to start using endearments with her? More likely, it had slipped out purely by accident. Regardless, she loved the way it sounded. "You are?"

"Relax, okay? I just wanted to get a rise out of you. Guess it worked." Still laughing, he stepped closer and took her by the hand, pulling her into the sunlit living room. From there, they could watch Tommy Lee at play on his hands and knees in the foyer, digging toy after toy out of the wooden chest Gage had designed to look like a fine piece of walnut furniture, which sat beneath a window on the far wall. "You two haven't had lunch yet, have you?"

"Lunch? No, but I can whip somethin' up if you'll just have a seat. Would you like to read yesterday's newspaper...again?"

"No." He shook his head. "What I *would* like is to take the two of you to Livvie's Kitchen for lunch. After that, I plan to release you to Livvie."

"Livvie? I don't understand."

He grinned. "Livvie is going to take you shopping. I believe your first stop might be Beitman and Wolf. I told her she should keep you out until your little heart can take no more, or until you've purchased the entire inventory, whichever comes first. Of course, she'll probably want to take you to J. C. Penney, or some of the other ladies' clothiers in town, but I'll leave that to Livvie. At any rate, I want you to buy some new work dresses, skirts, blouses, sweaters, undergarments...anything you need. You understand?" He looked at her feet. "You could do with some new shoes, too."

Dazed, Ellie looked down at her loafers. Her toes had nearly worn a hole in each one, and the soles were so weathered that her arches ached every evening. But then, was that so unusual after a long day of housework?

"I know what you're thinking—you can't leave the children, you have so many things to do, the garden needs weeding, et cetera, et cetera. Don't worry, I saw your list." He tapped the end of her nose and chuckled. "The kids are in my care tonight. After lunch, I'll take Tommy Lee back home with me and put him down for his nap, and then, when the other kids get home from school, I'll be here to greet them and make dinner. Like it or not, they'll be feasting on my specialty: spaghetti!"

Ellie could only smile, so overwhelmed was she by the prospect of an afternoon of shopping.

"You would not believe how excited that woman got when I asked her to go with you," Gage went on. "She started dancing a little jig right there in the middle of the restaurant. If Will hadn't had his hands covered in bread dough, I think he would have hauled out his harmonica and played a tune to match her steps. Anyway, when you're finished shopping, the Taylors will drop you back home. Will's got that new truck, and he said he needs a reason to drive it. Do you think five or so hours is enough time for you to pick out a new wardrobe? Livvie seemed to think it would be."

For the life of her, Ellie could not close her mouth. It simply wouldn't move. About all she could do was stare, speechless, and try to sort through the whirl of disbelief and delight that filled her mind. Lunch with her husband and then shopping with Livvie? Surely, she'd gotten herself stuck square in the middle of a dream, and a simple pinch to the arm would wake her up. So, she took a fold of skin between her thumb and forefinger and pressed. Hard. And nothing happened.

"Don't you want to say something?"

"Uh...yes, I do."

"Well?" He rocked on his feet, smiling expectantly.

"I couldn't...can't...I mean, it sounds lovely, but so extravagant. I've never—"

He shushed her with three callused fingers pressed gently to her lips. They smelled of fine wood and a hint of coffee, and she nearly kissed them. Yet she still found herself unable to move, her mouth or anything else.

"I'm way overdue in sending you on this shopping trip, El. It's past time you got some new dresses. We'll stop at the bank on our way to Livvie's and make a withdrawal. That way, you'll have a pocketbook full of cash to cover your purchases. I have a running account at Beitman and Wolf, as well as at J. C. Penney, so don't use your cash there."

Did he say a pocketbook full? And what was this business about running accounts? Why, even the wad of cash her mother had given her hadn't quite filled her pocket, let alone her pocketbook. Was he crazy? She didn't know if she should protest or burst out laughing. Never had she owned a store-bought dress, unless she counted those her mother had purchased at the secondhand store in Athens—and, of course, her wedding gown. Good gravy! She wouldn't even know how to act in a new dress. Surely, she would never do her chores in one, but then, hadn't Gage told her to buy some work dresses? What exactly was a work dress, anyway? If it came from a store, it was new and oughtn't be used for such things as dusting and sweeping.

Gage clapped his hands once then rubbed them together. "Well then, we best get a move on. My stomach's rumbling, and I know Livvie's probably standing at the front window waiting for the first glimpse of us."

"But I...." She cast a gaze downward. "I look ghastly."

He turned a crooked grin on her. "You look charming in my eyes, and that, dear wife, is all that counts." He turned toward the foyer. "Tommy Lee, you want to go eat at Livvie's Kitchen?"

His eyes lit up. "Can I have hambooger?"

"Hm. What do you say, *Mama?* Can he have a hambooger?"

Joy inexpressible welled up in her heart, and when Gage touched the small of her back as he ushered her out the front door, it came to her in a flash. She loved Gage Cooper with every fiber of her being.

Chapter Twenty

*Cast thy burden upon the LORD, and he shall
sustain thee: he shall never suffer
the righteous to be moved.*
—Psalm 55:22

When's Ellie comin' home?" Abe asked Gage for the dozenth time that evening.

"I can't say, exactly. I told Livvie to see that she bought herself a full wardrobe."

"What's a wardobe?" his spaghetti-faced three-year-old wanted to know.

"A bunch of clothes, dodo," Alec explained.

"Alec, don't call your brother names."

"Yeah!" Tommy Lee exclaimed.

"Tommy Lee, I will do the disciplining."

"What's dissipping?"

"Making you follow the rules," Frances chimed in, though she kept her eyes on the spaghetti she was twirling around her fork. "I miss Ellie's cooking," she said in a near whine. "But yours is fine, too, Daddy," she quickly added. "It's just that Ellie cooks like a chef in a restaurant."

"Wivvie's Westawant!" Tommy Lee exclaimed.

"Yeah, we know, you went there today," Alec grumbled.

"Go easy, Alec. He's just excited."

"When are you going to take *us* to Livvie's Kitchen?" Frances tried to fit her forkful of spaghetti into her mouth, but it slid off of the utensil onto her plate in a neat little pile. She sighed and tried again, this time cutting off a section with the side of her fork and then scooping it into her mouth.

"I'd rather go on another picnic," Abe put in.

"Don't talk with your mouth full," Gage reminded him. "I agree that another picnic would be fun. We'll put it on the calendar."

Alec picked up his water glass and slurped down half the liquid, then set it down with a thud and an aah.

"Do you have to drink so dramatically?" Strange how the return to single parenting, temporary though it was, immediately brought out his penchant for correcting his kids' every action. He wished Ellie would step through the door and relieve him of the responsibility. She'd been doing such an excellent job with the kids that he'd as good as handed over the reins.

But then, he realized it was much more than that. He missed her for her personality even more than for the magic she seemed to work with his kids, and he couldn't wait to get a glimpse of her. Would she walk through the door with a smile on her face and her arms full of shopping bags, or would she return sullen and empty-handed, having found nothing to suit her? He desperately hoped for the former, because her happiness had become one of his chief priorities.

For days, he'd been trying to analyze his feelings for Ellie, but he'd struggled to pinpoint the direction of his heart. One moment, he wanted to take her in his arms and reacquaint himself with those plump lips;

the next moment, he berated himself for robbing the cradle. Good grief! Ellie had never kissed anything but farm animals and feather pillows. Oh, and a fence post. Mustn't forget that.

After supper, everyone chipped in to help clean up, the boys washing and drying the dishes, Frances sweeping the floor, Gage gathering up the trash to haul out to the backyard burner, and Tommy Lee being his three-year-old self by announcing to all that he had to use the "johnny."

"Shall I go with you?" Gage asked.

"No!" He looked at Frances. Evidently, he was accustomed to being helped by a female.

Frances shrugged and handed off the broom to Gage. "There're some more crumbs under Tommy Lee's chair. Better take care of them before Ellie gets home."

"Oh." He nodded, taken aback. But something in him knew just what she meant, so he determined to sweep up every stray particle. Life had changed in a lot of ways over the past two months. His baby boy now used the toilet like a regular kid, his older sons worked dutifully at the kitchen sink with nary a grumble, and his once near-wordless daughter now freely told him what to do, and he obeyed!

Ellie finally returned at six thirty, a full hour after most stores closed.

His kids surrounded Ellie and showered her with a volley of questions—"Did you have fun?" "What'd you buy?" "Show us everything!" "Did you bring me anything?" "What's in that box?"—as they gazed in wonder at her armload of purchases. The sight was certainly foreign to them, for whenever Gage went shopping, he always brought home a single box or bag, never a bevy of merchandise. Ginny had never been much for shopping sprees, either, and she'd employed a seamstress to make most of the family's clothes.

Seated in the overstuffed chair in the parlor, Gage lowered his newspaper and smiled at Ellie. She cast him a sheepish gaze in return. "Livvie insisted I keep buyin', even when I wanted to stop. One little store even extended its hours for us."

He couldn't help the chuckle that rolled out of him. "That's exactly what you were supposed to do. I hope you found what you needed."

"I certainly did! I bought a few dresses, a pair of shoes, some skirts and blouses, and, oh, gracious, I can't remember what all because Livvie kept holdin' things up to me and sayin', 'This will do nicely,' and 'Oh, you must have this!' and then nearly forcin' me to buy whatever it was. She kept insistin' you wouldn't mind."

"I don't. In fact, she followed my instructions precisely."

"Let's look at all your stuff," Abe said, shifting his weight impatiently.

Frances took the liberty of unloading parcel after parcel from Ellie's arms and setting each one on the floor. Then, she knelt down and began peering inside the various bags. "This is pretty," she said, holding a yellow dress under her chin.

"Pwesents!" Tommy Lee squealed.

"Not for us, squirt," Alec told him. "Ellie went shoppin' for herself. You don't need somethin' every time somebody goes to the store."

Gage propped his elbow on the arm of the chair and rested his chin on his fist as a grin spread across his face. Alec and Abe had heard the same explanation from him countless times.

Frances continued pulling out purchases, including a fleecy robe, a slippery-looking nightgown, and some silky undergarments trimmed with lace. At the sight of them, the boys screeched and covered their eyes.

"Ick!" Alec exclaimed.

"Those are gross!" Abe affirmed.

Ellie's bronzed cheeks flushed a deep scarlet. "I didn't mean for you to see those."

"I think they're very pretty," Frances said.

"No, they're disgusting," Abe insisted, his face screwed up in a fierce grimace.

"Triple disgusting." Alec elbowed his twin, and Tommy Lee joined the two of them in moaning, though he had no clue what the ruckus was about.

Gage suspected they were more curious than anything but knew they would never admit it. He chuckled quietly, even as he scolded himself for imagining how lovely his wife would look in a shimmery negligee.

Ellie pulled herself together and reached down to pat Tommy Lee's head. "Well, I bet you won't think this is disgusting."

"What? What?"

"Well, Livvie and I didn't limit our shopping to clothes. We might have stopped at the candy store on Market Street...." She bent down, the end of her long braid skimming the floor, and picked up a white paper bag.

"Candy!" Tommy Lee clapped his hands together.

"You got candy? What kind?" Alec asked eagerly. He and Abe stepped closer for a better look, their disgust with the undergarments evidently past.

"I hope you like candy sticks. I bought several flavors."

"Mmm, we do!" said Frances.

"Oh, and let's see...." Ellie dipped her hand deep inside the bag and drew out a sucker on a stick. "I couldn't resist these lollipops. And there are two wrapped chocolates for each of you, includin' you, Gage." She glanced at him, and she might as well have reached out and grabbed his heart, so strongly did he feel the head-to-toe jolt. "Oh, and I've got a bag o' jelly beans, every flavor imaginable."

Cheers and applause filled the room, and as Gage sat watching his wife divvy out candy to his kids, he tried to remember what life had been like without her.

At the stroke of nine, when all four kids had been tucked in bed and prayed over, Gage beckoned Ellie back downstairs to the kitchen, where he insisted on making her a cup of tea.

"No, you've already done enough for me today," she said. "I'll make the tea."

"Well, all right, then. You won't get an argument from me. Meet me in the living room." He winked, relishing the blush it elicited.

The living room had been tidied up—toys put away, books neatly stacked, the afghan folded and laid over the sofa back, and all of Ellie's purchases carried up to her room. As he prepared to sit down on the sofa, he noticed a folded piece of paper on the floor, sticking out from under the coffee table. He leaned over, picked it up, and unfolded it without a thought. "My sweet Eleanor" was printed at the top in an unfamiliar script. He glanced toward the kitchen, where he could hear the sounds of water running, dishes rattling, and feet shuffling quietly across the linoleum. The letter must have come from her mother, and the thought of reading it tempted him mightily. What could it hurt? He was Ellie's husband, after all; didn't he have the right to read whatever her mother had written? The letter's contents could very possibly settle at least some of the questions that swirled in his head.

With the speed of a bullet, he started skimming the letter, running across innocent words and phrases like "Eleanor, you are married?" and "You with four stepkids I can't hardly emagine it" and "I have not missed a single day of reading my Bible." He found the scrawl a bit hard to decipher, especially with the number of spelling errors, but he made out most of it. And he felt plenty guilty for violating Ellie's privacy, yet something—sheer nosiness, or maybe just the desire to learn her deepest secrets—compelled him to read on.

He ran across a few names—Byron, then Walt and Mildred—and quickly grew confused. Why was Ellie's mother keeping her daughter's whereabouts from Byron? That was troubling, for sure. Gage knew that Ellie disliked her stepfather and even had recurring nightmares about him. What had the man done to chase her away from Athens?

Skipping further down the page, he read that "Byron and the others moved his still over to Curtis Morgan's farm." Byron ran a whiskey business? It wouldn't surprise him. Why, right here in Wabash, a fellow by the name of Orville Dotson had managed an illegal operation for years before the government had finally shut him down. Hungry for more information, he scanned further down the page.

"What are you doin'?" Ellie slammed the tray of teacups and saucers down on the coffee table and snatched the letter from his grasp. "Don't you know you're not supposed to read other people's mail?"

"Don't you know you're not supposed to withhold important information from your husband? You never told me Byron was in the whiskey business."

Her eyes flashed with alarm. "What else did you read?"

"Not enough, apparently. Who's Mildred?"

"Just the neighbor." She refolded the missive and held it behind her back.

Gage crossed his arms and squared his shoulders. "What's got you so riled? It's just a letter from your mother, isn't it? I would think you'd want me to read it."

"Well, you're wrong," she snapped.

"Who's Walt?"

Her eyes shut for a second, and Gage thought he saw her shudder. "Nobody. Now, can we please change the subject?"

"Not yet. Sit down." He pointed to the couch. "You've been evading my questions long enough, young lady, and I won't have any more of it. You are going to start talking right now, and if you don't, I'll wrestle that letter out of your hands, you hear?" He was half joking about the wrestling part, but he hadn't meant to come off sounding so harsh. At least he'd gotten her attention, for she plunked herself square in the middle of the sofa and folded her arms across her chest, still clutching the letter close to her, as if her life depended on safeguarding its contents. She dropped her chin and stared at her lap, putting him in mind of a pouty schoolgirl.

He eased down next to her and put his arm along the back of the sofa, then let out a long breath of air. "All right, Ellie. Start from the beginning."

☙

"I don't know exactly what you mean by the beginnin'," Ellie said, glancing up.

Gage cocked his head and raised an eyebrow, and her stomach turned over. "I think you do, but just in case you're a little hazy, how about we start with the day you left Athens? And don't give me any of that nonsense about how you decided it was time you struck out on your own. We've established that your stepfather is a no-good creep, that he was the primary reason you left, but something big happened down there to prompt you to leave in such a hurry, and now you're going to tell me what that was."

The taste of dread melted on her tongue, and she swallowed. "What if I can't?" She fidgeted with her skirt.

"You can, and you will."

Up until now, Gage had been patient with her, respecting her decision to keep quiet about her past. But this letter seemed to have pushed him over the edge. Still, she couldn't afford to reveal the truth. "I think the only thing for me to do is to pack my things and leave," she said quietly. Her eyes fell to her holey shoes. "I won't take any of the clothes I bought today, though. That would be like stealin'. And I'll need to return Livvie's coat...."

He closed his eyes and pinched the bridge of his nose. "What are you talking about?"

"We can get an annulment, since we didn't—"

"Would you stop talking nonsense?"

"It isn't nonsense, Gage. I'm as serious as a dead horse." She chewed her lower lip. "See, the thing is, if I tell you what happened, you'll not only tell me to leave; you'll push me out the door."

He touched her shoulder and gave a little squeeze. "I doubt it, Ellie. I married you for better, for worse, so believe me when I say there won't be any annulment."

She fingered the letter in her lap, turning it over and over as she deliberated. "Oh, here!" she finally said, tossing it at him. She sighed and buried her face in her hands as her heart thumped like a hammer in her chest. "Read it."

"Are you sure?"

"Hurry up!"

With her eyes squeezed shut, she awaited his reaction, listening to his steady breathing, hearing the rattle of paper, feeling his leg shift beside her.

"Phew!" he whispered moments later. Was that all he could say?

She separated her fingers slightly and peeked through at him. "Shall I start packin'?"

He turned sober eyes on her, but his breathing remained steady. "I need to get some things straight in my head."

She swallowed a hard, bitter lump that tasted like bile and uncovered her eyes, grabbing her braid to finger it.

"Just answer me yes or no, unless you want to elaborate. Okay?"

She nodded slowly and held her breath.

"Did Byron kill someone?"

Slowly, she bobbled her head up and down.

"Did you witness it?"

Another slow nod.

"Did you have anything to do with it?"

Ellie sat up straight and scowled. "With killin' him? No, of course not. I'm no murderer, Gage!"

"All right, settle down. I'm just trying to get to the bottom of this. So, you left Athens after witnessing this crime? Why not go straight to the authorities?"

Guilt coursed hot through her veins. "I know I should have, but, oh, I did something terrible, so I...I couldn't."

"You just said you had nothing to do with it."

"Not with the murder, but...."

He looked afraid to ask. "But, what?"

"The hole," she whispered. "I dug the hole and helped throw Walter Sullivan in it."

When she heard him gasp, the scream she'd kept pent up for weeks mounted in her lungs, and she had to plant her hand firmly over her mouth to prevent it from erupting.

"You *what*?"

"I...oh, Gage, I dug the hole! Did you hear me? I dug the hole!" Her voice had risen in pitch, and she might have shouted, if he hadn't gathered her to him and allowed her to bury her wails in his chest. "Y-you don't know Byron," she sobbed into his shirt. "He gets a strong hold on people and scares the life right out o' them, especially Mama and me. He...he put a gun to my head and made me dig." She sat back and looked at him through tear-blurred eyes. "Lord, help me, I'm just as guilty for doin' that as he is for murderin' Mr. Sullivan." The taste of bile crept up her throat, and she suddenly had the urge to retch. Pushing away from Gage, she ran to the front door, fiddled with the lock, yanked it open, and ran across the porch to bend over the railing and empty her stomach into the front flower bed.

Presently, a hand came to rest on her back, gently rubbing in a circular pattern. "Oh, sweetheart. Oh, honey." Gage pulled the hair away from her sweaty forehead and lowered his face close to hers. "Is it all out?"

She breathed hard and fast, gripping the railing with one hand and wiping her wet face with the other. "I...I don't know. I think so."

"Take some deep breaths. Try to relax." His hand continued to form tender circles on her back.

Ever so slowly, her senses returned, and she managed to bring herself to an upright stance. "Oh, my gracious. I'm sorry I did that."

"It's all right. Come on inside."

She leaned on him and followed his lead back into the living room, where he sat her on the sofa again. Beside her, he pulled her close and eased her head onto his shoulder. They sat in silence for a moment while he caressed her cheek.

After a few minutes, he cleared his throat. "You're not just as guilty as he is, Ellie. Shoot, I probably would have dug that hole myself if I'd had a gun pointed at my head."

Another sigh shook her body. "Thank you for sayin' that, but it doesn't hide the fact that I'm goin' to jail. And something else...I worked Byron's whiskey still. I didn't want to, but he forced me to help him. He always said if he went down, I was goin' with him."

"Well, he's a fool for saying that. You're not going to jail; I'll see to that myself. Who is this Walter Sullivan, anyway?"

"He was a crooked government agent. Don't know his title, exactly, but he worked for the department that enforces Prohibition. And that was a joke, too, because what he actually did was take money from Byron in exchange for keepin' his mouth shut about the operation."

"Bribery. There's more of that going on in the government than folks care to believe."

Ellie nodded. "On the day Byron shot him, he was demandin' more cash, which would have pretty much drained Byron of all his profits. It made Byron spittin' mad. I woke up one morning to a bunch of screamin' and shoutin' in the front yard, so I jumped out of bed, and the next thing I know, I'm huddled next to Mama, watchin' Walter Sullivan go down. Oh, my stars, all the blood...it was purely awful, I tell you. Awful!" She closed her eyes, as if that would make the memory disappear, but it only made it more vivid in her mind.

Gage's hand came down to rest in the center of her back again, bringing a tiny measure of comfort. "It's going to be all right, El. You have to trust me on this—and you have to trust the law. We're going to the sheriff's office first thing in the morning to file a report."

She sat up with a violent start. "I can't do that. *You* can't do that. I only told you because you forced me, but you have to hold the secret close to you, right here." She touched her hand to his chest, near his heart.

He covered her hand with his, gently intertwining their fingers. "This is not the kind of secret we can afford to keep."

"No, Gage, you don't understand. Byron is mean as the devil himself. If he finds out that I've reported him to the authorities, he'll kill Mama just to spite me, and then he'll come after me and kill me, too!"

"He won't have time to kill anyone, because the cops will stay ahead of him. You've got to learn to trust, Ellie. Let the law do its job. You've been carrying this burden too long, and now it's time to let it go." He raised his eyebrows. "It's especially important that you put it behind you before my mother arrives."

"Your mother? When is she comin'?"

He furrowed his brow. "She's arriving next Wednesday on the afternoon train."

She scooted away from him and turned to face him directly. "Next Wednesday? I hardly think I'm ready to meet her!"

"I'm sorry you feel that way. She's anxious to meet you, and the kids will be so excited when I tell them."

"Look at me, Gage. I'm nothing like Ginny."

He smiled and spoke softly to say, "No, you're not, but that won't matter to Claire Cooper. She's not an ogre. Matter of fact, I think you two will get along nicely."

"Not if she learns the truth about me. You're not goin' to tell her, are you?"

He hesitated a moment. "I don't see how we can avoid it."

"She can't find out! She'll hate me right off the bat."

"I won't say anything to begin with, how's that? We'll wait and see how things play out." He reached over and rubbed her shoulder. "My mother is a very forgiving person, Ellie. You'll see."

"But I've still got so much 'backwoods' left in me. Your mother is probably all refined and proper." She squeezed her eyes shut. "Suppose the sheriff decides to put me in jail till he sorts everything out. What sort of an impression will that make?"

"I can't imagine him putting you in jail, El."

"But he'll see me as an accomplice. I dug the hole, remember?"

"You were coerced. That doesn't make you an accomplice. You're worrying about things that haven't even happened, and it's almost a sure bet they won't. Sheriff Morris will probably ask you a few questions about what you saw, but he won't put you in a cell. I'll see to that." He reached out and touched the tip of her chin, turning her head toward him. "You just need to cooperate and tell the truth about everything. You'll do that, won't you?"

"Do I have a choice?"

He scratched the back of his head and studied her with pensive eyes. "You do want Byron put away forever, don't you?"

"More than anything! But Byron is a sly fox. He's very good at what he does, and that's cover his tracks. He's already moved his still."

"And you'll tell Sheriff Morris where he moved it to, and he'll contact the agents, and they'll go do their jobs. It's really not all that complicated."

"No? Like I said, you don't know Byron. He's a bad seed."

"Listen, Ellie." Gage turned so that their knees touched. "We're going to pray about this right now, and I want you to let God take this burden off your shoulders. Do you think you can trust Him to do that?"

The idea appealed more than anything, but it sounded too good to be true. The only one who'd ever borne her burdens was her mama, yet even she was powerless to fix this problem. "I guess I could try."

He squeezed her hand and bowed his head, so she followed suit, wanting with everything in her to put down every worry and care.

His prayer stirred her to the depths of her soul. *Oh Lord, may I one day have the gift of prayer?* she pleaded silently. Surely, praying required a gift, did it not? Gage prayed so eloquently, so effortlessly, for God to protect her and the whole family. He asked the Lord to grant her peace and strength, and then to give her an extra dose of courage when they went to the sheriff's office—courage to be completely candid about everything she'd witnessed back in Athens, and courage to trust that everything would turn out as it should. He thanked the Lord that Ellie's mama had found peace and forgiveness with the risen Savior and asked that she, Ellie, might also experience the ever-glowing light of God's love. At that, Ellie sneaked a peek at her husband, and a dozen questions tumbled through her mind. How could it be that just a few months ago, she'd been scraping by in a ramshackle house in the hills of Tennessee, and now, she was living in near luxury with a loving family to look after? How was it that she'd spent her life loving only her mama, and today, her heart seemed too small to contain the love she felt for Gage and his kids?

Part of her hoped that Gage would follow up his fervent prayer with a warm kiss of reassurance, and she even leaned toward him with lips slightly puckered. Instead, after saying "Amen," he held her in a warm embrace, the type she might have received from a close friend or brother. He then set her back from him and put his hands on his knees. "You best get a good night's sleep so you'll be rested and ready to talk to the sheriff tomorrow. We'll drop the kids off at school beforehand—they'll appreciate riding, for a change."

"Aren't they goin' to wonder where we're goin'?"

"I'll tell them we have an errand to run. They won't think anything of it."

"All right." She glanced down at her lap. How foolish to have thought he might want to kiss her again, especially if her appearance matched her still-damp eyes, which had to be puffy and red.

He stood up and extended a hand. "Come on, I'll walk you upstairs."

She accepted his help, relishing the strength of his grip. If he was going to walk her to her room, perhaps he intended to kiss her there! Her heart took a hopeful leap.

When they reached her door, however, he merely bent down and gave her a light peck on the cheek. Granted, it was nice, but it didn't compare to the kisses they'd shared just weeks ago. "I'll see you in the morning, Ellie. Try not to worry, okay?"

She gave a simple nod and stepped inside her room, hoping he hadn't detected her disappointment. Gracious, she'd just told him she'd witnessed a heinous crime; he had enough to digest without the complication of passionate kisses. Maybe he was even mulling over what he might do with her.

"Good night, then," she whispered.

"'Night," he said. "You should read from the Psalms before you go to sleep. It'll comfort you."

"I will."

When she closed the door, she listened to his retreating footfall, then shuffled across the room, climbed into bed, and opened her Bible.

Chapter Twenty-one

The LORD is slow to anger, and great in
power, and will not at all acquit the wicked:
the LORD hath his way in the whirlwind
and in the storm, and the clouds are
the dust of his feet.
—Nahum 1:3

The sheriff's office was small, smoky, and cluttered. A couple of deputies, each of them with a cigarette sticking out of the side of his mouth, sat behind desks stacked nearly to the ceiling with papers and folders. One of them glanced up when Gage entered with Tommy Lee on his hip and held the door for Ellie, while the other kept his face buried in his work.

A middle-aged woman with mousy gray hair pulled back in a bun and eyeglasses riding low on her nose stood up and approached the reception desk. "Can I help you?" Her expression was neither friendly nor reserved as her gray eyes roved from him to Ellie. She wore a drab brown dress that matched her personality.

"Is the sheriff in?" Gage asked her.

"Yep, he's back in his office. Do you have an appointment?"

"An appointment? I didn't know I needed one."

She straightened her shoulders and huffed. "The sheriff's a busy man. Have a seat, if you want."

"We'll stand, thanks." He hoped his reply made it clear they intended to wait, no matter how busy the sheriff might be. Next to him, Ellie's breaths came out fast and jagged. The sooner they got this over with, the better.

"Fine. What's your name?" the woman asked.

"Gage Cooper."

She gave a half nod and then started to turn, but she quickly reversed and faced him. "Are you that cabinetmaker with the shop over on Carroll Street?"

"Yes, ma'am."

"Humph. I've seen your work. Mighty fine."

"Thanks."

Across the room, one of the deputies glanced up. "My wife's been after me to have you build her a china cabinet. Her friend Phoebe Brackston just bought one from you. I s'pose those things run real expensive, eh?"

"That depends on the size you're looking for, but I'm not here to talk business." He turned to the mousy woman, who still stood there, listening. "Ma'am?"

"Oh!" The woman jumped to attention, her curtness replaced with a certain kind of respect. "Yes, sir. I'll let the sheriff know you're here."

A moment later, the woman came back and ushered them into Sheriff Morris's office. The rotund man stood and extended a hand over his desk. "Mornin', Gage. Good grief, I haven't seen you in ages. How goes it?" He cast Ellie a hurried, if not fascinated, glance, and nodded, almost making a triple chin of his double one. "Mornin', ma'am." Then, he chortled at Gage. "I heard you posted an ad for a wife awhile back. Looks like you found yourself a pretty little thing."

Gage nodded. "Yes, sir."

The sheriff looked over their heads. "Don't just stand there, Clara!" he barked at the mousy woman, presumably his secretary. "Bring us some coffee."

"Don't bother on our account," Gage quickly put in. "We won't be taking up much of your time, sir." He hefted Tommy Lee to his other hip, thankful that his typically chatty son was showing a reserved side for a change.

"No? Well, what brings you here? Have a seat right there." He gestured at the two chairs facing his desk. "This must be your youngest, eh? What's your name, young man?"

When Tommy Lee buried his face in Gage's shoulder, he didn't try to coax him out of his shyness. "This is Tommy Lee." He turned and smiled at Ellie, who looked to be in need of some reassurance. "And this is my wife, Eleanor."

Morris nodded, then sat down, picked up a box of Cuban cigars, flipped open the lid, and put it under Gage's nose.

Gage stared down at the stogies. "No, thanks."

Morris snapped the lid shut and set it back down. Then, he waved his hand at Clara, who still lingered, as if to shoo her away. "Close the door on your way out."

Gage heard her heave a loud breath and shut the door.

"Word to the wise," the sheriff said with an insolent smile. "Never hire your wife to work for you."

❊

Once Ellie had spilled the details of Walt Sullivan's murder and her role in helping to bury the dead man, her body and voice trembling with the retelling, the suddenly sober sheriff had plenty of questions for her: Why hadn't she gone straight to the Athens police? What had taken her so long to report the crime? And what could she tell him about Walter Sullivan? She answered each query to the best of her knowledge, and whenever her tongue seemed to falter, Gage spoke up to help clarify matters. Her head felt near to bursting when the interrogation finally ended. Even with Gage squeezing her hand to lend quiet strength, she held her breath as she awaited the sheriff's certain decision to hold her there, pending further investigation.

The sheriff scribbled a few more notes on a scrap of paper, then laid down his pencil and looked up. "I'll be in touch. You're free to go, but I don't want you two gettin' any ideas about skippin' town."

At those words, Ellie's stomach knotted, and a million prickly goose bumps sprouted on her arms.

Gage pushed back his chair, so Ellie did likewise, standing up beside him. "We have nothing to hide and no plans for going anywhere," Gage said. "Matter of fact, my mother is coming to visit next week, so we'll be sticking close to home."

The sheriff stood, pulling at his fat chin with his thumb and forefinger. "That took a heap o' courage to come in, young lady. I appreciate it. I'll be putting in a call to the Athens police department real soon here." He shook hands with Ellie and then Gage, whom she had to lean on as she made her way to the door, since her legs refused to work properly.

Outside, the sunless sky and cooler temperature added to Ellie's morose mood. She gathered her jacket collar to her throat and huddled closer to Gage.

"You did it, El," Gage said, putting an arm around her shoulder. "And you aren't sitting in a jail cell. Feel better now?"

Tommy Lee took one look at the concrete stairs stretching down toward the street and started squirming to be released, so Gage set him on the ground. "All right, you can walk, big guy, but hold tight to that railing," he told him, keeping a grip on his other hand.

"I will, Daddy. I good climber."

Ellie breathed in the crisp air. "Yes, I do feel better. Lighter."

He smiled. "You're still a little shaky. Here, take my arm." She complied, and together they descended the stairs toward his waiting Buick, parked parallel to the large brick building.

Near the bottom, Gage stopped and turned to her. "You did very well, Mrs. Cooper. I'm exceedingly proud of you."

She met his eyes and smiled for the span of three relieved heartbeats. "Thank you, Gage. I couldn't have done it without you."

And then, right there on the courthouse steps, in front of the pedestrians and passing cars in the street, he leaned forward and pressed his lips against hers. It was a soft, gentle kiss that ended far too soon, but it was a kiss, and she rejoiced in it.

At the car, Gage opened the door for Ellie to climb in, then set Tommy Lee on her lap. "How about a donut at Livvie's Kitchen before I head to work?"

"Donut!" Tommy Lee squealed.

"Really? You have time?"

"You bet I do. Besides, I want to personally thank Livvie for taking you shopping."

"I get donut, Daddy?" Tommy Lee persisted.

Gage tapped his nose. "For being such a good boy this morning, you certainly do get a donut—and some chocolate milk, if you'd like."

Tommy Lee bounced on Ellie's lap and clapped his hands.

Ellie looked up into Gage's warm eyes. "That would be lovely."

Something about the atmosphere in Livvie's Kitchen always put Ellie in a calm state of mind. At the sheriff's office, her nerves had been pulled as taut as harp strings, but now, she relaxed at the mere sights of Livvie talking to a customer and Will and Gus engaged in spirited conversation with some fellows seated on bar stools.

A few diners glanced up at their entry and smiled or waved, and Ellie smiled back, amazed at the feeling of acceptance she felt in the room. Considering the nature of her marriage to Gage, one might have expected at least a few critical stares, but, no—the folks of Wabash had been more than friendly, at least those she'd had the privilege of meeting.

"Well, if it isn't the Coopers, at least a portion of 'em," said Coot Hermanson, sitting at his favorite table by the door. His faithful dog stood by his side, seeming to wag his entire body.

"Hi, Coot." Gage extended his hand. "Good to see you."

"I've been runnin' into your wife from time to time, Gage. Mighty fine lady you latched on to, if you ask me. I hear she's been keeping them twins o' yours in line, too."

"You hear that, do you? You have a direct line with the school principal?"

"Ha! Not quite, no, but I hear a lot of good things, that's all. You want the latest news around town, it's best to check in with me before you go reading the *Plain Dealer*."

Gage shook his head. "You've always been a reliable source, I'll give you that."

While the two men chatted on, switching to shop talk, Ellie and Tommy Lee turned their attention to Reggie, petting him and scratching behind his ears.

"Ellie!"

She turned and saw Livvie rushing toward her with outstretched arms. The women embraced, and then Livvie stepped back and smiled admiringly at her. "My, my, don't you look stunning in that yellow dress, and with low-heeled pumps to match! We were smart to pick this one at Beitman and Wolf. Don't you agree, Will?" she asked her husband, who had come from the kitchen to join the little group.

Will flashed Ellie a grin of approval. "I would have to say she has never looked better."

Heat crept up her neck. Gracious, she didn't like being the center of attention.

"Looks like you're dressed for a very important meeting or event," Will added. "You three have some big plans for the day?"

It was a friendly, innocent question, but not one she felt inclined to address at the moment. What on earth would her new friends think if they learned that she had witnessed a horrid murder but hadn't had the courage to report it to the authorities until this very morning? Thankfully, Gage came to her rescue. "Just decided to bring my wife and Tommy Lee over here to sample some of Will's fine bakery items," he said, as casually as could be. "Heard those donuts he fries up are beating out the competition across town."

Livvie gasped. "Oh, my! Don't let Debbie Stine-hart get wind of that!" To Ellie, she explained, "Debbie opened her shop, Debbie's Delicacies, over on West Maple Street about a year ago, and already she has a reputation for baking the best donuts, cakes, breads, and cookies in town. Will even admits that he's hard-pressed to compete with her, although he still puts his best foot forward, don't you know." She laughed. "He and Debbie have a regular rivalry going on over their cookies, and it's become quite the joke around here. At any rate, I'll bring you one of Will's fresh-made donuts. What kind were you thinking? We have plain, glazed, chocolate, cinnamon-sugar, crème-filled—you name it!"

Tommy Lee's eyes grew to double their size. "Cinnmon sugar! My favorite."

"Tommy Lee," Gage said, a tiny frown furrowing his brow. He laid a hand on the boy's shoulder. "Wait your turn."

Livvie ruffled his hair and smiled. "Well then, cinnamon-sugar it is, young man!"

"Yippee!"

"And what about you two?" Livvie asked.

"I'll take a plain donut and a coffee," Gage said. "Ellie?"

"Uh, plain for me, too, please. And a cup of tea."

Gage nodded. "We'll take a glass of chocolate milk for Tommy Lee, as well."

Just as Livvie turned to head to the kitchen, Tommy Lee blurted out, "I go potty now!"

Livvie turned around and applauded him silently, while a few patrons nearby chuckled.

Evidently encouraged, he went on in a louder voice, "I'm thwee. I use the johnny!"

"Uh, buddy...." Gage looked to Ellie for help. "That isn't the sort of thing you announce in a restaurant."

"Why?"

"Because...people don't need to know."

"Why?"

"Because...it's a private matter."

"Why?"

Gage sighed and shot Ellie a fretful look, and she nearly laughed at his predicament. When she was about to take Tommy Lee by the hand and lead him outside for a quiet conversation, Livvie eased the tension by bending down and tousling his head. "Tommy Lee Cooper, I daresay you are shooting up faster than a cornstalk in late July."

"You gots a johnny?"

"Tommy Lee," Gage warned him.

"I do, indeed. Would you like to visit it?"

He hesitated. "Um, no. I just wants a donut."

More chuckles and amused murmurs filtered through the room. Gage shook his head, then took Tommy Lee and Ellie by the hands and led them toward a vacant table.

Coot Hermanson chortled loudly. "What you got there is a typical toddler, Gage Cooper. Why, I remember you at that age. You and them brothers o' yours done gave your ma and pa a run for their money.

Gage grinned at him as he pulled out a chair for Ellie. "Ah. So, what you're saying is, I'm getting exactly what I deserve."

"Something like that, yeah." The old man laughed and snorted, then stood and made for the door, Reggie following faithfully at his side. He said his good-byes all around and was still chuckling to himself when he exited through the squeaky diner door.

After their mid-morning treat, Gage dropped Ellie and Tommy Lee at the house before heading back to work for the remainder of the afternoon. Tommy Lee made a beeline for his toy box and started digging out his cars and trucks. A steady rain was now falling outside, which meant no playing in the dirt, but that was fine by Ellie. She would take advantage of Tommy Lee's containment by writing a letter to her mama. Keeping an eye on her charge, she sat down at the big oak desk, took out her writing tablet, and put her pen to the paper.

Dear Mama,

I was overjoyed to receive your letter. I'm glad you are managing without me. I miss you so much I can taste it. This will not be a long note because I want to send it out today, and the mailman will be here soon. I have to tell you something important. This morning, we went to the sheriff's office to report that I saw Byron kill Mr. Sullivan. I didn't want to do it, but I had to, since Gage came across your letter and I ended up telling him everything. I am very worried about you. Please be on your guard. I don't know how this will turn out, but Gage keeps saying that God is in control, and I know you believe that, too.

Gage gave me a Bible, and I've been reading it every day. God has been speaking to me in ways I can't even explain. I will write again soon.

Your loving daughter,
Eleanor

Chapter Twenty-two

For God so loved the world, that he gave
his only begotten Son, that whosoever
believeth in him should not perish,
but have everlasting life.
—John 3:16

The following day, a Saturday, Gage decided to do some much-needed maintenance around the house—painting the shutters, fixing a squeaky screen door, replacing a cracked windowpane, and repairing a step on the back porch. Meanwhile, he put the twins to work cleaning out the detached garage. Frances kept herself busy looking after Tommy Lee, while Ellie worked in the garden for a while and then alternated between washing loads of laundry and hanging the clean clothes on the line. It was a warm, breezy afternoon, the kind that made a body rejoice in simple pleasures.

Every so often, he caught Ellie's eye while she went back and forth carrying loads of wash, and they exchanged a smile. He hadn't planned to kiss her on the courthouse steps yesterday, but, ever since then, he hadn't been able to get the memory of those sweet lips off his mind. He shook his head and gave himself a mental scolding. Hadn't he decided not to complicate matters by taking their relationship to a deeper level, especially in light of all that Ellie had been through? Oh, she liked to give the impression of being independent and full of guts and grit—and, to her credit, she'd done a remarkable job of managing his kids and keeping the household running like clockwork—but, underneath, she was a tender shoot of a woman, not yet sure about the world around her, and she'd need to let down her defenses in order to learn to trust. This fact had been especially evident in the sheriff's office yesterday morning.

Did she trust him? Shoot, they didn't even share a bedroom. But he wanted to suggest they start doing so when his mother came to visit. He wanted to restore the library to its intended purpose and, more important, avoid Claire Cooper's probing questions about the state of their marriage. His mother, while she was respectful of her sons, had an unusual gift of discernment, and if she sensed even a degree of marital discord, she made no bones about confronting it head-on. He could almost hear her now: *"If you and Eleanor have had a spat, I want you to swallow your pride and make amends with her. You know the Bible says never to let the sun go down on your anger. Marriage isn't always easy, but sleeping in separate quarters is no way to settle a dispute."* The more he thought about it, the more he realized he must broach this subject with Ellie. He wouldn't insist on sharing the bed—a mattress on the floor would suffice for him—but it was crucial that they put on a front, at least for the duration of his mother's visit.

After he'd hammered a final nail into the bottom step, he stood on it to test the stability. Satisfied, he bent over to gather up the tools he'd used, then glanced at his wristwatch. Good. There would be plenty of time to visit the house where they would find "Free Puppies," as advertised on the sign tacked to a tree on the corner of Market and Thorne streets. Wouldn't his family, especially Ellie, be surprised when he insisted they all pile in the Buick and go for a ride?

He regarded the small outbuilding next to his garage. In years past, it had served as a chicken coop, but now it sat empty, save for a few storage crates and some unfinished furniture. With some rearranging, it could work well as a doghouse, unless his wife insisted on keeping the critter indoors. He wasn't big on house pets—or on outdoor ones, for that matter—and with his mother coming to visit, now really wasn't the best time to bring home a new puppy. But he had to believe that with everything Ellie had endured in the past months and relived in recent days, a dog would do wonders for her spirits, especially since she'd made essentially the same case to him before.

Things are about to get wild around here, he mused to himself, *but maybe it's time for a little craziness.*

❧

With supper done, the dishes washed and put away, and the hour yet early, Ellie suggested that the family gather in the living room to play a game of dominoes or to work on a jigsaw puzzle.

"Or we could play checkers," Alec said.

"Or we could work on my pink pillowcase," Frances chimed in. Ellie had been teaching her to sew, in an effort to encourage her to expand her interests beyond reading. Lately, all Frances wanted to do was sit at the sewing machine Ellie had unearthed from an upstairs closet and stitch fabrics.

"Dance!" Tommy Lee said, spinning in circles for a few moments before collapsing on the carpet.

"I have a suggestion," Gage said in an offhand manner.

Alec groaned and made a long face. "Please, no more chores!"

Gage chuckled. "As if I worked you to the bone. No, I have a different idea, and it involves taking a trip in the car."

Tommy Lee squealed and set off toward the door, as if already sensing an adventure.

"Where are we going?" Frances asked.

"You'll see." Ellie didn't fail to notice the twinkle in his eye, and she wondered what he was up to.

Incessant chatter filled the car while Gage steered them in the direction of downtown Wabash, but they'd driven only a couple of blocks when he made a left onto Thorne Street, then began braking at every house they passed.

"Why are you going so slow?" Abe asked, leaning forward in his seat.

"I'm looking for a certain house," Gage said.

"Why?" asked Alec. "Are we gonna visit someone?"

"Sort of."

"Darn. I thought maybe you were takin' us for ice cream," Abe muttered.

"Ice cweam!" Tommy Lee started jumping up and down in Ellie's lap. "I want ice cweam! I want ice cweam!"

"Settle down," Ellie said gently, holding him still. She cast Gage a sideways glance. "What have you got up your sleeve?"

Paying no heed to her question, he drove another block before slowing again, this time pulling into a driveway and then cutting the engine. "This is the house."

The kids craned their necks to get a better view. "Whose house is this?" Abe asked.

"I don't really know," Gage said, chuckling. "Didn't anyone spot that sign at the foot of the driveway?"

Everyone, including Ellie, turned full around, but all that was visible was the back of the sign. "What did it say?" Frances asked.

"It said...." Gage swiveled in his seat and gave each of the kids a sneaky grin. "Free puppies!"

"Huh?" the twins said in unison.

"Oh, Daddy!" Frances exclaimed. "Are we really getting a dog?"

Ellie felt her heart leap—and her jaw drop. She stared at Gage, speechless.

He sobered instantly. "You did say you wanted one, right?"

Just as when he'd told her he was sending her on a shopping trip, Ellie couldn't move her mouth, either to close it or to speak. Finally, she managed to swallow and nod. "Yes, more than anything," she whispered.

His smile returned, and a sigh of relief came out of him. "Well then, Coopers, let's hope there's a half-way-decent-looking little mutt left to take home." At that, they all scrambled out of the car, as eager as pups themselves.

❦

From the litter of six, they chose a black-and-white bundle of fur with a tail that had started wagging the instant he'd laid eyes on all of them—and hadn't stopped since. Abe immediately remarked that the dog's patterned coat reminded him of a checkerboard, so they unanimously decided to name him Checkers. On the ride home, he was passed from lap to lap, and when they returned to the house, Ellie and the kids played with him in the living room while Gage devised a makeshift barrier out of wood to keep in the kitchen. This he did to appease Ellie, who'd objected to his original idea of bedding him down in the shed. "He'll cry all night long if we keep him out there," she'd told him.

"He'll cry all night, regardless of where he sleeps," Gage had countered. "At least we won't hear him if he's in the shed."

But Ellie had been impossible to convince. "Gage Cooper! You can't expect a puppy that's been sleeping with its mother and littermates for the first two months of its life to suddenly sleep in a cold, dark shed."

Frances had picked up Checkers and held him to her cheek. "He can sleep with me."

"No, me an' Abe want him sleepin' with us," Alec had said.

"He'll not be sleepin' in anyone's room," Ellie had ruled. "We'll make a bed for him in the kitchen. Yes, he'll cry, and by mornin', you'll probably all want to take him back where he came from, but he'll adjust soon, you'll see. He'll need to go outside to relieve himself a couple o' times in the night, so it'll be easiest if we keep him in the kitchen. Gage, can you rig up something to block the doorway to the parlor?"

He'd run a hand through his hair and tried to frown but formed a crooked grin, instead. "Do I have a choice?"

"It's either that or let the pup have the run o' the house, in which case you'll probably step in a puddle outside o' your room first thing in the morning—or worse."

"I'll go get some wood," he'd said with a sigh.

As expected, Checkers cried on and off through the night. Every hour or so, Gage heard footsteps creep down the stairs and a voice speak in hushed tones, first Frances, then the twins, and then Ellie. He pictured each one picking up the whining pup, soothing his fears, and then either cleaning up his mess or, preferably, taking him outside to relieve himself. The kitchen door opened and closed at least a dozen times, by Gage's count, and he'd probably slept a total of sixty minutes from 9:00 p.m. till 3:33 a.m. Of course, he had no one to blame but himself for giving in to his wife's wishes for a family dog. Yet, as he lay there, staring at the ceiling and listening to someone shuffle around in the kitchen and then open and close the door—again—he realized he didn't have one regret. The joy this dog had already brought to the family, especially to Ellie, far outweighed any of Gage's misgivings. And the little mutt was rather cute, with his big, intelligent brown eyes, nice markings, and waggly tail, indicating his good nature. The yip didn't appeal, though—not when Gage looked again at his clock and realized they'd all be getting up for church in a matter of hours. Tommy Lee was probably the only one who'd enjoyed a full night's slumber. That boy could sleep through anything! Gage turned over on his side and pressed a pillow over his head, hoping to block the pup's barks, but it was useless. So, he threw off his blanket and tiptoed to the kitchen to give the little whippersnapper a good talking-to.

He should have known he'd find Ellie sitting cross-legged on the floor, two bare knees peeking out from her nightdress, with the puppy sitting in her lap and chewing on an old sock. "You are a little cutie, you know that?" she spoke to him in a sugary-sweet voice. "I haven't had a pup as cute and sweet as you since...well, I don't think I've ever—" She glanced up, her face registering surprise and then regret. "Oh, Gage...hi. Sorry about all the racket."

He leaned against the doorframe and held her gaze for several electric heartbeats. She looked down, breaking the spell, and pulled her nightgown over her knees.

"How's the little mutt doing?" he asked.

"He's happy as long as someone's with him. He hasn't had one accident in the house, either."

"That's because somebody's been taking him out every hour. You realize that you and the kids can't keep up that schedule forever, right?"

"Oh, I know. The novelty will wear off, and, pretty soon, he'll become mostly my responsibility, but I don't mind." She lifted the cuddly critter and nuzzled his furry side with her nose. Something in his gut hitched at the sight of someone with so much love to give. He wondered if her heart had reserved a sliver of that affection for him. Before he had time to process the question, though, she hit him with one of her own.

"You think Sheriff Morris has gotten ahold of the Athens police?"

"That's been on your mind, hasn't it? Well, I'll admit, it's been on mine, as well." He stepped over the barrier he'd built and strode across the room. Crouching next to her, his knee brushing against her side, he reached over and started massaging Checkers behind the ears. The pooch closed his eyes and snuggled more deeply into the well of Ellie's lap. "I expect he has. Who knows? Byron might be the newest resident of the local jail."

"I hope you're right. Will I have to go back to Athens to testify?"

"If you do, I'll be by your side every step of the way."

"But...your job! And the kids, the house...."

"Everything will work out as God sees fit. He has a perfect plan in all of this, Ellie."

"I know." She looked down, one of her braids falling forward in front of her shoulder.

Gage patted Checkers on the head and then snagged the end of Ellie's pigtail, instead, giving it a gentle tug. "You have to learn to let go of your worries. There's a Bible verse in First Peter that says to cast all your cares upon God, because He cares for you."

He touched one of her knees, which caused her to lift her chin, her chocolate eyes locking on his. "You make it sound easy."

"It is easy, really, once you make up your mind that you don't want to live apart from God's will, that you want Him to come into your heart and take full control of your life."

She gave a slow, deliberate nod. "I do want that. I just don't know exactly how to go about it."

He smiled. "Is that so? Would you like me to lead you in a prayer to seal the deal between you and Jesus?"

When she looked at him, her eyes shimmered with eagerness. "I would love that, Gage." And so, on the kitchen floor in the predawn glow of a Sunday morning, he took his wife's hand in his and led her in a prayer of repentance and surrender to the Savior.

Chapter Twenty-three

*The wicked, through the pride of his
countenance, will not seek after God:
God is not in all his thoughts.*
—Psalm 10:4

Ned and Bill's investigation slowed to a grinding
halt the following week, when severe thunderstorms
and strong winds whipped through East Tennessee,
downing power lines from Knoxville clear down to
Chattanooga and blocking roadways to the extent that
many of the agents were unable to make it to work.
So, until the streets had been cleared and electricity
had been restored, the most Ned could do was mull
things over in his head, review his paperwork, and
come up with various scenarios. He'd filed a missing
person bulletin with his superiors, but the weather
hampered him from pursuing any other avenues.

On Monday afternoon, he was sifting through
a swell of papers—Walter Sullivan's files, mostly
sketchy and incomplete—when a knock sounded on
his office door. He looked up and saw Russ Auten,
Sullivan's former partner, standing in the doorway.
"Hey, boss. I guess it's safe to say you've canceled
today's staff meeting?"

Ned gave a soft chuckle and nodded, motioning
the young man inside and inviting him to take a seat

across from his desk. He was glad for the distraction. "How'd you fare in the storm? Your family all safe?"

The fellow sat, crossed one leg over the other, and folded his hands. "We're all fine, thanks. Lost a few shingles off our roof, but that was the extent of the damage. Heard several areas south of us got hit really hard."

"Yeah, I heard the same. I was just thinking how grateful I am my house remained in one piece."

"Any news on Sullivan?" Auten asked. "I assume that's what you've been working on today."

Ned picked up a file from his desk. "Been going over his last entries, and they're all pretty vague. Here's one." He pulled a paper from the folder and started to read: "'Stopped in Benton. Thought I had a lead. Turned out to be nothing. Traveled up Highway Eleven to Sweetwater for a meeting'—he doesn't say who he's meeting with, of course—'and stopped for lunch at a diner'—doesn't give a name, of course." He tossed the paper aside, folded his arms across his chest, and sighed heavily. "I've got a bad feeling about all this, but nothing to go on."

"You figure he was taking money to stay quiet?" Auten asked.

"Yeah, and my guess is, he got a little too demanding."

"Any idea who was paying him?"

"I have a hunch but no proof. The guy even moved his still."

He heard another rap on his door. Herm Cushman, Ned's boss, stood in the entryway, a frown etched on his craggy face. "Just got some pretty gruesome news."

A knot formed in Ned's gut. "What is it?"

"I won't mince words," Herm said, stepping farther into his office. "Somebody just unearthed Walt

Sullivan's body in Athens. Fellow was out walking his dog, surveying the damage to his property, when the mutt started sniffing and digging. Supposedly, Walt's hand surfaced first, and the guy called off his dog. Made it down the mountain this morning to report his findings, and the cops went back up with him to investigate. Body was partly decomposed, but Sullivan's ID was in the pocket. You should drive down to the morgue in Athens to confirm his identity the first chance you get."

Ned swallowed down the bile that had collected at the back of his throat. "Where'd they find him?"

"Somewhere off a road called West Peak, in a cluster of trees."

"West Peak? Bill and I were just up there the other day."

"Well, don't bother trying to go up again. Fellow with the dog mentioned he barely made it down, for all the clogged roads, and when the cops came back to town, they reported the bridge went out soon after they crossed it. It'll be a few days before it's passable again."

"There must be another way up there."

"I imagine there is, if you happen to know your way around those parts." Herm rubbed his whiskered chin and raised his bushy eyebrows. "You know, I'm as anxious as you to get to the bottom of this thing, but our hands are somewhat tied right now. We'll bring in the Bureau of Investigation, and the Athens police will conduct a thorough investigation. May as well let everybody do his job. In the meantime, did Sullivan have any next of kin?"

"None that we know of, except...." Ned thought about Eileen Ridderman. "There is someone who'd probably want to at least know about his death."

Cushman looked only mildly interested. "Yeah? Well, somebody's got to plan the funeral. Soon as the coroner releases the body, we'll give the guy a decent burial."

As much as Walter Sullivan had been mistrusted and disliked by apparently the whole department, it was sobering to lose a fellow agent, no matter his popularity. Ned was almost certain that plenty of officers and agents would show at the cemetery to pay their final respects, whether or not they'd considered Walt a friend. The department followed a code of allegiance, and when a comrade fell in the line of duty, every man felt the loss.

Ever since hearing Cushman mention West Peak Road, Ned hadn't been able to get Byron Pruitt's face out of his mind. He wanted to be the one to tell him they'd found Sullivan's body and then watch for a flicker of angst in his expression. If that blamed bridge hadn't been washed out, he'd head up to West Peak right now. He couldn't even place a call to Eileen's mother. He supposed he'd have to drive over to Seymour and tell her to her face, first thing in the morning. Something told him the woman wouldn't be too brokenhearted over the news.

❧

Byron awoke with a start when a sound in the other room made him jolt upright. Ever since that thunderstorm and blasted tornado—or whatever it was that had roared through his property like an out-of-control locomotive—had turned his truck on its side, shattered a few windows in his house, and blown some shingles off his siding, he'd been jumpier than a jackrabbit in a jailhouse. Dazed, he glanced to the side and saw that Rita had left the bed. No surprise there. She rarely slept through the night, and she usually stayed on the couch, anyway, which was fine by him. He didn't give a hoot where she laid her head, as long as she stayed under his roof. Blamed woman had no place to go, anyway. And, even if she did, she didn't have a dime to her name. Come to think of it, he hardly had any money himself. With his whiskey still smashed to smithereens from the collapse of Curtis Morgan's barn roof, it'd be a while before he could get another one up and running and start the cash flowing again. But he'd done it before, and, he supposed, if he had to, he could do it again. Next time, maybe he'd build his still deep in the wooded hills, which the natives alone could navigate—or, better, in another state, where no soul knew him. Considering what he'd done to Sullivan and how those agents had come around, snooping for clues, it might be best for him to move on. Rita would hate it, of course, and she'd grumble all the way—if he took her with him. Maybe he ought to leave her here to fend for herself. Actually, that notion was downright appealing. She never said boo to him anymore, anyway.

Groaning, he set his feet on the floor and stretched his arms toward the ceiling. Then, he stood, his knees creaking like two old doors. Since he was awake, he figured he might as well take a trip to the outhouse, the sole building that the twister had left untouched.

He found Rita in the living room, curled up on the sofa with a book. A single candle burned on the table next to her. "What you readin' there, woman?"

She jumped as if she'd been scared by the devil himself and quickly tucked the book behind her. "What you doin', startlin' me like that?"

"Why *you* actin' all guilty?"

Alarm flashed across her face. "I ain't." She sat up, straightened her legs, and planted both feet on the floor, still concealing that book.

Byron swaggered across the room and gripped her arm till she winced. "I asked you a question, woman. What's you readin'? Nasty smut?"

She wrenched free of his grasp. "Absolutely not."

"Then, what?"

"You ain't interested, believe me."

"I am now, 'specially with you hidin' it like a bag o' gold or somethin'."

She gulped and pressed her back against the cushion behind her. "Git on back to bed, Byron."

He laughed, despite the utter lack of humor he saw in the situation. "Give it here, woman, 'fore I smack you." He extended his open hand.

"No."

Anger sizzled through his blood. "Don't be stupid. You know I'll yank yer arm right outta its socket."

"Then, that's what you're gonna have to do."

Blamed woman had a stubborn streak that stretched clear to the state line. He hauled her off the couch, and she cried out in pain. Good. She wasn't a light thing, but he still had strength enough to smack her around. She'd managed to grab the book, so he yanked her arm down and spun her body so that her back was up against his chest. It was a struggle, and it took some wrestling, but he finally wrangled the book from her grasp.

"Give it back!" she screamed. "So help me, Byron...."

He held it out of her reach and looked at the cover. "The Holy Bible?" He sneered. "When you start readin' this trash?" She grabbed for the book, so he turned away, and, as he did, something flew out from the pages and sailed to the floor. An envelope. She dove for it, but he lunged faster and snatched it first. When he saw the return address, a thrill rushed through his veins. "Well, whaddya know? Your little girl done took off for Wabash, Indiana! What'd she go up there for? Never mind; it don't matter none what her reasons were. What does matter is, I finally got me an address, no thanks to you. I happen to know of somebody who used to run a still up there, too. Ain't that convenient?"

"Who?"

"Somebody name of Dotson. Orville Dotson, to be exact." He held tight to the note, satisfaction and sick excitement stirring in his chest. Tears streaked down Rita's cheeks, but he didn't care. He studied the envelope again. "Eleanor *Cooper*? What'd she go change 'er name for?"

"She got married," Rita said quietly.

"Married?" He guffawed. "What kind o' fool would marry that no-good biddy?"

Rita bit her lip and blinked hard. "Don't call her that. Ain't nobody better, kinder, or sweeter than my Eleanor, and you know it. Some man in Wabash reco'nized those qualities and asked her to marry 'im."

"Is that so? Me, I think he jus' wanted a housekeeper he could work to the bone. Here, take your Good Book." He tossed the Bible on a chair and snickered. "But this"—he waved the envelope in front of her face—"this I keep. I been wantin' to git my hands on this here gem for a long time now."

"You give that back, Byron." She grabbed for the envelope, but he kept it out of reach.

When she started jumping frantically, he gave her a good shove backward into the coffee table. "Settle down there, woman, 'fore I whop you a good one. I need quiet so's I can think." He ran his hand down his whisker-rough face. "You gotta help me push the truck upright agin."

"What? You'd need a bunch of men to do that!"

"It ain't that heavy. Between the two of us, we can right the blamed thing."

"What's the point? It won't start."

"Won't know that till I set the crank. I'm pretty sure she'll start, but even if she don't, I know Curtis'll drive me down the mountain."

"Where you gonna go? What you gonna do?"

One corner of his lip curled involuntarily. "Stop askin' me so many questions. It ain't your business."

"It sure is. If you're takin' off, I'm goin' with you," she stated, calm as you please.

"My foot you are! You're stayin' right here. Who you think's gonna feed the animals?"

She ignored his question. "If you don't take me with you, I'll have Burt drive me to town, and I'll git on the first train to Wabash."

He cursed under his breath. "No, you won't, 'cause Burt's been laid up ever since a big ol' tree branch knocked him out in that storm. He ain't goin' nowhere, Rita."

Her composure turned to agitation. "Is he all right? How come I never heard 'bout it?" She continued trying to wrench the envelope from his grasp, but he kept it away from her.

"I don't know nothin' but what Curtis tol' me. Heard his ribs got broke and he's havin' problems with his lungs. The old geezer's 'bout ready to keel over, anyways. This'll just help 'im along."

"Burt Meyer is a fine man and a good neighbor."

She reached again for the envelope, and, this time, he gave her another good shove that knocked her backward, until her body came to rest against the dining room table. Breathless, she lowered her head and glared at him. So, she wanted to play, did she? It'd been a while since they'd had a good knock-down, drag-out fight, and he started itching for one.

With the back of her hand, she wiped a dribble of spit from the corner of her mouth. "If you think I'm about to sit back and watch you go after my girl so's you can kill 'er, you're crazy," she murmured through her teeth.

"Who said anythin' 'bout killin' 'er? I jus' want her home. You want to see 'er agin, don't you?"

A flicker of hope flashed on her face, but then it vanished, replaced by a hateful scowl. "I don't believe a word you say."'

"No?" He walked up to her and grabbed a handful of her thinning hair, thrilled to read sheer terror in her eyes. Leaning in close, so that their breaths mingled, he whispered in his most menacing voice, "You best keep yer big trap shut, you hear? If you go blabbin' anythin' to anyone, includin' them stupid neighbors of ours, you can be sure you'll never see yer girl again, and that's a promise. I git wind that you've talked and, so help me, she's a goner. I got connections, Rita—connections to the worst kind o' creeps you ever met. Even if I git into trouble, which I won't, you can bet yer sorry li'l face you'll never see the light of another day. I'll sic the hounds o' Hades on you, and you'll be kissin' this world good-bye. You got that, you li'l trollop?"

For a second, he thought she might defy him, but she simply bobbed her head up and down.

"Good. Real good." He released her hair and breathed a sigh of relief. "Stay here. I'm goin' out to the johnny. When I come back, I want you to fix me a good breakfast. I got me a big appetite all of a sudden."

When he returned to the house, it pleased him to find her huddled in a ball on the couch, fear still etched on her. "Git up now and make me my breakfast."

She rolled to her side and slowly stood up. "You talk big, Byron, but you can't get away with this. If you hurt my Ellie, it's all gonna come back on you, no matter if I tell or not."

"Shut up and make my breakfast."

"You oughtta just march down to the police station and turn yourself in. Things'll go easier for you if you do. You can tell 'em that Sullivan was takin' bribes, that you felt threatened, that he had a gun. Maybe they'll see it as self-defense or somethin'."

He gawked at her. "You're even stupider than I figured. I tol' you to plug that hole in yer face, but you keep runnin' off at the mouth, anyway. Maybe I need to whack some sense into you. What do you think?"

She turned and shuffled, slump-shouldered, to the kitchen without another word.

"That's more like it," he said, entering his cluttered bedroom. "I want bacon and eggs!" Outside the window, a bird chirped happily, as if to say that everything was right with the world. He had half a mind to get his shotgun and shoot the thing right through the window, but he didn't want to break another pane.

"I got one advantage over you that you ain't counted on before," Rita called out.

He gritted his teeth. So help him, he would kill her now if she didn't shut her yapper. He swallowed deep and walked back to the doorway. "Oh, yeah? What's that?"

"I got the Lord on my side." Grease sizzled in the pan, and the smell of bacon drifted toward him. "He'll protect me an' provide for me, of that I'm sure. And I'm believin' the same for my girl."

In spite of his ire, he gave a good belly laugh. Again, it wasn't the sort that stirred up any humor in his chest. As a matter of fact, her statement made the hair stand up on the back of his neck. "That's the biggest bunch of baloney I ever heard."

"We'll see, Byron Pruitt. We'll just see."

Chapter Twenty-four

*But if we hope for that we see not, then do
we with patience wait for it.*
—Romans 8:25

On Monday, Ned drove to Seymour to tell Mrs. Ridderman the news of Walter Sullivan's demise. As predicted, she didn't appear heartsick over it, although she was quite certain that Eileen would take it rather hard. Since the phone lines in Seymour hadn't been downed in the storm, she promised to call her daughter later that day to break the news to her. Ned assured her that he would let her know about the funeral arrangements, in case she wanted to attend on Eileen's behalf. "Fat chance of that happening, Mr. Castleberry," she said with a slight smirk.

On his way back to Athens, he stopped at the county coroner's office, but the secretary informed him that the coroner was gone on business and wouldn't return until Wednesday.

"What? You're kidding. I have some important dealings regarding that...that body they brought in."

"Hm. Walter Sullivan, you mean? Well, I can assure you, he's not going anywhere."

His mood was far from humorous, so he merely sniffed at her witty response. She must have sensed his annoyance, for she sobered her tone to add, "You can come back first thing Wednesday, if you like. I'll put you on his docket, or, if it's urgent, I can put you in touch with the district attorney's office."

"No need. If I'd wanted to talk to the D.A., I'd have gone straight there, don't you think?" She raised her chin and flinched a tad. "Do you have any idea when he plans to release the body?"

"I would imagine sometime Wednesday, or maybe Thursday. I'm typing up the report right now."

"Really? Can I see it?"

She lifted her eyebrows skeptically and sat up in her chair. "Sir, that is—"

"Classified," he said in unison with her. "I know, I know. Just tell him Ned Castleberry stopped in to see him, and I'll be back around nine Wednesday morning."

"Ned Castleberry? Aren't you the Director of Prohibition for East Tennessee?"

When he nodded, she moaned and then ripped a piece of paper out of a binder to hand over for his perusal.

After reading the report and then confirming Walter Sullivan's identity—quickly, for he didn't care to let his gaze linger on a partially decomposed corpse—Ned thanked the secretary and headed back to Knoxville. On the way, he decided to drop in on Bill and his wife, Elsie. Bill had taken a few days off of work to repair the storm damage his house had sustained. The road to the Flanderses' place had been mostly cleared, but the debris and fallen trees that filled the yards attested to the havoc that had been wreaked in the neighborhood.

When Ned pulled into the driveway, he found his friend standing on the seventh or eighth rung of a ladder, nailing a shutter back on. When Bill noticed him there, he gripped the ladder with both hands and began his descent. "Ned! What're you doin' out here, you ol' geezer?"

Ned leaned against his car. "The question is, what are you doing up there, and why didn't you call in the guys who specialize in this sort of work? You're not as spry as you used to be, you old codger."

"Hey, who you callin' a codger?" Bill gestured to his handiwork. "Do you mean to insinuate that I'm not competent to nail a simple shutter back in place?"

"I am, indeed. When I drove in, I noticed that the second one over the kitchen window is hanging a little askew."

Bill followed his gaze for a second, then laughed. "Is not!"

The front door opened, and Elsie peeked out her pretty head. "Ned Castleberry! It's about time you showed up to talk that man o' mine into hirin' somebody. I keep tellin' him he's goin' to fall and break a limb. You two want some lemonade?"

"That'd be great, honey," Bill said. After she closed the door with a whack, he looked back at Ned. "All right, I know you didn't come out here to critique my skill as a handyman. Tell me, what have I missed?"

❧

The Cooper family was busy all Tuesday afternoon getting the house ready for Grandma Cooper's imminent arrival on the Wednesday train. Gage came home from work early to put the finishing touches on his outdoor repairs, the twins pulled weeds and scrubbed down the porch, and Ellie and Frances polished the silver and dusted every nook, cranny, and crevice in the house. In the meantime, Tommy Lee made it his mission to chase Checkers all over the yard. It didn't take long for the two of them to wear themselves out, and they fell asleep in the hammock Gage had rigged between two trees in the front yard.

Of course, Ellie had been making preparations for several days, especially while the kids were at school. She'd planned menus and done the shopping, as well as baked a variety of breads, pies, and cookies. Still, with Tommy Lee to watch, as well as a new puppy underfoot, it was difficult to accomplish much more than that on her own.

She'd moved with a lighter step for the past couple of days, and she knew exactly why: she'd surrendered her life to the Lord. Oh, there'd been no obvious miracle, but what she had experienced ever since praying with Gage was a calm spirit and a transcendent peace she'd never known before. That didn't mean that her angst over what had happened in Athens had vanished completely, but the burden she'd carried for so long certainly felt lighter, now that she could share it with Jesus.

At six o'clock, they stopped for a supper break of sandwiches and canned peaches. "Come and eat!" was all Tommy Lee needed to hear to come bounding toward the house, Checkers close on his heels, tail wagging with excitement. The pup had adjusted well to his new surroundings and, thanks to everyone chipping in, hadn't had a single accident in two days.

While they were seated around the table chatting about school, their grandmother's impending arrival, the unseasonably warm weather, and Checkers' funny antics, the door buzzer sounded. Abe was the first to leap up from his chair. "I'll get it. It's prolly Ralph. I told him we might be able to play baseball later." Checkers followed behind him.

"Not tonight, I'm afraid," Gage told him. "You have more to do around the house before your grandma comes."

Abe came back seconds later, looking alarmed. "It's Sheriff Morris, and he wants to talk to you. What'd you do, Daddy?"

Ellie held her sandwich centimeters from her mouth, her appetite having taken a nosedive, and looked at Gage, unblinking. She set the sandwich back down on the plate. Had the sheriff come to take her away, then? Lock her in a jail cell because Byron had mentioned her role in either the murder or the whiskey still operation? Her stomach tightened in a knot of pain. *Lord, help me to stay calm.*

Gage pushed his chair back and laid his napkin next to his plate. "Everyone stay put. This should take only a minute."

Abe sat down again, and the conversation languished, as everyone looked to Ellie for a hint as to why the sheriff of Wabash might come calling. With her heart in her throat, she could barely swallow, let alone speak. She raised her water glass to her mouth as an excuse.

Thankfully, Frances filled the void. "He probably wants to ask Daddy to build him something."

"Yeah," Alec said, starting to giggle. "Like maybe a guillotine."

"What's that?" Frances wanted to know.

"It's something they use to cut off bad guys' heads. Our teacher told us there was this guy who got executed during the French Revolution, and they said after his head came off, his eyes kept blinking, and they—"

"Alec, that's enough!" Ellie nearly shouted as a jolt shook her body.

"But it's true! And the same thing happened to some lady named Maria something. Mr. Madison said they don't do that sort of thing anymore, though. Is he right?"

"I have no idea, but that's an awful thing to talk about at the supper table."

"Eww!" Frances moaned. "Now I'm going to have nightmares about it."

"No, you won't, because we're changin' the subject," Ellie insisted.

"I'll still see it in my sleep."

"I hope I do," Abe chimed in. "I like scary dreams! Well, I mostly like waking up to find out they weren't real."

Tommy Lee's eyes widened. "Whose head comed off?"

"Nobody's," Ellie said, touching his shoulder.

Abe contorted his face, spread the fingers of both hands in a spidery fashion, and bent over the table toward Tommy Lee. "A very bad, creepy criminal."

"Yeah, he prolly killed somebody," Alec added.

"Boys!" Ellie's patience had dwindled to a particle. At her harsh tone, the twins silenced themselves and went back to eating. She fingered the buttons at her collar and watched the kitchen door, awaiting Gage's return with a sense of dread.

When he finally returned, he simply sat back down and resumed eating, as if nothing had happened. He chewed a bite of his sandwich for a few moments before looking up and meeting each of the five pairs of eyes that stared at him. "What?"

Her throat as dry as stale bread, Ellie said, "What did the sheriff want?"

Gage shrugged. "Nothing much. He just wanted to pass on a message. Now, let's finish up here so we can get the rest of our chores done."

Nothing much, my foot! Ellie mused. His reply may have satisfied the rest of them, but it did not suffice to squelch her fears. She would get a more detailed answer out of him as soon as they were alone.

❈

When the kids were in bed, Ellie cornered Gage in the kitchen, just as he'd expected her to, and demanded an explanation for the true purpose of Sheriff Morris's visit. The two of them bundled up in jackets and went outside to sit on the porch swing, a quilt spread over their legs. The chill in the air almost compelled him to retreat inside, but he wanted to talk to Ellie without any chance of the kids overhearing.

He did his best to calm her fears as he informed her that the Athens police department was still ignorant of Byron's guilt in murdering Walter Sullivan, but Ellie reacted with as much indignation as he'd expected.

"Not one telephone wire is in working order in Athens, or a good deal of East Tennessee, for that matter," Gage explained gently. "They've had some severe storms down there. I asked Sheriff Morris why he hadn't sent a telegram, but he said even the wire service is cut off. The one thing that is working is the mail service, so he sent a letter to the Athens police. Then, today, he managed to get through by telephone to some department south of Athens—Bradley, I think he said—but it may be some time before this thing gets resolved. Apparently, several of the main roads were also washed out."

"Oh, dear. I hope Mama's all right! That house they live in is little more than a shack."

"I'm sure she's fine. Sheriff Morris said the word he got was that there were no casualties and that folks are making do." He put an arm around her trembling shoulders and pulled her close to his side. "Worrying isn't going to accomplish anything, Ellie."

"I know that. The Lord has been helpin' me learn to trust Him." She looked at her feet, which scuffed against the porch floor with every back-and-forth sway of the swing. Beneath the amber glow of the porch light, a petered-out Checkers slept. "It's not easy, though. I think I must find some strange pleasure in worryin'."

He chuckled. "That's human nature for you."

"Don't you ever worry?"

He thought for a moment. "I used to worry about my kids before I married you."

She turned to look at him. "Really? And now you don't?"

He shook his head. "You've done a great deal to ease my load, El. I know I've thanked God, but I don't know if I've ever thanked you for that."

"No need. Besides, I'm the one who should be doin' the thankin'. I needed a home, and you provided it."

"And I needed a caregiver for my children, and God provided you."

The swing creaked. "You're a very nice man, you know that?"

Gage chuckled. "Are you saying you've abandoned your first impression of me?"

Her breath warmed his cheek. "Well, I guess I did find you a little smug early on."

"Smug? Humph." He swallowed a chortle and began rubbing circles on her shoulder with his index finger.

"And you thought I was a little hillbilly. Do you still?"

"I never called you a little hillbilly. Young, maybe, but not a hillbilly."

"You may not have said it, but you probably thought it."

"So, you think you know me well enough to read my thoughts, do you?"

"I'm startin' to."

He studied her in the velvet richness of early evening, the lamplight casting long shadows, the sky just starting to flicker with a few stars. In a matter of weeks, the porch light would draw so many mosquitoes, they wouldn't be able to sit out here to enjoy the evenings. He stopped the swing with his foot. "What am I thinking now?"

Their gazes held for a couple of shivery breaths. "That it's gettin' downright chilly out here?"

"Nope. Well, it is a little nippy, but that wasn't my primary thought."

"Oh." She pulled the quilt up to her chin and puffed out her lower lip in a tiny pout. "You could be thinkin' how anxious you are to see your mama. I know I would be."

"I'll be happy to see her, but, again, that wasn't my number one thought."

"Hm. Well, I guess you'll have to tell me."

"Or I could show you." His hand detected a quiver in her shoulder as he lowered his head and kissed her earlobe. "I was thinking I should try to improve upon that kiss I gave you on the courthouse steps," he said huskily.

Ellie grinned. "It was a little skimpy, now that I think on it. But then, you told me I was too young and inexperienced to be kissin', so I thought you might want to wait till I got older before tryin' again."

She never failed to surprise him with the things she blurted out. He chuckled and kissed her neck, just beneath her jaw, then lifted his fingers to her chin, turning her face so that he could look straight into her deep, chocolate eyes with the sweeping lashes. "That's what I would do if I were smart."

"But you are smart, and kissin' me again won't change that. We are husband and wife, after all."

"We are, aren't we? When did you get to be so practical?" He dropped his lips to her waiting mouth, and his heart set off like some wild beast. *She's still just a girl, and I'm seventeen years older.* But the reminder didn't keep his trained lips from delighting in the touch of her untutored ones, his hands from turning her body to face his, or his arms from pulling her close—as close as two people could be without melting into each other. He let his feelings run away with him until common sense regained its hold and gave him the strength to set her back. There were things they needed to discuss, and they couldn't wait until tomorrow.

Her shoulders slumped. "Are we done already?" Her innocent tone made him smile but also emphasized again their stark age difference.

"For now. There's something else I want to talk to you about." He used his foot to start the swing again, and the squeak of the chain links was enough to wake Checkers. He got on all fours, stretched, and lobbed down the porch steps to sniff at the grass. Gage wondered briefly how to transition into what he wanted to say, but, after a moment, he decided just to go for it, hoping the intimacy they'd just shared would cushion the subject. He stretched his arm along the back of the swing, again dropping his hand to her shoulder. "I don't know if you noticed, but while you were getting supper ready, I...well, I cleaned up my downstairs bedroom...made it a library again."

Her gaze darted up. "You did? Well, that's...nice. Where did you hide everything?"

"I didn't hide anything, really. I returned the blankets and pillows to my armoire upstairs, cleared out all my personal items, and straightened my desk. No more makeshift bedroom. I'm surprised you didn't notice—you walked right past it, and I'd propped the doors open."

"Shall I go look at it now? You should have told me you planned to do that. I would've been glad to help out."

"Really?" When she started to stand, he pulled her back down. "Then, you don't mind?"

She tilted her head and tossed him a questioning look. "Why should I mind? It'll be nice not to feel like I'm trespassin' on private property every time I go in there to dust or to look for a book to read."

He breathed a bottomless sigh of relief. "I'm glad you see it that way. I've missed my room."

"Your room? You mean...oh!" Her eyes widened with understanding. "You want your room back! Well, that's fine, o' course. I don't mind movin' in with Frances. But, wait...where, exactly, did you plan to put your mother? I suppose the twins could both—"

"My mother usually stays with Frances. They enjoy that special time together."

"Yes, that makes sense. Well then, I shall take over the library. Gracious, it's my turn, anyway. We should've made the switch long ago. It's only fair—"

"Ellie. You just said how nice it is to have the library returned to normal."

"Well, it's not like I'm goin' to create any big disturbance in there. I'll keep my belongin's where they are, if that's all right with you, and I can carry a blanket and pillow down each night." She stretched out her legs, toes in the air, as they continued to swing.

Gage stopped working his foot, so they lost momentum, gradually slowing to a stop. Ellie planted her feet back on the ground and looked at him expectantly.

"It wouldn't look right to my mother, your walking down there with a blanket and pillow every night." He sighed and squeezed the bridge of his nose. "I don't want her thinking we're, you know, having problems so early in the marriage. She might start asking questions."

"Well, I won't let her see me go down there."

"Ellie, be reasonable. This is not that big a deal."

"Yes, it is." A cross between panic and confusion skipped over her expression. Hadn't she just kissed him with the eagerness of a child opening presents on Christmas morn? In fact, he'd been the one to draw the line on their moment of passion. "If you'll remember, that was part of the bargain, my havin' my own room," she pointed out.

"I know, and you have...up until now. Did you take that to mean forever?"

"Yes, o' course. Didn't you?"

"I don't know, exactly. I don't think I thought that far, but, now that I have, it seems to make more sense for us to share my room...not the bed, necessarily, but

the room. I'll sleep on the floor, of course. After my
mother leaves, we can go back to separate rooms, if
you want, but I'd like to keep the library functional.
Maybe I can rig up a room in the basement or something, though it's a little musty down there."

"What about the kids? Won't they wonder why
you've suddenly moved out of the library?"

"I'll think of some explanation."

"And Tommy Lee? How do you expect to keep him
from blurtin' somethin' out?"

"I'll just take my chances with him. I can't control
what comes out of that boy's mouth."

Her shoulders relaxed a little. After a couple of
quiet, thoughtful breaths, she nodded and said, "Well,
I suppose it might work. Do you have an extra curtain?"

"A curtain?"

"We'd need somethin' to separate our comin's and
goin's and our...well, our undressin'."

"We'll turn our backs to each other."

Checkers scampered up the steps again, ready
to play. Ellie gawked at Gage, ignoring the puppy for a
change. "You'll cheat!"

It was all he could do to keep from laughing aloud.
She was something else when she got riled up—and
she looked about seventeen, too. He grinned at her. "I'll
do my best not to."

Before he had a chance to hold her there, she
stood up and cast him a stern look, hands planted on
her hips like two handles on a piece of crockery. "Now
I know why you kissed me, mister...mister sneaky
pants! You're fixin' to have your way with me later."

"Huh?" He leaped up so fast that the seat swung
back and then forward again, knocking him in the

leg. "I had no such intention. And what's with 'mister sneaky pants'? Didn't you just tell me I was a very nice man?"

"A woman can change her mind."

He fortified himself with a deep breath as he considered his next words. "I merely think it's a little... well, silly for a husband and wife to be sleeping in separate rooms. Notice I said separate rooms, not beds. Like I said, I'll sleep on the floor."

"If you insist on comin' back to your room, then I'll sleep on the floor."

"What?" He came nose to nose with her on that one. "No, you won't."

"Will, too. I'm used to hard surfaces. In Athens, I slept on a thin straw mattress for years and survived just fine."

How had they gone from kissing to fighting in the span of a few short seconds? At their feet, Checkers whimpered and pawed at Gage's shins. He looked down in annoyance, then glanced back at Ellie. "I'll take the floor, you'll keep the bed, and I don't want to hear another word about it." He moved to the door and opened it, then waited for her to break her stubborn stance. "Go inside," he said, "please." Good grief! This was not the way he'd wanted to end the evening, playing the role of dictator.

Ellie stepped over the threshold and paused at the entrance to the library. "So, this is what a library is supposed to look like." She studied the space for a moment, then swiveled around, hands on her hips again. "It looks very nice." Checkers went to stand near her, and she patted his soft head. "Would you mind seein' to Checkers tonight? You'll need to refill his water bowl and replenish his food dish."

"Yes. I mean, no, I don't mind."

"Good." She turned back around and walked to the stairs. "I'm goin' up to my room to enjoy my last night o' privacy." At the first step, she paused and added, "And don't think you'll be kissin' me again anytime soon. I'm onto you."

He blinked twice and scratched his head, then opened his mouth for a rebuttal that never made it off his tongue.

Funny how, at the height of his frustration with his child bride, he also realized he loved her.

Chapter Twenty-five

For ye have need of patience, that, after
ye have done the will of God, ye might
receive the promise.
—Hebrews 10:36

Grandma Cooper's train arrived on the tail of a spring storm no one had seen coming. It had been a sunny morning until ten o'clock, when an army of gray clouds had crawled in and darkened the sky to a shade one might have called "midnight gloom." As the wind had raged, streaks of lightning had reached across the sky like unraveling skeins of yarn, all twisted and tangled, and they'd been answered by deafening claps of thunder that scared the bark right out of Checkers.

Gage came home from work at eleven thirty, stopping by the school to pick up the kids, for whom he'd requested an early dismissal. When it was time to leave for the train station, the family made a mad dash to the car but climbed in as drenched as wet rags. Of course, Tommy Lee thought the whole thing quite comical, and he laughed as he bounced along in his daddy's arms. Frances screamed with every mud puddle she ran through, and the cutest was Ellie, who'd decided to tie up her hair in some kind of bun but hadn't used enough pins to keep it intact. Half of her hair had fallen down her back by the time she reached the car. She sputtered about it all the way to the station, trying desperately yet fruitlessly to fix it as she fretted over what his mother would think. Gage eventually stopped insisting that she wouldn't care, for it was no use.

Meanwhile, the kids babbled on, first about the pounding rain but then about how excited they were to see their grandma. "I hope she brought us something," Abe said.

"She always does," Alec declared.

"I hope she brought me a book," Frances chirped.

"Well, don't go making that the first thing you ask her," Gage said as he cut the engine in a parking space not far from the platform.

Thankfully, the rain had slowed to a heavy mist on the drive over. The Buick's back doors opened and the kids filed out. Ellie, still fiddling with her hair and looking more rattled than he'd ever seen her—well, almost; she'd been pretty rattled last night—gave a loud gasp. "I don't think I can do this," she said in a wobbly voice. "I can't meet her lookin' like this."

"Of course, you can. You look so nice in that new blue dress."

Tommy Lee tugged on Ellie's arm. "Come on, Mama. Let's find Gwamma."

Gage met Ellie's panicked eyes once more. "Stop worrying your pretty head, El. She'll love you right off." *As I do.*

Not to be comforted, she reached for the strands of hair that hung about her face and tried cramming them back inside her disheveled bun. "You're just sayin' that."

"All right, I'm just saying it." He chuckled, even though he'd long known that it's never smart to laugh over a woman's woes. "Doesn't make it any less true. Are you still mad about last night?" It was a foolish question; he'd felt her cold shoulder at breakfast.

She sniffed. "I don't know. Have you changed your mind about...the arrangement?"

He shook his head. "It's best we share my room, El."

She took a big gulp of air and reached for the car handle, giving it a good shove with her shoulder. "Then, I'm still mad."

In the parking lot, he almost had to run to keep up with her—not easy, considering how heavy Tommy Lee was getting. "Well, could you not let my mother know? I'd like us to at least pretend to be a happily married couple."

"I'll do my best," she said without turning around.

❧

Ellie didn't know why she'd expected Claire Cooper to be judgmental or exacting, because it was immediately obvious that she was just the opposite. At the first sight of her, the children ran straight for her outstretched arms, and Ellie could see why. From the silver-haired top of her petite, slender frame to her shiny, patent-leather pumps, she had the words "warm" and "approachable" written all over her, not to mention "animated" and "loving." Ellie's mama was attractive, too, but years of toil and stress had erased much of her natural beauty. Not so this woman. Why, if she'd worried a day of her life or spent a minute too long in the sun, it certainly didn't show in the form of facial wrinkles. In fact, her hair was the only indication that she had probably reached her mid-fifties.

After giving the children her unbroken attention for several moments, commenting on their growth, tousling the twins' hair, giving Frances a kiss, and gathering up a giggling Tommy Lee, she finally looked up at Gage and beamed, then gave Ellie an equally warm smile. "I'd say it's time I met the other Mrs. Cooper, wouldn't you?" she said to the children.

"Who's Mrs. Coopa?" Tommy Lee wanted to know.

"Ellie, silly," Abe said, looping his hand through the woman's arm to travel the short distance. Gracious, if anybody had a mind to peel the kids away from their grandmother, he'd be hard-pressed to do it, and she felt a tiny prick of envy. She wanted the kids to love her like that, all of them.

"Hi, Mom." Gage stepped forward and embraced his mother, who never stopped smiling as she wrapped her arms around his back and squeezed. "Ah, Gage. So good to see you, son." Then, just as quickly as the hug had begun, it ended when she stepped away and planted her gaze on Ellie. "Now then, introduce me to your beautiful wife."

The rest of the day went by in a blur of activity, beginning with a lively lunch at Livvie's Kitchen, followed by a ride through town to show Claire all the newest establishments. And then, since the rain had let up and the sun had come back out, they stopped at the park by the river so the children could play on the swings and merry-go-round while the three adults sat at a picnic table nearby and visited. Finally, around four o'clock, Gage pulled the Buick into the Coopers' driveway, stopping next to his beat-up truck, and everyone got out. The twins fought over who would get to carry their grandma's giant suitcase into the house, but it ended up being too heavy for either of them, and so Gage did the honors.

Frances kept her arm linked with her grandma's as she walked her through the house, pointing out any changes they had made. Ellie wondered if she was surprised to see the framed picture of Ginny still on the mantel with the other family portraits, and no pictures of Gage's new wife to be found. It made sense, really, because even though Gage appreciated her, had even said how grateful he was to have married her, it was only because she'd filled his need for a nanny. That was how he still viewed her, then—as a nanny whom he got to kiss on occasion, when the feeling struck him. Well, she'd told him not to expect any more smooches in the near future, and she'd meant it. It was enough that she was playing along with the "happily married" charade for his mother.

Supper was simple—potato soup, salad, and fresh-baked bread—yet Claire raved about every aspect, especially the peach cobbler Ellie served for dessert. She even asked for the recipe. Of course, it was stored in Ellie's head, just like every other dish she'd concocted from memory, learned by cooking with her mama in their tiny kitchen in Tennessee. "I'll be happy to write it down for you, ma'am. It's in my head right now, and I actually didn't bring any printed recipes along when I moved up here."

"I see." She looked curious, perhaps wanting to probe further, but Gage cut her off at the bend.

"Ellie has done a fine job of keeping us all well-fed."

"She cooks the best chocolate cake," Frances said. The girl had vied for and won the seat next to her grandmother and had scooted her chair so close to Claire's that a single sheet of paper would hardly have fit through the crack. It was sweet to witness the mutual love between this grandmother and her beloved, adoring granddaughter.

Alec laid his napkin next to his plate. "You want to play carrom with Abe an' me tonight, Grandma?"

"Oh, you know I would. I've been practicing with your grandpa, knowing that you'd want to play. I do believe I've improved enough to win a match or two."

"Wanna race cars?" Tommy Lee asked next.

"I can't think of anything I'd rather do."

Not to be outdone, Frances said, "You want to see what I've made on the sewing machine, Grandma? Ellie's been teaching me. So far, I've made a pillowcase and a table runner, and now I'm working on some kerchiefs. In fact, I made one for you."

"You made one for me? Oh, my lands, I'm so anxious to see it, but that reminds me of something."

"What?" Alec asked, taking a swig of milk to wash down his last bite of cobbler.

"I have presents for all of you."

"Whee!" Frances cheered. "I knew you would. You always bring us something."

"Pwesents! Pwesents!" Tommy Lee chanted, banging his spoon on the table.

Claire laughed and stood up. "Don't anyone move," she ordered. "I shall return before you can say diddle-doodle-daddle-dee!"

And she did, bearing an armload of presents—a board game for the twins, a cloth doll for Frances, a wooden truck for Tommy Lee, and, for Gage, a shiny new hammer with his name engraved on the handle. He moved his hand over the tool and smiled. "Thanks,

Mom. I think I know why that trunk of yours was so heavy."

She gave a light laugh. "And for my new daughter-in-law." She turned to Ellie, extending a small package wrapped in yellow paper and tied with white ribbon. "Just a little something to welcome you to the Cooper family."

Ellie clamped a hand to her chest. "Oh, but you shouldn't have. We...we didn't get you anything."

"You most certainly did, when you all gave me the most heartwarming welcome at the train station. The gift of family is plenty enough for me. Now, go ahead and open it."

With trembling fingers, she untied the bow, which was somewhat flattened from being packed away, and held her breath. She couldn't even recall the last gift-wrapped present she'd received. The book her mama had splurged on three Christmases ago, perhaps? With the children all gathered around her for a closer look, and Tommy Lee trying to help her with the process, she glanced across the table at Gage and found him watching as intently as the kids, smiling and encouraging her with his eyes.

"Open it," Abe urged her.

"Yes, hurry," said Frances.

She returned her attention to the gift, her insides jumping with excitement, and peeled back the paper to reveal a beautiful silver box.

"Ooh," Frances said on a raspy breath.

When Ellie lifted the lid and saw a stunning silver necklace with a heart pendant, her own heart swelled, and words failed her. "Oh, my gracious."

"Do you like it?" Claire asked.

"I've never seen anything prettier. Is this really for me?"

"Of course, dear. If you look on the back, you'll see it's engraved with your initials, E. C."

She turned it over, and, indeed, there were her new initials, blurred by her misty eyes. It was hard to draw a full breath for all the emotion stirring inside her. She closed her fist over the charm and brought the necklace to her chest. "Thank you so much, Mrs. Cooper. I'll cherish it always."

"Please, not Mrs. Cooper. Claire will do fine—or even Mom, if you feel so inclined. Anyway, I'm pleased you like it. We have some dear friends who own a jewelry store in Chicago, and they helped me select the piece. Gage, help her put it on. I think it will look lovely with the scooped neckline of your dress."

He pushed back from the table and grinned at her. "It would be my honor."

They spent an evening of conversation and play in the living room, Claire updating Gage on his brothers, his father, and his nieces and nephews while the kids played with their new toys and games. Ellie listened with utmost interest, trying to imagine what it must have been like to grow up in a big family like Gage's, surrounded by love and attention. The only love she'd ever known had come from her mama—and her daddy, before he'd died. Aside from that, they'd stayed secluded in their mountain cabin, interacting rarely if at all with anyone else, excepting her classmates at school and, of course, the Meyers. But her schoolmates had always been more acquaintances than friends, and Burt and Mildred had never been overly sociable. The truth was, her closest friends had been farm animals.

She clutched the heart pendant at her throat and marveled at the instant acceptance she'd received from Claire Cooper. Could she ever call her "Mom," as the

woman had invited her to do? She practiced saying
it in her head while petting the canine companion in
her lap, but even that was difficult. Perhaps, in time,
it would become a natural thing.

As the late hour ushered in the darkness, Gage
caught her eye and nodded toward the kids to suggest bedtime. They weren't exactly on one accord with
each other right now, considering his determination
to move back into his room tonight against her wishes, but she couldn't deny that the children bound
them together in a way that overcame some of their
differences. She nodded back and took the initiative
to speak.

"You children better start putting your things
away and getting ready for bed. You have school tomorrow, don't forget." The mere mention of the word
"bed" reminded her of the awkwardness in store for
her and Gage, and she heard her pulse beating in her
ears. How silly to be skittish! It wasn't like anything
was going to happen, especially since he seemed to
be fine with her ban on kissing.

"Aww, do we have to?" Alec whined.

Tommy Lee yawned and rubbed his droopy eyes.
"I no sleepy," he moaned.

Claire put her hands on her knees and stood up.
"I, for one, am more than ready for bed. This has been
a very long day. A sound night's sleep, and I'll be as
good as new in the morning."

Her comment helped to get everyone moving,
and, soon, the living room had been put back to
rights, most of the lights had been turned off, Checkers had been taken out one last time and then put
in the kitchen behind his barrier, and everyone was
heading for the stairs.

"Daddy, are you comin' upstairs to sleep?" Alec asked.

At his question, Ellie stumbled on the steps, then quickly regained her balance, her heart having jumped to her throat.

"Well, I'm coming upstairs, of course," he answered in his smooth, deep voice. "I'm going to tuck you in, as I always do, and then go back downstairs to read for a while. Is that all right with you?"

"Sure."

And, just like that, the subject was dropped.

After bedtime prayers had been spoken and good nights had been exchanged, Gage followed Ellie down the dimly lit hallway to his room. At the door, she stopped and whispered, "Did you mean it when you said you were goin' downstairs to read?"

"I thought it would be best. I'll give you time to get situated under the covers, how's that?"

"Are you sure I can't sleep on the floor?"

He put a finger to her lips. "Shh. Positive. End of discussion."

She slipped inside the bedroom and closed the door behind her, then stood there listening to his retreating steps, before she made a mad dash for her nightgown and other toiletry items. She would complete her nighttime ablutions in record time and be under her blankets within three minutes.

By the time she heard Gage climbing the stairs, she was safely in bed, hair freed from its bun, quilts tucked up to her chin. She lay stiff as a corpse, staring at the ceiling and listening as he opened the bathroom door and started moving around, turning the faucet on and off, flushing the commode, and then running the water again. She wondered about what men did to prepare themselves for bed. Whatever it was, it didn't make a lot of noise; now, all was quiet, save for the tick of the windup alarm clock beside the bed—and her pulse still pounding in her ears. "Lord, help me," she whispered. "I feel like a bride on her weddin' night." *Which is plain ridiculous, really.* She rolled over and looked at the floor. There was plenty of room for him to sprawl out, and no need to give the matter a second thought. After all, he was her husband; it shouldn't have mattered one jot that they were sharing a room.

Minutes passed before she heard Gage open the bathroom door again, click off the light switch, and come padding down the hall. Outside the bedroom, he paused, then knocked quietly on the door.

A catch in her throat made her cough. "Come in."

The door swung open, and a tight gasp slipped past her lips. Mother of mercy, he was shirtless! She hadn't expected that. Byron was the only man whose bare chest she'd ever seen, and by accident; she'd made sure to shield her eyes ever since. He had rolls of skin and a forest of dark hair, whereas Gage's chest was mostly smooth, with a small clump of light hair in the center. As for loose skin, there was none to be found. She swallowed hard and set her eyes on the ceiling again.

"I didn't rush you, did I?"

"What? No, I had plenty o' time, thank you."

As he moved to the bureau, she stealthily turned her head to watch him move about. He opened the bottom drawer and pulled out a couple of blankets and a pillow. Then, he folded the thicker blanket in half and spread it on the rug, parallel with the bed, and tossed the pillow on top, at the same end of his "bed" as hers. She watched as he lowered himself onto the blanket to test it for softness. "Perfect," he said, angling her a grin. She averted her gaze to the ceiling, but it was too late. She heard his low chortle. "Shall I turn off the light now, or do you want to read a bit?"

"Do you?"

"I've already read."

"Then, you can turn it off."

"Would you like me to pray before we go to sleep?"

"I...yes, would you?"

He knelt beside her bed, as he did when he prayed with his kids. As was always the case, his prayer washed over her with power, and she marveled at the way he strung his words together with such articulation that it made her want to weep. How did he manage to draw her emotions up to the surface? Or was it Jesus working through his words? She had so much to learn about her newfound relationship with God.

When he spoke the final amen, he stood back up, walked over to the door, and put his finger on the wall switch. "Ready?"

No good-night kiss? Well, that was fine, of course; in fact, it was exactly what she'd insisted upon. "Ready." When the light went out, she freed her arms from under the covers, tugged the quilt up to her armpits, and waited for her eyes to adjust to the darkness. She could make out Gage lowering himself to his pathetic bed, plumping his pillow, and shifting back and forth before settling on one side, facing her. A tiny wave of guilt trickled through her for taking over his bedroom, his bed. But they'd made an agreement, and he was the one who'd broken it. The floor would have to suffice.

A silent tension enveloped them for a few minutes, until the clock downstairs gonged the tenth hour. "Gage?"

"Yes?"

"Thank you. For the prayer."

"You're welcome."

"I like your mother."

"Yeah, she's pretty great. Didn't I tell you not to worry?"

"Yes, and you were right. She's a wonderful person, and the children adore her. It will be so nice to have her around. How long will she stay?"

"I don't know. A couple of weeks, probably, until she feels like her welcome's run out."

In the hallway, a door opened, and someone padded down the hall to the bathroom. Next door, Ellie heard the whiffling sound of Tommy Lee's light snores. He'd been such a good sport, managing the entire day without a nap, but she had no doubt he would take an extra-long one tomorrow.

On the ceiling, a dancing shadow caught her attention, and suddenly she thought about all the nights Gage and Ginny had lain together in this very room, perhaps staring at that same shadow. "What was she like, Ginny?"

"Why do you ask that now?"

"I don't know...because I know you must be thinkin' about her, now that you're back in your old room."

He shifted some, and in the faint light coming through the window, she could see that he'd rolled onto his back with his arms folded behind his head. "Actually, she wasn't on my mind at all. You'll recall I slept in here for several years before you came."

"Do you still think about her often?"

"I think about her some, but certainly not all the time."

"I suppose you still love her."

"I love the memory of her, if that makes sense, but I don't ache over losing her like I did that first year. It's definitely gotten better." He yawned loudly, whether from fatigue or an attempt to change the subject, she couldn't tell.

"I'm sure the children miss her every day. I know I miss my mama so much, I almost taste it sometimes. Especially after meetin' your mother and seein' the love you and the kids have for her...it makes me ache to see my mama."

"I can imagine. We'll see about bringing her here to come visit sometime, or maybe even moving her here once that stepfather of yours lands himself in jail."

"Really?" She rolled on her side and hung her head over the bed so that she could get a better view of him. "Did you really just say that we could see about movin' Mama up here?"

He gave a quiet laugh. "That's what I said, El. Would you like that?"

"That's like askin' if I'd like ice cream every night before bed."

"Would you like that, too?"

"Well, no, but I'm just sayin'...gosh, thank you again." She flipped on her back and stared at the ceiling once more. "I sure hope the Athens police department gets word about Byron as soon as possible and puts him behind bars."

"I do, too, but let's try not to worry about it. We've done all we could on our end, and now it lies with the law. Try to trust the system."

"And the Lord," she reminded him.

"Yes, definitely the Lord."

The second hand on the clock ticked at least ten times. "I guess it's not so bad," she said. "What do you think?"

"About what?"

"Sharin' the room. It gives us each someone to talk to."

"Mmm-hm, it sure does." His voice had that drifting quality.

"Are you tired?"

"Sort of."

"Oh. Well then, I guess we should say good night."

Silence ensued, and she wondered if he'd fallen asleep. Apparently, her presence in the room did not have the same effect on him as his did on her.

"'Night," he finally said, his voice sounding distant. Well, phooey on him for being no fun!

When she rolled over to face the wall, bringing her blanket with her, she heard a new sound above the ticktock of the clock and realized something: Tommy Lee was not the only one in the household who snored.

Chapter Twenty-six

The foolishness of man perverteth his way.
—Proverbs 19:3

The funeral service for Walter Joseph Sullivan in Sevierville took place on a gray morning with dark clouds hanging in the sky like sodden washcloths, ready to drip at any moment. Solemn-faced officers and Prohibition agents had congregated around the gravesite, some with hands folded, others with umbrellas at the ready. A preacher in an ill-fitting black suit read a couple of Scripture verses and glanced intermittently at the wooden casket, as if the body inside was the one listening instead of the small crowd.

Ned shifted his weight from one foot to the other, snapping a twig beneath his shoe. Across the way, Bill removed his hat and mopped his brow with his sleeve. He kept his gaze trained on the preacher, but Ned knew that his mind was wandering, probably wondering what his wife was fixing for dinner.

Yes, he knew Bill, and he wasn't mourning Walt Sullivan—nor was anyone else, in all likelihood, with the exception of the young lady who hung on the outskirts of the throng with her mother and held a hankie to her nose, raising it every so often to dab her teary eyes. Eileen Ridderman wasn't overly attractive, by any means, with her disheveled mousy hair and timid demeanor. No wonder she'd latched on to Walt Sullivan—she probably had low self-esteem and struggled to find a man worth his salt, and so, rather than wait till one came along, she'd take up with the first one to offer a kind word. He gave his head two quick shakes for his heartless psychoanalysis, as if he knew the first thing about what went on in a woman's head. Shoot, most days, he could barely figure out his Marlene.

At the close of the service, Ned pushed through the crowd, ignoring a few of his cronies, to reach Eileen Ridderman and her mother before they left the cemetery. Not even Bill got the time of day from him as he followed the two ladies, who were headed to their car.

"Mrs. Ridderman," he called out.

The woman and her daughter stopped and turned. "Oh, Mr. Castleberry, I thought I saw you in that circle of mourners," said Mrs. Ridderman. "This is my daughter, Eileen, but I guess you already know that. As it turns out, she did want to pay her respects, so my brother drove her all the way from Florida. Of course, I couldn't let her come alone."

"Of course, you couldn't." Ned looked at the younger woman. "Hello there, Eileen. That was mighty nice of your uncle to do that. He must think the world of you. I'm Ned Castleberry." He extended a hand, but she didn't take it, so he dropped it back to his side. "I work for the Bureau of Prohibition. Your mother may have told you I was investigating Walter Sullivan's disappearance. At the diner in Athens where you used to work, I learned that you had a...well, some sort of relationship with him." He supposed it was a speck inconsiderate of him to question her at a time like this, but he wasn't sure when he'd have another opportunity to speak with her.

She sniffled, clearly still upset. "What about it?"

"Well, I wondered if you could shed any more light on who might have...uh, killed him."

"I told my mother everything I know, and I assume she relayed it to you."

"She did say that you'd mentioned his connections with a fellow named Byron. We now know him to be Byron Pruitt. That last name ring a bell with you?"

"What if it does? Is that going to bring Wally back?"

She really missed him, something Ned didn't understand. He decided to come right out and ask. "Mind telling me what Walter Sullivan ever did for you?"

Mrs. Ridderman looked equally eager to hear her response, the way she turned her full attention on Eileen, her arm hooked around her shoulder.

Eileen blinked back tears. "He was good to me... and kind."

"I heard he also had a mean side," Ned said gently.

The young woman's head shot up, and she glared at her mother. "What did you tell him?"

"The truth, darling." Mrs. Ridderman sighed. "I know Mr. Sullivan hit you on more than one occasion. You told me as much. Nobody was happier or more relieved than I when you left for Florida. That man was poison, and you know it."

Eileen's shoulders dropped, as did her chin. "He drank too much. When he was sober, he could be so sweet."

"Sweet" and "Walter Sullivan" didn't belong in the same sentence, in Ned's opinion, but to each his own. "So, this Byron Pruitt," he pressed, "can you tell me anything about him? Anything at all?"

Her mouth twisted as she thought, and then she shrugged. "Once, I heard Wally say he was meaner than a snake, but that he could handle him. That's about all I can remember him saying."

"Did Walter ever tell you what he did for a living?"

"He told me he worked undercover for the government, but he never talked about it, so I thought he had a very important job. I know he made a lot of money. He was always waving his cash around."

Ned blew out a long breath and scratched his temple. "That money did not come from the government, I'm sorry to say. If any agent in our department is rich, it isn't because of his salary. Most of us are underpaid, and some get greedy and seek out other ways to earn money."

She stared at him with crinkled brow. "How do you mean?"

"Well, they usually fill their pockets with bribes. To put it bluntly, miss, we believe Walter Sullivan was a crooked agent, that he accepted money from bootleggers in exchange for keeping quiet about their stills. In the case of Byron Pruitt, though, I'd say Walt chose wrong. Did he ever mention any other names that stood out to you?"

To say she looked stunned would have been an understatement, and there was a significant degree of sheepishness and self-blame in her expression. She put a hand over her gaping mouth and held it there a moment before dropping it. "He always just said he was good at his job, and that the government saw to it he was well compensated. I...I swear I didn't know, and, no, he never mentioned other names to me."

Ned figured he'd reached the end of the line concerning Eileen Ridderman. "Well, I thank you for your time, miss, and I...I'm sorry to have bothered you."

He turned to go, even took a few steps, but an exclamation of "Wait!" had him whirling abruptly around. "Yes?"

"I...I believe I have something that might help you."

"Really? And what's that?"

She reached into her purse and pulled out a small black book. "I told you Walt never mentioned names to me, but, well, this is some sort of record book that belonged to him. He always kept it close by, and I saw him write in it many times. He left it at my apartment but never came back for it. I know I should have turned it in when I first heard about your investigation, but...I don't know, I guess I've been holding on to it as a sort of keepsake." She actually clutched the thing to her chest.

"Eileen, give it to the man, for goodness' sake!" her mother spouted. "That could be important evidence."

Ned tried to contain his eagerness. "I'd be much obliged."

She nodded slowly and handed it over.

"Thank you. I'll take good care of it." He opened his suit jacket and stuffed the book into the inside pocket. Then, tipping his hat, he bid the ladies goodbye and headed back toward the cemetery, his step a little lighter.

❧

From his seat on the train, Byron looked out the foggy window at the scenery as it passed—old barns, acres of farmland, small towns, rivers, trees, and flat terrain. He had probably an hour yet to travel before reaching Wabash, and he was as eager as ever to get off of this rumbling train, with its piercing whistle that nearly ruptured his eardrums each time it sounded. He supposed that was what he got for sitting in one of the front cars, but he didn't care to move elsewhere, since his stomach was feeling far from settled, and doing so might prompt him to barf up that sour apple he'd eaten earlier. He wiped his brow, sweaty due to the cramped train car and his jumpy bundle of nerves. He had to get to Eleanor before the police found her, especially in light of the latest happenings. Last night at dusk, Curtis Morgan had come over all out of breath to tell him they'd found Walt Sullivan's body. Some mongrel dog had dug it up, and they'd already had a funeral.

"Today's paper said it was a gunshot wound to the chest what killed him," Curtis had said, eyes nearly bulging out of his head.

"Oh, yeah?" Byron had done his best to react with nonchalance. Thank goodness Rita had been out in the garden pulling weeds, or she'd have blown his cover for sure.

Curtis had pushed on the door to come inside, but it was latched, and Byron hadn't been about to unlock it.

"I wondered why that ol' fool stopped comin' around," Curtis had said, moving restlessly on the front mat. "But you said you paid him off good so he'd quit buggin' us."

"Yeah, and it worked, didn't it?"

Curtis had stood still and eyed Byron suspiciously. "Say, you didn't have nothin' to do with his dyin', did you, Byron?"

"Who, me? You kiddin'? 'Course I didn't!"

"I ain't got nothin' against breakin' the law to make booze, but murder...now, that's somethin' else altogether. I heard 'bout another feller got hisself kilt some months ago, and it gives me the creeps to think it could happen t' any of us. It's a risky business we're runnin', Byron. You gotta watch your step."

"You can say that again," Byron had agreed, keeping his poker face intact. "You know Sullivan was takin' bribes from lots o' moonshiners. You can bet your last cent he had a slew of enemies. Frankly, I'm glad somebody had the nerve to do 'im in."

Curtis had peered in through the screen. "You goin' somewhere?" He pointed across the room at Byron's bulging tote bag.

"Yeah, and I was hopin' you could drive me to the train station first thing in the mornin'. I was meanin' to come over to your place tonight to ask. Heard they fixed the bridge enough for traffic to come an' go. Me an' Rita, an' my horse, too, got my truck righted agin, but it don't work. Fool thing won't even turn over."

"I can drive you, yeah, but where you headin', and when you fixin' to get back? We got that new still to build, don't forget. I managed to salvage a few parts from the rubble, but most of it got destroyed in the roof collapse."

"Goin' up to Wabash, Indiana. There's a fellow up there name of Orville Dotson who used to run a pretty profitable operation. He's outta the business now, served some jail time, I guess, but Gomer Krebbs told me awhile back he's doin' some consultin' work now, all under the table, o' course, and I think it's worth my while to go talk to 'im."

"Yeah? Ol' Gomer makes a pretty penny. We oughtta just team up with him."

"What, an' share our profits? Bend to somebody else's rules?"

"Yeah, you're right. Best to keep our business small and in our control. Guess it couldn't hurt to talk to that Dotson fella for some pointers. 'Course, how smart can he be if he got caught?"

"I don't care about that. He's got some formulas for whiskey that ain't been tried down here. I figure we'll git an edge on Krebbs."

"Hm. Good thinkin'. What time's your train?"

"Seven, but I want to git there by six thirty to pick up my ticket."

"I'll be here a li'l after six, then. You can be glad the trains are operatin'. Wonder when they're fixin' to have them phone lines up an' runnin' again."

"Don't know, don't care."

Curtis had turned and looked toward the garden, where Rita was still bent over, pulling weeds. Fortunately, most of the bruises she'd gotten in their fight the other morning were hidden beneath her clothes, and the marks on her face weren't visible, thanks to the way her body was turned. "What's your ol' lady say 'bout you takin' off?"

Byron had sneered. "Again, don't know, don't care."

And that was the truth. He'd had it with Rita and her constant whining and nagging. He'd told her he was going to Wabash to have a nice little talk with Eleanor while she stayed home and tended the animals. If anyone came around asking his whereabouts, she was to say that he'd left town on business for a few days and hadn't told her where he was going.

The train chugged along for the next hour, and Byron must have dozed, because it seemed like only a minute had passed when that blamed whistle blew again and the conductor's voice boomed, "Wabash!"

As soon as the monstrous locomotive came to a shrieking halt, Byron stood up, got off as quickly as he could, and ran to the closest patch of grass to retch up his apple.

Chapter Twenty-seven

Be not afraid, only believe.
—Mark 5:36

*E*llie had always loved the sound of a train whistle—fortunate, because in Wabash, trains were always
coming and going, rocking the very earth beneath her
feet as they rumbled through.

"Train's leaving town," Gage said, as if reading
her thoughts, and braked to a stop at the new traffic
light at the intersection of Market and Wabash streets.
"Man, those things are loud. Most days, I barely even
notice them, but today the whistles just seem to pierce
the air."

"For me, trains always bring up childhood memories." Ellie was enjoying the ride with Gage—the only
drive they'd taken without the kids since getting married. It was nice to converse without having to compete
with bickering children and interruptions from the
backseat. They had escaped at Grandma Cooper's insistence when she'd heard Ellie mention that she needed to pick up a few grocery items. Why, she'd nearly
pushed them out the door, saying she loved spending
time with her grandchildren, and wasn't that exactly
why she'd come—to give the two of them a chance to
get away, if only just to make a grocery run? The notion

that Gage's mother wanted to give them privacy made Ellie blush. Yes, they were newlyweds, but, so far, the honeymoon had been completely platonic, except for a few scattered kisses. And even those had stopped altogether, even though they now shared a bedroom. Ellie almost rued the day she'd laid down that silly law.

The light turned green, and they advanced through the intersection, then slowed about one block later to turn left onto Huntington Street. "Tell me about those memories," Gage said.

She proceeded to tell him about the trips she'd taken into town as a child with her parents and how the trains had always fascinated her. "We used to stand there and count the cars, Daddy and me, and then we'd wait for the caboose to bring up the rear so we could wave at the fellow in that little car. I love the caboose, don't you? It's such a nice way to end a train."

He grinned and turned into the parking lot of Murphy's Market, a store that seemed to have a little bit of everything, from fresh produce to canned goods, from dairy products to random items, such as men's socks and nuts and bolts, displayed in bins smack-dab next to each other. Some days, Ellie just liked to go inside and wander up and down the aisles. Of course, she had to keep a close eye and a tight hold on Tommy Lee because the store fascinated him every bit as much as it did her.

Gage stopped the car and turned in his seat to look at her. "I think it's great how the simple things in life seem to bring you the most joy."

She shrugged. "Well, it's easy to find joy in the simple things when that's all you've ever known."

He reached up and tweaked her chin. "You're something, you know that? Come on, young lady. Let's go inside."

The evening air held a bit of a bite, so she gathered her sweater close to her neck as they crossed the parking lot. Tonight, there was no time for dawdling, since the store would close in twenty minutes. They collected their items efficiently and then stood at the cash register, waiting for Mr. Murphy to ring up their purchases and load them into a cardboard box.

"You two enjoyin' your evening?" the storekeeper asked.

"Very much, thanks," Gage said. He cast Ellie a private wink, which, as usual, sent a delightful sensation shimmying right down her spine.

Back at the car, Gage loaded the sack of sugar and the box of other items into the trunk, then opened Ellie's door. She'd needed to learn to wait for him to do that, rather than opening it herself, and she rather enjoyed his chivalry, an altogether foreign experience since the passing of her daddy.

Gage revved up the Buick and turned onto Huntingdon. "Have you ever been to one of those moving picture shows?" he asked her.

"Good gracious, no. They were just startin' to talk about buildin' a theater in Athens when I left, but I never would have considered somethin' so extravagant. I will admit, they sound intriguing. Imagine seeing a story played out on a big screen rather than simply readin' it in a book!"

"Yes, imagine."

They turned onto Market Street, passing Oh Boy! Produce, Bradley Drugstore, Kramer Cleaners, Crystal-Renee Beauty Shop, and Beitman & Wolf, where she and Livvie had spent a good deal of time, not to mention money. She smoothed her new skirt, relishing the texture of the fresh fabric. She'd never owned such fine clothing, and wearing it made her feel so much more ladylike. Even her manner of speaking was more ladylike, mostly because of her efforts to model the pattern of such people as Gage and Livvie. She fingered the ends of both her braids, which hung in front of her shoulders, and toyed with the idea of cutting them off in favor of short, stylish hair, like Livvie's. Her long hair was a nuisance, always getting in the way when she bathed Tommy Lee and otherwise tended him. Not only that, braids were hardly the fashion, and the only other pigtails she'd seen in town had been on the heads of little girls. Perhaps, if she gave her hair a bit of shape, her husband would start thinking of her more as a grown woman instead of a "young lady," as he often called her.

They passed the beautiful Hotel Indiana, and then Gage made a sharp turn into a parking lot across the street from the hotel. "What are you doin'?" Ellie asked.

She followed his gaze to the building outside her window. It had a bright sign that said "The Eagles Theater." Beneath that, the glimmering marquee read "Now Showing: Al Jolson – 'The Jazz Singer.'"

"Are we goin' inside?" she just about shrieked.

"No, we're going to sit out here and keep imagining what it would be like to watch a real picture show." He laughed. "Of course, we're going inside, silly girl. This particular show is a talkie, not a silent movie. I hear the music is great. I think you'll like it."

"*Think* I'll like it? I *know* I will!"

He smiled. "Stay put." After getting out of the car, he walked around to her side and opened her door, then stood there with an outstretched arm.

Stunned speechless, she merely stared at him.

"Are you coming?"

She blinked and placed her hand in his, allowing him to pull her out of the car and then link his arm with hers. "All right, young lady. Let's take you to your first picture show."

⁂

Gage couldn't recall having a better time at the theater, mostly because he'd never seen Ellie have so much fun. Her eyes stayed fixed on the screen, and her pretty mouth hung partially open, for the duration of the show. Why, he could have waved a hand in front of her face, and he doubted she would have noticed. Ginny had never watched the big screen with such utter absorption, and, while he had yet to take his kids to see a movie, he doubted even they would exhibit as much fascination as Ellie.

Whenever Al Jolson broke out into song and dance, she rocked her body back and forth and nearly clapped aloud, putting him in mind of Tommy Lee with her childlike excitement, and when a character rattled off a funny line, she laughed louder than anyone else, never seeming to notice the occasional audience member turning around to seek out the origin of that lively giggle. Oh, how he loved her! He'd wanted to kiss her for days now, but he'd respectfully opted to abide by her crazy "no kissing" rule so that she couldn't accuse him of taking advantage of her. Who had ever heard of a husband prohibited from kissing his own wife? Well, by gum, he could at least put his arm around her. And he did, about halfway through the movie, but she didn't react, so absorbed was she in the film. Apparently, his nearness didn't affect her nearly as much as hers affected him.

When the movie ended, they remained seated and watched the listing of the cast of characters, Ellie's jaw ever drooping in astonishment.

The screen finally went dark, but her eyes stayed glued in that direction. "Did you like it?" he asked.

"What?"

"The movie. What did you think?"

Finally, she looked over at him, her eyes shining in wonder. "Oh, Gage, it was the most marvelous thing I've ever seen. Can we go again?"

"Of course, if you're good."

She giggled. "I promise."

They exited the theater and wended their way through the lamp-lit parking lot along with a few fellow moviegoers, some of them holding hands, others just walking side by side, talking about the film and sharing the parts they'd most enjoyed. Gage decided to take her hand, and when he did, she glanced up and smiled. "Thank you for the evening. I hope your mother isn't worried about us."

"She's not."

"How do you know?"

"I told her I planned to keep you out awhile."

"You did not!" The marquee lights reflected off of her hair, making it shimmer like black gold. She looked at him with surprise in her eyes.

"Did, too." His side brushed against her, and something stole over him—a "fullness of heart" was the only way he could think to describe it. He wondered if she felt it, as well. When they reached the car, he opened her door, and the flowery scent that stirred up as she slipped inside teased his senses, just as it'd been doing all night. He closed his eyes for a moment, then closed her door so that she wouldn't see the foolish grin that had spread over his face.

The streets were mostly deserted on their drive home, save for a few cars and a couple of pedestrians on a late-night stroll. At the intersection of Market and Fisher streets, Gage slowed for the right-hand turn, and his eyes connected for a second with those of a woman walking alone on the side of the road. He could have sworn he'd seen a bruise as big as a baseball on her face, but then again, it could have been just a shadow. He glanced at Ellie to see if she'd noticed, but she was watching out the other window.

"That was odd," he said. "That woman back there looked a little desperate."

She sat up and swiveled her body to look behind them. "I don't see anyone. You really think she was in trouble? Maybe we should turn around and check to see if she needs help."

Gage looked to make sure no other cars were coming, then made a U-turn in the middle of the street. When he started retracing their path, though, he saw no sign of the woman. She'd vanished, maybe up an alley or behind a building. "I don't see her, either," he mumbled. "Strange."

"Was she someone you knew?"

"Nope, never saw her before, but that's not unusual. Wabash has a population of almost nine thousand. She wore a frumpy-looking coat, and I thought I saw a bruise on her face. Definitely looked lost."

"That's too bad," said Ellie. "I wish we could help her."

"Yeah, me too." A troublesome sense gnawed at him on the drive back home—and long into the night. Hours later, he lay on the floor, staring wide-eyed at the wall, where a shaft of light from a streetlamp had found its way through the window. Ellie's soft breathing eased his nerves a little, but that bedraggled woman's haunting expression made it impossible to sleep.

The next morning, Gage found himself driving up and down Fisher Street in his old truck, looking for her, as foolish as he felt doing it. Shoot, he couldn't even pinpoint the reason for his frantic need to find her. "Lord, I don't understand the notion that I ought to know that woman, but there's something about her that seems strangely familiar," he prayed as he pulled up to the curb outside his shop. "Please lead me to her, or, at the very least, keep her safe until someone else comes across her and recognizes her need."

Chapter Twenty-eight

These things have I spoken unto you, that
my joy might remain in you, and that
your joy might be full.
—John 15:11

Ned choked back the dust stirred up by the two police cars in front of him as they wound their way up the mountainside, then slowed to make the turn onto West Peak Road in the direction of Byron Pruitt's farm. They had evidence enough to arrest the fool, and Ned could hardly wait to watch the proceedings. That fellow was going down, and he was going to be there to witness it. When telephone service had been restored, Ned had received a call from the Athens police department, saying they'd heard from Sheriff Buford Morris of Wabash, Indiana, that Byron Pruitt could well be a suspect in the shooting death of government agent Walter Sullivan. Ned didn't know who'd made the claim or how the information had reached the ears of Sheriff Morris, but he had a sneaking suspicion that Pruitt's stepdaughter had fled there and filed the report.

He followed the other cars into the driveway and stopped, stirring up a cloud of dust around their vehicles. Then, he sat tight behind the steering wheel and watched as four armed officers emerged from the cars and made for the house, spreading out in various directions. One circled around behind the house, another went toward the barn, and the other two stepped up to the porch and knocked on the door. No one answered, so they knocked again and waited about twenty seconds, at which point one officer bellowed that they were coming inside. He gave the door a kick, and the thing came right off its hinges, falling in, so that he and his partner had to walk across it to enter.

Tension grew like a storm in Ned's chest while he waited to see some action. Minutes went by without anything happening, however, and when the two officers emerged from the house, weapons still drawn, he felt deflated. "Nobody's here!" one of them yelled from the porch.

"All clear out here!" called the officer who'd checked out the barn.

A loud tap on Ned's window nearly sent him through the car roof. While he collected his bearings, he tried to place the person on the other side of the glass. It was the neighbor they'd visited awhile back. "They lookin' for Pruitt?" she asked through the glass.

He opened his door and stepped out. "Howdy, ma'am. Yes, do you know where he is?"

"I got a good idea," she said. "I been feedin' the animals for the Pruitts. Here, you might be interested in this letter." She reached inside her dress pocket, pulled out an envelope, and handed it to him. "I took the liberty of openin' it, since Rita weren't here to do the honors. It's from her girl, Eleanor. You'll see by the return address she went to Wabash, Indiana." She pointed at the printing in the corner. "Right there's the address, case you're interested. This letter'll prob'ly tell you everythin' you want to know and then some."

He opened the letter and quickly scanned it, committing the address to memory.

"I'll take that," said an approaching officer. Begrudgingly, Ned passed it along, knowing he couldn't interfere with the department's investigation. It wouldn't keep him from making his own inquiries, though. "You think Pruitt went to Wabash?" he asked the neighbor.

"I know he did. Rita tol' me so. He means to get to 'er girl 'fore the law does, but she ain't gonna let that happen. Stubborn woman jumped on the train after Byron got on. 'Course, he don't know it. He'll be fightin' mad when he finds out she followed 'im. I took 'er to the station myself, even though I can't drive worth cat's spit. Burt's holed up at home with some broken ribs, so I had no choice. I made it, and that's what counts," she rambled.

Ned's mind started spinning. He turned to the officers, who'd been listening in. "You fellas best send word to the department in Wabash to be on the lookout for Byron Pruitt. And let them know that Eleanor Pruitt—"

"Cooper. Eleanor Cooper," the lady corrected him. "She's married now. I still cain't believe it, but it's true. It's right there in that letter."

Ned nodded. "All right, then. Eleanor Cooper. Let them know her life could be in grave danger."

The officer who appeared to be the one in charge frowned with annoyance. "You government agents are all alike. You think we don't know how to do our jobs. Why don't you go back to your tidy little office in the city and stick your face in some paperwork?"

Swallowing his irritation, he turned to the neighbor woman. "Thank you for turning in that letter, ma'am." He tipped his hat at her and then gave the officers a curt nod. "I hope you fellas can find someone to read it to you."

※

Thanks to Edith Nickerson's ongoing chatter and Fred's incessant hammering, Gage blocked out his former thoughts about the desperate-looking woman on the side of the road and tried to focus on his task—designing an armoire for a client in Ohio. Seated at his desk in the corner of the shop, he started drawing up the plans, using the eraser end of his pencil about as often as he used the tip, for his mind now filled instead with thoughts of Ellie and how she'd looked in the theater last night, all awestruck by the picture show. He wanted to introduce her to as many first experiences as possible, just so he could watch her eyes light up with excitement and that alluring mouth of hers drop open in amazement.

"I swear, you got more work orders here than Georgia has peanuts," Edith lamented while thumbing through a stack of papers. "How're you and Fred ever going to fill all these?"

"Patience, my dear, patience," Gage said. "Fred and I work as fast as we can. Isn't that right, Fred?"

"If we worked any faster, they'd have to ticket us for speedin'," he replied.

"Oh, pooh! Wouldn't hurt you to hire another body, you know," Edith pointed out.

"I've been thinking on that," Gage said. "You know anybody as talented as Fred and me?"

"Pfff," she snorted. "There's a whole town full of people smarter 'n you two, right here in Wabash. Oh, wait, you were talkin' about talent, not brains."

Gage laughed, taking her jests in stride. "While I'm at it, I just may look into replacing my secretary."

"Good luck in your search. Don't know a soul who'd put up with you two besides me."

"She's right, Gage." Fred set down his hammer and started digging in his toolbox. "We aren't that easy to get along with. You're always bossin' us around, and I'm always bellyachin' 'bout one thing or another."

"Not to mention always makin' a racket in here," Edith added.

Gage chuckled. "Yeah, somebody should really invent a method to build cabinets and such without the use of hammers and drills."

They kept up their good-natured banter for the next few minutes, until a knock sounded on the shop door. "Come in!" Edith called. "Door's always open!"

The door squeaked on its hinges, and a figure slowly came into sight: a haggard-looking, weather-beaten woman. What in the world? Speaking of mouths dropping open, Gage felt his chin fall nearly to his knees. It was *her*—the woman he'd seen on the street last night. His pencil slipped out of his fingers and bounced on the floor, and he didn't bother picking it up.

"C-can I help you?" Edith asked, her eyes wide.

"I...I came to see Mr. Cooper," the woman said softly. "Which one's he?" Her gaze flitted from Gage to Fred.

Gage pushed his chair back, the legs grating against the floor. "Uh, me, that's me. I'm Gage Cooper. I saw you last night...on the street."

"Oh, I didn't know.... I'd like to speak to you, if I might have a few minutes o' your time...outside, maybe?"

He didn't know this woman from the lady in the funny papers, but then, he recalled praying for her, even asking God to lead him to her—or, at the very least, lead her to safety. Criminy, hadn't he been out on Fisher Street just this morning, looking for her? Her showing up at his shop was more than a coincidence; it was a divine appointment, no doubt about it. But, why? "Sure," he said. "Here, we can just go in the back room and talk. How's that?" Ignoring the dumbfounded stares of Fred and Edith, he pointed to the door of the closet-sized room. "It's a bit chilly today. We'll be more comfortable inside."

"You want a couple of chairs?" Fred asked.

"Yeah, please."

Fred dusted off two wooden folding chairs with his bare hand, carried them to the tiny room, and set them up on the floor. "There you go."

"Thanks," Gage said.

Fred quirked his eyebrows and backed out of the room, closing the door behind him.

Gage gestured to one of the chairs. "Go ahead and sit. It's all right." Then, lowering his chin, he squinted and scratched the back of his head. "Am I supposed to know you? You look vaguely familiar."

She sat down and folded her hands in her lap. He noticed that her fingers were cracked and caked with grime. "No, we never met, but I...I sort o' feel like I know you."

"Really? How's that?" Her swollen cheek looked like it could use some ice.

"I'm Eleanor's ma."

His jaw dropped again. "You're...? What are you...? How did you...?" He managed to lower himself into the chair facing her.

"I followed my no-good husband to Wabash, but he don't know it. He means to harm Eleanor, I know he does, and so I had to come, you see, so I could warn 'er. Byron—that's my husband—done somethin' purely awful, Mr. Cooper."

"Gage, call me Gage, and I know. Your daughter already told me about the murder, and we've been to the sheriff."

"Haw! You have?" Her mouth flew open. "Well, okay then, that's done. Good. So, the police know what he did. But why didn't they come out an' arrest 'im?"

Gage sighed. "That's another story. Apparently, you had a bad storm, and the phone lines were down?"

"Oh, yes. It stormed somethin' awful."

"Well, that's why the Athens police didn't get the message, although maybe they have by now. How did you wind up here? And your face...how...?"

She reached up and covered her cheek with her palm. "Oh, this ain't nothin', really. Don't bother about it. As for how I found you, Eleanor told me in a letter what you did for a livin', even gave me the name of your place, so I just asked directions from somebody on the street. I came here last night when I got off the train... 'course, you weren't here. I just been kind of wanderin' around the town since then."

"Did you find someplace to sleep last night?"

"I don't have much cash on me, shamed to say, so I found a corner to huddle in. I may have dozed a little."

"No need to be embarrassed. You must be exhausted, and awfully hungry."

"Like I said, don't bother 'bout me. I just want to get the message to my girl that Byron's huntin' for 'er."

Gage thought his head just might spin right off his shoulders. "So, you're really Ellie's mom...Rita, right?" He was still trying to digest the fact that she was here in Wabash, let alone that Byron was, too.

"Yep." She fingered the fabric of her soiled skirt. "Can you take me to 'er?"

He wanted to ask her more questions, but he knew they were pressed for time, especially with Byron on the loose. "I will, of course. Do you have any idea where your husband might be?"

She frowned. "Not a clue, sorry to say. I followed 'im here, ridin' several cars behind 'im, and I watched as he got off the train. It looked like he'd got mighty sick, the way he was all bent over in the grass. I didn't want 'im to see me, so I sorta crept along beside the train and mixed in with the swarm of folks millin' about. Problem about that was, I lost track of 'im, an' by the time I got free of the crowd, he'd up an' disappeared." She paused, and then her expression brightened. "Wait! He mentioned somebody's name a couple o' days ago, some feller what used to run a still in these parts. His name's...oh, it's slipped my mind. Orville somethin'-or-other."

"Dotson? Orville Dotson?"

"That's it! That's the name. Anyway, I think he's got some kind o' connection with the guy. If I had to guess, I'd say he might be holed up there."

Gage had heard enough, at least for now. He stood up and extended his arm to the weary-looking woman. She merely studied his hand, and in that moment, the resemblance to Ellie was unmistakable. It was mostly in the eyes and the characteristic high forehead, as well as the tawny skin. Yes, she looked like she'd seen better days, but with some rest and tender loving care, he imagined she'd spring back to life.

He dropped his hand, figuring he ought to explain the plan. "Okay, Rita. Here's what we'll do. First, we'll go to the sheriff and tell him everything, and then I'll take you to my house, where you can reunite with your daughter, meet my mother, who just happens to be visiting, and get settled in."

"Your mother?" Her grimy hand shot up to cover her mouth. "Oh, I don't know...."

The truth was, he didn't know, either. Claire Cooper and Rita Pruitt were about as opposite as could be, socially speaking, but Gage had never known his mother to treat a soul unfairly, and he sincerely doubted she'd start now.

"Come on." He extended his hand once more. "We have things to do and places to go."

She finally reached up to take his hand and allowed him to help her to her feet.

When he opened the door, he found Fred and Edith pacing with feigned ignorance. They must have been hovering just outside the door and heard the bulk of the conversation. "Your lips are sealed," he ordered them with a glare.

"You bet they are," Fred said.

Edith pinched her thumb and forefinger together and ran them across her lips as if closing a zipper. "Not a word. Promise."

"Good. I'm heading out. Fred, work your tail off. I don't think I'll be back in till tomorrow. And give some thought as to who might work well with us in the shop."

"On a permanent basis?" Edith asked. She scooted to the door to open it, then turned and gave Rita one last, thorough look.

"Yes, full-time. I think we're going to need some help filling all the orders we've been getting, and I don't expect that to change."

"I've already got a fellow in mind," Fred said. "My nephew Justin. I've told you about him. He's a good, hard worker...talented, too. He's got a wife and a little kid."

Gage paused in the doorway and rubbed a hand over his bristly face. He hated to hire somebody sight unseen, but he trusted Fred. "Justin, huh? Is he available?"

"Far as I know. He's been workin' part-time over at the lumber company, but he'd like somethin' more steady. Does repair work on the side. He can fix anything."

"Anything?"

"Pretty much."

"Call him and ask him to fill in till we get caught up on our orders. If he works out, we'll keep him around."

Fred grinned and let out a breath. "You won't be disappointed. Now, sounds like you and your mother-in-law have a rather important agenda to tend to." Fred looked at Rita, who shifted nervously, her eyes on the floor.

His mother-in-law. Gage hadn't yet thought of her in that light, and the realization gave him a stronger sense of responsibility. "That we do." He placed his hand on Rita's back to usher her outside. "And we don't have a second to waste. I'll see you two later."

They exited the building, and Gage looked both ways before leading Rita across the street to his truck. Starting now, he would have to stay on the lookout for anything suspicious. Man, what he wouldn't do for an extra set of eyes in the back of his head.

❋

Byron kicked at the dirt as he ambled down the road on his way back to town from Orville Dotson's. What a waste that trip had been! He should have known the guy wouldn't give him the time of day, let alone offer him a place to lay his head. All he'd asked for was to stay a couple of nights, but the jerk had said he was trying to keep his nose clean and didn't want to get mixed up in any funny business. Byron had tried to assure him that he wasn't mixed up in anything, and all he wanted was a cot in some remote corner and maybe a little consulting on the side. "Consultin'?" The guy had given him a crooked stare. "If you're talkin' about moonshine, I don't do no consultin'. I might have, at one time, but jail done turned me around, mister. Now, if you're needin' some cheap place to stay, you might try the Dixie Hotel on Main Street, or there's the Sleepy Time Inn on Sinclair."

"Orville, who's at the door?" came a woman's voice, probably his wife's.

Orville had turned around briefly to say, "It's nobody, dear," then returned his gaze to Byron, giving him one of the most sinister glares he'd gotten in his life. "Now, git, you hear? And don't come back. I ain't in the business no more." At that, he'd closed the door in his face.

"Yeah, right. Once in the business, always in the business!" Byron muttered to himself as he scuffed along, dreading the four-mile trek ahead of him. He cursed that fool back in Athens who'd told him Dotson would welcome him with open arms.

When a car came along from behind him, he debated whether to dash into the bushes and hide or try to catch a ride. In the last second, he stuck out his thumb, and, lo and behold, the Model T slowed to a stop, and the passenger-side window was rolled down. "Where you headin'?" the old fellow behind the wheel asked.

"Just into Wabash."

The guy then reached across the seat and pushed open the passenger door. "Climb on in. I can take you right to the center of town."

⁂

Ellie enjoyed a morning of shopping with Claire and Tommy Lee, followed by lunch at Livvie's Kitchen. Next, they headed to the Crystal-Renee Beauty Shop, Claire having talked Ellie into getting her hair trimmed when she learned that she'd been entertaining the idea. "Have them take just a little bit off the ends," she'd said. "It'll give you some style, and then, if you decide you want it a tad shorter, you can always go back and have them cut off a little more. And if they happen to take a bit too much, well, the wonderful thing about hair is that it grows back." She'd made it sound so simple that Ellie had ignored any misgivings she might have had and agreed.

Tommy Lee fell asleep in the stroller as the two women made their way to the beauty parlor, window-shopping as they went. He snoozed on when they arrived at Crystal-Renee, where various women, stylists and patrons alike, hovered over him and whispered comments about how cute he was for the duration of Ellie's haircut. As she watched the dark clumps fall to the tile floor, she worried that she'd made a mistake, but a simple smile from Claire was enough to dispel her concern, at least for now.

"You have gorgeous hair," the girl trimming it said. "When was the last time you had it cut?"

"I actually don't remember. It's been a long time. My mama used to trim it for me."

"How about I give you some bangs?" she asked. "We can use the curling tongs to flip the ends under. Bangs are so popular right now, and so is the bob, but don't worry; I won't make you look like a flapper. You'll look more like a movie star."

Ellie doubted that. "Oh my, I don't know. This is all a little drastic for me." Already her hair felt a lot thinner. She longed to get a glimpse at the sides and back, but she was seated away from the mirror, so she had no idea how she looked. "Would I still be able to put my hair in braids?"

"Sure, but they'll be shorter. You can put it in a ponytail, too, or just pull it back with some combs. You'll love it. I think you'll find it very manageable."

Out of the corner of her eye, she looked at Claire. She was beaming. "You're beautiful," she mouthed.

Her mother-in-law thought she was beautiful? A tingle of excitement raced up her spine. And what of her husband? Gracious, it would all be worth it if he thought the same.

※

True to his word, the driver dropped Byron in the center of town. He muttered his thanks and climbed out of the car, and the fellow drove off. As he'd done yesterday after getting off the train, he made his way to a vacant alley where he could watch folks come and go but not worry about being spotted. The last thing he wanted to do was make a spectacle of himself.

His stomach growled, reminding him that it'd been several hours since he'd had breakfast, at a restaurant up the street—Livvie's Corner, or something like that. But he refused to patronize that place again, for he couldn't bear another round of interrogation from the cook: "Where're you from?" "You just visiting?" "You got a job in town?" "Where're you staying?" The guy's inquisition had made him eager to get out of there, so he'd responded as vaguely as possible, downed his waffles in record time, paid before receiving his check, and made a beeline for the door. He was longing for another meal, though, and he scanned the street for options. There was a produce stand across the road, but, considering his reaction to the sour apple he'd eaten yesterday, he aimed to stay clear of fruit for a while, ripe or not.

He fought back a yawn while watching the citizens of Wabash meander past, some with kids in tow, others carrying armloads of packages. He needed to come up with a plan, but it was hard to think on an empty stomach, not to mention a tired mind. He hadn't caught more than an hour of shut-eye on a hard park bench last night, and his body ached for sleep. Maybe he ought to hunt down another restaurant, hopefully one that was a little more obscure, off of the main drag. After that, he could go in search of a place to sleep. Just a few hours would put him in a better frame of mind for concocting the perfect plan. With his tote, which was getting heavier by the hour, thrown over one shoulder, he started to shuffle along, taking care to keep his head down. He had to be ready to make a run for it if someone started following him. Paranoia had set in since he'd learned from Curtis that Walt Sullivan's body had been found. Eleanor could blab at any minute. No doubt about it—the sooner he did away with her, the better. He fingered the envelope in his pocket, remembering the address: 742 W. Hill Street. It couldn't be that hard to locate her.

Up ahead, a couple of ladies stepped out of a store, one of them pushing a baby buggy the other gabbing nonstop about her companion's new hairstyle. He had to dodge sideways to avoid running head-on into the stroller. *Fool women,* he thought to himself. Why didn't people watch where they were walking?

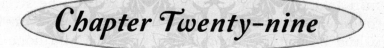

Chapter Twenty-nine

*Have not I commanded thee? Be strong and
of a good courage; be not afraid, neither be
thou dismayed: for the Lord thy God is with
thee whithersoever thou goest.*
—Joshua 1:9

Gage paced from one end of the living room to the
other, stopping every so often to peek out the front and
side windows, while Rita sat in a chair and watched
him, her hands clutched so tightly in her lap that her
knuckles turned as white as snow. "Where do you
think they could be?" she asked. "Do you think Byron already snatched 'er up? Oh, my gracious, this
is terrible. I hope he didn't take your mama an' son,
too."

"No, we can't jump to conclusions," he replied,
trying to keep his voice steady. "I'm sure all they did
was go for a walk. Maybe they went down to the park."

"But they shouldn't be out 'n' about at all, not
with Byron lookin' for Eleanor. He's so mean and dan-
gerous." She touched her bruised cheek. "I hate to
think—"

"Then don't think it, Rita. Try to remain positive.
The sheriff is out there right now, doing what he can to
locate Byron. He'll call in his detectives and deputies,

and together they'll bring him in." He pulled the curtain away from the window and gazed up the street for any sign of the women returning from town. It would be a rather long jaunt, but Ellie had done it many times, and he knew his mother enjoyed traveling on foot, so they probably would have thought nothing of the distance.

Checkers whined and fussed, so Gage picked up the little critter. It seemed that he only wanted to play, however, so he set him back down, only to watch him take up a rubber ball in his mouth and trot over to Rita.

With a sigh of resignation, Gage closed the curtain again. Worrying wouldn't accomplish anything. "Easy, Checkers," he warned the dog. Then, he smiled glumly at Rita. "Well, the least I can do is show you around the house. I have a strong hunch Ellie will want you to share a room with her, and I have no objections. Why don't I take you upstairs to your room and the bathroom, so that you can try to get comfortable?" He would leave it up to Ellie to tell her mother she needed a thorough washing.

"What? Oh no, I couldn't sleep with Ellie and separate the two o' you. Gracious, you're just married. I'll be more than content to just lie on that there couch for a few nights." She pointed to the sofa under the big front window. "Once this whole matter gets resolved, I'll be goin' back to Tennessee."

"Believe me, Ellie will want you close by, and I don't mind, really." He was tempted to add that Ellie would probably be glad to send him back to the library. "She's talked so much about you, and I expect she'll fall over in shock when she sees you." He just wished she would come through the front door in the next five minutes.

He picked up Rita's little knapsack and gestured to the staircase. "Come on. Let me show you the upstairs."

⁂

Ellie found the walk back home to be quite pleasant, even though a few clouds had gathered overhead, blocking some of the sun's warmth. Tommy Lee had awakened and was babbling nonstop, mostly about wanting to get out of the stroller, but Ellie insisted he stay put so that they could make it home as quickly as possible. He didn't like her answer, so he threw a little fit, something he rarely did unless he was tired. "He missed his usual nap," she said to Claire.

"No need to explain, dear. I know how it is when a child's schedule is altered. But I will say this: he's been good ninety-five percent of the time. Such a good sport, allowing us to cart him all over town! You're doing a wonderful job with him...and all the children, really. I'm amazed at how you've managed to bring our precious Frances out of her shell."

"Oh, I haven't done much of anything but love each one, and that's been easy."

When the house came into view, so did Gage's truck, and a mixture of surprise, excitement, and concern washed over her. She glanced at her wristwatch, which read twenty after two, an odd time for him to be home. Claire must have thought the same thing, for she said, "I wonder why Gage—"

Just then, the front door flew open, and he stormed down the porch steps, marching in their direction like a soldier on some important mission. "Where have you two been?"

His scolding tone brought them to a halt. "I asked Ellie to take a walk with me," Claire said. "We ended up in town for lunch and some shopping. Why? Is something wrong?"

"Yes, something's wrong. You shouldn't be out here in broad daylight."

Ellie felt her throat close up tighter than the lid on a Mason jar. "What's goin' on?"

He dropped his shoulders a notch and released a deep sigh—relief? Then, he looked at Ellie, his eyes roving up and down, as if seeing her for the first time. "You look...different. You cut your hair."

She would have preferred a compliment to a neutral observation, but now was not the time to fret over what he thought of her haircut. "Why did you come runnin' out here like the house was on fire?"

"Something's come up."

Seeing his forehead crinkle caused her stomach to tighten. "What is it?"

Gage looked left and right, as if searching for something. "Did either of you notice anything suspicious in town?"

"No, of course not," said Claire. "What's this about, Gage?"

"I want out!" Tommy Lee wailed, standing up and trying to climb out of the stroller. Gage bent over and hefted him out. "I have a bit of news," he said, holding the squirming boy in his arms. "Some of it's good, some of it's not so good. I'll give you the good news first, and the rest we'll discuss inside. Ellie, there's someone here to see you."

"Who...?" She followed his gaze to the house. Standing on the porch was—no, it couldn't be! She gasped and plastered a hand across her mouth. "Mama?"

"Yep, in the flesh. Go see her."

He didn't have to tell her twice. Forgetting her fear of the bad news, she set off on a sprint across the yard, bounded up the porch steps, and fell straight into her mama's waiting arms.

※

Gage had been on edge all afternoon, wondering how this thing was going to play out. He felt desperate to protect his family from that villain Byron and needed to come up with the best possible solution for ensuring their safety. While the kids played in the backyard, he and the other adults gathered around the kitchen table to discuss their strategy. He suggested they all take a train to Chicago tonight, thinking they could stay with his parents while they waited out Byron's arrest. And his mother fully agreed. But Rita said her sole reason for coming to Wabash had been to warn her daughter, and she wondered if it wouldn't be better if she just went back to Tennessee.

Her comment invited argument from Ellie, who wouldn't hear of being separated from her mother so soon, if ever. Her thinking was that they'd be better off staying put for the moment. After all, Byron wasn't after all of them; he just wanted her. She even suggested setting a trap that would draw him in and put him right in the path of the local law enforcement.

"A trap?" Gage raised his eyebrows. "No way am I allowing my wife to be used as bait for that maniac. There's no telling what he has up his sleeve."

Stubborn Ellie pulled back her shoulders, bit her lip, and then, out of habit, reached for her braid—and remembered it wasn't there. Gage grinned. Blamed if she wasn't prettier than a picture with her newly trimmed hair, turned under slightly at the ends, and those sweeping bangs that fell in gentle wisps across her forehead. There was no mistaking her for a mere girl anymore, and he aimed to tell her so when he finally got her alone.

Sheriff Morris stopped by while the family was cleaning up after supper.

"Why's the sheriff keep coming over?" Alec wanted to know. "Abe and I been real good in school lately. He's not checkin' in on us, is he?"

If the situation hadn't been so critical, Gage might have laughed at his son's worried expression. Instead, he ruffled his hair. "No, Alec. He just wants to chat with me a bit. I'll be out on the front porch."

"I'm comin' with you," Ellie said.

"No, you're staying here."

She handed her dishcloth to Rita and looked him square in the face. "I'm comin' with you," she repeated.

He blinked twice. "All right, but I'll do the talking."

She gave a huffy little breath, and he looked past her at Rita and Claire, both of whom lifted their eyebrows and shrugged.

Gage followed Ellie onto the porch and closed the front door behind him. "So, what's the latest, Sheriff?" he asked the craggy-faced man. "Did you go out to Orville Dotson's place?" On the chance that Pruitt was out there lurking in the shadows, he tugged Ellie close to his side, and she allowed it.

"Yes, yes, we did that, and Dotson said he sent him packing."

"And you believe him?"

"I've no reason not to."

"Did you search his place?"

"Looked around, yeah, but Mrs. Dotson said her husband didn't give the man the time of day. She's been making Orville toe the line ever since his stint in jail."

Gage had heard something similar regarding Dotson. Still, one couldn't be too trusting. Criminy, he didn't even trust Buford Morris entirely, not after hearing countless rumors about the lawman deliberately overlooking alleged bootleggers because he liked to imbibe with the best of them.

Ellie stepped away from Gage. "So, what are you goin' to do to find him, Sheriff? I want Byron Pruitt put away forever."

"I know, I know. We're workin' on it. Got word from the Athens police department that they're sending up a couple of detectives. They'll be here tomorrow to lend a hand with the investigation."

"That's good to know," Gage said.

The sheriff nodded. "Dotson told me he gave Pruitt the names of a couple of cheap motels in town, seeing as the guy needed a place to stay and didn't appear to have the money for anything fancy. I thought we'd check out the hotel registers. You're welcome to join us."

"And leave my family?"

"We'll be fine," Ellie said. "I'll draw the curtains and lock everything up tight."

"I can call a deputy to come stand guard outside," Sheriff Morris said. "I just thought you might want to take part in the investigation."

"I'd like to, but—"

Ellie lifted anxious eyes to him. "I think you should. What could go wrong? I'll have a deputy and two levelheaded women lookin' out for me. And the

Lord, of course. I'd say I'm more than covered." Her pretty lips curved into a grin. "You'll be better off huntin' down Byron than sittin' here stewin' about where he is and what he's up to. I'm not afraid o' Byron Pruitt. He's been terrorizin' me for the past eight years o' my life. I think I can handle a few more measly days. And I say 'days' because I'm confident you'll catch him soon, maybe even tonight. Byron tries to act smart, but he's really about as dumb as a bucket of doornails."

Sheriff Morris cleared his throat. "Well, time's a wastin'. You coming or staying?"

A pang of uncertainty speared him, followed by a wave of urgency. Ellie was right about trusting the Lord to watch over her. It dawned on him that he hadn't really prayed about this whole situation since learning that Pruitt was in town. *Lord, forgive me for neglecting to bring my burden to You. Please help me to trust You to keep my wife and family safe. And would You lend us wisdom in locating that awful louse Byron?* After his silent prayer, he looked at the sheriff. "You'll get someone over here to stand guard?"

"It's as good as done. One of my deputies will be over within the hour."

Gage waited for a strong sense of confidence to fill his being, but none came. He released a long sigh. "All right, but give me a minute with my wife."

With a nod, the man stepped off the porch to wait on the walkway. Gage put his hands on Ellie's shoulders. "Are you sure you're comfortable with this?"

"I'm sure. We'll all be fine! Like I said, I'm not afraid of that lunatic."

"Well, you should be. He's probably armed. Man, I wish I owned a gun, but I've never had need for one."

"And you don't now. We'll be careful," she assured him.

He smiled and brushed his fingertips over her smooth cheek, wanting to kiss her but deciding it wouldn't be prudent to put on a show for the sheriff. "You're quite a woman, you know that? And I do mean woman." A lump of emotion clogged his throat. "And I like that new haircut," he whispered, winding a few of her silken strands around his index finger. "It suits you."

She cocked her head. "Why, thank you. I...I wasn't sure what you thought."

Sheriff Morris coughed. "You comin', Mr. Cooper?"

He cast a glance over his shoulder. "Yeah." Then, he set his gaze on Ellie again, letting it linger there a moment. "I'll leave it to you to tell our mothers where I went, but don't let on to the kids, if you can help it."

"I'll take care of it. Now, go."

"Lock the doors."

"I told you I would."

"And close the drapes."

"Go."

With one last look into her shining eyes, he turned and loped down the stairs.

Chapter Thirty

What time I am afraid, I will trust in thee.
In God I will praise his word, in God I have
put my trust; I will not fear what
flesh can do unto me.
—Psalm 56:3–4

Ned packed his satchel with a couple of spare shirts and an extra pair of trousers. He didn't know how long he'd be in Wabash, or what kind of trouble he'd get in for going, but he couldn't just sit around the office waiting for word of Byron Pruitt's arrest.

"Here're some clean socks," Marlene said, entering the bedroom. "Fresh off the clothesline." She laid them neatly in a corner of his suitcase, then rearranged a few of his other items.

"Thanks, darlin'. I shouldn't be gone more than a few days. I'll find a phone and call you every night."

"You'd better."

"You do understand why I'm going, don't you?" He put his arms around her. "I have to see that Byron Pruitt is caught before he harms anyone else."

She laughed quietly against his chest. "And you want to make sure the job's done right."

"I guess you know me pretty well."

She pulled back and shot him an adoring smile, reaching up to cup one of his cheeks in her palm.

"About as well as anyone could after thirty-six years of marriage."

"Thirty-seven years next month," he said, rubbing noses with her.

"What time does your train leave?"

He glanced down at his watch. "Nine o'clock. I'm scheduled to arrive in Wabash at seven in the morning. I'll grab some breakfast when I get there and then head over to the sheriff's office."

Ever the fussbudget, she picked a piece of lint off of his shoulder. "I hope you can get some sleep on that train."

"That's why I got a berth. I'll sleep like a baby. Well, maybe not quite that good, since you won't be there."

"Oh, pooh. Since when have you needed me to sleep? I watch you nap on that chair over there from six to seven every evening, and you don't see me lying next to you."

They bantered back and forth like that until the time came for him to leave for the L&N Station. On the front step, he kissed Marlene good-bye, and when he pulled out of the drive and glanced back at the house, she stood there, smiling and watching, her hands stuffed inside her apron pockets.

Gage rode along with the sheriff and his deputy Dan Fett, whom they'd picked up at the station, from one hotel to the next, canvassing the cut-rate places Dotson had recommended to Pruitt, along with a few others that came to mind. But none of them had a guest registered under his name or even fitting his description.

"What else is there?" Gage asked from the backseat. "Do you suppose he's just hanging out on the streets? Maybe down at the tracks behind the train station with the hobos?"

Sheriff Morris slowed to turn east onto Maple Street. "That's a possibility. Let's head over there."

"There is that boardinghouse a block ahead," Deputy Fett mused. "We could check there on our way to the depot."

"Good thinking." Morris drove through the next intersection and pulled into a narrow parking space in front of Newberry Boardinghouse. Widow Newberry usually filled her rooms with upstanding characters who generally leased by the month—single men, for the most part. Gage couldn't imagine Byron hiding out in there, much less passing muster with Fern Newberry and her scrutinizing eye.

The three of them filed out of the car, marched up the tulip-lined walkway, and pushed through the double doors into the bright parlor. The focal point of the formal-looking, hardwood-floored room was a large brick fireplace surrounded by overstuffed upholstered chairs. The appearance of the parlor reinforced Gage's impression that it was too nice a place for the likes of Byron Pruitt.

"Can I help you gentlemen?" asked a young lady standing behind the reception desk.

"Hello there, miss," Morris replied. "You have any vacancies?"

"We did earlier today, sheriff, but not anymore."

"Oh, yeah? You mind telling me who took the last room?"

She pursed her lips and tipped her head thoughtfully. "Hmm...well, I can't say outright, but I can check for you. I just came in a couple of hours ago. I've been helping my grandma run the front desk."

"That's mighty nice of you. Would you mind checking?"

She crouched down, disappearing for a moment, and then stood up, plunking a large binder on the counter in front of her. She proceeded to skim through the pages with her slim, youthful fingers, finally landing on the one she wanted. Squinting, she ran her index finger down the page, stopping about three-quarters of the way from the top. "Well, it says here we had somebody by the name of Norman Booth sign in around two o'clock, but I can't guarantee he's in his room. People come and go all the time."

"Norman Booth?" The sheriff bent over the counter to have a look at the registry. "You don't see a Byron Pruitt anywhere on that page, do you?"

The girl looked again, her eyes narrowed in careful inspection. "No, sir. Nobody by that name."

"Sheriff, my wife's maiden name is Booth," Gage pointed out. "It's possible he used a different name to conceal his identity, and 'Booth' might have been the first thing that came to mind."

Morris eyed him with a calculating expression. "Yep, yep. That's a good possibility, all right."

Gage sighed. Buford Morris may have won the election for sheriff, but he sure wouldn't be winning any awards for his detective skills.

※

Byron started down the stairs, carrying his rifle in a sack, but he halted near the top when he heard the conversation taking place down at the front desk.

His stomach clenched tighter the longer he stood there and listened, craning his neck to make out the words.

"We're looking for someone named Byron Pruitt," said a male voice. "You got a key to the room of this Norman Booth? If he isn't there, we'd at least like to take a look around."

"I don't know," said a female voice. "I should call my grandmother."

"You don't have to call your grandmother. I'm the sheriff, remember? See this badge?"

"Sheriff, she knows that. She's just trying to be conscientious," said another male voice. "Young lady, we just want to check out this Booth fellow and ask him a few questions. Chances are, he's not the man we're looking for, but we need to make sure."

That was all Byron needed to hear. He tiptoed back up the stairs and raced to the end of the carpeted hallway, opened a window, and stepped out onto the fire escape. He reached the ground in seconds, surprised by his own agility, never mind that his lungs felt near to bursting. From there, he maneuvered down a shadowy, tree-lined alley behind several storefronts, then darted across a street to bolt down the next lane. After running some three or four blocks, he dropped to his haunches behind some trash barrels to collect himself. He clutched his burning chest and gasped for air, his throat as dry as chalk dust, his brow dripping with sweat.

After a few minutes, he slowly stood back up. Seeing no one coming, he made another mad dash across the next street and into an alley. At the next block, he saw a cab driver sitting atop a carriage hitched to two horses. Forcing a calm demeanor, he slowed to a walk and fixed his collar. "You open for service?"

The weary-looking driver came to life, donning a top hat and grabbing the reins. "Where you want to go, mister?"

"Seven forty-two West Hill Street."

"That'll run you fifty cents."

Rather than complain about the exorbitant rate, Byron opened the door, climbed inside, and slid along the worn leather seat. "Hurry it up, all right?"

"You got it, mister."

The driver picked up his whip and gave it a good, loud snap, and the carriage jolted forward, jostling Byron's already jarred nerves. "Let me off a block away from the house, though," he called to the man.

"Yes, sir. We should be there in about five minutes."

Five minutes wasn't much time for deciding on a plan, but it was all he had.

❧

After Ellie had privately told her mama and mother-in-law where Gage had gone, they'd decided it best to take the kids upstairs to wait for his return. Explaining why had been another story.

"Why do we gotta go upstairs?" Alec asked.

"Yeah, why can't we play in the living room, like we always do? Besides, our favorite radio show is gonna be on pretty soon, and we never miss that," Abe added.

"Well, we'll have to miss it tonight," Ellie said, drawing the living room drapes. Meanwhile, Mama went about closing all the other curtains and seeing that the windows were latched and the front and back doors locked up tight.

Claire put Checkers in his enclosure in the kitchen and switched off the light. "It'll be fun, you'll see,"

"Alec, don't call your brother names," Ellie said. "Your daddy is helpin' the sheriff find somebody."

"Who?" Abe asked.

She gave a quiet sigh. "Just...a man."

"He must be a bad guy if the sheriff's looking for him," Frances said somberly.

"Good thing me an' Abe haven't got in trouble for a long time, or the sheriff might be lookin' for us," Alec reflected.

"He wouldn't have to look far," said Abe, throwing a pillow at his twin and hitting him square in the face.

"Hey!" Alec hollered. "This is war."

He pitched the pillow back, but Ellie intercepted it. "No more roughhousin', fellas. How about I read a book to everyone?"

"Yeah!" they all cheered at once. Even Tommy Lee stopped what he was doing and raced over to climb onto Ellie's lap.

"Frances, do you have a book we all would enjoy?"

Frances looked through the small pile of reading material she'd brought into the room. "How about this one?" She held up *The Tale of Peter Rabbit.*

"Oh yes, I love that story," Ellie said, reaching for the book.

Downstairs, the puppy had started barking. Claire laid down her knitting and stood. "I think I'll go let Checkers out. I'll watch him from the back porch."

Mama jumped up from her chair, too. "Why don't I go? It's the least I can do. 'Sides, I left my bag in the kitchen."

Claire smiled. "We'll both go."

Ellie didn't like the thought of either of them leaving the room, but she didn't want to make an issue of it in front of the children, and there was safety in numbers, after all. She gave a hesitant nod and then watched them walk out the door.

"You see anything?" Sheriff Morris asked. He, Deputy Dan, and Gage had spent the last ten minutes rummaging through the room registered to Norman Booth, rifling through the fellow's suitcase, opening drawers, searching under the bed, emptying the pillows from their cases, and even checking behind the window shades.

"If we're wrong about Pruitt's alias, and some guy by the name of Norman Booth really is stayin' here, he's goin' to come back to a real mess," Deputy Dan reflected. "He'll probably call the sheriff to report a robbery!" He laughed at his own joke.

"He sure packed light," Morris said, ignoring the jibe and opening an armoire to look inside.

"Let's check the communal bathroom down the hall," Gage suggested.

"Are we done in here, then?" the sheriff asked.

Gage stared at him. "You tell us. You're the sheriff."

The fellow puffed out his chest in a show of self-importance. "Well, I think we've investigated every corner of the room. Let's close it up and check out that lavatory."

In the hallway, they passed a boarder, a thirty-something man, who obviously had just showered, considering his wet, slicked-back hair and the damp towel slung over his shoulder. He nodded politely, then stopped at the room next door to the one they'd just ransacked and turned a key in the slot. The sheriff stopped and swiveled. "Say, mister, you wouldn't happen to know anything about the guy who just checked into the room next to yours, would you?"

He pushed the door open a few inches and glanced up. "Can't say I do, no. I heard him talking to himself, though—the walls must be pretty thin. It sounded like a bunch of nonsense, like he was rehearsing for a play or something."

"Rehearsing, you say? Was there anyone else in the room?" the sheriff asked.

"Doubt it. His was the only voice I heard."

"Could you make out anything he was saying? You said the walls are thin."

"A little bit, but I'm not one to eavesdrop, so I went downstairs and listened to the phonograph. When I came back upstairs, it was quiet over there"—he chuckled—"till he started snoring. Guess he was getting a nap."

"Well, the words you did hear...what were they?"

The young man squinted in thought. "Well, let's see. He said something like, 'You ain't goin' to say one word, li'l missy. You remember what I tol' you would happen if you did.' After that, he cackled, like it was in the script or something, and then he said, 'You don't want nothin' to happen to yer mama, now, would you?' Like I said, I think he was practicing his lines. I hear there's a stage play starting up this weekend over at The Eagles Theater. Don't recall what it is, though. Sorry. You could probably check at the box office."

"Yeah, yeah, I'm sure we could. Thanks for your time, mister."

"Not at all." The fellow then narrowed his eyes as he looked toward the end of the hall. "Humph, that's really odd."

"What's odd?" the sheriff asked.

"The window at the end of the hall. I've never known Widow Newberry to leave it open like that."

"Where's it lead?" Gage asked.

"To the fire escape."

As the threesome scrambled back to the car, Gage's stomach swirled with uneasiness, and his mind raced with innumerable gruesome thoughts. Had Pruitt fled down those stairs? What if he was at the house already, beating down the door to get to Ellie? And what of his precious kids, mom, and mother-in-law? Were they all in danger? *Lord, please protect my family.* "We'd better get back to my house, Sheriff. I don't like what I just heard."

"Neither do I. I'll put the old jalopy into top gear."

All three of them yanked their doors shut, and Morris gunned the engine.

"No doubt Pruitt was rehearsin' his lines," said Deputy Dan, "but I think we can safely bet he wasn't practicing for some play."

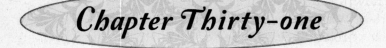

Chapter Thirty-one

For God hath not given us the spirit of fear;
but of power, and of love, and of
a sound mind.
—2 Timothy 1:7

*S*even forty-two," Byron muttered with satisfaction when he spotted the numbers on a post in front of a rambling two-story house about half a block up the road from where the cab driver had left him. He sneaked along in the shadows, thankful he'd worn black trousers and a dark shirt. Stars peppered the darkening sky, and sparse clouds partially hid the sliver of a moon, which further aided in his obscurity. He took care to watch where he walked but still managed to step on a stick, and the cracking sound sent a neighbor dog into a flurry of barking. Byron stood stock-still and waited, grateful when the owner stepped onto the porch and ordered the mutt to be quiet.

Parked in the Coopers' driveway was a car with someone sitting inside. He slipped behind a tree, then slowly poked his head out to survey the situation. The driver-side window had been rolled down so that the fellow could blow cigarette smoke out the opening, and it looked like he had a flashlight, pointed at—what was it?—a book. Had he been stationed there to guard the house? What a joke! Byron fought the urge to laugh. Like a prowling cat, he moved low to the ground and advanced on the car. The neighbor dog barked again, but the fool officer was so engrossed in his book, he paid it no mind.

Upon reaching the driver side, Byron slowly rose, and then, with the butt of his rifle poised, he said, "Good book?" The fellow gasped and turned toward Byron, who thumped him hard between the eyes, knocking him out cold. He fell in a crumpled heap across the seat. "You can finish it tomorrow."

Next, he wended his way through the dark yard, sorry that he hadn't snatched the flashlight from that dumb cop's hand. He tried to see inside the house, but the closed curtains made it impossible. So, he skirted the house, making his way to the back stoop, where he stealthily climbed the five cement steps. The screen door opened easily, but the interior door refused to budge. Next to the door, there was a small, uncovered window. Peeking inside, he saw a dimly lit entryway and, beyond it, the kitchen. Again using the butt of his gun, he jabbed a hole through the glass, then quickly reached a hand through the opening to unlock the door and turn the knob. *Easy as pie,* he thought, his adrenaline surging as he stepped inside, glass crunching beneath his shoe. A clock ticked above the stove. Eight thirty. He had to hurry before those men at the boardinghouse figured out where he'd gone. He tiptoed along, hoping not to step on a creaky spot, as he prowled the house in search of his prey: a girl with long, black braids and a sassy tongue.

※

"Shh!" Ellie hissed at the sound of glass shattering downstairs. "Don't move, and don't utter a single word, you included, Tommy Lee. I want all of you to get under my bed, and you're not to come out until I say so."

In spite of her warning, Tommy Lee whimpered, so she quickly crouched down beside him and whispered, "Honey, you've got to be brave." Then, seeing that all four kids were staring at her with wide, fearful eyes, she added, "Trust me, all right? God will protect us. I'm sure of it."

Alec nodded. "We'll be quiet. And, Ellie? Be careful, 'cause we love you."

"I love you, too, all of you." Then, standing, she skimmed the room for some kind of weapon, but all she could come up with was the wrought-iron lamp stand. She unplugged it, grabbed it off the dresser, and swung it over her shoulder, fists gripping the base in readiness to hurl it at the first thing that came through the door. Lord help her if it happened to be Mama or Claire. *Oh, where are those women?* Stepping forward, she turned off the overhead light, then muttered a quick prayer. "Lord Jesus, we need You. Please, please keep us safe." But, even as she prayed, beads of perspiration formed on her forehead, and her heart nearly pounded out of her chest as she fastened her gaze on the closed door.

※

A lamp in the spacious living room cast enough light to give Byron a decent grip on the layout of the house. The thought occurred to him that maybe Eleanor wasn't even here, but then, he figured she had to be, since they'd stationed that stupid cop in the driveway. She must be hiding, and the realization made his blood run hotter. Oh, how he loved a good game of hide-and-seek.

"Eleanor," he sang out. "I know you're here. Don't you wanna come out an' say hi to yer stepdaddy? I've missed you, and so has yer mama. Fool woman's been cryin' ever since you left." He maneuvered his way into the next room. "Can you hear me, Eleanor? How 'bout givin' me just a li'l clue as to where you are, so's I'll know if I should come upstairs? Come on, pretty please, with maple syrup?

"You got yerself a nice spread here. What'd you have to do to git this guy to marry you?" He lifted an expensive-looking crystal vase from the center of the dining room table and dropped it on the floor. It shattered with a crash so loud, even he jumped. "Oops. Clumsy me." He burst into unrestrained laughter, then quickly sobered and moved forward.

The ticking of the clock on the fireplace mantel, along with the barks of that blasted neighbor dog, were the only sounds that broke the eerie silence of the house. He advanced through the rest of the downstairs, still finding no one. So, he decided to go upstairs. Maybe he'd turn on a light up there, if he could find a switch. What could it hurt?

He felt his way to the staircase, taking care not to trip over anything. "I'm comin' up, Eleanor." His shoe located the bottom step, and he started climbing, his footsteps echoing like thunderclaps in a cavern. "You gonna come out so's I don't have to waste time lookin' for you?"

A muffled whimpering sound drew him to a halt. "I forgot you've got stepkids now. Well, that's all right. I ain't comin' for them, anyways. It's you I want, isn't it, Eleanor? Yep, you know somethin' you ain't s'posed to know, so I'm gonna have to keep you from talkin'. I sure hope you haven't talked already."

When he reached the top of the stairs, the glow of a lamp in the first room showed him he had to make a sharp right. He raised his rifle to his shoulder and proceeded down the hallway, his pulse pounding in his head.

"Hello, Byron." Someone stepped out of the shadows. *Rita?* It couldn't be. He squinted to make out the blurry figure at the end of the hall. "What in the—?"

"Put that gun down, you big fool, 'fore I shoot you. I always have been a better aim than you, and you know it."

He swallowed the bile that rose in his throat at the sight of his wife facing off with him. "Where'd you come from?"

She chortled. "Surprised to see me, are you? Did you really think I was gonna let you go after my girl? I told you I wouldn't stand for it, didn't I? I been bendin' to your every little whim for the past eight years, Byron, and I'm done."

"But I left you in—"

"Athens, yeah, but Mildred drove me down the mountain. Ridin' with her was even scarier 'n ridin' with you, but we managed just fine. I watched you git on that train, Byron, even saw you retch at the station once we got to Wabash. If you ask me, it was more nerves than anythin' what made you lose your lunch. You're a lot o' hot air, Byron, anyone ever tell you that?"

"Shut up," he ordered, cocking his rifle and fixing his aim on her. "It didn't bother me none doin' away with Sullivan. I could do away with you just as easy."

In the shadows, he heard the click of her gun, as well. The realization struck that she *was* a better aim, and faster, too. "Where you git that gun?"

"Where you think? I brought it with me, dodo, tucked in my bag. 'Course, I had to run downstairs to get it a bit ago. I figured it wouldn't be long 'fore you showed up here, and I wanted to be ready. We been hidin' at opposite ends, just waitin' for you."

His gut clenched. "Who's *we*?" A quick glance behind him revealed no one.

"Oops. Slip o' the tongue."

A shaft of light from another room down the hall blinded his ability to distinguish shapes and movements. Rita had the advantage, and that made him nervous. "W-where's that purty li'l Eleanor, anyway?" he asked, thinking to distract her. Why was he so nervous all of a sudden? "She's awful quiet, wherever she is."

"Don't matter where she is. You ain't gonna hurt her. This here's the end of the road for you, Byron."

Another tiny whimper came from the room just steps in front of him. He moved closer, preparing to open the door and peer inside.

"Stop right there, Byron, I'm warnin' you."

He didn't think she'd follow through. The only thing she'd ever shot was a target in his backyard. Granted, she was darn good at hitting the bull's-eye, but when he'd asked her to go hunting for their supper, she'd said she couldn't shoot a living creature. "Ha. You're a lot o' talk, too, Rita. You wouldn't shoot yer dear, faithful husband, now, would you?"

"Pfff. Don't ask me twice."

With his gun aimed at the door to the room where he'd heard a noise, he took another small step. A loud shot blasted through the hallway, and there was a searing pain in his wrist, which forced the gun from his hand. He looked down at the carpet, where a pool of blood was spreading. Jaw dropping in shock, he looked up again. "Rita? I can't believe you shot me, woman!" With his good hand, he gripped his injured wrist to stop the bleeding, but then came a hard, painful blow to his head, which traveled clear to his toes and made him crumple to his knees. "Who...?" And that's where his thought ended as his body fell forward, his world going black.

"That was a gunshot!" Gage shouted, taking off at a run toward the house, past the car of the deputy who was supposed to be guarding his family. He took the porch stairs two at a time and turned the doorknob, but, of course, it wouldn't budge; it was locked as tight as a drum, just as he'd ordered. He tried to peek inside a window, but, again, all the drapes had been drawn, leaving not a crack to see through. In a panic, he leaped off the porch, planning to dash around to the back of the house.

"Cooper, slow down!" the sheriff ordered him. "You don't know what you're gonna find in there. You could get yourself killed. You've gotta approach this with some measure of common sense."

But common sense didn't have much sway over his actions right now. "I've got to get to my family."

"Let me go first," said Sheriff Morris. "We're the ones with the guns."

"I'll cover you," said Deputy Dan, coming up alongside him.

Reluctantly, Gage followed them to the back door and waited while the sheriff and his deputy ascended the back stairs. "Looks like Pruitt broke the glass to get in," the sheriff whispered to his deputy as they stood on the stoop.

Gage's chest tightened into a hard, anxious knot. "Hurry up," he hissed.

"Shh," the sheriff said, turning the doorknob and advancing over the threshold with caution, followed by the deputy and then Gage. Broken glass crunched beneath their feet. Upstairs, a regular ruckus erupted, with pounding footsteps and loud female voices. Gage pushed past the two men and raced for the stairs, taking them like a deer.

Around the corner, he got a big surprise—a man lay facedown on the floor with blood oozing from his arm. Rita stood over him, pointing a pistol at his head. "Don't even think of risin' up, Byron, or I'll have my friend hit you again with that fryin' pan." The guy moaned and writhed in pain. "And quit yer bellyachin'."

Breathless, Gage asked, "Is everyone all right? Where're the kids and Ellie?"

"Good as gold," Rita answered with a smile. "I think they're in your bedroom."

"I'm bleedin' to death, Rita," Byron moaned.

"No, you ain't. You're goin' to jail, and I'll make sure you're good an' alive for the whole experience." When he cursed under his breath, she gave him a kick in the side. "Watch yer tongue. There's kids about."

Gage's mother had positioned herself behind Rita, her face as white as milk, her eyes about as big as the frying pan she held in her hand. Gage stepped around the fellow curled up in a fetal position, tempted to give him a good kick himself for breaking into his house and endangering his family.

Huffing, Sheriff Morris came around the corner, followed by Deputy Dan. "I'll take over from here, ma'am," the sheriff said, holstering his gun and producing a set of handcuffs. "I assume this is Byron Pruitt."

"You assume right," Rita said, backing off to let the sheriff do his job.

"Good work, ma'am. We could use you on our force." With that, Sheriff Morris set a booted foot in the center of Byron's back and hauled the guy's good arm out first, then the wounded one. Despite Byron's squalling and thrashing, he managed to slip on the handcuffs and drag him to his feet.

He looked to Deputy Dan. "Why don't you go back down and check on our friend Clint? He might need some assistance."

"No need." All heads turned down the hall. There stood the deputy, looking sheepish and sporting a monster-sized goose egg between the eyes.

"Can we come out yet?" came a muffled yell. It sounded like one of the twins.

Gage opened the bedroom door. "Get away!" Ellie screamed. Something hurtled toward him, and he raised a hand to deflect the object. It bounced off of his shoulder, knocking him sideways, and then crashed to the floor. "Ellie, it's me, Gage. It's over, honey."

"Ellie! You li'l she-cat!" Byron shrieked from the hallway. "I'm goin' to—"

"Shut up, Pruitt!" said the sheriff. "You're under arrest." They plodded down the stairs, the sheriff continually telling a muttering Byron to be quiet.

Gage looked at Ellie, who was trembling, one hand pressed over her mouth, her eyes filling with tears. When he closed the distance between them and wrapped her in a tight hug, her sobs turned into howls. One by one, the children crawled out from under the bed, looking pale and haggard, and Tommy Lee broke into a bawling fit to match Ellie's. Gage tried to gather the boy close while also holding Ellie, but soon his mother relieved him of the job by scooping up the screaming boy and carrying him into the hallway.

The twins ran for the door, but Frances huddled close to Gage's side. He put a hand on her shoulder and drew her close. "I was scared, Daddy."

"I know, punkin. But it's all right now. You're safe."

"Ick!" Alec exclaimed. "There's blood on the floor."

"We'll send somebody from the department over to clean that up for you, Mr. Cooper," Deputy Dan said to Gage.

"I appreciate that."

"Eww, there's blood everywhere!" Alec went on.

"It's disgusting," Abe confirmed.

Ellie's body felt suddenly limp in his arms, and he noticed she was covered in sweat. Glancing down, he saw that her eyelids were fluttering. "Ellie?"

Just as her legs gave way, he swept her into his arms, and then he laid her on the bed.

"Ellie!" Frances gasped.

In seconds, the deputy was at his side. "I'll call for a doctor."

Chapter Thirty-two

Fear God, and keep his commandments:
for this is the whole duty of man.
—Ecclesiastes 12:13

Dr. Wilson Trent arrived less than fifteen minutes later. He had been the Coopers' family physician for as long as Gage could remember, and he'd delivered each one of his kids, so he trusted him implicitly.

Dr. Trent quickly examined Ellie while Gage got him caught up on the recent happenings. "She's fainted, that's all," was his diagnosis. "But I'm going to give her a sedative, anyway. Considering everything you've told me, it sounds like your young wife has been through a lot in the past few months."

Frances climbed up on the bed to sit next to Ellie. "Is she going to be all right?"

The doctor tapped the girl on the nose. "You bet she will, but she's going to need your help around the house."

Ellie roused, looked around, and then immediately tried to sit up. "What...?" Her brow furrowed in confusion.

"Stay put, young lady," Dr. Trent said, reaching inside his bag. "I have a couple of pills I want you to take. Can we get some water?"

Alec, who'd been looking on with Abe, darted off. "Thank you!" Gage called after him, then surveyed the room. His mother sat in a chair near the door, holding a sniffling Tommy Lee in her lap, while Rita stood at the foot of the bed, chewing her lower lip, much in the way her daughter sometimes did. Abe stood across the room, casting worried glances at Ellie, and Frances, ever the little mother, still sat on the bed, rubbing Ellie's arm. The only one missing was Checkers, but he soon appeared, carrying an oversized bone in his mouth. Apparently, Gage's mother had locked the pooch down in the basement with his "prize," and there he'd stayed, oblivious to the drama unfolding upstairs.

After the doctor left, Gage chased everyone out of the room, saying he wanted some time alone with his wife. Everyone gladly complied, except for Frances, who hesitated in the doorway. "I'll be right back to sit with you, Ellie."

"All right, honey," Ellie said. "Thank you." As soon as Frances stepped away from the door, Ellie set anxious eyes on Gage. "I don't see why I can't get up. I'm fine now."

He lowered himself onto the edge of the bed and took her hand in both of his, rubbing her palm with the pad of his thumb. "You're not fine. Dr. Trent said you needed to rest, and I happen to agree with him. I'm making you stay in bed at least through tomorrow."

"What? But that's so silly. I have things to do."

"Actually, you don't. Our mothers have already volunteered to take care of the meals and household chores, and I wouldn't advise arguing with women who're skilled at wielding guns and fry pans."

She giggled. "Oh, my goodness, you're right." They shared a moment of lighthearted laughter, but she quickly sobered. "Gage, when I heard that window shatter, I knew it was Byron, and all I could think about was protectin' the kids."

"You did that. And I'm very proud of you."

"When our mothers went downstairs and didn't come back, I hoped they'd found a hidin' place. I didn't know they'd come back upstairs to waylay Byron, and I was so overcome with fear that I didn't hear any o' the goings-on in the hallway. Leave it to Mama to stay one step ahead. She knows how that connivin' rat works."

"And I guess you do, as well. You thought he was the one coming through that door when I opened it."

"I'm so sorry I hit you with that lamp! Did it hurt very much?"

"Oh, it was terrible. Awful. I can hardly stand the pain." He gave an exaggerated moan.

"Oh, you! I completely lost my head, didn't I?"

"Don't worry, it's right back where it's supposed to be." He reached up and tousled her freshly cut hair.

Ellie smiled and then stared off, as if sinking back into a deep hole of regret. "Sometimes, I worry I might actually hate him."

"Who?"

"Byron. Is it wrong to feel that way?"

He pondered her question for a moment. "He's a murderer, Ellie, and he's made life miserable for you and your mother. But to allow hatred and bitterness to consume you would be like giving him permission to remain in control. Do you want that?"

"I don't know how else to feel about him," she said, still staring off. "I can't love him."

"Well, maybe you don't have to love him as much as pray for him."

Her head snapped to Gage. "Pray for him? Why would I do that?"

He smiled. "Do you think God loves him any less than He loves you or me? Do you think Byron's any less redeemable than either of us, or that he doesn't need prayer as much as anyone else?"

She bit her lower lip and scrunched up her nose. "You make a good point, but...well, I guess he doesn't seem very redeemable to me."

Gage gave an inward sigh, understanding fully the way she felt. "The truth is, we're all God's children, created in His image, and He loves us all equally. It's just that many folks choose to turn away from that love."

"I'm glad I didn't."

He smiled and gave her hand a gentle squeeze. "I'm glad, too."

With a loud sigh, she pulled her arm away, turned onto her side, and tucked her hands beneath her cheek. He thought she made a fetching picture, lying there in a sliver of moonlight with her hair disheveled and her dark lashes shading her eyes. He wanted to tell her how much he appreciated all she'd done for him and his kids. Man, why didn't he just come out with it, tell her he loved her? About the time he got up the nerve, she yawned, and he suspected those pills from Dr. Trent were starting to take effect.

"Can I come back in yet?" Frances peeked inside the doorway.

Ellie turned and gave her a lazy smile. "Come on in, honey."

Frances scooted across the room to stand by the bed. "Is Daddy sleeping with you tonight, or is your mama?"

The unexpected yet completely innocent question created a strange tightening in Gage's chest. He would have liked to be the one to keep her company tonight, especially after the harrowing day she'd had. He ran his hand through his hair and smiled at the floor. "Well...."

"My mama," Ellie answered.

"Yeah, her mama."

🌱

Ned stepped off the train in Wabash under a dreary sky. It felt darn cold, too—maybe not to the locals, but to a Southerner accustomed to the temperature reaching 70 degrees by seven in the morning, this was no picnic. He drew his jacket collar close around his neck and surveyed his surroundings. First stop: coffee and a cinnamon bun.

He spotted a man preparing to board the train, probably traveling on business, from the looks of his suit and briefcase. "Excuse me," Ned said, and the fellow turned and lifted his eyebrows. "Can you suggest a place where I might get a light breakfast?"

"Sure thing, mister." He pointed west. "Up ahead, you'll come to Market Street. Walk a couple of blocks, and on your left you'll see a nice little diner called Livvie's Kitchen."

"Much obliged."

When Ned entered the little restaurant, he found it abuzz with patrons. To reach the hostess stand, he nearly had to step over a big black dog stretched out in the middle of the floor like he owned the place. A pretty woman with strawberry blonde hair and a pleasant smile approached him. "Morning," she greeted him. "Are you alone?"

"Afraid so."

She smiled. "You don't sound too happy about that." She led him to a small table along the wall and pulled out a chair. "Would you like some coffee and a newspaper to keep you company?"

"You've just read my mind and quite possibly stolen my heart."

She tossed back her lavish head of hair and laughed. "My husband won't be too thrilled about that." She pointed at the cook.

"That's all right. My wife back in Tennessee wouldn't be too happy, either."

She sobered just slightly. "Tennessee? I thought I detected a bit of an accent. You wouldn't be one of those Athens policemen arriving to escort that scoundrel Byron Pruitt out of our fine town, would you?"

This town was smaller than he'd thought. "No, I'm afraid I'm not. But I am an agent with the federal government, and I've been conducting my own investigation of Mr. Pruitt. So, they've already found him, have they?"

"Indeed they have. Big news this morning."

"Is that so? What happened?"

"Oh, gracious, I don't know too many details, only that his wife shot him in the hand last night."

"His wife...that would be Rita?"

"You know her?"

"Met her, sort of. I understand the daughter, Eleanor, lives here in Wabash."

"Yes, and she's become a dear friend. She's married to Gage Cooper, a fine craftsman who builds cabinets. From what I understand, this Pruitt fellow broke into the Coopers' house, apparently looking for Ellie."

"Well, I'll be. Guess that cuts my investigation short, doesn't it? Not that I'm disappointed, mind you."

"You say you're a federal agent?"

He nodded and grinned. "I sound a lot more important than I really am."

"Well, Mr. Agent, how about I bring you one of my husband's homemade rolls to go with that newspaper and coffee?"

"Now you're talking my language."

After breakfast, Ned asked his friendly server for directions to the courthouse. To say that he received a hearty welcome upon entering the office of Sheriff Buford Morris would be akin to saying that cows bark. The man resembled a beardless, grumpy Santa Claus with his double chin and round belly. When Ned introduced himself as the Director of Prohibition for East Tennessee, the fellow stood but did not shake the hand offered him. He'd received similar treatment from other law enforcement officials who didn't have much regard for Prohibition, as if Ned was solely responsible for passing the Volstead Act, but he'd grown a thick skin over the years and learned to slough it off.

"What's your business here, Mr. Castleberry?" the sheriff had grumbled.

"I understand you're holding Byron Pruitt in custody on burglary charges."

"That's right. What do you know about Pruitt?"

"He is the alleged murderer of one of my agents, and I'm interested in seeing him, as you can imagine."

"Ah, Walter Sullivan. Yep, know all about that case. Well, I have strict orders to release Pruitt to the

Athens police just as soon as they arrive." He looked at his wristwatch. "Expectin' them around eleven."

"You mind if I look in on him before they get here?"

The sheriff eyed him over his reading spectacles. "I s'pose that'd be all right. I'll get one of my deputies to escort you to his cell."

Byron Pruitt sat hunched on his cot in his ten-by-ten cell, his face looking especially haggard thanks to a covering of whiskers. When Ned approached, he squinted his bloodshot eyes and sneered. "You."

"You remember me, do you?"

"Pfff, you're that agent. What do you want?"

"Got something I wanted to show you in case you decide to plead anything other than guilty to murdering Walter Sullivan."

"Who's Walter Sullivan?"

"Uh-huh. You can play that innocent act with me if you want, but I got witnesses saying you knew him well."

His jaw twitched, and he stood up, wrapping his left hand around a cell bar and sticking his nose through the opening. The other hand bore a large bandage, probably covering his gunshot wound. The guard stood some fifteen feet away, no doubt all ears. "Yeah, well, big deal. That don't mean I killed 'im."

"From what I hear, your wife and stepdaughter say otherwise. Eyewitness accounts won't bode well for you in court."

"Ain't nobody goin' to believe two hillbilly women."

"No? That's not what I hear. Seems your step-daughter sent your wife quite a telling letter about how she went to the police and confessed everything about the murder, right down to the part about her burying the body while you aimed a gun at her. Why else do you think the sheriff hunted you down? It wasn't just for breaking and entering, Pruitt."

A trapped expression skittered across his dark face. "I don't got to talk to you. Guard, git him outta here."

The guard didn't budge. He just stood in his corner, feet shoulder-width apart, arms crossed.

"What if I told you there were other witnesses?" Ned pressed.

Panic swamped his expression. He turned his head and looked at the cement wall. "I'd say you was lyin'."

"You see this black book, Pruitt?" He held it at eye level.

Pruitt fixed it with a hard stare, obviously trying hard to conceal his interest. "Yeah, I see it. So what?"

"It belonged to Walter Sullivan. I got it from his girlfriend. It contains a number of interesting tidbits."

Pruitt's upper lip curled like a vicious dog's, showing yellowed teeth. "Got nothin' to do with me."

"Actually, it does, if you want the truth. There's a list of names and addresses in here. The government's been conducting its own investigation and discovered a lot of illegal stills across the region—your region." He lowered the book and flipped through it, then stopped and started reading, his index finger sliding down the page. "Here're just a few of the entries: Rory Johnston, Blackie Ferguson, Hubey Garvey, Randall Weston, Charlie Ford, and, hm, Byron Pruitt, to name a few. I can keep going, if you like, but it's really not necessary. After questioning each one of these bozos, it seems Walter Sullivan took a haul from him. As long as the poor mope paid him the right amount, he kept his yapper shut. There's one glaring problem on this page, though."

"Yeah? What's that?"

Clearing his throat for effect, he said, "Well, one name's been crossed out. You interested in knowing which one?"

Pruitt made a fast swipe at his sweat-beaded brow. "Not really."

Ned smiled for all of a second. "Somebody by the name of Alger Grant. And don't try telling me that name doesn't strike a chord with you, Pruitt, not when I've got a slew of witnesses who say they saw you gun him down in cold blood. Yep, another agent and I've been assigned to run our own investigation, apart from the Athens police." The beads on Pruitt's forehead expanded to the size of small bubbles that burst and made wet trails down his pock-marked face. Ned went on. "Seems Grant was getting close to throwing in the towel on his operation and turning Sullivan in. But you didn't want that to happen, did you? 'Cause that would have brought an end to your operation—your lifeblood. And so you took matters into your own hands. A couple of fellas even helped you bury the body." He couldn't stop himself from smirking. "Those fellas led us straight to the burial site, too. It's unfortunate they're wasting away in jail back in Athens now."

He stopped to take a breath and looked around the room. The guard still appeared to be listening in, but he'd maintained an expression of indifference. So, Ned returned his gaze to Pruitt. "There were a couple of fellas in your little circle who didn't like the direction things were going—Garvey and Weston, to be precise—so they made a habit of hiding out at your place when they expected Sullivan to show up. You guessed it—they saw you shoot him down. They didn't come forward, though, due to the threats on their own lives if they told. See, it's quite a mess, isn't it, Pruitt? You're deep in cow dung, wouldn't you say?"

Pruitt spat on the cell floor and shifted his weight. Then, he glared at Ned with hate-filled eyes. "What do you want from me?"

"What do I want? Humph. Well, it's really quite simple. I want you to plead guilty in the murder of Walter Sullivan so your wife and stepdaughter don't have to testify at your trial. See? I told you it was simple. They've suffered enough without having to face a judge and jury. Pleading guilty will give you a little bargaining leverage, maybe save you from the death sentence."

Pruitt snarled. "Maybe I want the death sentence."

"Ha! Nobody wants that, not even the fearless Byron Pruitt. Think about it. You'll have a few days to decide before I hand this book over to the Athens police. If you get yourself a lawyer real quick, you might be able to make your plea before they get their hands on it. But if you wait too long...well, let's just say I wouldn't want to be in your shoes." He turned and headed for the door, then paused for one final word. "And just in case you're the least bit curious about your cronies, at the moment, they're all sitting in cells just like you, their stills smashed to smithereens. And that goes for your friends Curtis Morgan, Herb Sells, and Hank Waggoner. It's a sad life, isn't it, Pruitt?" He gave a laugh of pure satisfaction, then tucked the book back inside his jacket pocket and left.

Marlene would be plenty happy when he called to tell her he'd be taking the afternoon train home again. He'd meant to pay a visit to Eleanor Cooper and her mother, but, really, what was the need? He'd done what he'd come here to do.

Chapter Thirty-three

We love him, because he first loved us.
—1 John 4:19

Ellie spent the next day in bed, per the doctor's instructions, but she didn't enjoy a minute of it. Whenever she closed her eyes, images of Walter Sullivan's lifeless body falling to the ground played over in her mind. So, she did her best to stay awake, refusing to take any more of those pills from Dr. Trent, which left her feeling groggy. Byron's arrest had brought everything to the surface, and even though he sat locked behind bars, she couldn't fight off the fear that he might figure out a way to escape and come after her again. Gage peeked in on her from time to time to remind her that she needed rest. She appreciated his concern, of course, but she would have preferred that he not treat her like one of his kids.

She had other visitors, of course, but none of them stayed long, probably at Gage's request. Even when Mama brought in a tray of lunch, she insisted Ellie remain in bed while she ate and then resume resting. "It's for your own good, honey," she said.

"Why do I need rest any more than you, or anyone else?"

Mama lowered herself into the chair beside the bed, folding her hands in her lap. "Well, for one thing, I ain't the one who collapsed last night. Nor do I got four kids to look after. You been under stress, darlin', and last night capped it off."

She nodded, understanding at least in part. "Mama, I need to ask you a question."

"I'm listenin'."

"Do you hate Byron?"

"Hate? Mercy, no. Hate is one o' them emotions that eats at you from the inside out. Since the day I asked God to take control of my life, He's been helpin' me harness my feelin's. Now, don't get me wrong. I don't approve o' one thing Byron done, 'specially the way he mistreated you all these years, and I surely don't love 'im in the way a wife's s'posed to love 'er man. But I'll never let hate be the force that drives me. That'd be like lettin' Byron win."

Ellie almost laughed. "Have you been talkin' to Gage? He said nearly the same thing last night."

"Nope. I been talkin' to God."

She let her mama's words digest for the rest of the afternoon. And, after lunch, she picked up her Bible and read from Psalms, finding particular comfort in Psalm 3:

> LORD, *how are they increased that trouble me! many are they that rise up against me. Many there be which say of my soul, There is no help for him in God. But thou, O LORD, art a shield for me; my glory, and the lifter up of mine head. I cried unto the LORD with my voice, and he heard me out of his holy hill. I laid me down and slept; I awaked; for the LORD sustained me. I will not be afraid of ten thousands of people, that have set*

*themselves against me round about. Arise, O
LORD; save me, O my God: for thou hast smit-
ten all mine enemies upon the cheek bone;
thou hast broken the teeth of the ungodly.
Salvation belongeth unto the LORD: thy blessing is upon thy people.*

In the late afternoon, she actually napped freely, and instead of having nightmares about Byron, she dreamt that Gage had swept her off to a remote tropical island where they walked the sandy beaches hand in hand, and palm trees swayed in the ocean breeze.

She awoke to the wonderful aromas of supper cooking and the sweet sounds of her family talking in hushed tones. Feeling like a new person, she threw off her blankets, made the bed, and got dressed in her blue gingham shirtwaist. She tiptoed to the bathroom, where she pulled a brush through her hair, fastening the sides with two combs, and splashed water on her face to freshen up.

Then, she snuck downstairs, pausing on the bottom step to peer into the living room. Tommy Lee sat in his daddy's lap, listening intently while Gage read aloud from a book of fairy tales, and the twins lounged on the floor, drawing pictures. She could hear voices in the kitchen—Frances, Claire, and Mama. If only they could know how much her heart leaped with love at the sight or sound of them.

She cleared her throat, and, like a rabbit, Tommy Lee hopped off of Gage's lap and ran to her, his arms spread wide. She crouched down and picked him up, whirling in a few circles, until dizziness overtook her. He cupped her face with his pudgy hands. "All better?" he asked.

She laughed, not having realized till now how very much she'd missed her family while she'd been laid up in bed. "Never felt better." Over his head, she shot a glance at Gage and found him smiling. Well, at least he didn't order her straight back to bed—good thing, too, since she'd already made up her mind not to comply.

Just as Claire was summoning everyone to the supper table, the door buzzer sounded. The twins raced to the door, while everyone else gathered in the living room to see who was stopping by. Sheriff Morris stood on the porch, and at the sight of him, Ellie's heart dropped, thinking something must be amiss. But he smiled broadly, so she relaxed. Gage invited him inside.

"No, thanks," the sheriff replied. "I won't take up any of your time." He turned his police hat in his hands. "Just wanted to let you know that Byron Pruitt is headed back to Athens in police custody. Also wanted to thank you for the part you all played in capturing the hoodlum...you in particular, Mrs. Pruitt."

Ellie looked at her mama. There was a glint of something indiscernible in her eyes—sadness? regret? loss?—but she shrugged and smiled weakly. "It weren't much, really. It was just a matter o' bein' prepared. I know how that conniver works, so I had that advantage. 'Course, Claire here did her part, whackin' 'im with that fry pan like she done."

Claire shook her head several times. "I still can't believe I did that."

"Nor can I!" Gage exclaimed. "You, who never even laid a hand to your own sons, even when we well deserved it. Not me so much as my brothers, of course," he added with a wink.

"Byron had a visitor this morning," the sheriff went on. "Some government agent connected with Walter Sullivan. Don't know what transpired between them two, but by the time the agent left, Pruitt's inflated view of himself had sprung a leak. I s'pose he got a good grip on reality. One thing's for sure: that fellow gave him somethin' to think about. Well, I'll be going now." He started to leave, then paused and turned to Ellie and her mama. "Oh, I would expect you'll both be notified of the court date. 'Course, due to spousal privilege, you'll have the right to refuse to testify, Mrs. Pruitt."

At the mere mention of a trial, a quiver of dread ran through Ellie's body, but her inward prayer—*Lord, I am determined to trust You with my future*—quickly soothed her tangled nest of nerves.

After the last of the supper dishes had been washed and put away, the twins asked to go play at a friend's house. "Be back by eight thirty," Ellie told them.

The boys exchanged a glance. "Ellie's back," Alec said with a grin.

That sparked an outburst of giggles from Claire and Mama, who had retired to the living room, Claire with her knitting, Mama with a pencil and today's issue of the *Wabash Daily Plain Dealer,* no doubt ready to tackle the crossword puzzle. Frances asked Tommy Lee if he wanted her to push him in the hammock, and he answered with a gleeful clap, so out the door they dashed, leaving Gage and Ellie alone in the kitchen to gawk at each other.

"Well," he said.

"Yes, well."

"You feel like a walk?"

"A walk? Oh!" She knew her cheeks must be flushing pink with excitement. How could they not, the way he looked in that pair of tan trousers and pale plaid shirt? He'd rolled the sleeves up to his elbows, and she couldn't help but notice his thick, muscular forearms, shaded with brown hair. Near his throat, where several buttons had been left undone, more hair showed, enough to require her to swallow hard and turn her eyes away. Good gracious, he was handsome.

"Are you too tired? Because, if you are—"

"No! I mean, a walk sounds lovely."

"You want to get a jacket?"

"Do I need one? We didn't tell the kids to wear theirs."

"It's been a pretty mild day. If you get chilly, we'll head back, how's that?"

Or you could put your arm around me. "That sounds perfect."

The night was, indeed, balmy and mild. As they strolled down Ewing Street and then turned right onto Main, heading north, until they arrived at the Wabash City Park, they didn't lack for things to talk about. Gage told her how he'd spent his day off, mostly working in the basement, clearing away clutter and measuring for an extra room that could serve as a bedroom. He figured he needed a place to stay for as long as her mother remained with them, and the space could also serve as his bedroom once his own mother went back to Chicago.

"We're fortunate to have a dry basement, no mold or mildew, as some are prone to collect," he said. "It can tend to get a little musty down there during the hot summer months, but that's easily handled with a good fan to keep things dry."

"That's good." Ellie hoped he wouldn't detect her disappointment. She'd actually been looking forward to sharing a bedroom with him again.

"Are you going to try to convince your mother to move up here?" he asked.

"I'd like to," she confirmed, "but I don't know if she'll go for it. She already feels like she's intruding."

"She's welcome to stay with us as long as she wants. And, later, if she'd like, I could help her find a nice little place in Wabash."

"Really, Gage? You would do that?" She stopped for a moment, and two squirrels engaged in a game of tag scampered across their path before she moved forward again. "Mama would have to sell the farm, which would be no trouble, I'm sure. The house is little better than a shack, but the barns are in good shape, and there's a lot of acreage. Plus, for as much as Byron nagged her about it, she never did transfer any of the deeds to his name. That house belonged to her and Daddy, and she didn't want to go through the legal hassle of changin' it. Byron used to get fightin' mad about that. He'd expected to get everything she owned by marryin' her, but she stood her ground, and I'm glad she did."

"That was smart on her part."

He put a hand at her back and guided her to a park bench. They sat down, and Gage stretched out his long legs in front of them, crossing one ankle over the other. Then, he reached out one arm and rested it along the back of the bench, just skimming her shoulders, while the other he lowered to the armrest. She straightened her skirt and clasped her hands in her lap, smiling up at the birds flitting about in the treetops, singing the finale to their lively chorus, which would end with the onset of dark.

"Did you have a good day of rest?" Gage asked.

"Well, I didn't expect to enjoy it, but I have to admit it was lovely. Late in the afternoon, I drifted into a slumber that was positively blissful. Thank you for insistin' I stay in bed for the day. It seemed to do the trick."

"You didn't see me, but I walked by once and saw you engrossed in your Bible reading."

"Did you? I took advantage of the time and read as much as I could. The Lord spoke to me about trustin' Him with all that lies ahead. Sometimes, I feel like a failure when it comes to trustin' Him fully. I get fearful of the future and forget that He's in control."

He rested his hand on her shoulder, and a spark of desire tickled her skin. "What are you fearing the most right now?"

"I guess goin' back to Athens. I know I have to go there at some point to collect the rest of my belongings, and if Mama sells the farm, I'll have to help her pack everything up. That part doesn't bother me, though. It's facin' Byron in that courtroom that I dread."

"Maybe we should pray about that."

She looked up at him, but the setting sun shining directly behind him prevented her from reading his eyes. "You mean, now?"

"Sure, if you'd like."

"That would be nice."

He tugged her close, lowered his face so that their cheeks touched, and then began to pray, asking God to remove her fears and give her confidence and courage for whatever lay ahead. He thanked the Lord for all that she'd done for his family and for the love and discipline she'd given to his children, and then he asked for divine direction concerning her mother, praying that, above all, God's will would be clear. After the amen, he gave her shoulder an extra-tight squeeze before sitting up again. It would have been the ideal time for a kiss, but, other than that, it was the perfect end to the day.

*

As they walked back to the house, Gage mentally kicked himself for not kissing Ellie on that park bench. He thought about taking her hand while they strolled along, but she'd tucked it deep inside her skirt pocket, derailing that plan.

Back at home, the twins had finished playing with their friend and were now lying on the living room floor, listening to a radio show, while their grandma knitted. She told them that Tommy Lee had already been bathed, and Frances was now reading him a bedtime story. Ellie's mother had retreated upstairs, as well, saying she was ready for bed.

"Want something to drink?" Gage asked Ellie.

"Iced tea would be nice."

He smiled. "My thoughts exactly." In the kitchen, he switched on the light and opened the icebox, moving a few items out of his way to reach the pitcher of tea Ellie had made earlier that evening.

From the cabinet beside him, Ellie took a couple of glasses and set them on the counter, her nearness affecting him more than he would have expected. When should he tell her how he felt about her? Right now? Tomorrow? Next week? Next month? What if the right time never came? They both sipped their tea, staring for three long seconds over their glasses at each other. Then, they lowered their glasses, and he wiped his wet lips. "Ellie, I—"

"What you got, iced tea? I want some!" Alec raced past them, opened the cabinet, and fetched a glass from the shelf. Abe soon joined him, and the boys chatted about the radio program, which was evidently some suspense story, and speculated about what would happen next.

Gage's mother entered the kitchen next, yawning. "I think I'll make some coffee. Anyone care to join me for a cup?" She glanced at the pitcher of iced tea. "Oh, I see you're all set. Did you two enjoy your walk?"

Ellie nodded. "Yes, very much." She took several gulps from her glass, apparently avoiding Gage's eyes. "I think I'll take the rest o' this upstairs and check on Mama. Good night, everyone." She nodded at Gage and his mother and then left the room, calling from the dining room, "Boys, you best get ready for bed just as soon as that program ends."

"We will," they chimed in unison. They took their drinks into the living room, leaving Gage with his mother.

"Why do I get the feeling the boys and I interrupted something?"

Gage drained his glass, rinsed it in the sink, and set it on the counter with a thud. "Because you did."

"Hm. Something important, I gather. Are you two getting along all right, Gage?"

"We're getting along fine."

"Mmm-hm. Is that why you're wound tighter than a violin string?"

He scratched the back of his neck and shook his head in frustration. "I don't know, Mom."

She pulled out a kitchen chair and pointed at it. "Sit."

Feeling like a kid under his mother's thumb again, he slumped into the chair. She joined him in another chair, her hands clasped atop the table. "All right. What's bothering you?"

He sat there twiddling his thumbs, trying to decide whether he was too old to confide in his mother. After thirty seconds' deliberation, he sighed loudly and blurted out, "I've never told Ellie I love her." There, it was out. He'd draw the line at letting his mother know he hadn't shared a bed with her yet. "I was about to tell her just a few minutes ago, but then the twins came in and spoiled the moment, and she hurried upstairs, as if she didn't want to hear it anyway. And maybe she doesn't. Maybe she's not ready to hear it...maybe she doesn't want the commitment that goes with a marriage based on love. Oh, she adores the kids, and she's wonderful with them, but there's no mistaking she enjoys having the bedroom all to herself...part of our marriage agreement, I guess." Too late, he realized he'd just alluded to the nature of their relationship. Well, he couldn't turn back now. "At one point, she even suggested an annulment, if things didn't work out, although I can't imagine her leaving the kids. She loves them so much."

"And they her," his mother said, patting the top of his hand. He found the gesture strangely comforting. "So, what you're saying is, you haven't consummated your marriage."

"She seems so young. I'm seventeen years older than she is." He sighed. "Sorry, Mom. This is pretty embarrassing."

"I'm not the least bit embarrassed, and you shouldn't be, either. As for her youth, it's completely irrelevant in this case. Eleanor is a very mature woman, if you'll notice, and age has very little to do with it. She's lived a much harder life than either of us, and that's forced her to grow up quickly, to develop wisdom about a lot of things...just not when it comes to matters of the heart." She patted his hand again. "You're going to have to court her, woo her. Men today don't take the time or make the effort to sweep ladies off their feet."

"Woo her? Really, Mom. I haven't heard that term in years." He felt foolish having to ask his mother what was involved in wooing. Great Scott, he'd been married before, but his relationship with Ginny had not involved a long-drawn-out courtship. They'd simply fallen in love at a young age, and marriage had followed as the next natural step. He swallowed his pride. "What sort of things do you suggest I do?"

Her gaze shifted to the ceiling as her lips curved up in a dreamy smile. "Well, flowers are a good place to start. Buy them as often as you can. Every day couldn't hurt."

"Flowers every day? Isn't that a bit much?"

"And a box of chocolates would be nice. And notes...yes, notes written in your finest hand and sealed in envelopes, taped to her bedroom door before you head to work. And gifts, too...special trinkets to signify that you're thinking of her, even while you're working."

"I already gave her an entire wardrobe."

A pair of creases appeared at the bridge of her nose. "Yes, out of necessity. When was the last time you came home with something romantic, like a piece of jewelry or a fine, leather-bound book?"

"I gave her a Bible."

"And I bet she cherished it, hugged it to her, like it was fine gold."

He reflected on the day he'd brought home Ellie's Bible and recalled how her eyes had glistened as she'd skimmed the pages, how her hands had caressed its cover, and how she'd thanked him, saying it was the loveliest thing anyone had ever given her. "I think I see what you mean."

"Good. And if I may add one more thing...?" She raised her graying eyebrows.

"Yes?"

"Don't choose the kitchen—when everyone's about—to be the first place you tell her you love her. Take her somewhere special, someplace you're certain she'll love. You're a creative, gifted, intelligent man, Gage. Surely, you can handle this without your mother's help."

He smiled, pressed his palms to the table, and pushed himself up, then stooped to give her a kiss on the cheek. "Thanks, Mom. I think I got it."

⁂

"I don't know, Mama. He gave me such a somber look tonight in the kitchen before the twins interrupted him." Ellie sat down on the bed beside her mother.

"Well, somber looks don't always mean somethin' bad. Maybe he was fixin' to tell you somethin' wonderful. After all, he did invite you on that nice walk."

True, but much of their conversation had centered on the extra bedroom he was planning to build in the basement. Ellie stood up to undress and slip into her nightgown while her mother resumed her Bible reading. She took a brush from the vanity and ran it through her hair, staring at herself in the mirror without really seeing. "He said the most wonderful prayer for me in the park. Oh, Mama, he's such a fine Christian man. I don't see how I can ever measure up."

Mama lowered her Bible and smiled. "Darlin', who said anythin' 'bout measurin' up? He knows you're new at this walk with God. Gracious, he's the one who introduced you to Him. Has he asked you to pack your bags 'cause you ain't quite good enough?"

"No...but he needs me to tend his kids, so why would he?"

"That man loves you, honey, he just hasn't figured out how to tell you yet."

Ellie laid her brush back on the dresser and returned to the bed, pulling down the sheets and crawling in. "You're somethin', Mama, always lookin' on the bright side. Who introduced you to Jesus, anyway?"

She gazed off for a moment, as if lost in the memory. "A complete stranger, actually. Byron dropped me off at Grover's Market one day 'bout a year ago, and he went on to the hardware. While I was standin' at the canned goods shelf, a lady comes walkin' up beside me. Next thing I know, she's talkin' to me 'bout the weather 'n' such. I enjoyed conversatin' with her, but I didn't want to loiter, 'cause I knew Byron would be back real soon. Well, I started to excuse myself, an' she just reached into her purse and handed me this book. I remember lookin' down at it and thinkin' to myself, *What kind o' book is that?* She must've read my mind, 'cause she said, 'It's a Bible, and it holds all the answers for life's troubles. I want to give it to you.' When I didn't take it right off, she said, 'Take it, please. Every mornin' I get up and ask the Lord how He wants to use me that day, and today, He just said, "Go buy a Bible, and I'll tell you who to give it to."' And then, she smiled real sweet-like an' said, 'And you happen to be that person.' And then, just like that, she walked out of Grover's, and I never saw 'er again."

"Oh, Mama," Ellie said in a whisper. "I love that story. God must really love us to put special people like that in our lives. Maybe she was an angel."

"She could've been, but then again, she could've just been somebody totally tuned in to God's voice. That's how I want to be, real tuned in, so I don't miss a word."

Ellie blew out a long breath. "Me too, Mama."

Her mama turned off the light, and they lay there in silence, mulling over their discussion, until Mama remarked, "Ain't it interestin' how Gage gave you your first Bible, and now you're a Christian yourself? God had His hand on both of us before we ever knew Him, Eleanor."

She stared at the dim circle of lamplight on the ceiling as her eyes filled with tears. "What an amazing thought, Mama. Simply amazing."

They fell asleep holding hands.

Chapter Thirty-four

And we have known and believed the love
that God hath to us. God is love; and he
hat dwelleth in love dwelleth in God,
and God in him.
—1 John 4:16

The following Sunday, by some miracle, all eight of them managed to fit into the Buick for the drive to church. There was plenty of giggling, snorting, and moaning, of course, and they must have looked a fine sight to anyone watching when Gage found a parking space and they all filed out. In fact, several church-goers did stop in the parking lot, their hands above their eyes to shield the sun, and gawk. Gage could do nothing but laugh as he watched the seemingly un-ending procession of passengers crawl out of the car, the mothers trying their best not to look wrinkled and awkward, the twins leaping over the floorboard and out the door to dash across the lot, Frances emerging cautious and wide-eyed, as if seeing daylight for the first time in years, and Ellie, his beautiful Ellie, set-ting Tommy Lee on the ground, then brushing herself off and gazing at the ground, he knew, to avoid the countless pairs of eyes that stared from the sidelines.

"You look beautiful, El," he whispered, looping his arm and inviting her to slip her hand through it.

"I do?" She squinted up at him, her brown eyes sparkling in the sunlight, her hair glistening like black gold, with curly wisps framing her face, the rest of it cascading down her back to just below her shoulders. "Th-thank you. And thank you again for that lovely bouquet o' flowers yesterday, and the box o' candy the day before, and...and the lovely note." Her cheeks flushed to a deep rose. "My goodness, I'm fine now. You don't have to keep coddlin' me."

"Is that what you think? That I'm coddling you?"

"Well, I...."

He came close to brushing her cheeks with his lips but stopped just short and whispered, "Wife, you have a great deal to learn, I can see that." He chuckled. "I care about you, do you know that? Deeply. And I plan to tell you just how much sometime very soon."

She let go a light gasp, and her dark eyes roamed his face, her blush deepening as she touched two fingers to her throat. "Oh."

He stood there, still waiting with outstretched arm, and she hesitated a moment longer before slipping her hand partially through. He tugged it the rest of the way and placed his hand atop hers, smiling, as they set off toward the church.

"Everyone is lookin' at us," she said, staring at her low-heeled beige patent-leather pumps.

"They're feasting their eyes on you."

"That's flattering, Gage, but I think a more likely explanation is that they all read the front-page article in Thursday's issue of the *Daily Plain Dealer*."

"I sure hope they did. The article was pretty thorough and accurate, except for that part about Sheriff Morris's untold bravery in taking down Byron Pruitt and hauling him off to jail. As I recall, he put the handcuffs on him *after* our mothers did all the work." He snickered, which finally wheedled a smile out of her. Good gravy, but she had the power to flip his heart inside-out with that sweet little grin.

As they neared the church, folks stepped aside, as if parting the waters. Gage beamed and greeted each one. "Lovely day, isn't it?" he asked, and, "Good morning, folks." Most everyone returned the greeting.

"Good morning, Mrs. Cooper!" said a female voice Gage recognized as belonging to Debbie Stinehart. The short-haired woman emerged from a small gathering of chatty ladies, a big warm smile on her face. "We're happy to see you." She extended a hand, so Ellie took it. "I'm Debbie. We want you to know we all heard about your awful ordeal, and we're so thankful you came through it relatively unscathed. If you don't mind, I'd like to stop over one day soon with a plate of homemade cookies."

Another woman with a baby on her hip—her grandchild, perhaps—stepped forward. "And I'm Marcia Tisdel. You should know nobody turns down Debbie's cookies. She's quite famous for them."

Ellie gave a light laugh. "I've been told as much, and I wouldn't even think of turning them down."

Gage inwardly thanked the Lord for everyone's kindness. "Nice talking to you ladies. And, Debbie? I'll look forward to those cookies myself."

She winked. "I'd best bake a triple batch, then."

When they had bid one another good day, Gage squeezed Ellie's hand. "Shall we go inside, Mrs. Cooper?"

There came another one of those devastating smiles. "Yes, indeed."

They corralled the kids and followed them up the church steps and into the sanctuary, where Gage spotted his mother and Rita seated in the pew they'd said they'd save for the family, five rows back from the front. He and Ellie ushered the kids down the center aisle, and then they all squeezed into the pew. Seated now, Gage glanced around and saw Will and Livvie Taylor and their brood sitting across from them, one row back. Livvie motioned for him to get Ellie's attention, so he gave his wife a light poke and gestured behind him. When she caught Livvie's eye, she smiled with delight. Livvie then blew her a quick kiss and mouthed "I love you"—the exact words Gage intended to say, sooner than Ellie imagined. He could only pray the Lord would enable him to articulate those words so as to sweep her off her feet.

Reverend White's brief sermon on forgiveness touched Ellie to the core of her being. He stressed the importance of acknowledging past hurts and then surrendering them to the Father, forfeiting the right to get even. She was almost certain he'd conferred with Gage or her mama, the way his message hit her square between the eyes. "The Bible tells us that God is love, and that we are to love the Lord our God with all our hearts," said the reverend. "It also tells us to love ourselves, our neighbors, and even our enemies. Yes, folks—our enemies."

Of course, Ellie could not stop thinking about Byron. She cast a sideways glance over the kids' heads at her mama, who was listening with rapt attention and nodding her head in agreement. Something entirely foreign to Ellie washed over her for the very first time—a sense of freedom and healing—and, in that instant, she knew she needed to write a letter to Byron, telling him she'd forgiven him. Gage had been holding her hand throughout the message, and she found herself giving it an extra-tight squeeze. He glanced down at her, but the tears she was holding at bay kept her from meeting his eyes.

"Do you want to see love acted out?" Reverend White continued. "Then, read First Corinthians, chapter thirteen, and you will get a detailed picture of what the apostle Paul was talking about when he said, and I paraphrase, that love is patient, kind, and selfless. It isn't rude, and it doesn't hold any grudges. It does not delight in evil but trusts and protects.

"As you dwell upon the truth of God's love, I want you to also think about what He did for us on the cross—how He willingly and selflessly gave Himself as a living sacrifice, dying a sinless death, so that we could experience His forgiveness, power, and might, and then, in turn, extend our arms of love and hope to a hurting world."

He picked up his notes, tucked them inside his big Bible, and quietly closed the Good Book, lifting his eyes to scan the sanctuary of parishioners. "There is a gentleman present this morning who has asked to take a moment of your time, and I'm honored to give him the pulpit."

Reverend White stepped aside, and, to Ellie's amazement, Gage stood and made his way to the front.

❊

"I'm sure you're all wondering what I've got up my sleeve by asking Reverend White for the use of his pulpit. Don't worry, I'm not about to continue his sermon. I'm no preacher." A few snickers arose, turning to all-out laughter when a fellow in the back blurted out,

"Amen to that!" It was enough to break the ice for Gage and calm his edgy state of mind.

He fixed his gaze on Ellie, whose face showed confusion and maybe a tint of worry, which he meant to erase in due time. "As most of you know, I posted an ad for a wife in Livvie's Kitchen some months ago. Many people told me it was a harebrained scheme, a ridiculous method to find and secure a nanny and housekeeper. I suppose it was a bit unconventional, but, looking back, I can tell you for certain that God had His hand on the whole process, because I found myself a wife I never would have met in the dating circuit. Now, don't get me wrong—I don't advocate proposing marriage to someone as a business proposition, and I seriously doubt Livvie Taylor will go for any more of those particular postings on her bulletin board."

"Amen!" This came from Will Taylor, triggering more titters and chuckles.

Gage grinned and went on. "Ellie has proven to be a wonderful mother to my children, a fabulous cook and housekeeper, and a caring wife. The problem is, we got married in such a hurry that our vows had little meaning at the time. In fact, I'm sorry to say the biggest thing going through my mind back then was how glad I was to have finally found a permanent nanny for my kids.

"For that reason—and, may I say, this will come as a complete surprise to my wife—I would like to invite all of you to our wedding...which is about to take place in the next few moments, if Ellie will consent."

To keep from trembling, he gripped either side of the pulpit, his hands turning sweatier by the second. *Lord, help me remain upright,* he prayed. *And an extra dose of courage would be helpful.*

"Eleanor Cooper," he said, fixing his gaze on her beautiful, tawny face, "I want you to know that I love you, and I was wondering if you would be my bride... again."

The room grew silent, and everyone turned his eyes on Ellie, awaiting her answer. When she smiled and gave a tearful nod, the congregation broke out in happy applause, and Gage released the breath he'd been holding.

When the audience quieted down, Gage said, "Could you come up front, honey?"

Never had he seen the twins sitting at such attention. Even Tommy Lee sat erect on his grandma's lap, obviously interested in the goings-on, especially when he saw his new mommy walking toward the front of the church. And Frances—ah, how she beamed, sitting there in between her grandmothers.

🌾

Ellie barely heard the reverend's words, although she repeated the vows after him in rote fashion while facing Gage, her hands grasped tightly in his. *Lord, is this really happening? Did Gage actually proclaim his love for me in front of the whole congregation? Are we really getting married all over again?* Joy unparalleled made her heart pulse with music.

"I now pronounce you man and wife—again," the reverend said with a grin. "Gage, you may now kiss your bride."

In what seemed like slow motion, Gage put his hands on her shoulders, his gaze riveted on her face, as if entranced. If her pulse didn't modulate into a slower rhythm right this minute, she feared her heart would burst straight through her chest. As he drew her closer, a buzzing excitement stirred like a swarm of bees in her stomach, and, when at last his lips made contact with hers, a shiver of delight fused her feet right to the floor.

There was an eruption of whoops and hurrahs from the pews—the kinds of sounds she didn't know were permitted in church unless they were part of the worship. But then, she heard a definitive "Praise the Lord!" and couldn't help but picture God smiling down in utter approval.

Upon concluding the kiss, Gage cupped her face in his hands and whispered, "Don't you dare faint on me again, Mrs. Cooper."

"I won't," she said with a giggle, even though her crazy heart kept up its erratic thumping, and the applause nearly drowned out her ability to put two thoughts together.

Reverend White hushed the crowd with an uplifted hand. "Even though this whole event has come as quite a surprise to many of you, Mrs. Cooper included, there are a few who knew about it—namely, the group of ladies who were gracious enough to prepare a delicious feast for all of us to enjoy. You'll find a number of tables and chairs set up in the yard behind the church, so, after I give the benediction, please join us and partake of this meal, as well as offer your congratulations to this fine couple."

After the benediction, the reverend motioned for Gage and Ellie to process up the center aisle, through the crowd of cheering, applauding congregants. Out in the narthex, he turned and looked her in the eye. "You're not mad at me for doing that to you, are you, El?"

She laughed. "Mad? I'm ecstatic."

His gaze turned hopeful. "Are you also a little bit in love?"

She sobered. "No." When his jaw dropped, she started to laugh. "I'm a lot in love, silly. I have been for ages."

"So have I!" He kissed her again, firm and full, warm and wet, right there in the church parlor.

"Ahem."

They pulled apart at the sound of Reverend White clearing his throat, but the preacher just grinned. "I thought I'd warn you, your well-wishers are on their way out."

They straightened, put on their smiles, and prepared to shake more than a hundred hands.

⁂

"I don't understand. Where are you takin' me?" Ellie asked, snuggled up close to Gage in the front seat of the Buick as they buzzed through Wabash later that afternoon, crossing the river on their way out of town. The traffic was light, and Gage was thankful, for it would make their trek to Indianapolis easy and uneventful.

"Have you ever stayed in a hotel?"

"What? No...unless you count the one I stayed at here in Wabash when I first arrived. Gage Cooper, what do you have up your sleeve?"

He angled her a crooked grin. "A lot of hanky-panky."

She gave him a playful slap and then leaned over to kiss his cheek. "I suppose I can expect a lot o' that in the days to come."

"You bet your sweet life you can. As for where I'm taking you, well, I'd like to keep it a secret." He wanted to surprise her, and he expected her reaction at seeing the regal-looking, eight-story Canterbury Inn on South Illinois Street would be even more animated than when she'd seen her first movie—a talkie, at that. His anticipation spread like wildfire.

His mother and Rita had been more than willing to take care of the household for a few days, and he had no qualms about leaving his business in the capable hands of Fred, Edith, and Fred's nephew Justin, who'd shown great promise so far. For the next four days, Gage's sole responsibility would be to whisk his wife away to places unknown.

When they reached the center of town, just as expected, Ellie's eyes lit up like two perfect diamonds as Gage pulled the car into the circular driveway of the regal hotel. "I can't believe it!" she whispered in his ear after a bellman opened her door, bowed, and extended a hand. "I feel like a queen!"

After they checked in at the front desk, they headed to their room by way of the elevator, and another awed expression lit Ellie's face when the doorman pulled down the lever to close them inside. "Oh, my gracious, we're movin'!" She giggled. "It tickles my stomach."

They walked down a long, carpeted hallway to reach their room. Gage turned the key in the lock, pressed down on the latch, and pushed open the big door. "Oh, Gage! Look!" She raced across the room like a child on Christmas morning and pulled back the heavy drapes to let in the late afternoon light. "It's glorious."

"Yes, isn't it?" But he wasn't thinking about the scenery when he came up behind her, wrapped his arms around her, and planted a kiss on her head.

Chapter Thirty-five

And be ye kind one to another,
tenderhearted, forgiving one another, even
as God for Christ's sake hath forgiven you.
—Ephesians 4:32

Their honeymoon was a blissful blur of rambling all over town on city buses to see the sights, kissing on street corners in broad daylight, dining at exquisite restaurants, taking in a symphony performance and an art museum, and sleeping late, lying in each other's arms.

When the time came for them to head back to Wabash, though, they both expressed excitement at seeing the kids again and regaining some normalcy. My, how things had changed between them—all barriers down, the light of their love shining in their faces, with no fear of what the other would think if one reached out to take a hand or puckered up for a kiss.

Wabash welcomed them home with a thunderstorm, but it didn't dampen their spirits in the least. Even when they walked through the front door on Thursday afternoon and found the house empty, they were far from disappointed. The kids were still in school, and they hadn't called to tell their mothers when to expect them, so they must have been out running errands with Tommy Lee.

Of course, Gage wasted no time in initiating a thorough kiss, long and fully satisfying. "I plan to do that in every room of the house, in case you were wondering," he whispered an inch from her mouth.

Ellie was more than agreeable to the idea, and so, from the library to the living room, the dining room to the kitchen, and even up the staircase, they christened each room with their kisses. In her bedroom— *their* bedroom now—he kissed her all the way across the carpet, then fell with her onto their neatly made bed, which soon became rumpled under their weight as he ran hungry kisses up and down her neck, over her eyelids, and on both cheeks, his breath warm and tingly against her skin.

Ellie wasn't sure how much time had passed when a door slammed shut downstairs, followed by a friendly bark from Checkers and the sound of footsteps and voices filling the house. "Daddy! Mama!" squealed a youthful voice.

Gage stilled, propped himself up on his elbows, and looked down at her, his mouth curving up at the corners. "Welcome home, Mrs. Cooper."

She returned the smile. "There's no place I'd rather be."

⁂

From his jail cell, Byron read for at least the dozenth time the letter from Eleanor dated May 21.

Byron,

I hope this letter finds you as well as can be expected. I want you to know that Mama and I are getting on well in Wabash. We plan to return to Athens soon and pack up all our belongings. You'll be interested to know she's selling the farm to Burt and Mildred Meyer, livestock and all. She got a very fair price for it, and the Meyers are eager to expand their property lines. Of course, they'll tear down the house but keep the barns.

My husband has been working with a real estate agent here in Wabash and has located a fine little house for Mama to purchase only a few blocks away from where I live, so Mama will be fine. She's also going to start working as a waitress at a little restaurant here in town called Livvie's Kitchen. I thought you would want to know that.

Byron, I don't know when they plan to hold your trial, but I'm no longer afraid to face you. I will tell the truth, not because I want you to suffer for the rest of your life, but because that is what the Lord expects from me: the truth. Mama and I have both discovered that living for Christ is the only way to find true peace and contentment. We also know that no one is exempt from God's love and forgiveness. I wanted to say that, Byron, because even though you must surely believe there is no hope, I want you to know there is. Mama and I have found it, and I know if you trust and believe, you will find it, as well.

*Mama and I are sending you a Bible, and
I hope that in the days and months to come
you will find it in your heart to read it. God
is good, and though you will spend your
remaining days in jail, He still has a plan for
your life. If you place your trust in Him, He
will grant you peace and, best of all, a home
with Him for eternity.*

*Mama and I do not hate you, Byron, and we
have agreed to keep you in our prayers.*

*Your stepdaughter,
Eleanor*

Byron folded the letter, stuffed it back in its en-velope, and then shoved the whole thing into his hip pocket, where he'd kept it for the past few days. He sniffed, his eyes shifting to the Bible lying atop the wool blanket on his narrow cot. Someday, when he got plenty desperate, he might open it and try to discover the mystery of what had drawn Rita and Ellie to its pages. But, for now, he'd just sit and stew—and wait for his sentencing date. Yep, plenty of time later for thinking about cracking open that black book.

❧

Ned paused from shuffling through paperwork to wipe his sweaty brow, wishing the overhead fan would do a better job of cooling his stuffy office. He'd opened his window, but any breeze it ushered in brought with it a barrage of distracting street noises—trucks rum-bling past, car horns honking, train whistles blow-ing. A knock came at the door, and he glanced up.

Bill Flanders leaned against the doorframe, a rolled newspaper under his arm.

"Hey," Ned mumbled. "You come in here to help me make some sense of this mess on my desk?"

"Nope. 'Fraid I got my own mess to deal with." He stepped forward and tossed the newspaper on the desk.

"Since when do I have time to read a newspaper?"

"That's the *Athens Daily Post*. It just came across Russ Auten's desk, so I asked if I could borrow it. I have a feeling you'll want to make time for readin' it—at least the front-page article."

"Oh, yeah?" He settled back in his chair and unfolded the paper, his eyes making a trail to the headline in bold. "Well, I'll be darned. Isn't that something? 'Byron Pruitt Pleads Guilty to Murder Charge,'" he read aloud. "'Waives right to trial, awaits sentencing.'" A smile found its way to his face, and he reached inside his pocket for the little black book he'd gotten from Eileen Ridderman.

"What's that?" Bill asked when he set it on the desk.

"Oh, just a little piece of evidence I forgot to give the Athens police department. I'll run it over there tomorrow."

Outside his fifth-floor window, a car horn honked, a siren blew in the distance, and noisy trucks rumbled past. Ned looked at his messy desk. "You want to go for a Coca-Cola?"

"You buyin'?"

"I think it's your turn." He stood and rounded his desk, slapping his friend on the shoulder as they made for the door.

"Naw, I paid the last two times."

"What? You're lying. I paid last time. Wednesday, remember?"

They passed Rosie, one of the secretaries, on their way to the elevator. "It's Bill's turn," she said without glancing up. "And it was Tuesday."

A Letter from the Author

My dear readers,

You may remember running across a secondary character by the name of Debbie Stinehart. If you'll recall, she vied with Will Taylor for the title of "best baker in town," with her specialty being cookies. Well, I'm here to tell you Debbie is no fictional character. In fact, she is my best friend—has been since 1976—and, to top matters off, she's an avid baker.

Debbie makes it her mission to bake cookies for, well, just about everyone she meets: from new families in the neighborhood to the pastoral staff of her church, from the hospitalized to the bereaved, from shut-ins to the sick in body and heart, and even for the healthy and happy. She has been known to drop off a platter of cookies on my doorstep, particularly when I'm in the throes of a deadline, and then call and tell me to look on my front porch. She'll say, "I didn't want to bother you, but I thought some cookies would inspire you as you write your final scenes!" In short, Debbie spreads joy and shares her love of God through what many like to call her "cookie ministry."

On May 20, 2010, Deb received a diagnosis of non-Hodgkin's lymphoma. Throughout her regimen of chemotherapy, her countless doctor's appointments and tests, her bouts of chronic sickness, her loss of hair, and her lack of appetite and subsequent weight loss, Debbie has never lost her faith in Christ. Nor has she diminished in her smile, her sense of humor, or her ability to lift the spirits of others with her baking skills.

And here is the best news of all: after several scans, she is now cancer-free, and her doctor recently told her that if her scans remain clear for the next several months, she will be considered completely cured! Now, that is something to shout about!

With a little "sneaking around," thanks to her daughter, Alyssa, I was able to confiscate a few of Debbie's best recipes, and, with mouth-watering joy, I share them here (with Debbie's approval, of course).

How about baking up a batch and then, in Debbie's honor, making a few home deliveries? You will make somebody's day, blessing tummy and heart alike!

—Shar

A Preview of Book Three
in the River of Hope Series

Chapter 1

June 1930
Wabash, Indiana

The blazing sun ducked behind a cloud, granting a smidgeon of relief to Sofia Rogers as she compressed the pedal to stop her bike and, in a most inelegant manner, slid off the seat, taking care not to catch the hem of her loose-fitting dress in the bicycle chain. She scanned the street in both directions, hoping not to run into anyone she knew. Then, she parked the rusting yellow bike next to a dilapidated truck. These days, she dreaded coming into Wabash, but she couldn't very well put off the chore much longer if she wanted to keep food on the table.

Her younger brother, Andy, had won the race to their destination, Murphy's Market. His equally corroded bike leaned against the building, and he stood next to it, his arms crossed, his freckled face alight with a prideful smile. When she approached, he picked up the burlap sack he used for carrying supplies. "Didn't I t-tell you I'd b-beat you?" Around the house, she barely noticed his stutter, because it manifested most obviously when they came to town and strangers were present.

"That's because you had a full minute head start on me, you rascal." Sofie might have added that her present condition did not permit the speed and agility she'd once had, but she wasn't about to make that excuse. "You just wait. I'll win on the way back home."

"N-not if I can help it."

She pressed the back of her hand to her hot, damp face and stepped up to the sidewalk. "We'll see about that, Mr. Know-It-All."

Andy laughed and pointed at her. "Now your face is all d-dirty."

She looked at her hands, still soiled from working in the garden that morning, and frowned. "I guess I should have lathered them a little better when I washed up." She bent over and used the hem of her skirt to wipe her cheek before straightening. "There. Is that better?"

He tilted his face and angled her a crooked grin. "Sort of."

"Oh, who cares?" She tousled his rust-colored hair. "Come on, let's get started checking off those items on my shopping list."

They headed for the door, but a screeching horn drew their attention to the street, where a battered jalopy slowed at the curb. Several teenage boys, their heads poking out through the windows, whistled and hollered. "Hey, if it ain't that stammerin' li'l m-m-monkey boy and his pretty, street-walkin' sister. Whoooo!"

At their crudeness, Sofie felt a suffocating pressure in her chest. With a hand on her brother's shoulder, she watched the car round the bend, as the boys' whoops faded into the distance.

"I hate those g-guys."

"'Hate' is a strong word, Andy. Once you give in to it, your heart turns sour, and you don't want that to happen."

"I c-can't help it. It makes me so m-mad when they tease you."

"Oh, phooey, don't worry about me. You're the one who's had to put up with most of their bullying. I wish with all my heart they'd quit. I don't know why people have to be so cruel." As if the baby inside her fully agreed, she got a strong push to the rib cage that jarred her and made her stumble.

"You all right?" Andy grabbed her elbow, looking mature beyond his mere ten years.

She paused to take a deep breath and then let it out slowly, touching a hand to her abdomen. Even after almost seven months of pregnancy, she could barely fathom carrying a tiny human in her womb, let alone accept all of the kicks and punches he'd been doling out on a daily basis. "I'm fine. Let's go inside, shall we?" She'd read several books to know what to expect in the various stages, but none of them had come close to explaining how deeply in love she already felt with the tiny life inside of her. Considering that she'd conceived from an act of brutality committed against her, she should have resented the baby, but how could she hold accountable someone so innocent?

Inside Murphy's Market, a few people ambled up and down the two narrow aisles, toting cloth bags or shopping baskets. Sofie kept her left hand out of view as much as possible, in hopes of avoiding the condemnation of anyone who noticed the absence of a wedding band on her ring finger. She felt no shame, but she'd grown weary of the condescending stares. Several women had tried to talk her into giving the child up for adoption, including Margie Grant, an old friend who had served as a mother figure to her and Andy after their parents perished in a train wreck six years ago. "That little one in your belly is the result of an insidious attack, darling. I shouldn't think you'd want much to do with it once it's born," Margie had said. "I happen to know more than a few childless couples right here in Wabash who would be thrilled to take it off your hands."

Because Margie was a loyal friend, Sofie had confided in her about the assault, including when and where it had occurred. As for revealing her attacker's identity—never! Margie had begged her to go straight to Sheriff Morris, but she had refused, and then had made Margie swear on the Bible not to go herself.

"That is a hard promise to make, dearest," Margie had conceded with wrinkled brow. "But I will promise to keep my lips buttoned. As for adoption, if you gave the baby to a nice couple in town, you would have the opportunity to watch it grow up. That would bring you comfort, I should think, especially if you selected a well-deserving Christian couple."

"I can't imagine giving my baby away to someone in my hometown, Christian or not."

"Well then, we'll go to one of the neighboring towns," the woman had persisted. "Think about it, Sofie. You don't have the means to raise a child. Why, you and Andy are barely making ends meet as it is. Who's going to take care of it while you're at work?"

"I can't think about that right now, Margie. And, please, don't refer to my child as an 'it.'"

The woman's face had softened then, and she'd enfolded Sofie in her arms. "Well, of course, I know your baby's not an 'it,' honey. But, until he or she is born, I have no notion what to call it—I mean, him or her."

"'The baby' will do fine."

Margie had chortled, then dropped her hands to her sides and shot Sofie a pleading gaze. "I sure wish you'd tell me who did this to you. It's a crime, you know, what he did."

"Margie, we've been over this. It's better left unsaid, believe me."

"But people will talk! Who knows what they'll think or say when you start to show? If they learned the truth, perhaps they'd go a little easier on you."

"No! I can't. No one must know—not even you. I'm sorry, Margie."

Rubbing the back of her neck, Margie had sighed in frustration. "You know I love you, Sofie, and so I will honor your wishes…for now." Then, her index finger had shot up in the air, nearly poking Sofie in the nose. "But if he so much as comes within an inch of you again, I want you to tell me right away, you hear? I can't abide thinking that he'll come knocking at your door. You must promise me, Sofia Mae Rogers!"

Sofie hid the shiver that rustled through her veins at the mere thought of running into that evil boy again. Why, every time she rode her bike to work at Spic and Span Cleaning Service on Factory Street, she couldn't get the awful pounding in her chest to slow its pace until she reached her destination.

"Show me your list, Sofe." Andy's voice drew her out of her fretful memories. She reached inside her pocket and handed over the paper. When he set off down an aisle, she idly followed after, her mind drifting back into its musings.

❈ ❈ ❈

Elijah Trent parked his 1928 Ford Model A, a generous gift from his grandfather, in the lot beside Murphy's Market. As he climbed out, he was careful not to allow his door to collide with a bicycle leaning nearby. It looked as if it had been through a war zone. He closed his door and took a deep breath of hot June air, then cast a glance overhead at the row of birds roosting on a clothesline that stretched between two apartment buildings across the street.

When he pulled open the whiny screen door, an array of aromas teased his nostrils, from freshly ground coffee beans to roasted peanuts in a barrel. As he stepped inside, a floorboard shrieked beneath his feet, as if to substantiate its long-term use.

"Afternoon," said the shopkeeper, who glanced up from the cash register, where he stood, ringing up an order for a young pregnant woman. Beside her, a boy dutifully stuffed each item into a cloth bag. The young woman raised her head briefly to Eli, who sensed a certain tenseness in her chestnut-colored eyes. Then, she shifted her gaze back to the clerk.

"Say, ain't you Doc Trent's grandson?" the man asked.

How did he know? "That I am, sir. Elijah Trent. But most people call me Eli."

The clerk stopped ringing items for a moment and gave him an up-and-down perusal. "Heard you're takin' over the old fellow's practice. That's mighty fine o' you. I understand you graduated with honors from the University of Michigan, an' you worked at a Detroit hospital for two years, but you were itchin' for a small town. Timing's good, since Doc's reti-rin'. S'pose you two been plannin' this for quite a while now, eh? Hate to see Wilson Trent retire, but most folks seem to think it'll be good to get in some new blood. Get it? Blood?" He gave a hearty chortle, causing his rotund chest to jiggle up and down.

Eli forced a smile. "It sounds like Grandpa's been keeping everyone well-informed."

"He sure has. Well, and the *Plain Dealer* printed that article 'bout you. It's sure as rain they'll be wantin' to interview you once you get yourself established."

The woman cleared her throat and lifted a hand to finger one of her short, brown curls. She kept her eyes on the counter, shifting impatiently, while the freckle-faced youngster poked his head around and met Elijah's gaze. They stared at each other for all of three seconds; then, the boy quickly turned away when Eli smiled at him.

The clerk resumed his task, so Eli reached inside his hip pocket and grabbed the short list his grandpa had scrawled in his somewhat shaky handwriting. In Detroit, he'd taken most of his meals at the hospital. Helping his grandfather in the kitchen would be an entirely new experience. At least it would be only temporary, until Grandpa's housekeeper of twenty-odd years, Winifred Carmichael, returned from her two-week vacation out West.

"You lookin' for anythin' in particular?" the clerk asked.

"Nothing I can't find on my own, sir."

"Pick up one o' them baskets by the door for stashin' what you need. Name's Harold, by the way. Harold Murphy. I've owned this place for goin' on thirty years now."

Eli bent to pick up a basket. He hadn't thought to bring along a sack in which to carry the items home. The store he had occasioned in Detroit had offered brown paper bags, but the trend didn't seem to have caught on in Wabash just yet. "Yes, I recall coming here with my grandma as a kid."

"And I remember you, as well, with that sandy hair o' yours and that there dimple in your chin."

"Is that so? You have a good memory, Mr. Murphy."

A pleased expression settled on the clerk's face. "You used to ogle my candy jars and tug at your grandmother's arm. 'Course, she'd always give in. She couldn't resist your pleadin'. Seems to me you always managed to wrangle some chewin' gum out o' her before we finished ringing her order."

"It's amazing you remember that."

"Well, some things just stick in my memory for no particular reason." He glanced across the counter at the freckle-faced boy. "Young Andy, here, he's the Hershey's Chocolate Bar type. Ain't that right, Andy?"

The lad's head jerked up, and he looked from Mr. Murphy to the woman beside him. "Yes, sir. C-c-can I g-get one today, Sofie?"

Her narrow shoulders lifted and drooped with a labored sigh. "I suppose, but don't expect any other treats today."

"I won't."

The brief tête-à-tête allowed Eli the chance to disappear down an aisle in search of the first item on his list: sugar. He found it about the same time the screen door whined open once more, with the exit of the young woman and the boy. Next, Eli spotted the bread at the end of the aisle. He picked up a loaf and nestled it in the basket, next to the box of sugar.

"Well, I think it's plain disgraceful, her coming into town and flaunting herself like that. My stars, has she not an ounce of decency?"

"I must agree, it's quite appalling," said another.

Eli froze at the sound of feminine scoffing from the other side of the shelving unit.

"I always did wonder about her and that pitiable little brother of hers, living all alone on the far edge of town. No telling what sort of man put her in a motherly way. Why, if I were in her place, I'd have gone away until the birth. Surely, she has relatives living out of state. She could have birthed the child, given it to some worthy family, and come back to Wabash, with no one the wiser."

The other gossip cleared her throat. "Perchance her 'lover' won't hear of her leaving, and she doesn't dare defy him. She always did come off as rather defenseless, wouldn't you say?"

"Yes, yes, and very reclusive. Never was one to join any charity groups or ladies' circles. Why, she doesn't even attend church, to my knowledge. As I said before, the whole thing is disgraceful."

Eli shuffled around the corner and stopped at the end of the next row, where he picked up a couple of cans of beans, even though they weren't on Grandpa's list, and dropped them into his basket with a clatter. The chattering twosome immediately fell silent. Eli cast a casual glance in their direction, and he almost laughed at their poses of feigned nonchalance. One was studying the label on a can, while the other merely stared at a lower shelf, her index finger pressed to her chin.

When Eli started down the aisle, both of them looked up, so he nodded. "Good afternoon, ladies."

The more buxom of the two batted her eyelashes and plumped her graying hair, then nearly blinded him with a fulsome smile. "Well, good afternoon to you." She put a hand to her throat. "My goodness, are you the young man we overheard Harold talking to? Doc Trent's grandson?"

"Yes, ma'am."

"Well, I'll be. You sure are a handsome young man." Then, she grabbed her left side and puckered her pouty lips. "I'm feeling a sharp pain right here. You don't think it's my appendix...?"

"Well, I—"

"Oh, for mercy's sake, Bessie, mind your manners." The second woman bore a blush of embarrassment. "Don't pay her any heed. She's such a tease." She extended a hand. "I'm Clara Morris. My husband, Buford, is the local sheriff. And this is Bessie Lloyd. Her husband owns Lloyd's Shoe Store, over on Market Street. Welcome to Wabash, Dr. Trent. We read about your arrival in the newspaper. I hope you find yourself feeling right at home here."

"I'm sure I will." Eli shifted his shopping basket and extended a hand first to Mrs. Morris, then to the obnoxious Mrs. Lloyd. He would have liked to remind them that two upstanding women in the community ought to put a lock on their mouths, lest they tarnish their own reputations, but he hadn't come to Wabash with the intention of making instant enemies, so he restrained himself. "Nice meeting you ladies. You have a good day, now. And, uh, if that pain in your side worsens, Mrs. Lloyd, please feel free to stop by the office. My grandfather will be happy to examine you. We'll be working together for a few months until he turns the practice over to me. Even then, he'll still be around for consultations."

"Oh, well." She laid a hand over her chest. "I'm sure I'll be feeling just fine in no time. Probably just a little...indigestion."

"Yes, that sounds likely." He glanced to his left and, seeing a shelf with maple syrup, snatched a can and tossed it into his basket. Casting them one last smile, he headed down the aisle in search of the remaining items.

"My, my," he heard Mrs. Lloyd say. "I think it may be time for me to switch physicians."

"But you've been seeing Dr. Stewart for years," Mrs. Morris said. "What about your gout?"

"Pfff, never mind that. I'd much rather look into that young man's blue eyes and handsome face than the whiskery mug of Dr. Stewart. Why, if I were younger...." Eli picked up his pace and made it out of earshot before she finished her statement.

Several minutes later, he'd rounded up everything on his list, so he made his way to the cash register. He could once again hear the voices of his new friends, and it sounded as if they'd selected a new topic of conversation. "I went to McNarney Brothers Meat Market yesterday," Mrs. Lloyd was saying. "Would you believe they raised the price of beef by five cents a pound? Don't they know times are tight? Before you know it, folks won't be able to afford to eat."

"She could afford to go a few days without eating," Harold Murphy muttered. His eyes never strayed from his task, as he keyed in the amount of each item before placing it back in the basket.

Eli covered his mouth with the back of his hand until his grin faded. He decided it best to keep quiet on the matter. Something else bothered him, though, and he couldn't resist inquiring. He leaned in, taking care to keep his voice down. "That girl...er, that woman, who left a bit ago, who is expecting...."

"Ah, Sofia Rogers? She was here with her little brother, Andy." Mr. Murphy rang up the final item, the loaf of bread, and placed it gently atop the other goods. Then, he scratched the back of his head as his thin lips formed a frown. "It's a shame, them two...well, them three, I guess you could say." He glanced both ways, then lowered his chin and whispered, "Don't know who got her in that way, and I don't rightly care. When she comes here, I just talk to her like nothin's different. Figure it ain't really my concern. I know there's been talk about her bein' loose, an' all, but I can't accept it. Never have seen her with anybody but that little boy. She takes mighty fine care o' him, too."

"She is solely responsible for him?"

"Sure enough, ever since...oh, let's see here...summer of twenty-four, it was. They lost their ma and pa in a train wreck. They'd left Andy home with Sofie for two days, whilst they went to a funeral, little knowing their own funeral would be three days later." The man shook his balding head.

The news got Eli's gut to roiling. Even after all those years of medical school, which should have callused him to pain and suffering, his heartstrings were wound as taut as ever. He needed to learn to toughen up. Accept that bad things happened to innocent people; that he lived in an imperfect world in which evil often won.

"Where do they live, if you don't mind my asking?"

"Out on the southwest edge o' town. River Street, I believe. Off o' Pike."

Eli wasn't yet familiar with Wabash, but his grandfather certainly was, having driven virtually every street within the town limits to make house calls. But what was he thinking? He ought to bop himself on the noggin. He knew next to nothing about this woman, and the last thing he needed upon taking over Wilson Trent's medical practice was a reputation for sticking his nose where it didn't belong.

Eli paid the shopkeeper and took up the basket. He had a good feeling about Harold Murphy. "Mighty nice meeting you, sir. I'll bring this basket back next time I come in— or shall I return it tonight?"

Harold flicked his wrist. "Naw, you bring it back whenever it's convenient for you. Nice meetin' you, too, young man. You give that grandfather o' yours a hearty hello from me."

"I'll do that." Eli turned on his heel and proceeded to the door, which he shoved open with his shoulder. The first thing he noticed when he stepped outside was the absence of the two bikes, and it occurred to him then that Sofia and Andy Rogers had ridden to and from Murphy's Market on those rickety contraptions. A woman in what looked to be her seventh month of pregnancy, riding a bike clear to the edge of town? In a dress? And in this heat?

This time, he did bop himself on the head.